LEATHER, LACE, AND LOCS

What Reviewers Say About
Anne Shade's Work

Love and Lotus Blossoms

"Shade imbues this optimistic story of lifelong self-discovery with a refreshing amount of emotional complexity, delivering a queer romance that leans into affection as much as drama, and values friendship and familial love as deeply as romantic connection. ...Shade's well-drawn Black cast and sophistication in presenting a variety of relationship styles—including open relationships and connections that shift between romance and friendship—creates a rich, affirming, and love-filled setting...(Starred review)"—*Publishers Weekly*

Masquerade

"Shade has some moments of genius in this novel where her use of language, descriptions and characters were magnificent."—*Lesbian Review*

"The atmosphere is brilliant. The way Anne Shade describes the places, the clothes, the vocabulary and turns of phrases she uses carried me easily to Harlem in the 1920s. Some scenes were so vivid in my mind that it was almost like watching a movie. ...*Masquerade* is an unexpectedly wild ride, in turns thrilling and chilling. There's nothing more exciting than a woman's quest for freedom and self-discovery."—*Jude in the Stars*

"Heartbreakingly beautiful. This story made me happy and at the same time broke my heart! It was filled with passion and drama that made for an exciting story, packed with emotions that take the reader on quite the ride. It was everything I had expected and so much more. The story was dramatic, and I just couldn't put it down. I had no idea how the story was going to go, and at times I was worried it would all end in a dramatic gangster ending, but that just added to the thrill."—*LezBiReviewed*

Femme Tales

"If you're a sucker for fairy tales, this trio of racy lesbian retellings is for you. Bringing a modern sensibility to classics like *Beauty and the Beast*, *Sleeping Beauty*, and *Cinderella*, Shade puts a sapphic spin on them that manages to feel realistic."—Rachel Kramer Bussel, *BuzzFeed: 20 Super Sexy Novels Full of Taboo, Kink, Toys, and More*

Visit us at www.boldstrokesbooks.com

By the Author

Femme Tales

Masquerade

Love and Lotus Blossoms

Her Heart's Desire

My Secret Valentine

Securing Ava

Three Wishes

Leather, Lace, and Locs

LEATHER, LACE, AND LOCS

by
Anne Shade

2024

LEATHER, LACE, AND LOCS

ISBN 13: 978-1-63679-529-4

This Trade Paperback Original Is Published By
Bold Strokes Books, Inc.
P.O. Box 249
Valley Falls, NY 12185

First Edition: April 2024

CREDITS
EDITOR: CINDY CRESAP
PRODUCTION DESIGN: SUSAN RAMUNDO
COVER DESIGN BY INK SPIRAL DESIGN

Acknowledgments

I would like to acknowledge the following ladies for taking time out of their busy schedules to speak with me about the world of Black burlesque performers and dommes:

Bleu Pearl (@bleu_pearl4)
The May Hemmer (@themayhemmer)
Domi (@domipastrami)
Ms. Kitty LaReaux (@thatheauxkittylareaux)

I truly admire your strength, determination, and talent. Thank you for your openness and honesty in discussing the trials, tribulations, and joy in what you do.

Dedication

The characters in this book are dedicated to
the Women of Color who were innovators in…

Burlesque:
Madeleine Sohji Jackson, Toni Elling,
Lottie "The Body" Graves, Miss Topsy

Kink:
Mistress Mir, Vi Johnson, Mistress Velvet, Venus Cuffs

Black Haircare:
Madam CJ Walker, Annie Malone, Lyda Newman,
Nobia A. Franklin

CHAPTER ONE

Golden felt her eyes beginning to close and shifted in her seat to wake herself up. Under normal circumstances these weekly meetings were quick, concise, and over within a half hour, but since Mark, their manager, was out on vacation it was up to his second in command, Chris, to lead the team meeting this week. He was the only person who could make finances boring for her. He'd been droning on in his nasally monotone voice for a good fifteen minutes giving his own report which, funnily enough, seemed to be a lot longer than the five minutes Mark usually gave everyone to give their update. Chris had saved his own report for last as if they were the opening act and he was the main event with his complicated spreadsheet and colorful graphs showing how well his numbers were compared to the overall department numbers. He then had the nerve to pause at the end as if waiting for applause before deciding he had tortured everyone enough to end the meeting.

Golden was glad she'd taken a seat by the door because she couldn't get out of there fast enough.

"Hey, Golden, wait up!" she heard someone call from behind her.

She turned to find her officemate Geoff jogging toward her. She liked Geoff. He was a good guy and had been the one to recommend her for the investment banking analyst position that she'd been working in for the past two years. They had been loan officers at Providence Bank where Golden had started as a teller right after high school and continued working after she graduated college with a bachelor of science in financial economics.

"I was about to stick my pen through my ear drums if I had to sit and listen to him drone on any longer," Geoff said as they walked to their shared office together.

Golden grinned in amusement. "Yeah, I think the Analyst of the Month title has gone to his head. He knows damn well he wouldn't have done all that showboating if Mark were here."

"Fortunately, I won't have to sit through another one of those with him."

Golden looked at him in surprise. "You got the job in private equity?"

Geoff smiled broadly. "Yep. With Mark's recommendation I was a shoo-in. In two weeks, you'll finally have the office to yourself. At least until my replacement is hired."

Golden pulled him into a brief hug. "Congratulations. You'll be rolling in the dough with the big boys now. Are you sure you're ready?"

Geoff snorted. "I was ready a year ago, but nothing opened until now. They said there may be room for another analyst in a few months if you're interested."

"No, I said I would give this position a solid three years before I moved on. Besides, I haven't decided if I want to do private equity or hedge funds."

"Well, you know who to reach out to if you decide equity is the way to go."

"Definitely. I'm sure Lana will be thrilled about the change. She and the kids will get to see more of you."

"Yeah, she's definitely been holding it down. I'm going to head outside to call and tell her."

"Tell her I said hi."

Geoff nodded, placed his notepad on his desk, and left the office. Golden sat down with a weary sigh. She had three due diligence calls scheduled until four thirty then a five o'clock meeting scheduled with the Equity Capital Markets team to go over market updates and case studies for her newest client. She wouldn't be leaving the office before seven, then had to be back in tomorrow to finish two pitches she had to make in Chicago and St. Louis next week. She didn't know how Geoff had managed marriage and fatherhood working this job for three years. Their hours were brutal with working twelve-hour days and most weekends and unless you were lucky enough to get assigned to a nearby region, there was a lot of travel. Golden was assigned to the Midwest which she didn't mind so much considering Geoff had been handling the Southwest region and spent more time away from home than she did. She also didn't have a wife and kids to consider because there was no time for a romantic life. What free time she had she tried to make sure to spend with her family, sleep, and squeeze in a workout.

Golden's computer dinged to remind her of her video conference in fifteen minutes. She had just enough time to refill her coffee mug and order lunch from the cafeteria to pick up and scarf down between calls. Despite the long hours, frequent travel, and sometimes tedious days of due diligence calls, she liked her job. Especially the six-figure salary and great benefits that made it all worthwhile. It had afforded Golden the opportunity to purchase a two-family home in Jersey City last year for a good one hundred thousand dollars less than what she would've paid for a single-family in Brooklyn. She moved her mother into the one-bedroom apartment on the first floor while she and her best friend and roomie Melissa occupied the two-bedroom on the second floor.

Golden had kept the promise to take care of her mother and brother that she had made to her father before he passed away fifteen years ago. Scholarships and grants helped to pay her way through school so that she was able to use her salary from her teller job to put toward helping her mother pay bills. They were able to keep her father's death benefits in a savings account for her mother to use as she saw fit. She chose to use the funds toward what scholarships and grants didn't cover for Drew's tuition to Massachusetts Institute of Technology. Drew had fought the idea when their mother told him what she planned to do, but she reminded him of what their father said about him being gifted with his big brain and that he expected him to do amazing things with it. She couldn't imagine he wouldn't have wanted the money to be used for anything better. Drew couldn't say no after that. Golden managed to keep her online classes going while working and graduated with her degree in financial economics and was quickly promoted at the bank to a loan officer. Drew graduated two years later at the top of his class and was snatched up by a major technology company he had been interning with to work full-time as a web developer. She knew her father would be proud of what they had accomplished.

Golden frequently thought about what she had given up, but she would squash the ache and regret down because it had been a necessary sacrifice to get her family to where they were today, that's all that mattered. At least that's what she convinced herself after all these years. It didn't matter that she'd given up her and her father's dream for her to become a professional dancer or that he had made her promise not to let anything take away that dream. None of that mattered because she had also promised him that she'd take care of their family and that trumped the first promise. Unfortunately, thoughts of her father brought the memory of the day he died so clear in her mind that it played like a movie in her head.

❖

Fifteen Years Ago

Golden ran up the aisle to her father and jumped joyfully into his waiting arms.

He squeezed her tightly. "You did it, baby girl. I'm so proud of you."

She had just completed an audition and been accepted into the American Music and Dramatic Academy.

"You looked awesome up there, Golden. They would've been crazy not to accept you," Drew said as their father released her.

Golden gently punched her younger brother in the arm. "Aww... thanks, Drewski."

Her father continued smiling broadly. "Have I told you how much you remind me of my great-aunt Dinah?"

Golden tapped her chin as if she were trying to remember even though he said it after every audition or competition. "You may have mentioned it."

Her father chuckled. "Go grab your stuff and we'll stop for ice cream to celebrate."

Golden gave him one last hug then ran happily to the dressing rooms located backstage. There she found a folder with "Welcome to the American Music and Dramatic Academy" in gold font on the cover filled with everything she needed to know about the academy, her scholarship, and scheduling her orientation. Golden couldn't imagine ever being as happy as she was at that moment.

After celebratory hot fudge sundaes, Golden's father decided to stop at the bodega around the corner from their apartment to pick up her mother's favorite ice cream so that she wouldn't be left out of the celebration when she got home from work. While Golden and Drew sat in the car waiting, she decided to call her best friend Melissa to tell her the exciting news.

"It's about time someone recognized how talented you are," Melissa said.

Golden smiled in appreciation. Being friends with Melissa was like having her own personal hype girl. Golden's other friends didn't understand why she was friends with the shy nerd that they saw, but underneath the conservative clothes, glasses, and studious ways was a witty, caring, and beautiful person. Melissa had Golden going to art museums, reading Audre Lorde, and focusing more on her schoolwork. She considered Melissa the yin to her yang. They were like two halves of a really cool and smart person.

"So, what are we doing tonight to celebrate?"

Melissa snorted. "I don't know what you're doing but I have a report due tomorrow for my Honor's English class that I have at least a dozen more pages to write before I'm finished."

"Girl, you're pulling straight As in that class, one late assignment won't kill you. C'mon, it's teen night at Black Light. We haven't gone there in ages. Pleeeease," Golden begged her.

Melissa chuckled on the other end. "Yeah, okay."

"Great! I'll see you at six."

They said their good-byes and Golden smiled thinking about the fun they would have later. She looked across the street wondering what was taking her father so long. The sound of three loud pops came from the direction of the store. A moment later, two men ran out the propped open door and down the street followed by her father who stumbled out brandishing his service revolver pointed in their direction as he yelled for them to stop. Golden sat frozen watching the scene in disbelief as her father collapsed to his knees holding his hand over his chest. He turned in her direction, their gazes met and Golden couldn't get out of the car fast enough. She ran across the busy street narrowly missing getting hit by oncoming traffic. She faintly heard Drew yelling for her, but all she could focus on was the light going out of their father's eyes as she knelt beside him before he fully collapsed onto the sidewalk.

"Daddy?"

"Hey, baby girl, I'm so sorry for ruining your big day," he said weakly.

"No, it's okay. You're gonna be okay…SOMEBODY CALL 911!" Golden pressed her hands over the spreading circle of blood beneath his shirt turning the soft white into a muddy red.

"Dad? No no no no…" She looked up to see Drew take his hand, shaking his head vigorously.

Golden heard the wail of sirens in the distance, but she knew they wouldn't make it in time. There was too much blood and her father's smooth brown complexion was turning an ashen gray.

He reached up to stroke Golden's face. "My golden child. I love you and am so proud of you. Don't let anybody take your dream away, you hear?"

Golden's vision blurred with tears as she nodded. "I promise. I love you too, Daddy."

He turned to Drew. "I love you, son—" He coughed, and blood lined his lips. "I'm so proud of the man you're becoming. God gifted you with that big brain of yours for a reason. You're going to do amazing things; I just know it."

"Daddy…please don't go," Drew said desperately.

Their father gave him a soft smile. "You and your sister take care of your mother and each other," he said before his eyes fluttered closed just as the police car pulled up to the curb.

❖

Golden's vision blurred with unshed tears, and she quickly wiped them away with the back of her hand. She chose the right promise to keep. The other would've brought too much heartache. After that day, just putting on her dance shoes had made her weepy. The joy she had carried so long from dance had turned to heart-stopping grief because her father, a former dancer before Golden's arrival, had been her biggest cheerleader. Her passion for dance had died with him. Golden stood, picked up her coffee mug, and headed to the breakroom. She needed to shake off the emotions that were coming on by focusing on work. The one advantage of a busy work schedule was that you didn't have time to think about broken promises or regrets.

Golden didn't make it home until close to eleven p.m. because Chris decided as he was leaving the office that the team needed to redo a pitch for an upcoming initial public offering and he wanted to have the new draft ready for Mark to review when he returned on Monday. Since she was flying out Monday morning and still had her own presentations to finish, Golden stayed to get her part complete so that she wouldn't be in the office all weekend. As she pulled into the driveway, she wasn't surprised to see her mother's apartment was dark. With Golden paying the bills now her mother didn't need to work, but she insisted on continuing to do so. Golden didn't fault her because she knew her mother was not cut out to be a lady of leisure. Fortunately, she was able to find a position at a hospital in New Jersey in the maternity ward, but it didn't change the long shifts she sometimes took. She wasn't as tired as she used to be working as an ER nurse, but the maternity ward could sometimes be just as busy as an ER. Getting out of the car, she gazed up and noticed her apartment lights were still on, which meant Melissa was home.

After living with her mother and brother for so long, Golden had looked forward to finally having her own place, but when Melissa was kicked out of her parents' home after finally coming out to her family, Golden took her in. Melissa had insisted that it only be for a few months until she could find something that wouldn't leave her broke every month. That was six months ago. Golden didn't insist on her leaving because their schedules rarely synced up enough for them to see each other for more than a day. Melissa worked as a household manager for a New York executive's family and stayed at their home during the week then stayed at the apartment on the weekends and holidays. Golden liked having the company and knew Melissa was still reeling from her family ostracizing her. She was already considered a part of their family, so it only seemed right that they embraced her when her real family turned her away.

"Honey, I'm home," Golden announced as she walked into the apartment.

"Hey, stranger." Melissa was lounging on the sofa with her hand deep into a bag of chips.

Golden dropped her bag by the door and flopped onto the sofa beside her, then took the bag from Melissa and grabbed a handful before handing it back to her. "How do you manage to eat shit like this and stay so slim?"

"Because those damn kids' schedules run me ragged so I don't have time to eat most of the day." Melissa dipped a chip in a jar of salsa propped between her thighs.

Golden shook her head. "I don't know why you put up with them."

"For the same reason you put up with working twelve hours a day, practically six days a week. The money."

"You got me there. Are we still on for our appointments with Zoe on Sunday?"

"Yeah. She called earlier to confirm. She also wanted me to remind you to bring the wine."

"Don't I always? We still need to plan this year's girls' trip."

Melissa looked at Golden skeptically. "Are you going to have time? Last year's scheduling fiasco almost had us spending the weekend at the airport waiting for you."

Golden waved dismissively. "That won't happen again. Unlike last time, I've requested the time off far enough in advance to make whatever arrangements need to be made to cover for me at work."

"Okay, we'll see. Your mom cooked tonight. Turkey chili and cornbread. I brought some up for you. It's in the fridge."

"Thanks. I'll eat it tomorrow. Right now, I just want to sleep." Golden snatched one last chip from the bag then stood to leave. "I'll probably be gone by the time you get up. I plan to only be at the office until noon. Maybe we can meet up to grab a bite to eat after."

"You know me. I don't have any plans. Just let me know where and I'll meet you there."

"We seriously need to get you a love life."

Melissa quirked a brow. "Look who's talking. When was the last time you had a date?"

Golden grinned. "Probably more recently than you."

Melissa stuck her tongue out at her. "Good night, bitch."

"Good night, bitch," Golden responded affectionately.

❖

All joking aside, Melissa wished it were that easy to find her a love life. It wasn't like she didn't want one. Up until she recently came out, dating had been difficult because she had sort of still lived at home, renting the apartment upstairs from her parents, but she didn't really have a private life. She couldn't bring anyone back to her place, and after a while, the few relationships she attempted didn't work out because she still hadn't come out. No one could understand, in today's world, how a woman her age could still be in the closet. Melissa had been honest enough with herself to know that no one was keeping her from being her true self except herself. Yes, years of homophobia from her family legitimately kept her from coming out while she still lived at home, but once she was earning a salary that gave her the means to move out, just four months later, she ended up right back at home when her mother had a stroke.

Melissa had been guilted by her stepfather, Reverend Joe Walker, into moving back to help take care of her. She spent months working a full-time job as a personal assistant, which sometimes led to working late nights or coming in early mornings while caring for her mother on nights and weekends as the reverend ran the streets as if everything were normal. Fortunately, Melissa had been able to convince him to let her live in the studio apartment on the second floor that had recently been vacated, but he still charged her the same rent he would any person off the street. They also had a nurse during the day while Melissa took over as soon as she got home, but she would end up paying the overtime needed for the nurse to stay or work over the weekend if she wanted to have at least the semblance of a social life.

That was five years ago. Within a year, her mother had recovered as much as her body could with minor mobility issues. Melissa had continued helping in the evenings with preparing dinner and taking her mother to bible study, choir practice, and her women's meetings at the church. She somehow found time to hang out with Golden and Zoe and even go on some dates, but living at home hindered her from opening to something serious. Then she met Leah Edwards, a contractor doing renovation at the home of the family she worked for. Melissa had tried to wave off Leah's flirtations, but her sexy butch demeanor and Melissa's loneliness had won the battle with the part of her that stubbornly insisted on remaining closeted until she could move away from home.

In the beginning, Leah had been fine with Melissa not being out, assuming it was just with her family, not still so far in the closet that she was paranoid about even going out and being seen on a date with another woman. Leah put up with not being able to pick Melissa up at work or her house when they went out, not being able to go to any part of Brooklyn on dates or give Melissa gifts in fear that her stepfather would find them. She'd once come home early from work to find him snooping around her apartment. He had claimed that there was a leak downstairs and wanted to make sure it wasn't coming from her bathroom, but since she caught him walking out of her bedroom, she knew he was lying.

The final straw for Leah happened almost a year into them dating. Melissa had rarely been around Leah's friends except to occasionally meet up for drinks so, against her better judgment, she had agreed to go to a friend's birthday party. Melissa still felt horrible just thinking about that night.

❖

Melissa hesitated as she and Leah were about to enter Marco's apartment. Leah took her hand and gave her an encouraging smile.

"Babe, it's gonna be okay. You know my friends, they like you, what's there to worry about?"

Melissa gazed nervously at the door. "It sounds like a lot of people in there. Maybe you should stay, and I'll just grab a car home."

Leah's smile faltered. "Melissa, please, I'm tired of having to hide away every time we see each other. I've spent more time in my apartment since I started dating you than I have in the three years I've lived there. It's somebody's home. I can't imagine you would run into any of your stepfather's cult followers here."

Melissa looked guiltily down at the bottle of wine she held. Leah was right. She had been more than patient with Melissa and her paranoia. She was developing serious feelings for Leah and knew that it was time to put her big girl panties on and accept how things were.

She gave Leah a nod and smiled. "Okay."

"That's my girl." Leah leaned in to place a soft kiss on Melissa's lips.

Melissa wasn't good with public displays of affection, but she refrained from turning away. The party was in full swing when they walked in. The open loft layout of the apartment allowed for what had to be at least thirty people already there to gather without making it difficult to walk through. Melissa had no idea how popular Leah was until she was hugged, gripped up and fist-bumped by practically everyone they passed as they made their way through the room to locate the guest of honor.

Melissa blushed with embarrassment as some of Leah's friends teased her that they thought Leah had made her up because they hadn't met her in the time they had been dating. They finally found Marco setting out food on the kitchen island with two women.

He clapped happily. "Melissa! I'm so glad you made it!" He introduced her to his mother and sister then pointed toward a table nearby set up as a bar for her to place the wine she'd brought as her and Leah's BYOB contribution.

As Melissa maneuvered to the table, she heard a familiar laugh and stopped to listen curiously. When she didn't hear it again, she continued. On her way back, she heard the laugh again and looked around because there was only one man she knew who laughed like that. She had seen him spend hours trying to perfect his favorite comedian, Eddie Murphy's laugh. Her heart skipped when she spotted her stepbrother Duane. He was standing next to the sofa with his hand intimately massaging the nape of a man who had to be half his age. The man had his arm around Duane's waist staring up at him adoringly as her stepbrother spoke. Then he responded, and to Melissa's further disbelief, Duane, who was a minister at the family's church and married with three kids, turned to him, and lowered his head for a kiss.

Melissa turned away from the scene before the kiss was done and hurried back to Leah. She couldn't let Duane see her here and have him running back to their parents to tell them.

"Leah, I'm sorry, but I need to leave."

"Leave? We just got here. Are you okay? You look like you're going to be sick," Leah said in concern.

"I just saw my stepbrother Duane," Melissa whispered.

Leah's brow furrowed in confusion. "Are you sure it was him?"

"Yes. I don't want to ruin your night. You stay and I'll just get a car or take the train home." Melissa tried to keep the rising panic from her voice. The longer she stayed the better chance Duane would see her.

"Didn't you tell me that Duane is one of the head pastors at your stepfather's church and has a whole family?"

"Yes." Melissa didn't know what that had to do with anything.

"So don't you think he'd probably be more worried about you seeing him than you should be about him seeing you?"

To a rational person, Leah's logic would make sense, but Melissa wasn't feeling rational. "Either way, I need to leave." She turned to Marco with a tentative smile. "Have a happy birthday."

Melissa walked away not even looking to see if Leah followed. Just kept her head down as she made her way to the door. She walked out into the hallway and took a shaky breath of relief.

"I can't do this anymore, Melissa."

She turned to find that Leah had followed her. The look of resignation on her face told Melissa that she'd finally reached the point where dating her was no longer worth it.

"I'm sorry," Melissa said shamefully.

Leah sighed with frustration. "You need to stop apologizing and find a way to either accept that this is who you are or spend the rest of your life alone. This is partially my fault because you warned me, and I didn't listen. I foolishly thought that I could be the catalyst that brought you out in the open, but obviously your issues are far too deep for me to be the one to do that."

Leah grasped Melissa's hands. "Babe, I love you and I hate that this is the first time I'm saying it, but I need you to know it because it's also the reason I can't do this anymore. I worked too hard to accept who I am to be pulled back into the shame and fear of the closet, and I need to be with someone who is in that same place in life."

Melissa's chest felt tight, and she couldn't speak past the lump in her throat, so she just nodded and gave Leah's hands a squeeze. Leah gave her a sad smile, pulled Melissa close, and pressed a soft lingering kiss to her lips before turning away. The sound of joy and laughter that drifted into the hall as Leah opened the door was like a knife to Melissa's already breaking heart.

❖

Leah never knew, but she was the catalyst for Melissa to find self-acceptance. After spending weeks wallowing in self-pity and regret at losing such a wonderful, loving, and understanding woman, Melissa found a therapist and started the slow and painful process of unpacking all her mental and emotional baggage. When she finally found the courage to come out to her family, she hadn't been surprised but was still hurt by their reaction. Her mother had just sat quietly with a look of disappointment. The reverend angrily accused her of lying and deceiving them all these years and that he wouldn't allow that nastiness in his house. He'd given her a month to vacate the apartment she was renting. Joe Jr. had smirked knowingly, and Duane had refused to look at her as he continued shoveling food in his mouth as if acknowledging her would've forced him to reveal his truth as well. Melissa felt that after the cruel way her stepbrothers had treated her growing up that she didn't owe them anything, but she had kept Duane's secret. That was his burden to bear, and it wasn't her place to add to it by telling him what she'd seen.

When Golden had offered to take Melissa in, she couldn't have asked for a better place to lay her head as she began this new chapter in her life. The Hughes family had always been the family of her heart, and for the first time since she was five years old, Melissa was finally living in a loving and supportive environment that allowed her to relax and be herself, which was probably why she was hesitating with even looking for a place. It didn't hurt that Golden wasn't pushing her to go either, although she did encourage Melissa to call Leah. She had been tempted so many times to reach out to her, but she felt that she still had a lot to work through on loving herself before she would be in a good place for a romantic relationship, and she was fine with that. She was happy, she was surrounded by her found family, had wonderful friends and a good job. There was nothing more she could ask for.

CHAPTER TWO

Heeey!" Zoe greeted Golden and Melissa as she unlocked the door to her salon. She was closed for business on Sundays but made exceptions for them because it also gave them a chance to hang out since they were all so busy.

Melissa pulled her into a hug. "Hey, girl!"

"What up, chickie," Golden said when she stepped in to greet her with a hug as well.

"You don't know how glad I am to see you two. I need you to talk me out of putting my child up for adoption," Zoe said as she locked the door behind them.

Golden chuckled. "What did my sweet Kiara do now?"

Zoe looked at her as if she'd said the sky was green. "Sweet? That child stopped being sweet the minute she turned fourteen. She had the nerve to tell me I needed to get a love life of my own, so I'd stay out of hers. I would've knocked her into next week if I wasn't afraid what the medical bill would be."

Melissa snickered, then shifted her face into a mask of sympathy at the annoyed look Zoe gave her. "She's a teenage girl coming into herself and testing her boundaries. I'm sure it wasn't said in a mean spirit."

"And what would your mother have done if you had spoken to her that way?" Zoe asked Melissa.

"Probably would've called the reverend to come pray over me because I wouldn't have said something so disrespectful unless the devil got my tongue," Melissa responded nonchalantly.

Zoe frowned. She had learned about Melissa's oppressive childhood a few months after they'd all started hanging out together. They were at Zoe's place and had gotten ridiculously drunk one night. Melissa had panicked about going home in such bad shape and having to hear a sermon from the reverend on the sins of alcohol. Zoe had suggested they all stay at her place. After Golden and Zoe had finally gotten Melissa to sleep, Golden told her about Melissa's devoutly religious family and upbringing. Melissa would sometimes make jokes about it or casual comments like she'd just done, but Golden and Zoe knew she still hurt from it.

"Is she right? Are you all up in her love life?" Golden asked.

"I'm her mother. I'm supposed to be all up in her love life."

"That's true, but there are ways to be involved without controlling it. I think you've been open and honest enough with Kiara for her to make the right decisions for herself. You have to show her that you trust her enough to do that," Golden suggested.

Zoe thought about that as she gathered the things she would need for Golden's hair. Golden sat in the chair first since her naturally curled style would take much less time than Melissa's waist-length locs.

Zoe sighed. "I guess you're right. I might've overreacted to the situation because she ultimately made the right decision."

"What happened?" Golden asked.

"She was supposed to be going to a sleepover but had gone to a party with her girlfriends to meet some boy. The boy turned out to be a jerk when he convinced her to go up to a bedroom to just talk, but that wasn't what he really wanted to do. Fortunately, those self-defense lessons Drew gave her came in handy. From what she told me, she left him holding his nuts and bawling like a baby in the middle of the room. She called me to come pick her up, and instead of listening, being happy that she was okay, and proud of how she defended herself, I grounded her for lying about the party that placed her in the situation in the first place." Zoe draped a cape around Golden.

"Well, grounding her for lying seems to be fair, but I think you should also tell her how proud you are of how she handled the situation and that you only got mad because you love her. I think that will take the sting out of the punishment," Melissa said.

"She may also be right about your love life. I think we all need to take Miss Kiara's advice and get love lives of our own. I know it's bad when my mother is asking me about dating apps for seniors," Golden said.

"Are you serious? Ms. Carlin trying to get out there?" Zoe said.

Golden smiled. "Yeah, girl, and I don't blame her. Daddy's been gone for fifteen years, I don't think even he would've wanted her to be alone for this long, but I think she's been using needing to take care of us as an excuse, and now that Drew and I are taking care of ourselves and her, she no longer has that to hide behind."

"Good for her. I think she deserves to find love just as much as anyone, no matter what age she is. Shoot, she's even more beautiful now than when I first met her," Melissa said.

Golden wrinkled her nose in disgust. "Ugh, Mel, even after all these years I still can't deal with your crush on my mother. It's just gross."

Melissa chuckled. "Hey, at least I'm not trying to be your stepmom."

Golden frowned at her. "Don't even joke about something like that."

"Considering that would take Mel actually admitting that she likes Ms. Carlin and taking action to pursue her, I don't think you have anything to worry about," Zoe said.

Melissa picked up a curler from a nearby cart and threw it at Zoe. "Y'all ain't right. Let me at least have my crushes in peace."

Zoe chuckled. She'd had plenty of girlfriends in her life but nothing like the friendship she shared with Melissa and Golden. Probably because it was the first adult friendship she had. She'd lost many of her childhood and college friends after getting pregnant and was no longer partying and hanging out. The ones she did still speak with were more acquaintances than friends since starting their own families. Melissa and Golden had become more like sisters Zoe never had and she treasured that. She thought back to how she had met Golden who had helped Zoe find a way to make her dreams come true.

❖

Zoe crossed her legs to keep them from bouncing nervously as she and her mother waited to be seen about getting a small business loan. She looked at the clock on the wall, took out her phone to text her grandmother that they were going to be late and to ask if she could pick up Kiara from daycare. Zoe hated not being the one to do it, but without this loan there was no way she would be able to provide herself and Kiara with the life she envisioned for them. A life that she knew she was going to have to provide alone since Kiara's father, Ray, left them high and dry when Zoe told him she was pregnant two years ago. Zoe's mother told her she needed to file for child support, but she decided that if Ray didn't want to be in his daughter's life, then she didn't want his money.

Zoe was just starting on the road to get her business degree before heading to cosmetology academy with plans to take over her family's salon when she graduated. A baby fit nowhere in either of those plans, but she was determined to make it work on her own. She didn't return to Temple University in the fall. Instead, she transferred her credits to New York University to finish school. The only time Zoe took off from school was the eight weeks she needed to recover from having Kiara. She received her bachelor's degree in business management and immediately enrolled in cosmetology school. She worked in the family's salon as receptionist, shampoo girl, and doing whatever other odd jobs needed to be done to help pay for diapers and formula while her mother and grandmother lovingly took on babysitting and supplying Kiara with anything else her little heart desired. Zoe's mother even added Kiara to her health insurance so that Zoe wouldn't go broke with what little money she was making from covering doctor appointments.

Now her mother was looking to retire soon and leave the salon in Zoe's hands which was why they were at the bank trying to get a loan to cover the upgrades she wanted to make. She gazed down at the folder in her hand. She had worked on her business plan for two months making sure she had answers to every question that would be asked.

Zoe's mother placed a hand on her knee. "Stop fidgeting. You're making me nervous."

"Sorry. I just need this to work so that we can get the Hair For You product line off the ground. That can't happen with the current salon setup."

"I know, but worrying yourself sick isn't going to help. We've already got Mr. Steinman offering the second floor of the building at a much lower rent than we expected because of how long he's had the salon as a tenant. Even if we can't get the loan, I'm sure Grandma and I can dip into the salon's emergency fund to handle at least half the renovations needed. The rest we can take care of once profits start coming in."

"No, Mommy, I can't let you do that. Taking you and Grandma's hair products off the salon's shelves to a wider distribution was my idea so I should be the one taking responsibility for funding it."

"Okay, but it's there if you need it."

Zoe laid her head on her mother's shoulder. "I know, Mommy. Thank you."

"Ms. Grant."

Zoe looked up to find a well-dressed woman who couldn't have been much older than her walking toward them with a bright smile. She and her mother stood.

"Technically, we're both Ms. Grant," she said, accepting the woman's hand in greeting. "I'm Zoe, this is my mother, Sandra."

"Nice to meet you. I'm Golden Hughes. I'll be assisting you with your loan request. If you'll follow me, we can see how Providence Bank can help you."

"She's young and Black like you. Could be a good sign," Zoe's mother whispered as they followed Golden.

Zoe held up her hand with her fingers crossed. They stopped at a partitioned desk.

"What can I do for you today?" Golden asked once they were all seated.

Zoe offered Golden her business plan, then gave her pitch which included financial and future expansion plans.

"Well, Ms. Grant, just from my brief perusal, I can see you've got everything very well thought out. It's a solid plan and the amount that you're asking is more than fair. Let's see what we can do."

Golden asked all the necessary questions to fill out the application and do a credit check. Zoe had two outstanding student loan payments but other than that, her credit was very good, and her mother's score was almost perfect so she couldn't imagine them being turned down until she saw Golden frowning at her computer monitor.

"Is there something wrong?" Zoe asked.

Golden turned to her with a smile that didn't hide the concern in her eyes. "If you'll excuse me for just a minute, I need to check something."

After Golden left, Zoe was very tempted to peek over at the monitor but didn't think that would look good if she got caught. "I wonder what that's about?"

Her mother sucked her teeth in disgust. "I can give you one answer." She raised her hand and pointed to the back of it.

Golden frowned. "You think we're about to get turned down because we're Black?"

"Lenny from the barbershop across the street said he and a few other Black-owned businesses in the area had applied for loans at this bank over the years, and no matter how good their credit was or how much collateral they had they were turned down. I didn't say anything because I had done some research and found out that they had cleaned house with management and hired more Black folks. But I guess that might have been for appearances."

"Let's not jump to conclusions. Maybe there was a glitch in the system that she needed to speak to someone about."

Zoe was determined to remain hopeful despite the concern from what her mother said. It wasn't unheard of for a bank, especially a small one not connected to any of the major national banks, to discriminate against the very people in the community they did business with. A moment later, Golden returned looking as if she were trying to hold her temper in check.

She sat down with a tired sigh. "I'm sorry but we're not able to approve your loan. You have a large amount of student debt and a few late payments on it that concern the bank's managers. They feel it would be too risky to loan you the amount that you're asking for."

Zoe tried to hide her disappointment. "Okay, so how much would they be willing to loan us?"

Golden glared at something past Zoe and her mother then looked back at them. "Five thousand."

"Five thousand! You're joking, right?" Sandra said angrily.

Zoe placed a calming hand on her mother's leg. She didn't want to make a scene which would happen if she didn't check her mother now.

"That would barely cover the updates needed on the salon equipment alone." She felt like she wanted to cry. "Thank you, Ms. Hughes."

They stood to leave. "Zoe."

"Yes."

Golden looked warily past them again then moved from behind the desk and handed her a card before whispering, "Give me a call after three o'clock today. I might have a way for you to get the assistance you need." Then she gave her a friendly smile and offered her hand. "Thank you for coming."

Zoe gazed down at the business card with the bank's logo and Golden's business contact information in the typeset and another phone number written neatly at the bottom of the card. "Thank you. I'll do that."

❖

Golden had connected Zoe to an angel investor group where she was introduced to Alex Prince of Prince Property Management Group who invested in her plans only asking for ten percent of the profit made from Hair For You's product line. Now, ten years later, Zoe was opening a Hair For You II Salon in northern New Jersey and the Hair For You product line was one of the top selling natural hair care lines for Women of Color in the industry. Hair was Zoe's passion. Following her passion and finally seeing it all come to fruition thanks to Golden and her Angel Investor friend as well as gaining two wonderful friends in the process proved that there was nothing else that she would rather do.

"I have an idea. Next Friday I'm going to a client's birthday party. Why don't you guys come as my guests? It would be a chance for us to get out and have some real fun. Something we haven't done since our last girl's trip," Zoe said.

"I'm all for it. What about you, Mel?" Golden said happily.

"Are you sure it would be okay for you to bring both of us? Party invites usually give you a plus-one, not plus-two."

"It's a charity event. I'm sure she'll have no problem with my donation from purchasing an extra ticket. There is absolutely no excuse you could give me that I would accept as reasonable, so I won't take no for an answer," Zoe told her.

Melissa worried her bottom lip with her teeth.

"Pleeeease, Mel," Golden pleaded.

Melissa sighed in resignation. "Fine, but I'm going to need to do some shopping because I have nothing to wear."

"I never say no to a shopping expedition," Golden said.

❖

Golden walked into the supper club where Zoe's client's birthday party was being held and felt like she'd just stepped back in time. The club was decorated like something out of the gilded age with detailed moldings, gilded walls, high ceilings with grand crystal and gold chandeliers and sconces, and luxurious fabrics draped along the huge windows with the décor done in creams, blue, and white. It was elegant and rich without being ostentatious. At the far end of the room was a staircase lined with white wrought iron railings that led to a balcony overlooking the dining area. A jazz band played on a stage beneath the balcony and what she assumed was a performance stage sat along a wall at the end of the staircase.

Everyone was dressed in stylish evening wear that evoked the theme of the night, the Harlem Renaissance. Golden was glad she and Melissa had decided to go shopping earlier in the day because the Halloween flapper dresses that they had from a 1920s theme party a few years back would have been too tacky for this crowd who looked more like the high society Renaissance crowd than the dance hall crowd that the flappers in that time had migrated to. Golden wore an ankle-length gold sequin and ivory satin evening gown with a low-cut v-neckline and cap sleeves, opera-length black satin gloves, a double strand ivory pearl necklace and matching bracelet, black and silver vintage chandelier earrings, and black stiletto Mary Jane pumps. She had managed to tame her thick curls into finger waves in the front and pulled the rest back into a chignon. She loved the style of the dress because it accentuated her curvaceous figure and narrow waist but also had more give than it looked for dancing.

"Okay, who is this client of yours?" Melissa asked, a tremor in her voice as she gazed nervously around at the large crowd of people mingling about.

She wore a gold sleeveless dress with a modest v-neckline with black and gold sequin and beads arranged in an art deco design and fringe along the knee-length hem, similar black gloves as Golden, a triple strand ivory pearl choker with matching bracelet and pearl drop earrings, black stockings with a seam up the back and a pair of black low-heeled pumps. Both she and Zoe had styled their locs into intricately twisted buns at the backs of their heads, although Melissa's were so long that she had to leave some hanging down her back in a long, thick braid so the bun wouldn't weigh her head down on her neck. She looked fabulous, but Golden could tell she was nervous about the fitted dress accentuating her soft curves.

Zoe looped an arm through each of theirs to lead them farther into the room. "Her name is Belinda. Her wife, Ebony, is throwing this party for her."

Zoe's slim frame was draped in a sleeveless above-the-knee-length black glitter sequin cocktail dress that was covered in tiers of fringe from neckline to hem that undulated with her every move. She wore a silver pearl and rhinestone necklace with matching chandelier earrings, and a pair of rhinestone high-heeled sandals with an ankle strap. She looked like she fit in well with this crowd. As Golden looked around, she recognized several famous faces and suddenly stopped short at the sight of two R&B artists she'd recently discovered and fallen completely in love with.

"Is that the Rhythm Twins standing over by the piano?" she asked in amazement.

"Oh, yeah. Ebony is their producer," Zoe said matter-of-factly as she continued pulling them in that direction.

"Wait, this is Ebony Trent's wife's party?"

Zoe grinned mischievously. "Yep. Did I forget to mention that?"

Golden bumped Zoe with her hip. "Uh, yes!"

"Does it matter? They're people just like us."

Melissa snorted in derision. "Who just so happen to be rich and famous. I think I need to go to the bathroom." She attempted to break off from their little group, but Zoe was stronger than she looked and held tight.

It wouldn't have mattered anyway because they were spotted by the guest of honor who squealed in delight as she hurried forward to meet them. Zoe released them to step into her open arms.

"Zoe! I'm so glad you could make it. I've been getting compliments on my hair all night, so I need to steal you away to introduce my fabulous stylist to some industry folks," Belinda said. Her locs were twisted into an elegant updo with red and black glittering gems laced throughout to match the red and black beading on her gown. Zoe's hair artistry, especially when it came to braids and locs, was fabulous.

"Well, before you do, allow me to introduce my best girls in the whole wide world." Zoe waved Golden and Melissa forward. "Belinda Trent, this is Golden Hughes and Melissa Hart."

Golden offered her hand in greeting and Belinda waved it off and pulled her into a hug, followed by a bashful Melissa.

Belinda smiled broadly. "I've heard so much about you two that I feel like I know you already. Let me introduce you to my wife, then I'm going to leave you in her hands while I steal Zoe for a bit."

Belinda looped her arm through Zoe's as she walked back toward the group she had been with. Golden and Melissa followed dutifully behind them.

Melissa moved closer to Golden. "I really do need to go to the ladies' room. I don't feel well."

Golden grasped her hand and gave it a quick squeeze. "Breathe. It's just your nerves. Zoe is right. They're just regular folk like us. They just happen to be famous."

"Yeah, that helps."

Golden chuckled, but her stomach was doing flips as they reached the piano and Belinda began the introductions. Meeting Ebony was cool, especially since she and her father used to listen to her music, but the Rhythm Twins, Jade Sloan and Kendra Elmwood, who weren't twins or even related, had her feeling like a teenager finally getting to talk to her crush for the first time.

Belinda introduced Zoe and Melissa first, then smiled broadly as she introduced Golden. "And this is Golden Hughes. I've been told she's a big fan."

Golden felt her face flush hotly. She knew Zoe had something to do with that little introduction.

Jade took her hand. "It's a pleasure to meet a fan, Golden. Is that your real name?"

Golden knew from watching interviews of the Twins that Jade was of mixed heritage with a Japanese father and African American mother. She stood a few inches taller than Golden with a slim athletic figure, smooth bronze complexion, angular features, and deep brown, almost black eyes. She was dressed in black pin-striped slacks, a matching vest with a pocket watch hanging on a gold chain from a buttonhole to a small pocket of her vest, a white shirt with the sleeves rolled up to reveal slight but muscular forearms and the buttons at the collar left open where a red paisley tie loosely lay. Her jet-black hair was styled in a straight bob combed over to one side with a shaved undercut. Golden tried not to get lost in the dark pool of her cat-like eyes and thick lashes.

"Unless my family has been lying to me all these years, yes, it is."

Kendra playfully pushed Jade aside and took Golden's hand. "You'll have to excuse my rude friend. She's got no home training. It's a pleasure to meet you, Golden."

Kendra's sexy smile was just as hypnotic as Jade's eyes. She was the same height as Jade and dressed in a similar outfit except her pants and vest were light gray. That's where the similarities in the Twins ended. Kendra had a dark mahogany complexion, broad-shouldered muscular figure, round face, dimpled cheeks, a fade haircut, and soft brown eyes.

"It's a pleasure to meet you all as well." There was something about the way Jade and Kendra looked at her that made Golden feel as if they were the only three in the room.

"Um, sorry for interrupting, but do either of you know where the ladies' room is?" someone asked softly. Golden gave a quick glance to find Melissa standing beside her. She had forgotten she was even there. Kendra smiled at her, and Melissa looked bashfully away.

"Just past the entrance," Kendra said.

"Thank you," Melissa squeaked before turning to walk away.

Golden found herself nervous about being alone with Jade and Kendra. "Melissa, wait, I'll go with you."

Melissa looked relieved when Golden joined her. They made their way through the crowd, past the entrance where a line of guests was still queued waiting to get into the club, to a long hallway where the restrooms were located. They joined the line leading into the ladies' room.

"Are you okay?" Golden asked Melissa who looked a little green around the gills.

Melissa fanned herself with her hand. "I'm fine. I just felt weirdly out of place."

Golden took her hand. "Mel, you belong here just as much as any of those people. We're guests just like them."

Melissa gave her hand a squeeze then released it. "I know. I guess it's just been a while since I've really been out, and the fact that there are people I see on television or whose music I listen to on a regular basis in the same room is surreal. I just needed a minute to catch my breath."

"Why don't we get a couple of drinks to relax. I promise not to leave your side. If you decide that you want to leave, we'll just find Zoe, thank her, and head out. I'm sure she'll understand."

Melissa nodded. "Okay. Unless you need to go, we don't need to wait."

Golden looked at the half dozen women in front of them and stepped out of line. "No, I'm good for now."

They walked out into the main room toward the bar, ordered glasses of wine, then found a quiet little area to stand.

"I noticed the Twins were checking you out like you were the main course on the menu," Melissa said teasingly.

Golden grinned. "You think both of them were?"

"Yeah, because as soon as they laid eyes on you no one else seemed to exist."

"That's because of what Belinda said about me being a big fan. I'm sure it was nothing more than them humoring a groupie." Golden secretly hoped it was more than that, but she wouldn't say it out loud. Despite spending many moments imagining being with them individually while she listened to their smooth, sexy voices, seeing them together in person brought kinkier thoughts to mind.

"They're even more attractive in person. If you had a choice, which one would you pick?" Melissa asked as if reading her thoughts.

"I'm not interested and I'm sure they've probably forgotten me already with the number of fans they meet on a regular basis."

"Yeah, okay. They were practically drooling when you walked away."

Golden looked at Melissa in surprise. "Really?"

Melissa grinned knowingly. "Not interested, huh?"

Golden rolled her eyes. "Shut up." She spotted Zoe walking toward them.

"There you two are. Let me grab a drink and then we can head to our table. The dinner and show are about to start."

They waited for Zoe to get her drink then followed her to a table located a few rows back from the performance stage and the head table where the guest of honor and her guests were seated. Their table included them and three other guests who didn't look to be anyone famous. Introductions were made all around as they sat down.

Melissa leaned in toward Zoe whispering excitedly, "Isn't that celebrity chef Chayse Carmichael?"

"Yes, and that's her wife, Serena. You already met the Twins, and next to them is Pure Music's CEO, Cass Phillips, and her fiancé, Faith Shaw."

"I'm sure glad we're not at that table," Melissa said with relief. "Although, from the way they're looking over here, I think the Twins wished we were."

Golden gazed up from the menu card she had been reading to find Jade and Kendra grinning at her. Jade gave her a wink and Kendra blew her a kiss before she quickly brought her gaze back down to the menu as her face flushed hotly.

"Girl, your face is as red as the roses in the centerpieces," Zoe said humorously.

"Y'all ain't right," she said, despite the smile on her face.

Fortunately, the servers came around to take everyone's order from the three options on the menu, sufficiently distracting Golden's friends from teasing her. During their meal, she would peek up to find either Jade or Kendra watching her. It wasn't long before she was exchanging flirtatious glances with them. Once dinner was cleared the lights were dimmed and a spotlight shone on the bandstand where a woman who could be Lena Horne's twin, dressed in a beautiful glittery, slinky black gown stood at the microphone. The band played the opening refrain of Anita Baker's "Sweet Love," and she joined in singing with a smoky, sultry voice that made Golden feel like she really had been transported back to 1925 Harlem. Then the spotlight slowly moved up to the balcony above.

Striking a sexy pose on the balcony was a beautiful Black woman dressed in a black glittery gown with spaghetti straps, a glittery black corset around her waist, and hip high slits up both sides. She also wore long black gloves and a matching cloche skull cap with sculpted locks of hair coming out the side of the cap to curl along her cheeks and forehead. She slowly descended the stairs with the spotlight following her to the stage as the singer crooned. The woman began a sexy, burlesque style striptease that had Golden enthralled. Where pole dancing was about pole tricks to entertain the audience, burlesque was more about slow, subtle body movements that were meant to entice and tease. It allowed the performer to be playful and witty with her actions as she performed a slow striptease, and Golden loved it.

She gazed around the room and noticed how rapt everyone was then back at the performer and something old and almost forgotten rose within her. It started in the center of her chest and spread outward through her torso, into her limbs and shoved all thoughts but one from her mind—the urge to dance. Not like the kind of dancing she did in the rhythm and movement classes she took as part of her fitness routine or sweaty mindless dancing she did when she and her girls ventured out to a nightclub. She had that old feeling she used to get when she danced before her father passed away. In her mind, she saw herself clear as day on a stage again but not with one of her complicated choreographed contemporary routines. She saw herself as if she were the woman spotlighted, tempting and teasing her audience and seeming to gaze at each of them as if she were there for them alone. She controlled the crowd as if she were a charmer and they were all a roomful of snakes at her command.

"She's amazing," Zoe said in awe.

Golden smiled. "Yes, she is."

Melissa bumped her with her shoulder. "I recognize that look. It's about time."

Golden gazed over at her in confusion. "What look?"

"The look you used to get when your dad took us to see Alvin Ailey performances. Like you're dreaming of the day you'll be on that stage."

"Considering this isn't Alvin Ailey, I think you're mistaken." Golden turned back toward the performance.

"I could see you up there. I always thought you moved so sensuously when you danced, you've got a natural hourglass figure without even needing a corset, and those dreamy amber eyes and sexy mouth would have all these folks drooling."

Golden snorted in derision. "Yeah, right. I don't think so."

Despite her response, an idea was niggling its way into her head.

"What are you two going on about?" Zoe asked.

"Golden is thinking about becoming a burlesque dancer," Melissa answered.

Golden rolled her eyes. "I am not."

"Oh my God! Yes! I can totally see it," Zoe said excitedly.

Golden looked from one to the other. "Have you two lost your minds? I'm not going to leave a six-figure-salary job to shimmy, shake, and strip for a living." When she turned back to the stage, the performance was ending with the dancer striking a seductive pose once again. She was stripped down to red rhinestone pasties covering her nipples, red lace G-string panties, and her heels. It had only been a four-minute performance, but she received resounding applause and whistles. What followed were three more diverse and fabulous performances, one of which was an amazing aerial burlesque performed by another curvaceous Black performer to "El Tango de Roxanne" from *Moulin Rouge*. Golden was completely hooked after that, but she attempted to hide it because she didn't want Melissa or Zoe bugging her about it.

After the performances and cake, the rest of the night was dedicated to drinking and partying the night away. As Golden danced with Zoe and Melissa, Jade and Kendra walked over, grasped her hand, and led her away from them. She was placed between them as they smoothly danced around her, giving her the opportunity to dance with each of them without her having to spin in a circle. When the band switched into a samba Jade, who was facing her, took her hands while Kendra placed hers on Golden's hips. The three of them moved as if their rhythm were synced as one as they danced a bachata. She was spun around for Kendra to now take her hands and Jade grasped her hips. It wasn't much different than when she had danced with multiple partners back in the day, but the smoldering looks and sexy grins they gave her had Golden's whole body flushed with desire. When the song came to its closing refrain, they smoothly spun her a few more times as if they knew she was an experienced dancer and wouldn't fall over from dizziness, then each grasped one of her hands, placed their other hand on her back, and expertly dipped her. That's when Golden noticed that no one else was dancing. They were all gathered around to watch her, Jade, and Kendra and were now giving them a round of applause. She would've expected to feel embarrassed but instead she felt that wonderful high she used to feel after a performance as well as desire for the two women she'd partnered with.

"I think we need to take Miss Golden on the road with us, Jade. What do you think?" Kendra gave her a wink.

Jade's full lips spread into a sexy grin. "Hell yeah. What do you think, Ms. Golden? Wanna make this duo a threesome?"

Golden didn't miss the double entendre in her question and was tempted to say yes, but she had a feeling these two were double trouble. "I think we need to give our audience a bow, then I need to call it a night. I have work tomorrow."

They both looked disappointed but grasped her hands and joined her in a bow. The band transitioned into a slow R&B number, and Golden took that moment to make her escape. "Thank you for the dance."

She attempted to slip her hands from theirs as couples began to come together and dance around them. Kendra led them off the dance floor with Jade still holding her other hand, trailing behind her. Somehow Kendra located Melissa and Zoe and steered them in their direction.

Zoe greeted them with quiet applause. "Okay now! You all looked like you belonged on *Dancing With the Stars* out there."

Golden rolled her eyes. "Are y'all ready to go?"

"Yes, but we didn't want to ruin your fun." Melissa gave her a knowing grin.

"We're trying to convince Golden to go on tour with us, but she's playing coy," Kendra said, both she and Jade were still holding Golden's hands.

Melissa quirked a brow. "Did she tell you she used to be a dancer?"

Golden's gaze narrowed in warning.

"I knew it by the way those hips were moving and how you managed those spins at the end so gracefully. You holdin' out on us, Golden?" Jade said.

Golden smoothly slid her hands from theirs and moved to stand with Melissa and Zoe. "That was a long time ago and I really do need to get home. It was a pleasure meeting you."

Kendra chuckled. "I think we've just been dismissed, Jade."

Jade sighed dramatically. "I guess our charm doesn't quite go with Gold."

Golden grinned at her pun. "It's not you. I'm just not in the market for charms of any kind right now."

Zoe reached into her beaded reticule and pulled out a phone. Golden immediately recognized the purple case as she handed it to her. "Why don't you exchange numbers? You know, just in case you change your mind."

Golden gave Zoe a look that warned her she was going to pay for that later, then turned back to Jade and Kendra with a smile. "Yes, why don't we exchange numbers."

Kendra smiled. "May I?" She pointed toward Golden's phone.

Golden unlocked and handed it over. Kendra opened her contacts, typed in some information, then passed her phone back to her.

"I added both of our personal cell numbers in case you might like to grab a cup of coffee sometime," Kendra said.

"Which we sincerely hope you do because we would really like to get to know you," Jade said.

Golden could see the sincerity in their gazes. They weren't just looking for a groupie booty call. They genuinely wanted to spend time getting to know her. As appealing as their invitation was, she didn't have time to pursue a relationship with anyone, let alone this tempting pair because Golden had a feeling they came as a package deal.

"That's sweet. My job pretty much takes up ninety percent of my life, but I'll keep that in mind. Good luck on your tour." Golden was mentally kicking herself as she blew them off as nicely as she could.

Jade smirked. "We can take a hint. It was a pleasure meeting you, Golden." She took Golden's hand and raised it toward her lips for a soft kiss on her knuckles.

"Yes, it was." Kendra stepped forward and placed a lingering kiss on Golden's cheek.

"Ladies," they said in unison with a nod to acknowledge Melissa and Zoe before walking away.

Melissa sighed dreamily. "Girl, you are all kinds a fool for letting them get away."

"Who are you telling?" Golden watched them disappear into the crowd feeling a twinge of regret.

CHAPTER THREE

It had been three weeks since the party, and Golden found she couldn't get two things off her mind—the Rhythm Twins and the burlesque performances. She decided there was only one thing that she could do something about without getting herself caught up in something she wasn't ready for. She looked up the club where the party had taken place, found out who the performers were, then did a social media search for them and reached out to the first performer, known as Opal, to ask where she had trained. To Golden's surprise, the woman responded immediately with information for a studio where she taught burlesque dance classes. She was happy to learn that there was a class on Sundays, which was perfect since she didn't think she would be able to do any of the weekday evening or Saturday classes because of her work and travel schedule. She signed up for the class that Sunday before she could change her mind.

The day of her class, Golden told Melissa and her mother she was going to work out at the gym, which was normal for her if she didn't get much time to do so during the week. She took the train into downtown Manhattan. When she arrived at the studio, Golden thought she had walked into the wrong place as there were several women dressed in dance leotards and heels who looked far from being amateurs taking a class, and another three were performing tricks on three of the four poles in the center of the studio. Opal had told her to dress comfortably as if she were going to work out so Golden wore a sports bra and leggings. She started to leave until she caught sight of Opal waving her over toward a group of ladies she stood with.

"You're Golden, right?"

Golden accepted the hand Opal offered in greeting. "Yes."

Opal gave her a smirk. "When I saw your IG pic, I remembered you from the Trent party. You and the Rhythm Twins put on quite a show."

Golden smiled. "You saw that, huh?"

"Oh yeah. The three of you together was stunning. It was like you were moving as one. I could also tell you've had some dance experience."

"Yes. I trained in ballet, jazz, contemporary, hip hop, tap, and even a little ballroom."

"Do you still dance?"

Golden shrugged. "Unless you call a rhythm workout class every now and then or out clubbing with my girls dancing, nothing full-time since I quit fifteen years ago."

"Really? Then you must be a natural because you move like you've never stopped."

"Thank you. Was I mistaken in thinking this was the burlesque class tonight?" Golden asked, indicating the women on the poles.

Opal waved dismissively. "You're good. They take both my pole and burlesque classes. They're just warming up. Did you happen to bring a pair of dance shoes? If not, I can loan you a pair from the extras I keep in back."

"No, I'm good." Golden pointed to her bag which held a pair of low-heeled dance shoes she'd bought earlier in the week. She had made sure to break them in by wearing them around the house when she got home after work.

Opal nodded. "Excellent. You'll fit right in. Everyone here has some dance experience, so this should be a great class. In the meantime, introduce yourselves and we'll begin shortly." She gave Golden and the other ladies a smile and left the group to speak with the women on the poles.

"So that was you dancing with the Twins?" said a young woman who looked Golden up and down curiously.

"Uh, yes. Were you at the party?"

She looked back at Golden in amusement. "I wish! No, it's all over social media." She pulled her phone out and handed it to Golden.

From the view of the person recording, Golden saw them working their way through the crowded dance floor to stop at the edge of the circle that had formed around her, Jade, and Kendra as they danced. She didn't recognize the woman in the video as herself. That woman moved with a wild abandon and sensuality and a look of utter joy that surprised Golden to realize was coming from her. Jade and Kendra obviously had some Latin dance experience with how expertly they moved and passed her back and forth. Was this what others saw when she danced? To see what she felt on the inside shown so obviously on the outside made her crave that feeling again. She missed the thrill she used to get from dancing. The ability to lose herself and escape from the outside world, just for a little while, and enjoy just being free and physical. She felt an inkling of that while she watched Opal and the other burlesque performers and when she danced with Jade and Kendra.

When the video ended, she handed the young woman the phone with an embarrassed smile. "I had no idea anyone recorded it."

"The Rhythm Twins were asked about it on their radio interview this morning," another of the women in the group said. "You three were hot together." She offered Golden her hand. "I'm Santee."

Golden accepted it. "I'm Golden."

Santee was the same height as Golden, with a lean, svelte dancer's body, platinum blond hair styled in a short pixie cut, sun-kissed tanned complexion like she'd just stepped off a beach, and deep blue eyes. Santee introduced her to the other ladies in the small group. All were professional dancers looking to expand their skills with the recent popularity of burlesque. All had also seen the video and wanted to know if she was dating either Jade or Kendra.

"No. I'd just met them that night. It was one dance then I had to leave."

The first young woman, Brandy, who had shown her the video looked as if she didn't believe her. "You all look like there was more than just one dance between you."

"They were very nice, and it was fun but really, that's the extent of my time with them," she said, although, in the back of her mind she wished otherwise, as she hadn't stopped thinking about them since that night. She'd avoided the temptation to stalk them on social media which was probably why she missed the video of them going viral and had to talk herself out of calling them.

"Well, we better get ready. Opal is a stickler for starting on time." Santee thankfully put an end to Brandy's prying.

Brandy shrugged, then walked away with the remaining young ladies following her. It was obvious she was the leader of their little pack.

Santee sat on the floor to change into her shoes. "These young girls are always so ready to spill the tea."

Golden grinned at hearing this blonde hair, blue-eyed chick talking about spilling the tea like she was down with the culture. "I think it's more like the six degrees of separation theory. If I was dating one of the Twins, they could say they were connected to them because they know me."

"I guess. So, if you were dating one of them, which would it be?" Santee gave her a teasing wink.

Golden chuckled. "If I was dating one of them, which I'm not, I wouldn't kiss and tell."

Santee nodded. "Good answer."

Once they were both in their dance shoes, Golden and Santee joined the other ladies in their class. Santee introduced Golden to the ladies that had been on the poles at her entrance and she found that other than Brandy and her little twenty-something clique, they were all in their thirties. Golden felt much more comfortable knowing that. Once she got started it was like her body remembered just what to do and she was able to pick up the moves quicker than she expected. By the end of the two-hour class, Golden was thoroughly hooked on burlesque.

"You're a natural," Santee said as they were gathering their things at the end of class.

Golden felt her face heat with a blush. "Thank you. You're not so bad yourself. Do you do this for a living?"

"Not right now, but I am planning to switch careers soon to join Opal's troupe."

"What do you do now?"

"I'm a Rockette."

Golden gazed at Santee in surprise. "Really? I mean, I could see with those legs, but what makes a Rockette want to become a burlesque dancer?"

"Being a Rockette isn't all that it's hyped up to be. It's seasonal work that I have to audition for every season no matter how many years I've been doing it. Fortunately, I've made it every season for the past six years. Once I've made it past auditions, there's six weeks of rehearsals before the shows open which consist of six hours a day, six days a week. Once the show opens, then it's performing between two and four shows a day with only an hour and a half break between shows. On top of that, the salary is only about $39,000 annually so I work in the wardrobe department for the Broadway show *Wicked* to make ends meet between seasons."

"Wow, I had no idea."

Santee shrugged. "Don't get me wrong. I love it, but I'm getting too old for this life. Time to make room for the young and eager Brandys of the world."

Golden gazed over at Brandy showing off her pole skills as one of her girls recorded it, no doubt for all her social media fans. "I think the Brandys of the world may be a little too lit for the sedate life of a Rockette."

Santee grinned. "Yeah, you're probably right there."

Golden watched Brandy perform a death drop and shook her head in amazement. Burlesque was definitely more her speed.

❖

Melissa grinned knowingly as she listened to Golden excitedly talking about her burlesque class. She loved seeing that spark in her eyes again. She knew Golden had been trying to hide how much she missed that part of her life, but she also knew Golden better than she knew herself sometimes. Despite why she'd stopped dancing, doing so had left a big hole in Golden's heart that she seemed determined to fill with either more work or meaningless hookups. Melissa sometimes wished she had something in her life to be that passionate about. She was great at her job, but that's all it was to her, a job. A means to pay her bills and live. It didn't bring out any of the joy she saw in Golden's face when she talked about dance or Zoe's when she talked about hair. When she had mentioned this to her therapist, she had suggested that Melissa find a hobby or something outside of work and her friends that could bring out that passion she craved. So far nothing appealed to her, so she stopped trying.

"Are you ready for your interview tomorrow?" Golden asked.

Melissa sighed. "As ready as I'll ever be. I appreciate you setting this up."

"You need to get away from that family. You've somehow gone from house manager to nanny. Those kids are gonna run you ragged in another year. Vivienne's kids are all grown, and her grandkids live out of state, so you won't have to worry about trying to take anybody to a soccer practice or cello lesson again."

"You're making it sound like I got the job already. It's just the first interview."

Golden waved dismissively. "You're a shoe-in."

Melissa chuckled. "Thanks for the vote of confidence. We'll see."

The next morning, Melissa arrived fifteen minutes early for her two o'clock interview with Vivienne Baxter, the owner of Art is Life Gallery in Soho. Golden had told her that Vivienne was a stickler for punctuality and believed in the adage that early was on time and on time was late. Golden had also tried to get her to loosen up her conservative wardrobe as Vivienne was a very bohemian and fashionable woman, but Melissa was there to show professionalism which is what Vivienne had said was most important to her when they spoke briefly on the phone last week. She chose to wear a burgundy skirt suit, blush pink button-down blouse, and burgundy flats which she believed was both fashionable and professional enough to satisfy the colorful Vivienne Baxter.

She walked into the gallery to find Vivienne sitting at the front desk on a call. She smiled at Melissa and pointed toward a nearby seating area. Vivienne joined her a short time later. She was a tall, elegant woman with short salt-and-pepper natural hair, smooth, pecan complexion that made her look decades younger than her reported age of seventy, dressed in a bright and colorful Moroccan print shirt and wide leg palazzo pants, wedge heeled sandals that must have added another three inches to her tall height, and chunky hammered gold jewelry adorning her ears, neck, and wrists. Melissa felt at ease with her bright, friendly smile as she offered her hand, wrist jingling with bracelets, in greeting.

"You must be Melissa."

Melissa stood and grasped her hand. "Yes. It's a pleasure to meet you, Mrs. Baxter."

"Please, call me Vivienne. Have a seat. Since the temp I was supposed to have today was a no-show we'll have to do the interview here instead of my office."

"Whatever works for you."

Vivienne tapped on the tablet she'd brought over with her. "You have a short but impressive resume. I know both gentlemen you've worked for and the fact that you've spent eight years with Ron Lee's family is a major feat. He's a hard-ass in his business and personal life."

Melissa smiled tentatively. She didn't think bad-mouthing her current boss would win her any points with Vivienne. "He can be demanding, but I mostly work for Mrs. Lee."

Vivienne smiled knowingly. "Diplomatic and loyal, I like that. I see you also minored in event management. That's excellent as this position requires coordinating many gallery and personal events for me. I've already spoken with the first employer you've listed, and he had nothing but rave reviews of you. You also come highly recommended by Golden, and despite your friendship, I know she wouldn't send you my way if she didn't think you'd be a good fit. So, tell me—"

The sound of a buzzer interrupted them. Vivienne looked at her phone. "Shit. That's the bell for the back door. I have an exhibit being delivered and set up. Damn temp is screwing up my whole day. This is going to take some time. I'll understand if you can't wait," she said in frustration.

"I can wait. I took the day off, so I don't have anything else on my schedule."

Vivienne looked relieved. "Great. There's a kitchenette down the hall. Feel free to grab some coffee or a beverage. I'll try to be as quick as possible."

Melissa watched her hurry off toward the back of the gallery. Once she was out of sight Melissa collapsed back into the chair with a sigh of relief. She knew it was a necessary evil, but she hated the whole process of interviewing for jobs. It was just as bad as dating. You meet to see if you're compatible, it goes great, then you nervously wait around for days for them to call you back. If they do, then you're either lucky enough to get a second interview or they're telling you that they're just not that into you. Then there are those that ghost you because they don't even think you're worth that call to tell you they're not into you.

She and Vivienne hadn't spoken long before the interruption for Melissa to get a feel if she was into her, but it was starting off well so she could only hope. She needed a change. The family she worked for demanded too much of her time and energy. Living with them during the week meant she was on call practically twenty-four hours a day. She wasn't a social butterfly, but she at least wanted to have more than two days a week to decompress and have the semblance of a life outside of work. It also didn't help that as her employer's children got older their cuteness wore off and their privilege and entitlement had begun to kick in and was wearing on her last nerve. She'd become a glorified chauffer and nanny, spending more time running them around than managing the household which was what she'd originally been hired to do when she accepted the job eight years ago.

Melissa stood and wandered around the nearby exhibits. The gallery was big, taking up at least two storefronts. Most of the art was Afrocentric in style, but there were many other general looking pieces. One exhibit caught her eye. Despite knowing she was the only one in the gallery,

Melissa looked around to see if anyone else was there before approaching the alcove where it was located. There were several large panels that took up the entire alcove. They were all black-and-white photos of the same muscularly toned woman dressed in a black strapless leather corset, black leather booty shorts, spiked heel stiletto thigh high leather boots, a leather mask covering the entire top half of her face and head, and a long ponytail coming out of the back that brushed the top of her rounded behind.

The first picture featured the leather clad woman standing with one booted foot propped on a stool, while a man knelt in front of the stool licking the toe of her boot. The next picture featured her sitting in a cushioned chair with another woman sitting beside the chair with her head in the woman's lap as she was being stroked and a man curled around her feet. The third picture featured a third man on all fours drinking something from a bowl on the floor as the woman propped her foot on him just as she did the stool in the first picture with her stiletto heel dug into his back. All the models were dressed in cat ears and whiskers, leather harnesses, and jock straps for the men and a G-string for the woman. The last in the series featured the woman standing in a tall spread-legged stance holding a flogger with arm-length tassels in both hands as the four models knelt at her feet.

There were a couple of things that stood out for Melissa. The first was the confidence and power in the woman's eyes and smile as she stared directly at the camera. As if she were challenging the observer to join in her little game. The second was the adoration in the models' expressions as they gazed up at the woman. Even the man drinking from the bowl had such a look of pleasure on his face that Melissa felt compelled to turn away but found she couldn't. Although she couldn't fully see the woman's face, there was something familiar about her. It was as if she saw herself as the woman holding such command and presence from her adoring audience. She looked for the small plate that would tell her the name of the exhibit. It was located just inside the entrance and read:

Cat Lady–1976

J. Marshal, Photographer

Melissa turned back toward the last photograph and felt something deep within her clawing to get free.

"Hello," someone called.

Melissa shook herself from the hypnotic glance of the Cat Lady and hurried out of the alcove, her whole body flushed with embarrassment as if she'd been caught doing something she shouldn't. Standing at the entrance of the main part of the gallery was a courier.

"Hey, sorry. I didn't see anybody at the desk, so I walked in. I have a delivery that needs a signature."

"Oh, the owner is indisposed at the moment," Melissa said.

The guy offered her his clipboard and pen. "Can you just sign for it? I'm running behind as it is, and I can't afford to come back later."

Melissa hesitantly took the clipboard and signed where he asked. She handed it back to him and he handed her an envelope. "Thanks, miss." Then he hurried out of the gallery.

Melissa walked over to the front desk, not even looking at the envelope. It wasn't her business. She probably shouldn't have signed for the delivery and just gone and gotten Vivienne, but she didn't want to leave the guy standing there alone in the gallery. Just as she dropped the envelope on the desk, the phone rang. She wasn't going to answer it. That seemed like overstepping for someone who was only there for an interview. It stopped ringing but then began again, not even a minute later. Melissa looked toward the door, willing Vivienne to come through, but that didn't happen. With a sigh, she hurried around the desk and spotted a piece of paper right next to the phone with what looked like instructions. Melissa guessed it was probably supposed to be for the temp that never showed. She picked up the phone.

"Art is Life Gallery. How may I help you?"

"May I speak with Vivienne please. This is Howard Linder."

"My apologies, Mr. Linder, but Vivienne isn't available to take your call at the moment. May I take your number and have her call you back?"

"Yes, but in the interim, would you please tell me if exhibit 2340 is still available?"

"Uhm, yes, please hold and I'll locate that information for you."

Melissa put the call on hold and looked down at the instructions on the paper. Halfway down the sheet was a bullet about exhibit listings and the title of the spreadsheet where the information was located. She moved the mouse to wake up the computer to find that the document was already open on the screen. She did a search for the number Mr. Linder had given her and found what she needed. She took him off hold.

"Thank you for waiting, Mr. Linder. Yes, exhibit 2340 is still available."

"Excellent. Please have Vivienne call me at her earliest convenience to discuss the purchase of all three paintings in the exhibit." He gave Melissa his phone number, thanked her, and hung up.

Melissa had no sooner hung up than it rang again. This time she didn't hesitate to answer. She'd already signed for a package and taken one call, what was another going to hurt? It was a woman asking for availability to rent the gallery for an event. Melissa put her on hold, checked the cheat sheet to find the name of the program used for events, opened it up, found the calendar, but didn't see anything about pricing.

"Bottom right drawer. Folder labeled events."

She looked up to find Vivienne leaning casually along the wall with a grin. Melissa's face heated with a blush of embarrassment.

"Thank you." She located the folder and found a laminated sheet with pricing information. After giving the caller the information, she was asking for, Melissa proceeded to book the event in the system following the instructions on the sheet. The caller thanked her and hung up.

Melissa stood and turned to Vivienne. "My apologies if I've overstepped. The phone kept ringing and I didn't want you to miss anything important."

"No worries. You did great. I truly appreciate you stepping in. I walked out as you were finishing up the previous call. Was it anything important?"

Melissa turned and tore off the top sheet of the message pad she'd used and offered it to Vivienne. "Howard Linder called to inquire about purchasing all the paintings from exhibit 2340. He asked that you give him a call to discuss further."

"Nice! He's anal about speaking to an actual person and refuses to leave voicemails so if you hadn't been here, I would've missed the call. That's a ten-thousand-dollar sale you just made, Melissa." Vivienne smiled.

Melissa's eyes widened in surprise. "Ten thousand dollars?"

"Yes. Howard Linder is the art buyer for Prince Property Management's luxury resorts. He had been eyeing those paintings for one of their new resorts down in the Caribbean."

Melissa's heart skipped a beat at the mention of Prince Property Management. A bittersweet memory from fifteen years ago came to mind, and she quickly shook it off before the melancholy she usually felt after such memories took hold.

Melissa pasted on a pleased smile. "That's amazing. Oh, you also received a delivery." She picked up the envelope that she'd signed for and gave it to Vivienne. "I wasn't going to sign for it, but the messenger said he couldn't come back today."

"You have been busy in the time I was gone."

Melissa smiled sheepishly. Vivienne opened the envelope and pulled out what looked like a check and whistled.

"This is a check for a sale I've been trying to make for months now. The artist was about to pull their exhibit because they were growing frustrated with the back and forth with the buyer. I had all but given up and was going to be reaching out to someone else I thought might be interested." She grinned happily at Melissa. "How soon can you start?"

Melissa chuckled and Vivienne quirked a brow. "Oh, you're serious," she said in disbelief.

"Very."

Melissa found it difficult to believe that Vivienne was offering her the job already. "But we never finished the interview."

"What better way to know that you can handle the job than what you just did. You stepped up with confident professionalism when you had every right to just sit and ignore what was going on around you. Besides, I think you just might be my lucky charm." Vivienne walked over to the desk, picked up a pen and pad, and wrote something down before tearing off the paper and offering it to Melissa. "That's with full medical benefits."

Melissa looked down at the number on the paper and felt like she needed to pinch herself to make sure she wasn't dreaming. Vivienne was offering to pay her twenty thousand more than her current salary with medical benefits that she was currently paying for out of pocket.

She smiled broadly. "How does two weeks work for you?"

Vivienne gave her a playful pout. "I guess I'll survive a couple more weeks without you."

"I truly appreciate this opportunity."

"My pleasure. I'll email you the job details and all the employment paperwork. Just fill it out and bring it on your start date. Will a schedule of eight a.m. to six p.m., Monday through Friday, with some late evenings and weekends for coordinating personal and gallery events work for you?"

The thought of having her weeknights back for herself was the icing on the cake for Melissa. "Yes, that's fine."

"Excellent." Vivienne offered her hand. "I look forward to working with you, Melissa."

Melissa accepted her handshake. "As do I, Vivienne."

CHAPTER FOUR

Melissa gathered her things, barely containing her excitement as she practically floated from the gallery. Talking about being at the right place at the right time. Melissa had ignored her innate cautiousness about answering Vivienne's calls and she was glad she did. Although, hearing that one of the calls was from Prince Property Management threw her for a bit of a loop. During her train ride home, she wondered how Alex Prince, whose family owned the luxury residential and commercial real estate and property management firm, was doing. It had been fifteen years since the day she let the one who could've been her first real romance walk out of her life.

Melissa had first met Alex during her senior year in high school when she and Golden used to go to teen night at a neighborhood club called Black Light. Alex was the resident DJ at the club as well as for the college party circuit. She was also an acquaintance of Golden. Melissa vividly remembered that first look at Alex. She was of South Pacific heritage, was a good two feet taller than Melissa, with thick, wavy, shoulder-length black hair, dark golden bronze complexion, small hoops, and studs going up her left ear, and a diamond stud on her right nostril. She had beautiful chocolate brown eyes, full smiling lips, white even teeth shining brightly and softly dimpled cheeks. She wore a pair of bright blue Nike Zoom KDs with red trim, a pair of skinny jeans the same bright blue as the sneakers encasing long, shapely legs and slim hips, and a fitted red T-shirt tucked into the jeans and emphasizing a narrow waist and small breasts. The short sleeves had hugged her toned arms and broad shoulders. Melissa wouldn't call her beautiful in the feminine sense of beauty. She was more handsomely beautiful, if that was a way that could be used to describe a female.

Melissa had barely been able to look her in the eye and squeak out a hello in greeting. Amazingly, that hadn't deterred Alex from making it a point to seek Melissa out every chance she got just to say hello or for a brief chat. Then they exchanged numbers and began texting and calling each other. Melissa had been determined that they would never be more than friends, but as much as she tried, she couldn't control the direction her heart was going even though they had not gone out once in the months they talked. Then Melissa had found out she had gotten accepted into Howard University and Alex insisted on taking her out to celebrate since Golden was at her AMDA audition. They had spent the late morning and early afternoon at Luna Park in Coney Island and had been having a wonderful time until Melissa's fear of being outed shot the day to hell.

❖

Melissa and Alex finished out their day on the Ferris wheel. Their hands were mere inches apart on the seat between them. Melissa bravely slid hers over to cover Alex's hand. She turned, giving Melissa a sweet smile, and flipped her hand over to grasp hers.

"Can I kiss you?" Alex asked.

At a loss for words, Melissa nodded in response. Alex leaned in toward her and Melissa met her halfway. It was her first kiss. When their lips met it was as if Melissa had been waiting her whole life for this moment. Alex's lips were just as soft and warm as Melissa had imagined they would be as they pressed softly against hers. It was gentle and brief but still left Melissa dizzy with desire for more when it ended.

"That was my first kiss," she admitted with a shy smile.

There was no surprise or judgment in Alex's eyes. "Well then, let's make sure it's a good one."

She leaned in toward Melissa again, but when their lips met this time Alex expertly coaxed more than just a simple peck from her. With her inexperience, Melissa gave Alex the lead as her body was set ablaze from head to toe and an arousal like she'd never felt when she touched herself overwhelmed her. If she had known kissing felt like this, then she would have done it much sooner. Not knowing what do with her hands, she grasped Alex's shirt at the waist, gripping the material tightly as if she needed to hold on to keep from floating away. Melissa did her best to match whatever Alex was doing to her lips. She was practically panting when Alex slowly ended the kiss. Melissa gazed at her in dazed confusion.

Alex grinned. "I didn't think you'd want an audience."

That's when she noticed the Ferris wheel had begun to move again. "Oh…yeah…thanks."

Melissa scooted over as far as the seat would allow, her body heated with embarrassment now instead of arousal as she stared unseeing as the view of the ocean was blocked by other cars on the wheel.

Alex grasped her hand again. "I hope you're not regretting that."

Melissa gazed over at her and was surprised to see her looking a little unsure. Not something she was used to seeing from the usually confident Alex.

Melissa smiled hoping it would reassure her. "Not at all. This is just new to me."

Alex nodded. "I understand."

They spent the remainder of the ride in silence, hands still grasped even after they climbed out of the car and made their way to the boardwalk. Still feeling the effects of their kiss and enjoying the warmth and softness of Alex's hand in hers, it took a moment for Melissa to realize that someone was calling her name. She looked in the direction the voice was coming from and turned to see Mrs. Washington, head of the board of deaconesses and a major gossip in her stepfather's church, waving and walking toward them as she practically dragged her grandson along with her. She jerked her hand from Alex's as if she'd been burnt and stuck it in her jeans pocket.

"I thought that was you," Mrs. Washington said, giving Alex a cursory glance. "We don't see you working at the church much lately."

Melissa gave her a pleasant smile that she wasn't feeling in the least. "Good afternoon, Mrs. Washington. With graduation a month a way I've been focusing on school and studying for my finals."

"I see." She gazed at Alex again, giving her a more detailed look than her previous glance.

Alex's attire was not necessarily masculine but would probably be considered that for someone like Mrs. Washington who Melissa had never seen in pants even during the church picnic. She could see the wheels turning in her beady little eyes.

"Grandma, you said you would take me to get cotton candy," the little boy whined, attempting to tug her back the other way.

Melissa took that opportunity for them to make their escape and moved to walk past Mrs. Washington. "Well, it was nice to see you, Mrs. Washington."

"Yes. Be sure to tell your mother I said hello."

"Will do!" Melissa gave a wave without looking back.

If there weren't so many people to wade past, Melissa would've been running to get as far away from Mrs. Washington's prying eyes as possible.

"Melissa, slow down. I seriously doubt she can still see us," Alex said.

Melissa stopped and turned to her, not surprised to be greeted with a hurt expression. "I'm sorry. I saw her and just freaked out."

"I'm not gonna lie and say it didn't sting a little when you dropped my hand like I was going to infect you with gay cooties, but I understand. I don't expect you to be taking me home to meet the family, but after our day together and that kiss, I didn't think you'd be so embarrassed to be seen with me."

Melissa reached for Alex's hand, then withdrew it and balled her hand at her side. "No, I'd never be embarrassed about being seen with you. I was just worried about her seeing us holding hands, that's all."

Alex gave her a sad smile. "Yeah, that's all. I had fun today. Call me when you're ready to do more than just hang out."

She walked away, leaving Melissa standing alone on the boardwalk fighting to hold back tears of frustration threatening to spill.

❖

That felt like a million years ago. So much had happened after that. Golden's father had died that very afternoon, so Melissa had focused on being there for her friend, then exams and graduation followed along with the devastation of learning that her stepfather was refusing to pay for college unless she stayed within New York because his scam of a church was about to be audited. With the income the church and her stepfather's other side hustles brought in, she knew financial aid wasn't even an option. She threw all her emotion into staying strong for Golden and keeping herself from being overwhelmed with the disappointment of not being able to finally escape the restrictive existence of her home life. In the end, she had pretty much ghosted Alex too, afraid of facing those feelings as well.

Melissa knew, shortly after that day, that Alex had given up her dream of becoming an international DJ to help with her family's business and had become quite successful as a commercial real estate agent. When she started seeing Alex posting pictures on social media with some hot supermodel-looking chick, Melissa knew that it was too late to even think about reaching out to her and had unfollowed all her accounts. She had avoided hearing anything that had to do with Alex Prince or Prince Property Management until she and Golden became friends with Zoe and she learned that Golden had connected Zoe with Alex's angel investment group. Curiosity had gotten the best of her, and she did an internet search for Alex. It seemed she was doing very well for herself. She was the vice president for commercial and leisure real estate at Prince Property Management, was engaged to be married to a gorgeous European runway model, and her angel investment group had helped to turn around many failing Black-owned businesses throughout the tri-state area.

Alex also looked even better than she did when they had last seen each other. The fashionable suits, gorgeous evening gowns, and even her casual attire seemed to all enhance her femininity. Melissa thought it was sexy but not as sexy as the masculine and androgynous attire she wore during her days working as a DJ. As Melissa had flipped through Alex's social media pics, she had thought something about the way she smiled looked false. But it could've just been wishful thinking on her part because she wasn't the one making Alex smile. Melissa had allowed herself a day of regret over letting Alex get away, then had continued doing the work she needed to be in a place so she could welcome the kind of relationship that she had avoided all those years ago.

Now, with this new job opportunity, she could finally step out of her comfort zone and live the life of freedom and independence that she'd been wanting since graduating high school. If she was lucky enough to find an Alex of her own, then she'd be ready this time.

❖

Zoe finished putting the dishes in the dishwasher, then walked to Kiara's room and knocked on the door.

"Hey, KiKi, you wanna watch a movie with me tonight?"

The door opened just wide enough for Kiara's head to poke through. "Did you forget I was going to the movies and then spending the night at Nyema's?"

Zoe frowned. "Oh, yeah."

"Why don't you call Auntie Mel and Auntie Golden and have a girls' night or something."

"Maybe. I was hoping to hang with you tonight." Zoe realized how desperate that sounded before she even finished the sentence.

Kiara shook her head. "Mom, you really need to get out and find some type of hobby or something. Grandma and I worry about you wanting to spend more time with us than getting a life of your own."

This was one of those times Zoe wished she had treated her daughter like the child she was while growing up rather than like a little adult. "Um, excuse me? I have a life, thank you very much."

Kiara looked at her skeptically.

"Do you need a ride to Nyema's?" She asked, changing the subject before she could be lectured by her own child.

"No, her mother is picking me up and dropping us off at the theater."

Zoe tried her best to hide her disappointment. With Kiara's busy schedule of indoor and outdoor track, the debate club, and her social life, Zoe didn't see much of her. "Okay, well, have fun."

Kiara gave her a cheerful smile. "Thanks." Then shut the door in Zoe's face.

Zoe went to the living room, sat down, and pulled up the streaming menu. She scrolled through the movies available, but nothing appealed to her. At least nothing she'd want to watch alone. As she was deciding between another gaggy romantic comedy or explosive-filled action movie, her phone buzzed. She snatched it up at the sight of Melissa's name.

"Hey, girl, I thought you were working tonight?" she said.

"I am, but I thought I'd call you to see if you want to come to the exhibit opening tonight since I figured you're probably sitting at home alone moping."

"Kiara called you, didn't she?"

"Yes, but only because she loves you."

Zoe snorted in derision. "She's just trying to get me out of her hair."

"C'mon. You can come to the exhibit, then we can grab dinner after."

"Fine," Zoe said with exasperation.

Why was everyone trying to turn her into a social butterfly? Of course, she enjoyed going out occasionally, especially the girls' trip she, Golden, and Melissa took every year, but what was wrong with wanting to stay home and enjoy spending time with your family? Her mother was even pushing her to start dating again, something she hadn't done in at least six years, unless you counted the two or three hookups a year that she had, one of which was usually during the girls' trips, when being celibate just wasn't cutting it. Zoe felt her family and her business were more than enough to keep her happy, and she got companionship from her friends. There was just no desire for her to add a full-blown relationship into the mix.

After Zoe finished her call with Melissa, she was heading to her room when Kiara exited hers.

Zoe stopped in front of her with her arms crossed and an annoyed glare. "Did you seriously call Mel to get me out of the house?"

Kiara shrugged, looking as nonchalant as if Zoe had asked her if she'd fed the cat. "Yep. You weren't going to. I texted Auntie Golden first, but she's traveling. She was the one who suggested I call Auntie Mel."

She loved her child, even when she was impertinent. Zoe opened her arms and Kiara grinned and walked into her embrace, wrapping her arms around her waist.

"Have fun. Remember you promised to help in the salon tomorrow so don't be late." She placed a kiss atop Kiara's head and released her.

"I won't. Love you, Mom." Kiara gave Zoe a peck on her cheek and disappeared down the hall.

Two hours later, Zoe arrived at Art is Life gallery and joined the line of people waiting outside to get in. It moved quickly so she didn't wait long before she was giving the man at the door her name. He checked the list in his hand, gave her a smile, and opened the door for her. She had texted Melissa that she was there as she was standing in line so she wasn't surprised to find her waiting.

Melissa pulled her into a hug. "Hey! I'm so glad you made it."

"Me too. I realized on the way here that we haven't seen each other since you started this job a month ago."

"The adjustment from being an overpaid babysitter and gofer to being a real personal assistant to an adult with adult responsibilities has been intense, but I love it."

Zoe cocked her head to really look at Melissa and noticed something different about her. An air of confidence that she'd never shown before. "Yeah, I can tell. You look genuinely happy."

"You know, I am. Although I work for her, Vivienne treats me as her equal. She even gave me part of the commission for the paintings Alex's company bought."

"Wow. Really? That was generous of her. Good thing you decided to answer the phone."

"Who you telling?" Melissa looped her arm through Zoe's, leading her toward the crowded main gallery. "Let me quickly show you around, then I'm going to have to desert you to check on the caterers."

"You go do what you have to do. I can manage on my own. We'll see each other after."

"Are you sure?"

Zoe nodded and shooed Melissa away. "Girl, go."

"Okay. Here's a brochure of the exhibits including the one featured for this evening. If you're tempted to buy anything, let me know and I can point out the pieces for under a thousand." Melissa gave her a wink. "Enjoy!"

Zoe watched her walk away then merged with the guests mingling around the gallery and spotted a bar nearby. She ordered a glass of chardonnay and gazed down at the cover of the brochure Melissa had given her. It featured a beautiful bronze bust of what appeared to be a Woman of Color with a smooth bald head, actual wood gauge earrings in both lobes as well as several small silver hoops along the ear lobes, a wood bull ring in her nose and a silver stud on her nostril. Her head was tilted back with her eyes closed and her mouth was slightly agape. She looked to be in the throes of something pleasurable, giving Zoe a small tremor of pleasure as well. The caption from the photo read:

Artist–Iman Daniels
Pleasure

Zoe gazed around the room to see if she could locate where the piece was and determined it must be where a small group of people were gathered near the archway of the second half of the gallery. She made her way over to find a woman in the middle of a circle of guests standing next to the very sculpture on the cover of the brochure. The sculpture turned out to be a self-portrait of the artist herself. She was an attractive woman who looked to be in her mid-twenties, with a deep golden-brown complexion, wearing the same exact jewelry as the sculpture version of herself with the addition of a beaded choker holding a wooden disk with a carving of a woman's profile. She was dressed in a plain white fitted tank top, baggy, wide leg black jeans that rode low on her hips with the hem brushing the floor and held up by a leather belt. Black combat boots were peeking out from beneath the hem of the pants. She had just been asked who her inspiration was for getting into bronze sculpting.

"Thomas Blackshear. This piece," she indicated the bust, "was inspired by his sculpture titled *Romance.*"

Zoe smiled. She had a whole collection of Thomas Blackshear figurines on display in her living room.

"It's obviously a self-portrait. You titled it *Pleasure.* Can we assume that's what was happening at the time?" a woman asked with a flirtatious smile.

"Art is interpretive, if that's what you think, then who's to say it isn't true." Iman gave a mischievous wink to her audience. They chuckled in response. "Now, if you'll excuse me, nature calls."

As Iman walked away, Zoe found herself admiring the slow, lithe way her long-limbed body moved, the sexy sway of her hips, and the way she threw her head back when she laughed as people stopped to speak to her along the way. There were a few other things Zoe had noticed as Iman had spoken to the small gathering. Her smooth bald head that glistened under the lights, her wide-set expressive eyes that crinkled at the corner with her easy smile, and the fullness of her lips. Zoe turned away and had to shake herself from the images that came to mind of what those lips could do. She had been without physical companionship too long.

It also didn't help that despite hair being her passion, a bald head was her weakness. Zoe loved the feel of her palms running along a bald scalp. Feeling the warmth of body heat coming through the bare skin, tracing the shape, and indentations if there were any, along the scalp. There was a brave vulnerability in the act of shaving the head. A shedding of something holding the person back and baring their soul for the world to see. Zoe had been tempted a few times to shave her own head but didn't feel as if she had the confidence to pull it off. Iman definitely did, and it intrigued Zoe as she looked at the artist's other works near the bust. There were several small sculptures and a few oil paintings. The one commonality was that a powerful Black woman was featured in each piece with titles such as *Strength, Power, Prayer,* and *Love.* One painting featured a topless blood-splattered warrior woman with a shield strapped to her back, holding a spear at her side with a baby bundled in a blanket across her chest while a chaotic, bloody battle was fought around her. The title was *Black Motherhood.* The look of anguish on the mother's face while blood dripped from her matted hair down her forehead as she gazed down at her child who peacefully lay suckling from her breast wrenched Zoe's heart.

It was the darkest and most graphic of the paintings and had Zoe wondering why that was so different from the others. What was happening in Iman's life that her works of strength and feminine beauty turned into this dark creation?

"What do you think?" someone said from behind her.

Zoe turned to find Iman stepping up beside her, then gazed back at the painting. "I think it's honest, horrific, and beautiful. It's the reality of the Black mother trying to protect her child from the cruel and harsh truths of this world. An endlessly fought battle with no winning sides."

"Well, damn, it's like you were in my head when I painted it."

Zoe chuckled. "No, just a Black mother seeing herself."

"A lot of people don't see past the violence and blood."

Zoe shrugged. "Like you said, art is interpretive."

Iman turned to Zoe and offered her hand. "Iman Daniels."

Zoe faced her and took her hand. Iman's grasp was firm. Her palms warm and soft. "Zoe Grant." She quickly glanced at Iman's smooth head, wondering what she moisturized it with to give it such a natural shine.

"It's a pleasure to meet someone who can see past the obvious to the truth lying beneath and also happens to be extremely beautiful. The depth of your cheekbones, the long line of your neck, even the prominence of your collarbones are like something I could've sculpted."

Zoe's face heated with a blush as she giggled like some silly young girl. "Thank you."

Iman slowly released her hand but continued watching Zoe as if she were studying her. "Have you ever considered being an artist model?"

Zoe felt as if she were being stroked with Iman's intense gaze. "Uh, no."

"You should. I know this is probably going to sound like some pickup line, but would you consider modeling for me?"

Zoe looked at her skeptically "Seriously?"

"Seriously. Sit for me. I swear that there will be no nudity involved. I'll understand if you say no, but know that it will probably break my heart if you do." Iman pouted playfully.

Zoe chuckled. "Well, I certainly don't want to be the cause of breaking your heart. How about we meet to discuss it before I decide."

"Okay. I'm free after this and there's a coffee shop up the street." Iman quirked a brow in challenge.

Zoe found her determination sexy. "I'm supposed to be going to dinner with my friend Melissa, Vivienne's assistant."

"Oh, well, since I like Melissa, I won't insist you blow her off for coffee with me. We can exchange numbers to set something up soon."

"Okay." Zoe put Iman's number in her phone then texted her so that she would have hers.

"I'll be waiting for your call, Ms. Zoe." Iman gave her a wink before walking away to mingle with her other admirers.

Zoe decided to explore the other exhibits on display but found herself looking for Iman as she did, hoping to catch a glimpse of the sexy artist. It wasn't until the crowd had thinned out to a few tipsy stragglers that security had to nudge out the door that Zoe spoke with Iman again while she was waiting for Melissa to finish up. The artist was with a small group of people heading toward the entryway.

Iman grinned at her. "Hello again."

Zoe willed herself not to blush. "Hello. I heard you had a good night. Sold *Motherhood*."

"Yes. I hadn't really expected to. I've exhibited that piece many times, but it's never sold until now. I think you're my good luck charm."

"I would've bought it myself if I could."

"I appreciate that. Call me soon."

"I will."

Iman nodded and headed toward the exit with her friends. They all, including Iman, looked to be at least ten years younger than her. Too young for her to have thoughts of running her hands over the artist's bald head as Iman licked her way down her body and settled between her legs. Zoe had to force herself to look away from Iman's retreating figure. She'd definitely gone too long without sex and needed to rectify that before she even thought about calling Iman to meet for coffee.

CHAPTER FIVE

Several weeks after beginning burlesque classes, two events occurred that steered Golden in a direction she hadn't planned. The first was a call from the head of private equity where her former co-worker Geoff had gone, asking if she was interested in joining the team. The salary alone would be foolish to turn down, but the opportunity for minimum travel, fewer late nights, and getting her weekends back was just as tempting. Her only hesitation was that she'd promised herself she would give her current position three years, but the second event that occurred seemed to be pushing her to take it. She was feeling that old passion for the burlesque classes that she used to feel for dancing. It was as if she had found that piece of herself that she lost all those years ago with her father. Golden's family and friends noticed the change in her as well. She talked more about the classes and the shows she went to see than she did work. She even set up a studio in her basement so that she could practice on the days leading up to her Sunday classes. With the thought of having more time to dance, Golden was leaning heavily toward accepting the new position.

"So, what's keeping you from taking it?" her mother asked as she helped her prepare Sunday brunch.

Golden shrugged. "I guess I feel like it might be too soon to move on."

Her mother turned, cocked a hip against the counter, folded her arms, and quirked a curious brow at her. "Too soon for who?"

Golden attempted to avoid her mother's gaze. "I feel like I'd be abandoning Mark. He's been good to me these past two years. Entrusting me with clients he wouldn't normally assign to someone with my minimal experience that first year."

"Yeah, and it paid off. You've brought in more business than even that idiot sniffing around him like a dog in heat."

Golden grinned. "Chris is just eager to prove himself. Most of us came through the loan department together so he doesn't have that camaraderie with Mark that we do."

Her mother turned back to her task of rolling out biscuit dough. "Well, I think Mark will understand. Besides, we seem to see less and less of you these days between work and dancing. Not that I'm complaining about the latter."

Golden was surprised at how thrilled her mother had been about her taking up burlesque dance. Then she'd reminded Golden about the old videos of her great-aunt Dinah that her father had given her, but she'd never watched after he died. Fifteen years ago, she had stored all her dance gear and the four VHS tapes of Dinah in a box and tucked it away in the bottom of her closet. She hadn't looked at the box again until they were moving to their current house where she had once again stashed it in the back of her even bigger closet. When her mother had mentioned the videos, Golden had dug them out that night and sat with her mother to watch them since she still had a VCR. The videos were grainy like most film was from that time, but there was no mistaking the beauty of the woman on the screen as she moved across the stage, playing to whoever was recording her.

Golden had seen what her father had when he told her that she reminded him of their distant relative. She saw herself in the way her aunt's hips moved, the flow of her arms, even the teasing smile on her face. Although she might not resemble Dinah in looks, watching her movements was almost like looking in a mirror. They watched all four videos that had been filmed at the Moulin Rouge after she had moved to Paris. Golden and her mother held each other and cried after. They had been a piece of her father that he had gifted to her that devastating day. It had also been a release of grief and regret that Golden had been holding on to all these years. She let it go with a renewed sense of purpose and a dedication to fulfill her and her father's dream in the best way she knew how.

She had devoted her time memorizing the very seductive routine that was rumored to have been what drew her aunt's longtime companion, Celine, to her when they first met. Then she had performed it in class, and Opal offered to hire her on the spot to be a part of her dance troupe. Golden had laughed it off. Now she was thinking that if she took the new position in private equity, she could possibly dance part-time. Maybe one or two nights a week.

"I can practically hear the wheels turning," Golden's mother said. "Just take it. We're in a good place, there's no need for you to continue working so hard." She placed a flour-covered hand on Golden's cheek. "It's about time you finally followed your joy in life. Mark will survive losing you, but you may not survive the regret you'll have if you don't take the opportunities you're being given."

As usual, her mother was right, and it seemed her friends and her brother agreed when she mentioned it to them during brunch. Santee had joined them, fitting right in with the crazy group.

"After your solo last week, I for one, think you just need to leave corporate America altogether and dance for a living," Santee said.

Zoe raised her hand. "Can I second that motion? Melissa sent me the video of you practicing downstairs and I'd hire you for any and every party I'd ever have."

"You know I always thought you should've continued dancing," Drew said.

Golden quirked a brow at Melissa who sat quietly sipping a glass of wine. "What? My opinion about you dancing hasn't changed in the years we've known each other so there's no need for my input."

❖

A week later, after returning from a business trip, Golden accepted the job in private equity. Out of guilt, she gave Mark four weeks' notice to help interview for her replacement and ease the transition of her accounts. She also began training more seriously to become a part-time dancer with Opal's Dolls, an all-Persons of Color burlesque troupe. Golden had learned that other than Opal and the two other performers she had seen perform the night of Belinda Trent's party, there weren't as many well-known Black performers as she would've expected. There were a handful of well-known performers such as Audrey Love, Miss Vera Valentina, and Gigi Holiday who traveled and performed in upscale venues located in New York, Chicago, and Las Vegas, but not many Black performers reached the level of success they had. It was why Opal started her troupe, to help bring more burlesque performers of color to a wider audience.

Golden made it a point to support her fellow performers by going to their shows and considered it as part of her training so that she could get a feel for what the crowds enjoyed most. It also gave her the opportunity to learn more about burlesque and the many forms. There was classic burlesque, which was what her aunt Dinah had performed. That was about captivating the audience with the art of the slow striptease. Then there was modern burlesque which was more about the choreography than the striptease. Nerdlesque was about parodying pop culture and merging it with the traditional style of burlesque. There was gorelesque, which involved dark, horror themes such as vampires and blood. Golden had seen one of those performances and as much as she admired the ladies who performed it, she found she couldn't even sit through the entire show.

Tonight, she sat at a quiet corner table at the burlesque club she'd first fallen in love with the dance watching Opal perform when someone tapped her shoulder. She looked up and was surprised to meet the hypnotic gaze of one of the last people in the world she expected to ever see again.

"Fancy meeting you here," Jade said.

Golden turned to her left to find Kendra with that smile that always made her ache to have her whisper seductive words in her ear.

"Evening, Ms. Golden. Mind if we join you?" Kendra asked.

"Uh, no, not at all," Golden stammered.

The table was a small cocktail round for two which made for tight seating. Kendra grabbed an empty chair from a nearby table and sat down.

"Jade and I were just talking about our dance on the way here and who do we see as soon as we walk through the door? Our beautiful dance partner who left us with nothing but a viral video to remember her by."

Jade pouted playfully. "Not even a text to say howdy-do."

Golden felt her face heat with a blush and gazed down at her glass of seltzer as if hoping she could find the confidence she suddenly lost when Jade and Kendra sat down. "Yeah, I've been busy. My work doesn't leave me much room for a personal life."

"We can understand that. So, are you working now?" Kendra asked.

"Well, technically, no. I'm sort of in training." Golden pointed toward Opal on the stage.

"Training?" Kendra looked over at the stage, then back at Golden wide-eyed. "You're training to be a burlesque dancer? That's cool."

Jade gazed at her. "So, what do you do when you're not dancing?"

"I was working as an investment banking analyst, but I recently started a position as a private equity analyst."

Kendra looked at her dreamily. "Smart, talented, and beautiful. I think I'm in love."

"That makes two of us," Jade said with a wink. "So, Ms. Golden, what are you doing the rest of the night?"

"Catching the train back to Jersey and calling it a night. I have an early morning meeting."

She actually had nothing on her schedule tomorrow, but Golden had a feeling that going anywhere with Jade and Kendra would find her forgetting she even had a job.

"Allow us to chauffeur you home. We're much safer and faster than the train since we won't have to make any stops," Jade said.

Golden quirked a brow. "Safer, huh?"

Kendra placed a hand over her heart and raised her other hand. "We swear to be perfect gentlemen. After all, our video with you has gotten us more attention for our recent surprise album release than the hints our publicist dropped. We have to thank you somehow."

Golden looked from one to the other. Both held equally sad puppy dog faces that she just couldn't resist. "Okay. I would much rather take my chances with you two than the creeps on the late-night PATH train."

Jade smirked. "Thank you. I think."

"Now, if you two don't mind. I'm supposed to be learning, not being distracted by troublemakers."

"Our bad. Just act like we're not even here." Kendra covered her mouth and Jade covered her eyes.

Golden chuckled. These two were definitely trouble, but she found herself even more drawn to them than she was when they first met. Although they did sit quietly watching the show with her, Golden found their mere presence distracting. The Rhythm Twins were knocking Golden's internal rhythm all out of whack. Her heart skipped a beat if she happened to catch one of them watching her intently, her body grew hot each time one of their knees or legs brushed up against hers under the table, and she found the way they would lean in toward each other in whispered conversation weirdly attractive.

After the show, Jade and Kendra waited as Golden went backstage to say hello to Opal. Normally after watching one of her shows, she would just wait until her next class to see her and discuss the performance, but Golden needed a moment to clear her head after being in the Twins' presence. She chatted with Opal and the other performers for about ten minutes before deciding that it would be rude to keep Jade and Kendra waiting much longer because she was too chicken to face them.

"There she is. We thought you might've snuck out the back door," Kendra said.

"I was tempted to," Golden quipped.

Jade frowned and placed a hand over her heart. "Are you trying to break our hearts?"

Golden chuckled. "I'm trying to make sure you two don't break mine."

Kendra took Golden's hand and looped it through her arm. "Ms. Golden, if you let us, we'd treasure you like the rare gem that you are."

Jade took Golden's other hand and looped it through her arm. "We'd give you the world. All you'd have to do is ask."

Golden gazed from one to the other and knew from their suddenly serious expressions that they meant what they were saying. She was rendered speechless and looked shyly ahead as she allowed them to escort her out of the club and to their waiting vehicle where an Amazonian of a woman stood by and opened the door for them. Kendra climbed into the back seat, first followed by Golden, then Jade, leaving her sandwiched between them, which seemed to be the running theme for the three of them. Golden was afraid to admit she liked it. She gave their driver her address, then attempted to ignore the way Kendra's and Jade's pants legs brushed along her bare thighs, the heat radiating off them and warming her in some very intimate places. She needed something to distract her from the desire welling within her.

"So, tell me something about yourselves that hasn't already been written or reported about you." She was hoping casual conversation would be enough of a distraction until she arrived home.

"That we're homebodies," Kendra said. "There's a perception that all we like to do is party and have a good time and we've embraced that to help sell records, but Jade and I would much rather be sitting at home bingeing on our favorite shows or reading a good book."

"Yeah, and if I could walk around in a T-shirt, sweats and a pair of Uggs all day, I'd be in heaven," Jade added.

Golden grinned. "So, you're not the fashion-obsessed closet designer *XXL* said you are?"

Jade snorted. "I haven't designed my own wardrobe since my mom used to buy me Garanimals. Kendra has pretty much been dressing me since we were kids. She's also the one that works with our stylist to choose our outfits for appearances and concerts. I don't even know how that rumor got started."

"Is the story that you've been best friends since the womb true?" Golden asked.

Jade nodded. "Our mothers met at a birthing class and became friends when they found out that they lived just a block from each other. Other than Kendra being born a week before me, we've shared practically every day together. We went to the same daycare and were in the same classes throughout elementary school. People actually thought we were related because our mothers would sometimes dress us in the same outfits. When we got to high school is when our separate personalities showed, but we were still finishing each other's thoughts and sentences and basically were inseparable."

Kendra picked up the story from there. "We even came out to our families at the same time. We purposely chose to go to the same college where it got so bad that we always ended up liking the same girl and had to flip a coin to decide who would be the one to ask her out. When we started performing, using Twins in our group name was a no-brainer because we felt like we were twins born from different parents."

Golden found their story fascinating. "Do you live together as well?"

"We share a house in LA when we're there and mostly stay at Jade's when we're here. She's got a whole ass house in Long Island while I'm still living in a ridiculously overpriced loft downtown. If we need space from each other which, believe it or not, we sometimes do, then we have our own places to go to," Kendra explained.

"Do you still have to flip a coin to choose who will date someone?" Golden asked half-jokingly.

Jade grinned. "No, our individual tastes have changed over the years, but there have been a few times when we've found ourselves attracted to the same woman, but we no longer flip a coin."

Kendra's hand had been resting on her thigh. She shifted it so that her pinky was drawing lazy circles on Golden's thigh just below her skirt's short hemline. "We usually give her two options. She can choose which one of us she would prefer or, if she's willing, share her."

Golden gazed at Kendra and the intense expression on her face made her mouth go dry and her heartbeat speed up. "Oh," she managed to croak.

Jade's warm hand lay fully on Golden's other thigh. "Which option do you think you'd choose, Golden?" Her voice had taken a low husky quality that gave Golden shivers of pleasure.

Golden cleared her throat nervously. "Are you asking out of curiosity?"

Kendra caressed Golden's thigh, matching the same rhythm Jade had begun on her other. "We're genuinely asking. We both have been attracted to you since the night we met and thought the feeling had been mutual until we didn't hear from you. Then when we saw you tonight, we had to be sure because normally when we get a vibe from a lady it's usually right. Tell us we're wrong and we'll drop you off at home with a hug and leave nursing our broken hearts all the way back to LA."

Golden was so distracted by their touch that she couldn't focus on how to answer. She had been asked twice before which of the Twins she would choose to date, and she knew even then that there would be no choosing because she saw them as if they were two parts of one being. When they shifted their hands to continue their soft strokes just above her inner thighs, Golden's head fell back along the seat. Her brain was telling her that she needed to put a stop to their obvious seduction because it would only lead to trouble, but her body had other plans.

"I just assumed you came as a package deal," she said breathlessly.

"Only if you want it," Kendra said.

"Do you want it?" Jade asked.

They were only touching her from her inner knee to mid-thigh yet Golden was growing wetter and she was practically squirming on the seat. "I don't know if I can handle it."

"We'll be gentle," Jade said before Golden felt their lips press against her cheeks then along her neck.

Their movements were so in sync it was as if they had choreographed it like a dance break in their videos. Golden was panting and gripped both of their thighs as she tried to hold back the orgasm fighting to come through.

"What's your answer, Golden?" Kendra whispered in her ear.

"Me or Kendra?" Jade whispered in her other ear.

Feeling their lips brush along her ears, hearing the sexy timbre of their voices, Golden couldn't deny the truth any longer. "Both," she moaned and was rewarded with her face being turned toward Kendra for a passionate kiss then Jade for another as their long fingers moved under her skirt. Golden spread her legs to give them free rein as they stroked her through her soaked panties.

She didn't care that they were in the back seat of an SUV with the driver sitting within arm's reach or that Kendra and Jade were probably experts at seducing women like this all the time. All she cared about was the pleasure coursing through her like a wildfire as her lips were passed from one to the other and their fingers played her pussy and her clit as if they were playing their keyboard and guitar. They were both sucking gently on her neck when her orgasm exploded as if that wildfire had hit a tanker full of gasoline. Golden cried out, digging her nails into Kendra's and Jade's denim-clad thighs. As her orgasm subsided, Kendra's and Jade's hands rested lightly against her thighs as they peppered soft kisses along her neck and face before placing a final one on her lips.

"You are so beautiful," Kendra said.

"Glowing just like your name," Jade said.

Golden was still experiencing aftershocks from her orgasm and found that she couldn't form words. The Twins seemed to understand. Kendra readjusted her skirt and she and Jade simply grasped her hands and laid their heads on her shoulders as Golden noticed that they were exiting the Holland Tunnel and entering Jersey City. They were only five minutes from her house, and she was wondering if Kendra and Jade were going to have to carry her in because she wasn't sure if her legs would work. They pulled into her driveway and Golden noticed only the living room light on in her apartment, which meant Melissa must have gone to bed and she could sneak in without having to talk about her night.

Kendra and Jade sat up and Golden gazed shyly from one to the other. "I would invite you up, but I have a roommate."

Jade grinned. "That's okay. We have an early flight in the morning and there is no way we would make it on time if we came up."

Jade's door opened and she climbed out then offered Golden her hand. She took it, almost blushing at remembering where those long, manicured fingers were just moments ago. Just as she exited the car, Kendra came around from the other side.

"Any chance you can fly to LA for a few days with us?" Jade asked.

Golden smiled. "I wish I could, but I have too much going on at work and have a few bookings coming up with Opal's troupe that I need to get ready for."

Kendra sighed. "I guess we'll have to continue this when we swing back through here during the tour. That's why we're going to LA. We need to get ready for our first show there in a month."

"I heard. Starting in LA and working your way across the country, then heading to Europe," Golden said.

Jade nodded. "Our last stop in the US is New York. We can save VIP tickets for you and your friends. It includes backstage passes."

"As much as I would love that, Melissa, Zoe, and I will be heading to Turks and Caicos for our annual girls' trip at that time."

Kendra frowned. "Well, that sucks. For us, not for you. Turks and Caicos is paradise."

"Okay, how about this. We should be back here in six months for a break before we head back to LA. You can come spend the weekend with us at the house on Long Island," Jade offered.

A lot could happen in six months, but the hopeful looks on their faces warmed her heart, and the still lingering desire she felt after the car ride warmed a more intimate area. "I can't promise anything, but I will do my best."

Kendra chuckled. "I guess that's better than no."

Jade took a step toward Golden, gently grasped her chin and gave her a soft, lingering kiss. She then stepped aside for Kendra to take her place and do the same. "Good night, Golden," they said in unison.

Golden felt a little unsteady. "Good night, Jade and Kendra."

She turned slowly so she wouldn't embarrassingly trip over her own feet as she walked to her door. She could almost feel their eyes on her and knew they were watching her because she didn't hear the car doors open and close until she walked into the house. She peeked through the curtain to watch the black SUV pull out of the driveway and disappear down the block. She rested her forehead against the cool glass and sighed dreamily wondering what kind of craziness she was getting herself into.

Chapter Six

S ix months into her job as Vivienne's personal assistant, Melissa, still enjoyed it as much as she did when she first started. She managed Vivienne's personal life as well as her business life, and getting to know the dynamic woman and sharing her world was such an eye-opening experience for her. She was still a bit of an introvert in social settings, but under Vivienne's mentoring, Melissa was able to break free of her shyness in business settings as she was the first face and voice people met for the gallery. Talking on the phone had never been a problem. It was always face-to-face encounters that triggered her shyness because she felt too seen. It stemmed from years of being watched and judged by her family. Fortunately, she still had her therapist in addition to Vivienne's motherly encouragement to help her work through it. Vivienne had also encouraged her to take art business courses at Christie's and Sotheby's auction houses and helped her find a pricey but nice studio apartment within walking distance of the gallery. Melissa loved having her own place to do as she pleased. Having her own space to just sit and decompress after spending most days talking with people was a gift that she still found hard to believe she had.

Of course, Melissa missed having Golden's and her mother's company sometimes, but they were just a train ride away if she needed that familial love that her own family seemed incapable of providing. She stopped going to the family church years ago and only attended Sunday dinners once a month, if at all. She no longer desired to subject herself to the snide comments from her stepbrothers about her sexuality, despite one of them still living on the down-low. There was also her stepfather taking credit for her career success because he believed that if he hadn't forced her to stay local for school then she wouldn't have taken up administrative studies. Finally, there was her mother's lack of interest in anything that Melissa did. Those two hours drained her, so she had decided that it wasn't even worth it to maintain a relationship with her family.

Melissa's life was what she had dreamed of when the prospect of leaving home for college shone brightly in her future before it was snatched away by her stepfather. The only thing missing was romance, which was the reason she was standing in front of her mirror frowning at her reflection as she tried to figure out what to wear for drinks with a woman she matched with on a dating app Golden had insisted downloading onto her phone and setting up her profile for. This was Melissa's third match meet-up in the past month. The first two had not worked out at all. One had been an hour late for their meet-up with only a breathless apology, then spent most of their dinner together distracted and checking her phone. After dinner she politely thanked Melissa who was barely out of her seat before the woman practically ran from the restaurant. The next day Melissa noticed her profile had disappeared from the site.

When the second date showed up to meet Melissa for drinks, she looked a good twenty years older than her picture, seemed to have had a few drinks before she even got there, and finished off a bottle of wine within an hour of her arrival. Melissa had gone to the bathroom and texted Golden to call her in five minutes. When she did, Melissa acted as if there was an emergency and that she needed to leave. The next day she received a message from the woman asking if they could meet again and Melissa politely told her that although she enjoyed meeting her, that she didn't feel it was a match. She was called a bitch in response and hadn't heard from the woman since. With such utter disasters, she didn't have high hopes for tonight, but Golden told her it wasn't uncommon to suffer through a few bad dates before a good one came along. Melissa was of the mindset that three strikes and she was out. If this evening went in the direction of the other two, then she was done.

After trying on one more outfit, she settled on a deep green wide-leg jumpsuit with a tie neck-bow, long balloon sleeves, and a keyhole cutout and button closure at the back. The jumpsuit emphasized her long legs and made her appear to be taller than she was. She added a pair of cognac faux leather ankle boots with a pointed toe and four-inch heel. Melissa's clothes might have been conservative but what personality her clothes lacked was always made up for in her shoes. Because of her petite height she had always loved good high heels. She finished off her look with her long locs pulled back into a loose ponytail, gold earrings, and burgundy lipstick as her only makeup. She didn't want to go all out if the evening was only going to end up being a bust. Satisfied with her look, she grabbed a jacket and headed out.

A short time later, she was sitting at a table in Ginger's Bar, one of the last few lesbian bars left in New York. Melissa, Golden, and Zoe tried to make it a point to meet there as often as they could when they needed a night out. It was why Melissa had chosen the bar. If the night didn't work out, Golden said to text her, then she and Zoe could meet her there for drinks. It was still early so the bar wasn't crowded and Melissa made sure to sit where she could see the entrance. A few moments later, her match walked in. Riley Colbert, thirty-five-year-old self-professed geek working as an IT technician while trying to get into the computer gaming field. A former college basketball player who still enjoyed a weekly pick-up game, raised in a devoutly religious family in the Midwest, and stayed in New York after graduating NYU. Other than their similar upbringing, Melissa couldn't figure out why Riley had swiped right on her profile, but they'd had a great video conversation before Riley had asked if she wanted to meet up. She had said yes not just because of their conversation but also because Riley sort of reminded Melissa of Alex with her tall athletic build, androgynous appearance, and a wonderful smile whose genuineness had shown in her eyes.

Melissa stood and waved so that she would spot her and received a bright smile in return. Riley's long stride brought her quickly across the room to Melissa. She offered her hand in greeting.

"You're even more gorgeous in person."

Melissa accepted her hand, smiling bashfully. "Thank you."

"I see you haven't gotten a drink yet. Allow me, what can I get you?"

"I wanted to wait for you. A glass of pinot is fine."

Riley nodded. "I'll be right back."

Melissa watched her walk to the bar. The sight of Riley's tight round behind in her fitted jeans made her flush with warmth. She quickly turned away. She had willingly gone celibate after her relationship with Leah, not wanting to give any part of herself to someone if she wasn't ready for it to be more than a hookup. With her life finally moving in the direction she wanted she still wasn't quite sure she was ready for a relationship, but she at least thought it would be nice to start thinking about having some type of romantic companionship. A few moments later, Riley returned with their drinks.

"One pinot grigio for the lady and an IPA for me." Riley sat down and took a sip of her beer. "I can't believe I've never been here before. This looks like a nice spot to hang out."

"Yeah, my friends and I come here often. It's been around for about twenty years and one of the last remaining spots for lesbians so we try to make sure to support it whenever we can."

"That's cool. I'll have to add this to my bar-hopping list. So, have you met many other women through the app?"

Melissa tried to keep her expression neutral. "A couple."

Riley chuckled. "That bad, huh?"

Melissa grinned. "I didn't say that."

"You didn't have to. I've been there. Several times."

"Several? Why do you continue using the app?"

"Because it's fun. I'm not trying to find the love of my life. I just want to meet some ladies, have fun, and enjoy life. I've got too much going on for anything more serious than that."

On their introduction call, Melissa and Riley had just talked about their likes, dislikes, their childhood, and their careers. She thought it was too soon to ask about relationship goals especially after how bad her last two dates went, but hearing Riley say that she wasn't looking for anything serious eased her mind.

"Is that a deal-breaker?" Riley asked.

"Not at all. I am curious to why you chose me. I was told by one woman I contacted *no offense, but you look like the U-Haul, wifey type.* Her words, not mine."

Riley's eyes widened in surprise. "Are you serious? She was probably just intimated by your profile and that you reached out to her instead of the other way around."

"She did question why I messaged her if she hadn't swiped me first."

"Well, for the record, I don't know how she got U-Haul from pictures of you on a Jet Ski and lounging on a beach with a cocktail." Riley looked amused.

Melissa's face heated with embarrassment. "My friend insisted on using pictures from our vacation when she helped me set up my profile. She said they would give me a laid-back vibe. I felt like it was false advertising."

"It certainly made me swipe right. Why would you think it was false advertising? You looked like you were genuinely relaxed and having fun. Unless the pictures were doctored to make it look like you were on a white sand beach and clear blue waters when you really weren't."

Melissa smiled at Riley's overly exaggerated squinted glare of suspicion. "No, I really was on a beach in Turks and Caicos. It was last month during our annual girls' trip."

"There you go. It's not false advertising if it's true."

"I guess you're right. By the way, I'm very happy with where I live so I'm not looking to pack up a truck and move any time soon or to be someone's wifey. Like you, I'm not looking for anything serious."

"That's good to know. Now that we've got that out of the way why don't we grab something to eat? There's a great Mexican restaurant up the block, then we can come back and check out the karaoke."

"Okay."

❖

Melissa was having so much fun that time got away from her. After watching Riley put on her own Bruno Mars concert, to the delight of the crowd, she realized it was almost eleven. She had to be at work early to help Vivienne set up a new exhibit, so she needed to end the evening.

She gave Riley a round of applause as she approached their table. "If Bruno ever needs someone to cover for him, I'll be sure to recommend you."

Riley laughed. "Thanks. Are you sure you don't want to get up there?"

"Positive. Unless I'm with my girls I'll just feel ridiculous. Besides, I'm going to have to call it a night. I've got an early start tomorrow."

"I understand. How are you getting home?"

"The train. Less expensive and no traffic."

"Well, then I insist on escorting you home to make sure you arrive safely."

Melissa gave Riley a shy smile. "There's no need to do that. I'll be fine."

"I'm sure you will, but what kind of date would I be to send you off into the bowels of the subway system this late without an escort?"

Melissa found that she couldn't say no to that broad happy smile that reminded her so much of Alex. "Okay."

Forty-five minutes later, they were standing in front of her building.

"Now who's going to escort you back to Brooklyn?" Melissa joked.

Riley shrugged. "I'll be good. Thank you for an unexpectedly fun evening."

"Did you have a backup plan as well?" Melissa grinned.

Riley chuckled. "Yep. My brother was supposed to call with an emergency if he got a thumbs down text from me. What about your backup?"

"My friends were going to show up to crash my date if I had texted 911."

"I'm glad neither of us enacted our in case of emergency plan."

"Me too. Thank you for a fun evening."

"I hope we get to do it again. No pressure though."

"I appreciate that. I'll call you soon."

Melissa nervously wondered if she should kiss Riley good night or give her a friendly handshake. Riley decided for her when she grasped Melissa's chin, lowered her head, and pressed her lips on Melissa's. It was a sweet, chaste kiss but it still managed to spark something in Melissa that quickly roared to life. Riley's lips had barely left hers when Melissa grasped the back of her head and urged her to lower it once again. She didn't miss Riley's grin before their lips melded for a slow, passionate kiss. Then Riley's arms wrapped around Melissa's waist and pulled her close. She could practically hear her body screaming "YES, IT'S ABOUT DAMN TIME!"

"Would you like to come up?" Melissa said against Riley's lips.

"Only if you're sure."

Melissa stepped out of Riley's embrace to take out her keys. She unlocked the door, then reached for Riley. "I'm sure."

Giving her a sexy smile, Riley took her hand and allowed Melissa to lead her into the building. Melissa couldn't believe she was being so bold. As the elevator opened and they got on, her nerves began getting the best of her, but they were quickly dispelled when the door closed, and Riley backed her into the wall kissing her hungrily. Melissa's panties were wet before the elevator dinged for her floor. They walked with their arms around each other with Riley's hand moving down Melissa's back to her ass and back up. The warmth of her broad hand further stoked the fire of desire in Melissa. They barely made it through her door before Melissa turned and began unbuttoning Riley's shirt.

In the past she had never been the one to initiate sex or be the one in control while it was happening. But she had noticed something lately, particularly when she was masturbating, that had never happened before her job with Vivienne changed her life. She no longer held herself back from pleasure. She had spent so much of her life being controlled that she had feared losing control. Now she gave herself permission to just enjoy a feeling, savor a taste, or simply be in her feelings without being told it was wrong to do so. Touching herself was no longer just a way to relieve horniness. It was now a way to bring pleasure when she desired it and her orgasms had become so much more intense since she no longer held herself back out of shame and fear. This would be the first time since discovering this freedom that she would be experiencing sexual pleasure with someone other than herself, and the anticipation of it drove Melissa's current boldness.

She opened Riley's shirt then slid her hands inside to run her fingers down her sculpted abs. The feel of skin along her fingertips made Melissa's nipples tighten. She moved closer to slide one hand up and down Riley's back, then reached up to grasp the back of Riley's head to lower it for a kiss. This time Melissa's kiss matched the hunger she felt from Riley. She tore her lips away and led Riley to the partitioned bedroom area. Once there, Melissa turned to Riley and noticed something she hadn't before. There was an eagerness in Riley's gaze that she recognized. It was in the series of photographs at the gallery of the woman and her "kittens." They looked at the Cat Lady the same way Riley was gazing at her. Melissa's clit jumped at the connection. She had pictured herself as the Cat Lady many times during her self-pleasuring.

"Tell me what you want," Riley said, as if reading Melissa's thoughts.

Melissa removed her jacket and sat on the end of her bed. "Take off your clothes. Slowly."

She felt a little embarrassed by her attempt at sounding as commanding as she imagined the woman in photographs might sound until Riley smiled and slowly undressed. By the time she stood naked before her, it took all of Melissa's willpower not to just strip off her own clothes and beg Riley to fuck her. Besides, the Cat Lady would never beg anyone to do anything. If she wanted to get undressed, she wouldn't need to lift a finger. Being in control thrilled Melissa.

"Now undress me." This time her voice carried genuine command with no hesitancy.

Riley knelt before, lifted her foot, slowly removed her boot and sock, then pressed a kiss to the ball of her foot. Melissa bit her lip to keep from moaning in pleasure.

"Hold it together, girl. You're the Cat Lady. You're in control," she told herself.

After repeating the same with Melissa's other foot Riley stood and offered Melissa her hand. Melissa took it and Riley helped her stand. With a slow, methodic purpose that made Melissa lose her focus on staying in control, Riley undressed her as if she were unwrapping a treasured gift. By the time Riley's fingers slid into the waistband of her panties, Melissa's body was humming with desire. She watched as Riley knelt before her and slid her panties down her legs until Melissa could step out of them. Once she did, Riley remained there gazing up at her expectantly. That's when she remembered she was supposed to be channeling the Cat Lady.

Not quite bold enough to say what she wanted Riley to do, Melissa sat on the edge of the bed, spread her legs, grasped Riley's head, and eased it toward her. Riley nodded and licked her lips before she shifted to sit on her heels as she eased closer to the gap in Melissa's thighs. She lowered her head and her warm breath made Melissa's sex throb. As Riley began to slowly stroke Melissa, her orgasm built so quickly and was so intense that she was seeing stars. When they cleared, Melissa gazed down the length of her body at Riley who still knelt there licking her inner thighs in that slow, leisurely way cats cleaned each other. Every nerve ending in her body vibrated as she felt another orgasm building. Control, Melissa repeated to herself in her head as she placed a hand on Riley's head to stop her.

"Lie down on the bed," Melissa said breathlessly trying to regain control of her voice and the situation.

Riley placed one last kiss on the inside of Melissa's thigh then climbed onto the bed and lay on her back. Leah had called Melissa a pillow princess because she seemed to like receiving pleasure more than she gave. But that wasn't the case. Melissa was just too shy and embarrassed to ask what pleased someone so that she could do it. She always felt awkward, trying to do to her partners what was done to her because she didn't think she was doing it correctly until Leah also told Melissa that when she wasn't biting the pillow, she was actually pretty good at giving head as long as she wasn't stuck in her own head. She looked at Riley, her long lithe body almost taking up a good length of the bed as she patiently waited for her. Melissa was stepping aside tonight to allow the bold leather mask wearing mistress who eased her way into her head to take over.

Melissa touched, licked, and teased Riley to the height of pleasure then stopped and started over again. Riley whimpered and moaned, but she never once asked Melissa to stop. She seemed to enjoy being brought to the edge of orgasm only to be denied. Control was what Melissa wanted and Riley was handing it to her without question. Finally, when Melissa could no longer hold back the release she was also denying herself, she lay atop Riley, slid two fingers into her dripping sex and rode her until they were both shouting with desire. After, Melissa eased her fingers out of Riley and slid off to lie beside her. Riley grasped the hand Melissa had pleased her with, brought up to her mouth, and sucked her fingers clean.

"Earlier you asked why I chose you."

Melissa turned to her side to look at Riley. "Yes, and I don't remember you answering."

Riley grinned. "I didn't want you to walk out before our date even started."

"Why would I have walked out?"

Riley turned her and propped her head on her hand as she met Melissa's gaze. "Because I saw something in your eyes and in the cockiness of your smile that told me you would not only be fun to hang out with but also enjoyed having control."

"You got that from a few pictures?" Melissa chuckled nervously.

"I'm a submissive and as one, I'm good at reading whether someone else is one or not. Your profile comes off as someone who's quiet, sweet, and easygoing, which was probably what that chick that said you were wifey material was talking about. But your pictures said something else. Those pictures captured the real you. That's probably why your friend chose them for your profile."

Melissa felt oddly exposed. She got up from the bed, grabbed her robe from a nearby chair, and put it on as if she were donning a shield of protectiveness.

Riley sat up. "I'm sorry. Did I say something wrong?"

Melissa smiled and waved her off. "No, I was just a little chilly."

Riley looked at her curiously. "Do you know what I meant about being a submissive?"

Melissa knew. She wasn't a complete prude. "Yes, but I'm not what you would call dominant."

Riley smiled. "Well, if you aren't you sure could've fooled me after what just happened. I gave you control, and you ran with it."

Melissa's face heated with a blush. "I think we should call it a night. Let me call a car for you. I know you said you'll be fine, but it's the least I can do since I'm the one that invited you to come up."

"That's nice of you, but I can order one." Riley climbed out of bed and gathered her clothes. "If you could just point me to the bathroom, I'll be out of your hair shortly."

Melissa realized how dismissive she just sounded, but she wasn't ready for a conversation like that even if she had just had sex with the woman. "Just past the partition on the right."

After Riley went into the bathroom, Melissa went to the kitchen for a drink of water. How was it possible for Riley to see what she saw from Melissa's pictures? Until tonight, Melissa never recalled showing any dominant tendencies in any part of her life. Her sudden controlling nature tonight had more to do with the memory of the Cat Lady exhibit than some hidden need to be dominant. Riley had to have misread what she thought she saw. That's it. No need to dwell on it. Satisfied with that reasoning, she grabbed a bottle of water for Riley and waited for her in the main living area.

Riley came out of the bathroom a short time later. "I hope you don't mind that I used your mouthwash."

Melissa offered her the bottle of water. "Not at all and I'm sorry for being so rude. I wasn't kicking you out. I just have an early start tomorrow."

Riley accepted the water, smiling knowingly. "Thanks. No worries. I understand." Her phone dinged. "My car is downstairs. I had a great time. I hope you did as well."

Melissa couldn't help but smile. "I did. Thank you." She walked Riley to the door.

Riley turned and gave her a brief kiss. "Call me if you want to explore your dominant side a little more."

She gave Melissa a wink and walked out the door. Melissa spent the rest of the night tossing and turning, her mind reeling from Riley's words and her secret obsession with Cat Lady.

❖

"Vivienne, may I ask you a question about the Cat Lady exhibit?"

Melissa and Vivienne were finishing up with the setup of their newest exhibit.

"Of course, although I'm surprised it took you this long to acknowledge you even saw it."

Melissa looked up to find Vivienne smiling. She quickly looked away as her face heated with embarrassment. "I was just curious why it's never been for sale."

"That's what you're curious about? Well, it was a gift from my late husband. He was the photographer."

Melissa looked at Vivienne in confusion. "I thought your husband's name was Joshua Baxter. It says the photographer was J. Marshall?"

"J. Marshall was his photographer pseudonym. As you know, he came from a wealthy family in the pharma industry where he also worked, but that wasn't his passion. He loved photography, but his family wouldn't hear of him leaving the fold to become a starving artist as they put it, so he did it on the side. His other passion was the kink lifestyle, so he combined the two and sold his work under J. Marshall. Marshall was his middle name."

"That's an interesting gift to give to your wife."

Vivienne smirked. "Not when she's the one that modeled for it."

"You're Cat Lady?" Melissa practically shouted.

"The one and only. There, is that straight?" she asked as she stepped back from the painting she was hanging.

It took Melissa a moment to register what she had asked. She barely looked at the painting before nodding. "Yes, it's fine. So, were you into the kink lifestyle as well?"

"Yes, it's how we met." She turned to Melissa with a fond smile. "That's a story for another time. The Cat Lady series is just the first in a whole portfolio of kink art he did."

Melissa was rendered speechless for a moment as she digested what Vivienne was telling her. This sophisticated, elegant woman used to be a dominatrix and Joshua Baxter, the mild-mannered millionaire and philanthropist she'd read about, was a kink photographer.

Vivienne looped her arm through Melissa's. "Come, we have some time before we open the doors. I think you're ready for another reveal."

"There's more?" Melissa said worriedly.

Vivienne laughed. "Oh, darling, that was just the tip."

She led Melissa out the front door of the gallery, locked it, then to the building next door. Melissa had always been curious about what lay behind the bright red door. To Melissa's surprise, Vivienne slid a key into the lock. They walked into a large waiting room elegantly decorated with an antique gold chandelier hanging from the ceiling, cream leather sofas and chairs around the perimeter, and gold accent pieces. The only art on the walls were watercolor paintings of serene landscapes. At the far end of the room was a red leather wrapped reception desk with gold studs along the perimeter of the top of the desk. As she and Vivienne drew closer, she noticed the studs were pointed as if deterring anyone from standing too close. Finally, on either side of the desk were two more red doors.

"What is this place?"

"As you know, thanks to my generous late husband, I have been able to invest in various business ventures. Well, this was my very first business venture and the one I treasure even more than the gallery. Melissa, welcome to the Red Dahlia Social Club."

Melissa gazed at Vivienne in confusion. "This is one of your businesses. I look at your business portfolio regularly and I've never seen anything about the Red Dahlia Social Club. I've never even seen you come over here."

Vivienne grinned mischievously. "That's because this little gem is not on the portfolio you have access to. The Red Dahlia Social Club was a wedding gift from Joshua, so it was never put on the portfolio I started when I joined Level Up Investments, Alex Prince's angel investor group."

Melissa didn't understand what this was all about. "Why would you need to keep this a secret from me? I have access to your medical records. You can't get more personal than that."

"My dear Melissa, the Red Dahlia is a social club for people with very discerning tastes."

It took a full minute for Vivienne's explanation to register. "This is a sex club!"

Vivienne rolled her eyes. "Such a vulgar description. No, it's not a sex club, it's a fetish club."

"Isn't that the same thing?"

Vivienne sighed. "No, it's not. Maybe you weren't ready for this."

Melissa didn't like the regret she heard in her voice. "I'm sorry. I didn't mean to disappoint you."

Vivienne looped her arm back through Melissa's and led her back toward the entrance. "Oh, honey, you haven't disappointed me. I was just so excited to share this with you that I might've rushed it." She patted Melissa's hand. "We'll talk more about it when you're ready."

As Vivienne opened the door to leave, Melissa gazed back at the two red doors, then quickly looked away. No matter what Riley thought she saw in Melissa, she knew she wasn't, and didn't think she'd ever be ready to see what was behind those doors.

CHAPTER SEVEN

Zoe stood beside Iman gazing in wonder at the painting she had just completed. "It's so weird to see my face looking back at me from a painting. And it's so realistic. I feel like she's going to jump off the canvas."

"Does that mean you like it?" Iman said.

"I love it. It's amazing. You're amazing."

Iman grinned. "I'm just glad you finally agreed to pose for me."

Zoe smiled at the painting. "So am I."

When Zoe met Iman at her gallery showcase five months ago, she had been intrigued by the artist and her work, but she never saw herself granting Iman's request for her to pose for a painting. She had left the gallery for dinner with Melissa that night thinking that she would never see Iman again. Then a couple of months later, while out with her friends, Melissa told her that the gallery had finally sold Iman's *Pleasure* bust. Zoe had been happy for Iman. If she'd had an extra eight hundred dollars lying around, she would've bought it herself. She told Golden and Melissa about Iman's request and they immediately said she should do it. They had exchanged numbers, but Zoe had never called her for that coffee to discuss modeling for her and Iman hadn't called her to follow up with it. She'd basically left the ball in Zoe's court.

Zoe had texted Iman the following day asking if she was still interested in coffee. Iman had texted back that she'd love to, but it would have to wait. She was in Africa for a month but would call Zoe as soon as she was back in the States. Instead of calling, Iman surprised Zoe by showing up unexpectedly at the salon on a busy Saturday afternoon.

❖

"Okay, Mrs. Harris, let's get you to your granddaughter's birthday party looking fabulous."

Mrs. Harris patted her salt-and-pepper curls with pride. "Zoe, I don't know what I'd do without you and those miraculous hair growth drops. This time last year I was practically bald. Now look at me."

"It's not a miracle, just a little love and attention."

She walked over to the reception desk where her daughter was collecting payment from another stylist's customer.

"Thank you, Tara. You're all set for next month at the same time. Have a good weekend," Kiara said pleasantly.

The customer thanked her and left.

"Okay, I should have a gap in appointments right now so that I can get some paperwork done."

"Yep, you've got an hour until your next appointment. I brought that salad you asked me to pick up on the way here. It's in the fridge."

"I knew I raised you right."

Zoe placed a kiss atop Kiara's head then headed upstairs. Since the Hair By You distribution crew were off on Saturdays, Zoe liked to work from her office there more than the one in the busy salon. She stood in the middle of the open space filled with pride at what she and her mother had accomplished since Alex Prince's investment. Taking up the far end of the space were floor to ceiling shelving with boxes of Hair For You products waiting to be shipped via their online store or restocked in the salon downstairs. The middle of the space was the packing and distribution hub, and to the right of the entrance was her office and the large product development room next to it where current products were mixed and new products were created. They were outgrowing their current location so Alex was looking into industrial commercial spaces in Brooklyn and Staten Island to move their packing and distribution hub to. Once that move was completed, Alex suggested converting their current space into a spa, something that had been in Zoe's original business plan. Alex Prince truly had become Zoe's business guardian angel, and she could never thank Golden enough for bringing her into their lives.

With a contented sigh, she headed for her office and began the task of playing catch-up with her bookkeeping. Alex had suggested that she hire someone to do it, but Zoe didn't want anyone but Grant eyes touching their finances. Her mother usually did the books, but she had been visiting family down south with her grandmother for the past couple months, which was why they were behind. She grabbed the salad Kiara brought her and settled in to try to squeeze her late lunch and work in at the same time. A half hour later, the office phone rang. Zoe was about to ignore it until she saw that it was the internal line from the salon.

"Hello."

"Hey, Mom, sorry to bother but you've got a walk-in."

"Can't someone else take them?"

"She's asking for you. Says she came here straight from Africa." Kiara sounded amused by that last statement.

Zoe smiled. "I'll be right down."

She hung up before Kiara could respond, shoved what was left of her salad back into the bag, tossed it, then rushed to the bathroom to check her appearance. She had a bit of green in her front teeth and her hair was piled messily atop her head. Zoe ran back to her office, grabbed the mouthwash she kept in the drawer, then went back to the bathroom to rinse. Once she was confident that she didn't look like she had things growing from between her teeth, she picked up a bottle of loc oil from a basket of products they kept in the bathroom, unraveled the nest on her head, spritzed her palms with the oil and smoothed it through her hair as she detangled her locs. When she was finished, they flowed down her back with the light scent of frankincense and myrrh. She took a whiff of the oil left on her hands to relax her then washed it off and hurried back down to the salon.

When she walked in, there was Iman looking just as good as she did when Zoe first met her. Her bald head glinted under the light as well as the gold jewelry in her nose and ears, and she wore a pair of pink, turquoise, and black Kente print overalls with a long-sleeve black T-shirt and high-top sneakers. She was standing at the desk holding Kiara's rapt attention. As she approached, Zoe understood why. Iman was describing a safari that she had gone on. Kiara had dreamed of going on safari, which Zoe had promised would happen soon. Iman spotted her and turned, giving Zoe a guilty smile.

"I know I said I'd text when I got back, but Melissa mentioned that this was your salon, which is a small world because I pass it all the time since I live just a few blocks from here, so I thought I would just stop by. I realized now that might have been a mistake judging by the full house."

Zoe gazed around. Three people sat in the waiting area while all but Zoe's station had a customer in the chair.

"Yeah, we're a little busy today. I do wish you would've called or texted, but I have a few minutes before my next appointment."

"Oh, Mom, Candace rescheduled. She's having car trouble," Kiara said.

"Oh, okay. Well, I guess I have more than a few minutes."

Iman smiled broadly. "Enough to grab a cup of coffee at the Starbuck's on the corner?"

"Yep, her next appointment isn't until four now," Kiara answered for her with a mischievous gleam in her eye.

Zoe gave Kiara a look that said they would be chatting about this later. Then turned to Iman. "Looks like I'm free."

"Great." She walked to the door and held it open for Zoe. "Sorry for dropping in like this. I just wanted to see you."

"It's all right. My eyes were starting to cross staring at numbers while I was catching up on paperwork. Did you really come here straight from your trip?"

Iman gave her a look of chagrin. "Technically, I dropped my luggage off at home first then walked over."

Zoe smiled. "I see. Why were you in such a hurry to see me?"

"Because I was hoping you were going to agree to model for me."

"It's a likely possibility. We can discuss it over a mocha latte."

❖

By the time they had finished their coffee Zoe had hesitantly agreed to model for Iman, but it didn't actually happen for another month because Iman had to fly to the West Coast and Zoe was heading to the Caribbean with Golden and Melissa for their girls' trip just a couple of days after she returned. Now it was complete and Zoe stood looking at herself as one of Iman's warrior women, standing in a tall wide-legged stance with her locs blowing back in the wind, wearing a bra-like top with an armor breastplate, a long skirt with thigh-high slits, and thigh-high boots, holding a giant comb like a spear in one hand as an army of Black women stood behind her, all with natural and protective hairstyles, holding their own comb spears ready for battle. Their enemy was a giant faceless feminine figure standing menacingly before the warrior and her army with a long mane of straight hair whipping in the wind like serpents, her body draped in swatches of fabric with *shame, lye, relaxer, weave, wig, hot comb,* and *curling iron* imprinted on the swatches. As with all of Iman's paintings, it sent a powerful message about the Black experience.

"Have you chosen a title?"

Iman tilted her head and stared quietly at the painting for a moment, then smiled and nodded. "*Savior.*"

"Why *Savior*?"

Iman turned on her stool to face Zoe. The look in her eyes gave Zoe butterflies. "A savior is a person who saves another person or an ideal. You save Black women from the shame we were made to feel over our natural hair. You free them from the confines White society has laid upon us and show them their God-given beauty. If that doesn't describe a savior, then I don't know what does."

Zoe's face heated with a blush. "You give me far too much credit. I'm just a hairdresser."

Iman stood and gently grasped Zoe's face. "You are so much more than that," she said, placing her lips on Zoe's for a kiss that left her tingling from head to toes. "Feels like I've been waiting forever to do that." Grinning, Iman released Zoe's face and slid her hands to her shoulders.

"No need to stop now."

Zoe wrapped her arms around Iman's waist, pulled her flush against her body, and renewed their kiss. For weeks, while she posed in a sports bra and biker shorts, Zoe had been surreptitiously watching Iman as she first sketched then painted her portrait. Because the salon was closed on Mondays it was the only day that she could take an hour or two to meet Zoe at her apartment after her classes. She found it endearing the way Iman's brow would furrow in concentration as she sketched or painted and the intensity with which she would focus on Zoe to make sure she was getting a feature right was very sexy. When Iman would walk over to make a minor adjustment to the angle of Zoe's head or placement of her arm, her soft touch would send currents of desire firing through Zoe. Hell, she had even realized that the graceful way Iman stroked her paintbrush across the canvas was a turn-on. Now, after weeks of vivid sexy dreams and keeping her attraction to Iman in check, Zoe could no longer hold it back.

Within a matter of minutes, clothes were quickly shed, and Zoe was being lowered onto the futon in Iman's studio slash guest room. Nothing was said verbally, they communicated through lips, hands, and tongues. Zoe watched Iman's smooth head descend her body and reached down to run her hand over it. Something she'd been wanting to do since she met her. Iman moaned against Zoe's lower belly, the vibration of her mouth and the feel of Iman's warm scalp against her palm had Zoe moaning as well. Iman's tongue stroked then slid into Zoe's slit and Zoe almost bucked her off the bed. It had been so long since she'd had anything but her fingers or a vibrator down there that her inner walls clenched, and her orgasm was quaking through her before she could even register what was happening. She opened her mouth, but no sound seemed to come out for almost a full minute. When it did it was in a series of "ohs" in short succession that grew louder as her orgasm seemed to go on forever.

As the tremors in her body began to subside, Zoe gazed down at Iman grinning up at her, her lips, and the area around them shining with wetness. With the right touch, Zoe's orgasms could get messy.

"Are you always that sensitive?"

Zoe chuckled. "It's been a while and it doesn't help that I've fantasized about this moment since we first met."

Iman's eyes widened in surprise. "Really?"

Zoe nodded.

Iman made her way up to lie beside Zoe. "I have a confession to make. I've fantasized about you as well."

Zoe reached up to stroke Iman's head. "What was your fantasy about?"

"Painting you."

Zoe smiled. "Well, I guess both of our fantasies have come true."

Iman shook her head. "That's not the kind of painting I was talking about."

She slid off the bed, walked over to a shelf of paint supplies, and grabbed what looked like a large makeup case. She brought it over, knelt beside the bed, and opened the case for Zoe to see. Inside were about two dozen colorful jars.

"I also do body art. When you started posing for me and I got to see your gorgeous body, all I've wanted to do was paint you."

Zoe gazed at the body makeup curiously. "You'd paint my entire body?"

"Well, not EVERYTHING. I keep a supply of those disposable thongs that tanning salons use for anyone that models for me. Or if you'd feel more comfortable in briefs, I have a supply of those as well."

Zoe was intrigued by the thought of becoming a human canvas. The idea of feeling Iman's paint brush stroking her body made her flush with desire. "Okay. I'll take a thong."

"Cool!" The smile on Iman's face was like a little kid who had just been told they could have candy. "If you don't mind, you can hop in my shower and rinse off. The paint adheres better on clean skin. Then you can meet me in the living room."

"Okay."

Zoe got up and headed out of the room to the bathroom. She found it interesting that she didn't feel the least bit embarrassed about walking around Iman's apartment without clothes. She always had her mom, Kiara, or both around so she wore at least a robe when going in and out of the shower. Iman's easy-going free spirit tapped into Zoe's. The one that she'd stored away after she began dating Kiara's father, Ray. She had been so uninhibited before that, especially after realizing she was bisexual. Her first two years of college had been the most promiscuous and outgoing time of her life. Not wanting to be labeled a stereotypical bisexual woman who just slept around with any and everybody, Zoe might not have limited her options, but she had been careful with who she was promiscuous with. She had even spent one spring break at a clothing optional resort with a couple she had been sleeping with just before Ray entered the picture. Zoe liked that version of herself and was excited to tap back into her.

Iman's bathroom had a large walk-in shower with a soap dispenser adhered to the wall. There were three different options, moisturizing unscented, moisturizing scented, and sensitive skin. She chose the sensitive skin soap since she assumed moisturizer would affect how the paint adhered to her skin. After a quick scrub and rinse, she found Iman, who wore her painting overalls and nothing else, had moved all the furniture aside and was spreading a paint-splattered sheet in the middle of the now open floor. Then she grabbed a stool from the kitchen counter and set it in the middle of the sheet.

Iman offered Zoe a clear plastic square which she opened to find a flesh-colored disposable thong. It covered the important bits but that was about it.

"You can sit on the stool. I'm going to start with your face and work my way down," she gave Zoe a teasing wink then began laying out her supplies on the coffee table.

There were colorful paint options, brushes, makeup sponges, a spray bottle, and a few washcloths.

"Are you ready?" Iman asked.

"I guess so."

"Okay. It should only take two hours. Just like with your posing for my painting, I'll give you a break at least every half hour, but if you start feeling restless or stiff before then, let me know and we'll take a break."

"Got it." Zoe was feeling excited about the task ahead.

Iman finished Zoe's face with the speed and efficiency of an experienced makeup artist. Zoe wished she could see, but Iman wouldn't let her until she was finished with everything. Time seemed to stand still as Iman began her bodywork starting on Zoe's neck. Zoe closed her eyes and allowed the various sensations from paintbrush bristles tickling across her skin, light pressure of sponges dabbing at various places, and the soft swipe of a damp washcloth to lull her into an almost meditative state of arousal.

Iman leaned in and whispered, "Stand up please," in Zoe's ear as if she didn't want to disturb her.

She took Zoe's hands to assist her off the stool, which she appreciated as her legs trembled from a combination of sitting too long and the intense arousal she felt.

"Do you need to take a break?"

Zoe licked her lips with a shuddering breath. "No. I'm good."

Iman quirked a questioning brow but released Zoe's hands to continue her work. She moved from Zoe's abdomen to her lower torso and down her right thigh with long brush strokes. Zoe held back a whimper as she felt the brush stroke through the thin thong material covering her pubic area. She kept her eyes closed not only so that she wouldn't be tempted to see what her body looked like but also to avoid looking at Iman who she knew from the feel of the brush as she painted a detail on her hip, was kneeling before her.

"*Voilá.* Don't look yet. Let me get a mirror so you can see the full effect."

Zoe could hear her hurrying out of the room and took that moment to try to calm herself. She could feel the moisture between her legs and was glad for the paper thong or the proof of her arousal would've been dripping down her thighs. She heard Iman return with the sound of something being dragged.

"Okay, open your eyes."

Zoe opened them to find Iman standing before her holding a full-length mirror. She looked with amazement at her reflection. She was a human painting of a bouquet of full, lush red roses that popped against her dark complexion, with a monarch butterfly fluttering above them. The butterfly took up the entire top half of her face. She closed one eye to notice that with her eyes closed, her face all but disappeared within the butterfly's features. Along the right side of her neck was a rose bud that hadn't bloomed yet with the stem disappearing amongst the blooming flowers and leaves that covered her shoulders, chest, and forearms. From beneath her breast to her abs were the stems and more buds. The remaining length of the stems and thorns traveled over her pelvis, pubic area, and right thigh, ending at her knee. It was the freakiest and sexiest thing she had ever seen.

"This is amazing!"

"I'm so glad you like it. I knew the red would work well against your skin tone."

Zoe somehow tore her gaze away from her reflection and looked at Iman. "I wish I could just walk around like this instead of wearing clothes."

Iman grinned. "Now that would be a sight. I did an exhibit once with human canvases painted as some of the most classical art pieces in history. That was sooo much work. I don't do that stuff anymore. I just do stuff like this, photograph it, and sell the prints."

"Did you want to photograph me?"

"Only if you're okay with it, but this would just be for me. Not to sell."

Zoe struck a pose. "I'm ready for my close-up."

Iman laughed. She dragged the mirror back down the hall and returned with a professional camera. She posed Zoe with her arms slightly raised to make it seem as if the bouquet were spread out and the butterfly on her face was hovering amongst the blooms.

"Okay, close your eyes. Beautiful. Got them."

Zoe opened her eyes, walked over to Iman, and pressed a soft kiss to her lips. "This is one of the most entertaining days I've had in a long time. Thank you."

Iman pulled her close. "It's not over yet. Now I get to wash all this lovely paint off you."

She set her camera down and led Zoe back into the bathroom. She turned on the water, slid her overalls off and stepped into the shower, offering Zoe a hand. Once Zoe joined her, Iman shifted her so that she was standing just enough under the spray of water to get most of her body wet but not the locs Zoe had piled atop her head earlier. Then she grabbed a large sponge from the rack hanging on the shower head, squeezed soap from the dispenser onto it, and began to gently scrub the paint from Zoe's body. It washed away easily, leaving a wet trail of red, green, and brown snaking along the floor and down the drain. Zoe was so turned on that she backed Iman into the wall, kissing her as if she really were the butterfly still painted on her face sucking nectar from the roses it had been hovering above. When she ended the kiss Iman was grinning with butterfly colors smeared across part of her face. Their shower was cut short as they clumsily made their way into Iman's bedroom rather than her studio to finish what they had started earlier.

❖

Zoe returned home just in time to get dinner started before Kiara came home from practice. Her body still thrummed from her very eventful session with Iman. She quickly seasoned some chicken, wrapped two sweet potatoes in foil, then put them in the oven hoping she had enough time for another shower. Although she had managed to quickly wash the paint off her face before she left Iman's she didn't have enough time for another shower to avoid smelling of sex while she and Kiara had dinner. Zoe was rushing past the front door to head to the bathroom when Kiara walked in.

"Oh, hey, Mom."

Zoe pasted on a smile and turned to face her. "Hey, kiddo. You're home earlier than usual."

Kiara dropped her backpack on the storage bench just inside the door and sat down to take her shoes off. "Yeah, it seems half the team is down with that flu bug going around so Coach ended practice early."

"Oh, okay. Are you feeling all right?" More concerned about Kiara getting sick than how she smelled, Zoe walked up to her and felt her forehead.

"I'm fine. You had me get the flu shot last month, remember?"

"Yes, but that doesn't mean you can't get it. It just means it won't be as bad."

Kiara playfully swatted her hand away. "I'm fine, Mom, really."

"Okay. Well, dinner is in the oven. I was just going to jump in the shower. Can you keep an eye on it?"

"Yeah, you have paint or something on your neck," Kiara said with a knowing grin as she walked past her.

Zoe's face grew hot with embarrassment as she made her way to the bathroom. Well, at least Kiara only noticed the paint. Although there was no telling what was going through her child's mind as to how the paint got on her neck. Kiara knew Zoe was posing for Iman and despite her age, wasn't so naïve as to not put two and two together about what else might have been going on. Since Kiara was keeping an eye on dinner, Zoe took her time in the shower making sure to scrub any section of her body paint might have been overlooked. As she did, she smiled at the memory of what Iman's poor bed sheets looked like after they had sex before they finished their shower together. Not only had they not washed off all the paint, but they also hadn't bothered drying off. The sheets were wet and very colorful, which was how most of the paint Iman hadn't had a chance to wash off before Zoe attacked her came off. Other than when she hung out with her girls, Zoe had been sincere when she had told Iman that it had been one of the most entertaining days she'd had in a long time.

She came back out to find Kiara setting the table. "Dinner will be ready in five. I made a salad to go with the chicken and potatoes."

"Great. Do you want iced tea? I can make a pitcher."

"Can you do the half and half with lemonade?"

"Yep."

Zoe made the pitcher of lemonade iced tea with just a touch of sweetness just the way Kiara liked and set it on the table. Once the food was ready, they worked together to set it out for their meal. Zoe made it a point for them to sit down together like this for dinner as often as possible. It was a tradition with her parents that she had carried over when she had Kiara. These days, with their busy schedules, it usually only happens once or twice a week. Zoe treasured these moments because it gave her and Kiara time to catch up with each other.

"Do you think the team will be ready for the meet this weekend with so many people out sick?"

"Coach thinks we should have enough by then to cover the events we're registered to compete in."

"That's good. Melissa and Golden plan to be there to cheer you on."

"Cool. So, what's up with you and the artist?"

Zoe shrugged. "I'm modeling for a painting. You know that."

"I also know that posing for a painting usually doesn't require the model to be painted."

Zoe gazed up to find Kiara grinning. She grinned as well. "It's nothing serious and up until today I was just posing."

"Okay, step aside, Stella, Mom's finally getting her groove back."

Zoe rolled her eyes. "I should've never let you watch that movie with me."

"I think it's great. You're a grown woman with grown woman needs. There's nothing wrong with that."

Zoe looked at her daughter and once again wondered if treating her like a little adult rather than a child had been a good idea. "And what do you know about grown woman needs?"

Kiara chuckled. "Don't worry, Mom, dating and sex are at the bottom of my priority list. I'm not trying to ruin my Olympic dreams by getting pregnant. No offense."

"None taken and I'm glad to hear that. You know that you can come to me if you do decide to take that step, right?"

"I know. In the meantime, you have my blessings to keep doing you. It's past time that you did."

Zoe laughed. "Thanks."

CHAPTER EIGHT

When it came to anything to do with dance, Golden never did it halfway. Once she had burlesque down to appearing as if she'd been born to it, she extended her repertoire by learning aerial burlesque. She was the only one in Opal's Dolls who offered such an act and quickly became one of the most sought-after performers in the company. It got to the point that she was performing at private parties and clubs all over town, including becoming a regular performer at the very club where she had been introduced to burlesque. Golden was working her day job Monday through Friday and performing Wednesday through Sunday nights and she loved it. She knew how fortunate she was to have been mentored and trained by Opal, one of a select group of big-named Black burlesque performers. Many Black performers weren't afforded access to the contacts and introductions that Golden and her fellow performers had working for Opal. She hoped to change that someday by heading her own troupe. Until then she planned to get whatever status she could as an Opal Doll to get to that level.

Golden was backstage getting ready to perform her aerial act at a celebrity fundraising gala when her phone buzzed. She smiled as Jade's name flashed. She swiped the phone to answer and put it on speaker.

"Hello, stranger. How's the tour going?"

"Hey, beautiful, it's good. So good that we've extended a couple of dates and won't be able to meet-up as we planned."

Six months ago, Jade and Kendra asked her to meet them during their brief break after the tour. That meet-up was supposed to be next weekend.

"I'm a bit disappointed but happy that your tour is going so well."

"Yeah, I guess. We were really looking forward to spending some quality time with you. The video calls and texting these past months aren't enough. We need to see you."

"Yeah, we miss our golden girl," she heard Kendra say in the background.

"Aww, that's sweet." Golden missed them too, but she wasn't going to admit it.

Since the night Jade and Kendra had given her a ride home from Opal's show, then expertly seduced her in the back seat of their limo, she had done her best to keep things casual between them when they started texting and calling her while they were on the road. Because both her and the Twins' schedules were so busy, the video calls only happened once a week if that. Most of their communication was via group text messages between the three of them, which was daunting enough to keep up with. They ranged from a simple "Good morning, we just wanted to let you know we were thinking about you" to deep, thought-provoking conversations about something in the news or life in general. Golden learned that their party anthem stage personas were far different from the intelligent, thoughtful women she was getting to know these past six months. In the beginning, there were times when they attempted to turn a late-night video call into something sexier, but she always managed to steer them away from that and they fortunately let it go without a fight. Golden was disappointed she wouldn't be seeing them, and not just because she was ready to continue what they had started in the back seat, but also because she genuinely liked them.

"We'll plan for something after we get back, we promise," Jade said.

"Don't give your heart away to anyone else while we're gone," Kendra said.

Golden chuckled. "I'll do my best, but if I happen to meet Janelle Monáe and we hit it off, then I can't make any promises."

They both laughed. "Shit, if that happens, we'll wrap a bow around you and deliver you to her doorstep ourselves," Jade said.

"You two are silly. I've gotta go. I'm on stage in fifteen minutes."

"I would say break a leg, but those legs are too beautiful to wish that on. Have a good show," Kendra said.

"Thanks. I hope the rest of your tour is just as successful as the first part."

"We'll call you at the end of the week," Jade said.

They said their good-byes and Golden hung up feeling a little lonely not knowing when she would see them in person again.

❖

"I think someone is falling for the Twins," Melissa said.

"I wouldn't blame her if she was," Zoe said.

They were in Brooklyn at their favorite brunch spot, and Golden had just told them about her conversation with Jade and Kendra.

Golden rolled her eyes. "I am not falling for them. They're friends, just like you two are."

Melissa snorted. "We've never seduced you in the back seat of an SUV."

"Or invited you to spend a sex-filled weekend at a mansion in Long Island," Zoe said.

"Who said anything about a sex-filled weekend? I think your little fling with Iman has turned you into a sex fiend," Golden said.

Zoe laughed. "First, we all know what was supposed to happen this weekend if the Twins' tour hadn't been extended. Second, Iman hasn't turned me into a sex fiend, she just reminded me of who I used to be."

"A sex fiend," Melissa teased her.

Zoe tossed a fry at her which plopped into Melissa's water glass with a little splash.

"Good Lord, I can't take you two anywhere," Golden said with laughter.

Melissa plucked the fry out and set it on a napkin. "Speaking of Iman, when do we get to see this mysterious portrait that you posed for?"

Zoe shrugged. "Whenever she's ready to show it. She's gearing up for another exhibit and thinks she may add it to the pieces she'll be showing."

"Well, be sure to let us know when and where," Golden said.

"Will do. How are things going with your art classes, Mel?" Zoe asked.

"I should be finished by the end of the month. Vivienne wants me to try doing some curating, but I'm not sure I'm ready for that." Melissa had completed all the courses Vivienne had recommended with flying colors, but she was hesitant to step out of her comfy assistant role to add such important responsibilities as curating and choosing pieces for the gallery.

"Girl, if Vivienne thinks you're ready then you're ready. Don't start doubting yourself again. By the way, how's the dating app working for you?" Golden said.

Melissa shrugged. "I don't think it's the right thing for me. I'd rather meet someone the old-fashioned way."

She hadn't told them about Riley yet because she felt like it would lead to a conversation that she wasn't ready to have. Not that there was much to tell. She and Riley hadn't seen each other since that first night, but they had spoken when Melissa called her after finding out about Vivienne's secret life and social club that she had found herself growing more curious about lately.

Golden frowned. "Are you sure you want to give up after just a few bad dates?"

"Yeah, you've gotta dig through some coal before you find a diamond," Zoe said hopefully.

Melissa gave them a smile of reassurance. "I know you guys mean well and that you care about my happiness, but I'm fine, really. I'm happy with my life right now and don't need a woman to complete it."

Golden grinned and raised her hands in surrender. "In other words, get off your back and let you live your life. Got it."

Melissa chuckled. "Exactly. Now, tell us about your upcoming trip to California for the Hollywood Burlesque Festival."

Melissa sighed inwardly with relief that she had managed to deflect their conversation away from her love life. She didn't think her friends would judge her if she told them what was going on, but she felt like she needed to figure this situation out by herself.

❖

Later that night, Riley knelt before Melissa showing her how to put on a harness and dildo. When they had spoken last, Riley suggested that Melissa explore her curiosity and happily volunteered to assist her. Melissa still couldn't believe that she'd let Riley talk her into meeting at an adult toy store to buy the contraption she was now standing in.

"How's it feel? Are the straps tight enough? Too tight?" Riley asked, gazing up at her.

Melissa frowned. "It feels weird."

"You think it feels weird, go stand and look at yourself in the mirror."

Melissa walked to the full-length mirror in the corner of her bedroom. The dildo bounced with each step which caused the ridged saddle base attached to the back of it to rub against her clit and surprising her enough that she had to stop to control the sudden rush of pleasure vibrating through her sex. She looked back wide-eyed at Riley who grinned knowingly.

"Told you," was all she said.

Melissa continued her walk but slower to keep the dildo from moving too much. Once she stood before the mirror and saw herself, she laughed aloud. It was the freakiest thing that she'd ever seen. From the waist up were the obvious signs that she was a woman, but below the waist was a black jockstrap in which a very realistic looking six-inch penis that almost matched her skin tone perfectly extended from. It even had a set of balls hanging from it. She started to reach out to touch the dildo, then hesitated, not sure what to do.

"You can touch it. It is yours, after all. You paid for it."

Melissa looked at Riley's reflection as she sat cross-legged on the bed grinning.

Melissa returned her gaze back to her reflection, tentatively wrapped her fingers around the dildo, and just held it. She'd never touched a real penis, so she had nothing to compare it to, but Riley had assured her it felt like the real thing. The fact that she knew that surprised Melissa because she couldn't imagine Riley ever having been with a man, but she also knew you couldn't judge a book by its cover. Melissa ran her hand up to the tip of the dildo and back to the base, the saddle lightly bumping her clit and made her shudder with desire. Was this why men always had their hands in their pants? Did it feel this good to them when they stroked themselves? She turned and walked back to Riley, holding the dildo in place to avoid the stimulation from the saddle.

"Do you know how fucking sexy you look right now," Riley said, moving to sit on the edge of the bed, her face mere inches from Melissa's torso as she gazed up at her hungrily.

Melissa felt a surge of power as Riley looked at her that way. Something shifted in her. It was as if she became someone else.

"You want to kiss it?" she asked Riley, her voice taking on a deeper tone.

Riley licked her lips. "Yes."

Melissa grasped the dildo at the base and tilted it up toward Riley who lowered her head and pressed her lips to the tip before wrapping them around the head, holding Melissa's gaze while she did. Melissa continued holding the dildo in place as Riley stroked the head up and down with her lips. After a few moments, she released it and Riley's lips glided slowly to the base and slowly back up. She repeated the movement, holding still for the barest of moments when she reached the base so that it pressed Melissa's clit. She moaned and grasped Riley's head, forcing her to speed up her movements.

"Oh yeah…just like that," Melissa said as the ridged saddle bumped a steady rhythm against her clit until her sex was throbbing with her oncoming orgasm.

She didn't know how she managed to stay on her feet as her body exploded and she felt her own juices pouring down her inner thighs. As the aftershocks shuddered through her body, she gazed down at Riley and saw such an eagerness to please that reinvigorated her.

"Lie face down on the bed," she commanded Riley who excitedly did as she was bid.

Melissa climbed onto the bed, came up behind Riley, and slid a finger into her sex. She was so wet Melissa knew she wouldn't need the lube that Riley suggested she buy. She grabbed one of her pillows and, knowing what Melissa was going to do it with it, Riley lifted her hips for Melissa to slide it under and spread her legs so that her ass was raised, and sex displayed. Melissa moved up between her legs, grasped her dildo, and rubbed the head in the jewels of moisture glistening on Riley's pussy lips until she moaned with pleasure.

"Tell me you want it," Melissa said.

"Yes, please. I want your dick inside me," Riley begged.

Melissa smiled, feeling that power again, her own clit hardening as if it were the dildo that she grasped in her hand to guide, and slowly slide into Riley's sex all the way to the hilt then slowly withdrew just to the tip.

"Oh, fuck, yeah," Riley moaned.

Melissa grasped Riley's hips, slid the dildo back in, and pressed against Riley's sex to feel the saddle against her clit. She was still so sensitive after her recent orgasm that it wouldn't be long until she came again. Melissa didn't want to come yet. Not until she had Riley begging for her own. So, she gained control of her body to prolong her own pleasure then continued to slowly thrust in and out of Riley until she was whimpering and her pussy was dripping all over the dildo.

"What do you want, Riley?"

"I want you, Melissa. I want you to fuck me…hard." Riley thrust her ass back against Melissa.

She slowly withdrew again but thrust back inside Riley with a little more force. She continued that until the bumping from the base began bringing on her second orgasm, so she sped up the pace with Riley thrusting back to meeting each stroke.

"YES! OH FUCK, YES!" Riley shouted just before her body stiffened then convulsed with her orgasm.

Melissa's came a moment later, her nails digging into Riley's hips as she ground against her. As they both trembled, Melissa withdrew the dildo and collapsed on her back beside Riley with a satisfied smile. Yes, she definitely enjoyed being in control.

❖

Zoe lay tangled in Iman's bedsheets as she bathed in the afterglow of their all night sexcapade. It was their last night together before Iman left next week to spend a year living in Africa.

"I'm hungry. Are you hungry?" Iman asked.

"I could eat."

"Yes, you can." Iman grinned and winked. "How does waffles, turkey sausage, fresh fruit, OJ, and coffee sound?"

"Sounds good to me."

Iman grabbed her phone off the nightstand and placed their order through a delivery app. "Done. Now, I have a present for you."

She scrambled out of the bed and jogged out of the room. Zoe watched her with an amused smile. She adored Iman's energy, she was always shifting and moving, but Zoe knew that it would drive her crazy if they were seriously dating. The only time Iman seemed to be still, and calm was while she painted or sculpted. She hurried back into the bedroom holding a brown paper wrapped item that was shaped suspiciously like a large picture frame. Zoe sat up to lean back on the headboard.

Iman handed the parcel to her. "For you." She sat cross-legged beside her on the bed wearing a broad smile.

"What is this?"

"Only one way to find out. Open it!"

Zoe laid the package on the bed and pulled up the taped flaps in the back so she wouldn't rip the paper. It was just as she suspected, a picture frame. What she hadn't expected when she turned it over was what was in the frame. It was the painting she had posed for. She looked wide-eyed at Iman.

"I can't accept this."

"You can, and you will. You can hang it in your salon."

Zoe gazed at the warrior version of herself ready for battle in awe. "This should be hanging in a gallery somewhere, not my salon."

"Why not? It'll be appreciated more there than in a gallery where only a select few will see it or bought by some rich person who will hang it and forget about it until someone came by and commented on it."

Zoe's vision blurred with tears. She laid the painting back down and leaned over to pull Iman into a hug. "Thank you so much."

"You're very welcome."

"How much time do we have before the food arrives?"

"At least thirty minutes, why? Do you want to add to the order?"

Zoe got up and placed the picture in a nearby chair then returned to the bed and took Iman's face in her hands. "I just want to show the right amount of appreciation for such a wonderful gift."

Iman wrapped her arms around Zoe's waist. "I think that's plenty of time."

A few hours later, Zoe walked into her house to find her mother sitting on the sofa with Kiara sitting between her legs as she braided her hair.

"Hey, you two. Mommy, why didn't you guys just go down to the salon."

"Hey, sweetie. It's easier this way," her mother said.

Zoe grinned. She knew her mother liked braiding Kiara's hair at home because it not only gave them time together but also reminded her of the nostalgia of doing Kiara's hair when she was little. Kiara gave a distracted wave as her thumbs worked as nimbly across her phone's keyboard as her mother's fingers worked through her hair.

"There's pizza in there if you're hungry."

"No, I ate already." Zoe held back a smile remembering this morning's meal that didn't just include food.

"What you got there?" her mother asked.

"It's a gift from Iman."

Kiara found that interesting enough to look up from her phone. "Is it one of her paintings?"

Zoe set the painting that Iman had rewrapped for her to keep safe as she headed home. She removed the paper and held the painting up for her mother and Kiara to see.

Kiara's eyes widened in surprise. "She gave you THE painting?"

"Yes. She felt like it would be appreciated more if I had it than if some stranger bought it."

Zoe's mother looked from the painting, up at her, then back. "The details, how she captured your likeness is so amazing. It's more like a photograph than a painting."

"That is so cool. My mom is a piece of art," Kiara said.

Zoe chuckled. "I wouldn't go that far."

"Where are you going to hang it?" her mother asked.

"In the salon. Even if it isn't being displayed in a gallery, it should be seen."

"I agree. Right above the reception desk so that it's the first thing people see when they walk in," Kiara suggested.

"That's a good idea, Kiki." Zoe hadn't thought of that. She was thinking of placing it above the dryer station as that had the most wall space in the salon area, but displaying it right as folks entered would have more of an impact.

Her mother nodded in agreement and went back to braiding Kiara's hair. "I like that. It will let them know that Hair For You is so serious about haircare that we'll go to battle for you to protect it."

Zoe set the painting against the entertainment center then sat beside her mother gazing at it thoughtfully.

"Are you going to miss her?" her mother asked.

"Yes, but not in the way you might think."

"I think Mom is going to miss the adventurous side Iman brought out in her," Kiara added sagely.

Zoe gazed down at her daughter in amazement. "You are too grown for your own good."

Kiara shrugged. "Blame you and Grandma."

"I think she's right. Since you started seeing Iman, I noticed that bold confidence you had before Ray entered the picture was back. You were fearless growing up and had almost been the death of me and your father on many occasions. You always knew what you wanted and were never afraid to go after it. Even when you sat us down at fourteen years old, told us that you liked boys and girls, and that if we loved you, we would accept you no matter what. It was with a confident self-awareness that many adults coming out don't have. After you started dating Ray, your light slowly started to dim. As pissed as I was that he walked away from you and Kiara, I was also relieved because I knew that if he had stuck around, he would have dimmed Kiara's light also." Her mother wiped away a tear.

Zoe had no idea her relationship with Ray had affected her mother that way. "Mommy, why didn't you ever say anything?"

Her mother gave her a sideways glance. "Would you have listened? Like I said, when you wanted something there was no stopping you. You thought Ray was what you wanted and nothing I could've said would've changed that."

Zoe knew she was right. "I'm sorry."

"There is no need for you to be sorry. The one good thing Ray did was give us this little spitfire." Her mother gave Kiara's hair a gentle tug and Kiara grinned. "Also, it's obvious Ray hadn't been able to extinguish your light completely because I can see Iman spotted it as soon as she saw you and displayed it in that painting before she even helped you to rediscover it."

Zoe looked back at the painting now recognizing the image of the woman she had wanted to become before Ray's control, then motherhood had changed her. Iman had told Zoe once that she was just as much of an artist as she was, they just used different media. She said Zoe needed to embrace and release the free spirit that lay dormant within her.

"You know, I was thinking of entering the fantasy competition at this year's Bronner Brothers' hair show. What do you guys think?" Zoe asked.

Kiara turned so quickly Zoe's mother lost her grip on the patch of hair she was braiding. "Yes! Do it!" she said excitedly.

"I think that's an excellent idea. Competing in that show was one of your biggest dreams after I took you to your first one when you were little. It would also be great advertising for the salon."

"Especially when you win," Kiara said confidently.

Zoe laughed and gazed back at the painting. If she didn't know any better, she would swear her likeness was smiling proudly at her.

CHAPTER NINE

S he just gave it to you?" Melissa asked as she gazed up at Iman's painting hanging behind the reception desk at the salon in amazement.

"Yes. I still can't believe she just handed it to me as I sat naked in her bed."

Golden chuckled. "Well, if there's any reason to gift a masterpiece to someone, I guess months of great sex would be it."

Zoe gave her a playful shove. "That's not why she gave it to me. Not that I'm saying the sex wasn't great because it was, I just think it became such a personal piece for her that she couldn't bear to watch it go to a stranger."

Melissa patted Zoe on the shoulder. "Uh-huh, keep telling yourself that." She went and sat in Zoe's chair at her station.

Zoe took one last look at the painting then joined Melissa. Golden followed and sat at the station next to Zoe's. After all these years, they continued with their once-a-month Sunday hair appointments and were the only ones in the salon.

"Are you going to miss her?" Golden asked.

Zoe rolled her eyes. "Why is that everyone's question? Yes, but not because I had romantic feelings for her. I just enjoyed the ease of our friendship with benefits. We both knew that what we shared wouldn't be more than that, and it was very freeing."

"Well, at least one of us has been getting some while Melissa and I are out here living like we made some celibacy pact," Golden said wistfully.

Melissa gave a nervous chuckle. "Yeah, right?"

Golden's gaze connected with hers and there was a look of guilt in her expression before she looked away to focus on her phone. What could their little Mel possibly be guilty about? Golden decided not to blow her up. Despite their long friendship, they both deserved to have their secrets sometimes.

"Golden, you could be getting some twice over if you chose." She gave Golden the side-eye.

Golden snorted. "And how do you suggest that happening? Jade and Kendra are amid the biggest tour of their career. They're not even in the country right now."

"Bitch, they offered to fly you to London for a long weekend," Melissa said.

"The same weekend as the New York Burlesque Festival where Opal's Dolls were performing. I couldn't miss that opportunity."

"Okay," Melissa said skeptically.

"Besides, I think Jade and Kendra are looking for more than a weekend of sex. Our conversations have less sex and more substance. They've recently started talking about polyamorous relationships they've been in and what did and didn't work for them," Golden said.

"Is being in a throuple something that interests you?" Zoe asked.

Golden had been asking herself that question recently. "It hadn't even crossed my mind before meeting Jade and Kendra."

"And now?" Zoe asked.

"Now, I could see myself doing it, but it scares the crap out of me. That's a lot of intense emotions in one relationship. How'd you do it when you were with that couple back in college?"

Zoe grinned. "That relationship had nothing to do with emotions. It was purely for sex, but that doesn't mean that throuples based on love don't work. I'm sure there's something you can find on the internet about it."

"Yeah, I found a couple of websites and articles about polyamorous relationships. Of course, there are good and equally bad stories. Most of the bad ones seem to be from couples where one was coerced into it by a partner who just wanted an excuse to cheat," Golden said.

"That's messed up. The shit people do to others just to appease their own selfish needs," Melissa said bitterly.

"Well, fortunately I wouldn't be worrying about that with Jade and Kendra," Golden said.

Melissa gave herself a little shake then smiled. "True. To be surrounded by all that sexiness and love is a dream. It's not my cup of tea but I could see the appeal."

Golden saw the appeal as well and was so tempted that she, Jade, and Kendra were scheduled to have a video call late Friday night to talk about what was developing between the three of them and what was going to happen once Jade and Kendra finished their tour in a few weeks. She steered their conversation to the safer topic of what they were going to do for their next girls' trip.

Later that evening, Golden logged on to her laptop to order material for a costume that she was having custom made when something on the newsfeed popped up and caught her attention. *R&B duo Rhythm Twins accused of sexual harassment by backup singer.*

Golden's heart caught in her throat as she hesitated to click on the story. It would probably make more sense to reach out to Jade and Kendra instead of reading what was probably some sensationalized news story posted to get clicks. Gazing down at the time displayed on the corner of the screen, she calculated that it was after midnight in London. Jade and Kendra would more than likely still be at their concert afterparty. She clicked the story before she could change her mind. Afterward, she wished she hadn't. The predatory way that the woman described Jade and Kendra harassing her didn't sound like the women she knew. But then again, what did she really know?

Her relationship with them was mostly long distance, which obviously hindered really getting to know a person. Jade and Kendra had both told her that they weren't the party girls they portrayed in their music, that it was an act. Couldn't they be acting with her as well? Would it be fair for Golden to discount the woman's accusations because she thought she knew Jade and Kendra? Look at all the women whose stories were discounted because the person they accused was a celebrity? There were also accusers who were in it just for a payday. Could this woman be one of those? Golden picked up her phone. She knew Jade and Kendra wouldn't see her text until late, but she felt compelled to at least let them know she'd read it and wanted to talk. The ball was in their court now. Would they call her back right away to explain it all away? If so, then what?

Golden tried distracting herself with a movie but found she couldn't concentrate. Then she went to her basement to practice a routine for an upcoming show but that didn't help either, so she went to bed. She tossed and turned until her phone buzzed at one in the morning. She stared at Kendra's name on the screen for a moment, not sure if she wanted to answer, then she snatched it up and swiped to answer the call. Kendra's face popped into view with a look of relief.

"I didn't think you were going to answer for a minute," she said.

Golden switched on her nightstand lamp. "I almost didn't."

"We wouldn't blame you if you hadn't. Jade is on the phone with our attorney now or she would be on the call with me. Just so you know, we were blindsided by the story. Our agent wasn't even given a heads up that it was coming. Some reporter called her asking if we had a response to the accusations."

"I hate to ask this, and you can tell me it's none of my business, after all, you guys don't owe me any explanations about what you do, but is any of it true?"

Kendra didn't immediately respond, chewing her lip in contemplation. Golden's heart felt as if it were being squeezed in a vice grip as she waited.

"Not the harassment, at least not on Jade's and my part. We did regularly hook up with Fiona through most of our U.S. tour. Then Jade and I started talking to you more and saw the possibility of what we could have with you and ended things with her. She didn't like it and kept harassing us. The incident she described in the article didn't go down like she said.

During our tour in Chicago, we came back to our room after rehearsal to find her waiting in Jade's bed. Unlike what she reported, neither of us laid a finger on Fiona. Jade threatened to call security if she didn't leave. She threw a fit, cursing us out, threatening to sue us, even said she would go to the tabloids and scream rape if we didn't at least compensate her for the time she spent with us."

"She blackmailed you?"

Kendra sighed tiredly. "Pretty much. She wouldn't leave until we gave her five thousand dollars. I called our manager Trish, explained what was going on, and despite advising us against giving in to her demand, she transferred the money to Fiona's account. She finally left, we fired her from the tour, and thought it was all over until this story broke. Jade and I never held her against her will or forced her to do anything. Everything that happened was with Fiona's consent."

Golden almost sighed aloud with relief until she realized what Kendra said. "You said you two were sleeping with Fiona through most of your tour. Does that include when you were coming to New York at the time you were asking me to spend a weekend with you?"

Kendra looked guiltily away from the screen.

"Wow, okay. Look, I don't fault you and Jade for falling into ready-made pussy. It isn't like we're exclusive. Hell, you can't even call what this is dating, but I don't like being played or made a fool of. I told you early on that the biggest turn-off for me with any relationship, friendship or romance, is dishonesty. If you can't be up front with something like that while we're friends, then how can I trust that you'll be honest with me while we're in a relationship?"

"You're right," Kendra said dejectedly. She looked like she was trying to hold back tears. "I'm sorry that we weren't honest with you. Sometimes we get caught up in the bright lights and it ends up biting us in the ass. We do care about you, Golden, a lot, and would never want to do anything to hurt you."

Golden could tell she was sincere, but it didn't change the decision she'd just made. "I care about you and Jade also, but I think we need to keep things between us casual. You guys have a lot going on, as do I. I can't see a romantic relationship working out under the circumstances."

Kendra gave her a sad smile. "Yeah, maybe you're right. You're a special woman, Golden, who deserves to be treated like the queen you are. I wish Jade and I could've been the ones to do it."

Golden's heart felt as if it were shattering. "I do too. You and Jade take care." She hung up before the tears could fall.

Golden didn't understand why this was hurting so much. It wasn't like they had already been dating. She had only spent the past eight months talking to Jade and Kendra regularly, getting to know each other while they carved out a comfy corner of her heart and settled in while she wasn't looking. Golden curled up in the bed letting the tears soak her pillow as she nursed her first heartbreak since she'd lost her father.

❖

Melissa smiled down at the text message she'd just received from Riley who was loving her new life in California. A few months ago, she had been offered the opportunity to partner with a startup to get her own tech company off the ground. Now she was living her dream in the heart of Silicon Valley. She missed her but was also happy for her. Riley had been the first friendship she had developed outside of the one she had with Golden. Like Zoe's relationship with Iman, Melissa understood that what she had shared with Riley wouldn't last. They both benefited from their friendship with benefits. Melissa discovered her sexual self and Riley got the casual relationship she'd been searching for. With Golden and Zoe so busy with their own things, Melissa had enjoyed the companionship without the romantic ties that she shared with Riley was what she missed most.

She set her phone aside and pulled up the Sotheby's website to see if there were any new courses for her to take. Vivienne came breezing in a few minutes later looking fabulous as usual. Today she was dressed in a black maxi dress with large bright red and orange flowers and red headwrap.

"Good morning, darling. How was your weekend?" she asked as she came around the desk to place an affectionate kiss on Melissa's cheek.

"It was good. How about yours?"

"Excellent. Van came to town. This is the first I've left the house all weekend." Vivienne gave her a wink.

Melissa chuckled. Van was her little boy toy. He came up from Miami every other month to spend the weekend with Vivienne who still had a very active libido for a woman her age. She refused to see anyone local because she didn't want to be bothered. It was easier when there was no chance of running into each other or dropping in unannounced to see her. Melissa could only hope she had the freedom and life Vivienne had when she reached her age.

"That explains the glow you've got going and I don't mean those bright ass flowers."

Vivienne laughed. "They are bright, aren't they. It's so gloomy out I thought I'd bring the sunshine to work with me. I have a favor to ask and hear me out before you say no."

Melissa looked at her skeptically. "Okay."

"Shari, the receptionist at the Red Dahlia, had a family emergency and I have no one available to cover while she's out. Would you mind doing it? It's just sitting at the reception desk Wednesday to Sunday evenings answering the phone, making appointments, greeting the members, making sure they are set for their appointments, then doing a walk-through at the end of the night to make sure nothing, or no one, is left behind. The cleaning crew come in after closing, but they have their own key so you wouldn't have to worry about them. Unless it's a particularly busy night, which Saturdays tend to be, you should be out by ten at the latest. If it's busy, then you could be there as late as midnight. Shari expects to be back in two weeks." Vivienne had a hopeful look on her face.

She had done her fast-talking sales pitch on Melissa, not giving her a chance to interrupt with the negative response she was probably expecting. "Okay," Melissa said, surprising them both since she hadn't even given herself time to think about it.

"Oh, okay, that was easier than I expected. Well, I'll call Afrodite, to let her know to meet you tomorrow morning at ten to show you the ropes without the interruption of members, then you can sit with her all day Wednesday to see what it's like while we're open for business before the evening shift. Does that work for you?"

"I guess if it works for you. That means I won't be here those two days."

Vivienne looked amused. "I think I can handle it. I really appreciate this. I won't look a gift horse in the mouth by asking what made you say yes so quickly."

Melissa was relieved because she had no idea why she had. "I made coffee and brought those muffins you like from the bakery around the corner. Let me know when you're ready to go over your calendar for the week."

She could see Vivienne knew she was attempting to avoid the subject. Thankfully, she nodded and headed back to her office. Alone again, Melissa gave herself a moment to think about what she had just agreed to. She was going to be working at a fetish club. It was only two weeks and at the reception desk, but still, it was a fetish club. She felt her cheeks flush hotly as a nervous giggle bubbled up. One of many thoughts that came to mind was the fun Riley would have hearing about this.

The next morning, Melissa stood in front of her closet staring at her wardrobe. What did one wear to be a receptionist at a fetish club? Vivienne said she wouldn't be seeing any members today, so she chose a simple black belted coat dress and a pair of black leather knee-high boots. As she gazed at her reflection in the mirror, she changed her mind. The outfit seemed a little too on point. She looked as if she was going rip her coat dress open to reveal a leather harness and corset. She changed into a white blouse, black slacks, and a pair of black patent leather platform pumps. As Melissa walked past the gallery Vivienne stood at the window smiling like a proud mother watching her child go off to school. She even gave Melissa a thumbs-up which made her chuckle and relax a little. Standing at the red door, she took a deep breath and pressed the bell. The door buzzed and she walked in to find a crew of three cleaning the foyer and a woman who looked to be about her age standing at the reception desk.

"I'm going to assume you're Melissa. I'm Afrodite," she said, offering her hand as Melissa approached the desk.

Melissa accepted it. "Yes. It's nice to meet you."

Afrodite's nails were a good two inches long, pointed, and painted a bright hot pink. Her complexion was deep ebony, her hair was styled in a perfectly coiffed afro that haloed her heart-shaped face, her eyes were almond-shaped and a beautiful chocolate brown, and her hot pink lips spread into a broad cheerful smile with bright even teeth. Her love of hot pink was further shown in the catsuit that hugged her generous curves and leather ankle boots. The color looked wonderful against her dark skin.

Afrodite gave Melissa an appraising look. "You're as gorgeous as Vivienne said you were."

Melissa was surprised to hear that Vivienne talked about her that way. "Thank you. You're stunning yourself."

"Now that we've acknowledged our Black Girl Magic, why don't I give you a quick tour before we start on the boring stuff." Afrodite, still holding Melissa's hand, guided her around the desk to the red door on the right.

Melissa hesitated and Afrodite gazed back at her. "It's okay. There's nothing behind that door that will bite. Unless you want them to." Afrodite gave her a wink.

Melissa chuckled nervously, but she allowed Afrodite to lead her through the door. The hall was covered floor to ceiling in an off-white damask wallpaper with three more red doors on either side with a gold number on them. Afrodite stopped in the middle of the hallway.

"These are our playrooms. The office, guest showers, and owner's suite are on the other side down that hallway." She indicated where the hall turned to the left. "You can also access them from the other red door in the waiting room. Would you like to peek in the playrooms? They're empty now."

Melissa felt her face flush. "No, thank you."

Afrodite grinned. "You really are vanilla. It's cute."

Afrodite's tone wasn't insulting, but Melissa didn't think being vanilla was what you wanted to be known for while working here. She didn't respond, just followed her down the other hallway. There was a set of stairs leading up to another level which was their next destination. The stairway curved around and ended at a shorter hallway with two more doors on either side, then it opened to a room decorated in the same cream and gold décor and furnishings as the waiting area downstairs with a small platform in the center of the room.

"These two rooms are for those with voyeuristic and exhibitionist tastes." Afrodite walked further into the open space. "This is our party room where we hold our socials, entertain groups and even rent out to members for private events."

As they walked toward the platform, Melissa noticed a steel hook and clamps hanging from the ceiling. There were also clamps attached to the stage.

"Feel free to ask any questions you like."

Melissa figured Afrodite must have noticed her looking at the strange attachments. Although Riley had told her quite a bit about the BDSM culture, she had only scratched the surface of it, not getting into the hardcore stuff. Melissa had wanted to know more but had been afraid to go down that rabbit hole of internet search. Here was her opportunity to do it without possibly being spammed by fetish sites or having her search engine filled with stuff she wouldn't want anyone to know she was looking at.

"What are the clamps for?" she asked quietly.

"It's used for a suspension bar, or suspension cuffs for live performances during our socials and when we're giving demonstrations to novices interested in dabbling with kink play."

"You give classes?" Melissa said in disbelief.

"Yes, we have one scheduled this Sunday afternoon. You should come. It's an hour before your shift so you'll be here already, and I'll be the instructor."

Melissa looked from Afrodite to the stage, and this time when her face flushed it wasn't out of embarrassment.

"Maybe I will."

"Good."

Afrodite looped her arm through Melissa's, steered her toward the back wall, and pressed her finger against a notch in the chair rail. To Melissa's amazement, a hidden door popped open.

"This is our host domain. Hosts are what our kink workers are called. During events this door is hidden by a curtain so that we can discreetly come and go when needed."

They walked into a large dressing room that resembled something out of a Victorian boudoir with red damask wallpaper, pink velvet antique stools, and divans in the middle of the room. The far wall had ten individual dressing tables with red velvet chairs and antique gold filigree mirrors, the wall to the left displayed ten full-length versions of the dressing table mirrors, and to the right was an archway with red velvet curtains that led to another short hall with two more red doors.

Afrodite continued her tour down that hall. "The door on the left is where our bathroom and showers are located, the one on the right is our break room. Any questions before we head back down?"

So many, Melissa thought, but kept all but one to herself. "I take it you're not just a receptionist here."

Afrodite smiled. "No. I manage the club for Vivienne. It's why you haven't had to deal with anything to do with this aspect of her business. Not everyone is comfortable with discussing kink let alone looking at it as a legitimate business. Just like any other hospitality business, the Red Dahlia provides a service to those in need of an escape or pleasure. Vivienne's last assistant quit when she found out about this place. Said she couldn't work for a pervert."

"Wow, that was harsh."

"Yeah. The fact that you didn't run the minute you found out about it meant a lot to her, which is why she trusts you enough to ask you to help. It's kind of tricky to find a temp to work here." Afrodite smiled.

Melissa chuckled. "I guess so."

"Well, that pretty much concludes our tour. Can I get you a water or something before we head back down to get to the everyday chores?"

"Yes, thank you."

They stopped in the break room which offered a variety of snacks and beverages as well as microwaveable meals in the freezer in case a host was pulling a late night. It was obvious Vivienne took care of her employees, no matter what capacity they worked for her. Melissa grabbed water and a granola bar since she had been too nervous to eat breakfast this morning. The last hour they spent together was going over what would be Melissa's daily tasks, which as Vivienne told her, included answering calls, booking, and confirming appointments, greeting members, and connecting them with their hosts upon arrival and final walk-through at closing. Afrodite told her that she would stay until closing for the first three nights just in case Melissa ran into any issues. After that she would be on her own.

It seemed simple enough, but considering where she was, Melissa still felt nervous, especially at the thought of dealing with the members. What kind of people paid for such services? She felt foolish asking such a question, so she decided to set her judgment aside until tomorrow.

"Well, that's it. Any other questions?"

"Not that I can think of."

Afrodite nodded. "As I said, feel free to ask me anything. Even the little bit of information I gave you today is a lot for someone not in the kink lifestyle."

"Is that why you called me vanilla?"

"Yes, but it wasn't meant to offend you. Being vanilla just means someone who is only into normal," she used finger quotes, "sexual behavior. I could be wrong about you, but I'm usually pretty on point when judging if someone is actively into kink. That doesn't mean you wouldn't enjoy it if you tried it. It just means that you're presently not into it."

Melissa and Riley had done some soft bondage play, but what they did was probably foreplay for what happened at the Red Dahlia. "I see. Well, I better get over to the gallery. I'll see you tomorrow."

"Melissa, one last thing. Do you have anything…less matronly…to wear?"

Melissa gazed down at her attire. She wouldn't call what she was wearing matronly. Then she looked back up at Afrodite's bright sexy attire.

"I'm sure I can find something."

"Great. See you tomorrow!"

Melissa left and stood outside the club for a moment wondering what she'd gotten herself into. It was too late to back out now. With a sigh of resignation, she walked next door to the gallery.

"So, how did it go? Did Afrodite show you the ropes? Pun intended." Vivienne smirked.

Melissa walked behind the desk, stored her purse in the drawer, and sat down to get her delayed day started. "It went fine. She gave me a tour and went over my duties. It's a beautiful establishment."

"Thank you. I like to think so. What did you think of the playrooms?"

"I didn't see them."

"You said Afrodite gave you a tour. How did you not see the rooms?"

Melissa refused to meet her gaze. "I'm only going to be working there for a couple of weeks. I didn't feel it was necessary for me to see all of that."

"I guess." Vivienne sounded disappointed.

Melissa gazed up at her and could see it on her face. Vivienne had become a mother figure to her. Melissa disliked the thought of disappointing her. "I'll check them out tomorrow. Today was a lot for a vanilla person like me." She grinned.

"You may be vanilla, but I recognize a streak of flavor that my mentor in Paris recognized in me." She gave her a conspiratorial wink.

First Riley, now Vivienne saw something in her that she still didn't quite recognize herself. "I'm probably going to visit that boutique around the corner during lunch. Afrodite suggested I wear something less matronly."

Vivienne laughed. "What wouldn't be considered matronly next to that vibrant woman. Why don't I go with you and help you find some things you can mix and match with what you already have to bump up your wardrobe from fashionably conservative to sexy conservative."

"That's a fashion category I've never heard of."

"Think 1950s movie secretary."

Melissa laughed. "This should be interesting.

CHAPTER TEN

The next morning, Melissa had a few of the outfits laid out on her bed that Vivienne had insisted on buying for her. She said it was compensation for what she was doing. There were also the separate pieces Vivienne had suggested would be great to combine with the rest of her wardrobe to sexify it as she put it. The outfit she was considering for her first day was a sheer black dress with a long sleeve button-down blouse, belted waist, flowy pleated knee-length skirt, and a removable slip underneath. She thought it would go perfect with a pair of black suede platform sandals with a stacked four-inch leather heel that she'd just bought last week. Melissa's shoes were always the most flamboyant thing about her wardrobe.

Vivienne had also insisted that she go for a mani-pedi after work, which she did. Her nails supplied the only pop of color, a blood red that she matched with a lipstick they were selling as well. She twisted and knotted part of her locs into a high updo and left some hanging down her back. As she gazed at herself in the mirror, the red lips and nails made her feel bold, her updo added to the height she had from her heels, and the sheer dress made her feel sexy. When Melissa had told Riley about what she was doing Riley had predicted that this would be the first step into a world that Melissa would thrive in. She had also asked Melissa to send her a pic of her outfit. It was six in the morning on the West Coast so she doubted Riley would be awake already, but she took a mirror selfie and sent it anyway.

As she looked down at her phone, she saw Golden's name under Riley's in the text messages. There were several times last night when she wanted to call Golden and tell her what was happening, what she'd been feeling and why she was being drawn to do what she was doing, but something always stopped her. This experience was something of her own that she wanted to explore on her own, something she rarely did throughout her life. She was sure one day she would be ready to tell Golden and Zoe, but until then she gave herself permission to keep this little secret to herself for as long as possible.

When she arrived at the Red Dahlia, she punched a code into a keypad located beneath the doorknob that Afrodite had given her. It was a totally different vibe from the one she had entered yesterday. The lobby was empty, the lights were softly lit, new age music played quietly through hidden speakers, and the room smelled of sage and lavender.

"Good morning." Afrodite entered through the door on the left. She wore hot pink again, but instead of a catsuit her attire was a leather bustier top, miniskirt, and thigh-high pointed toe stiletto boots.

"Good morning."

"I love the outfit. It's like a sexy secretary. The evening clients will love it. They're usually our more discerning business members. Now, the first thing on today's agenda is introducing you to the crew."

"Okay. Maybe, after, I could look at the playrooms. I mean, if I'm going to be doing walk-throughs each night, I'm going to see them anyway."

Afrodite smiled knowingly. "That makes sense."

They continued up to the second floor into the hosts' room and were greeted by the sound of Cardi B's "WAP" bumping through the room. Ten men and women in various stages of undress occupied the space, filling it with chatter and laughter.

"Good morning, children!" Afrodite said loud enough to be heard over the music.

All ten, no matter what they were doing, including two men who had been bumping and grinding on each other to the music, suddenly stopped, turned toward Melissa and Afrodite, bowed their heads as if they were in the presence of royalty, and said, "Good morning, Mother Afrodite," in perfect unison.

Melissa realized the music had also been muted. Afrodite waited a beat before responding. "Children, I'd like you to meet Melissa. She'll be covering for Shari while she's away. You all know who Melissa is to our Mistress, and I expect you to treat her with the same deference as you do me, understood?"

"Yes, Mother Afrodite," they all responded again.

Melissa looked from them to Afrodite and back. Was this the control and power Riley had said was within her? She couldn't imagine commanding such respect.

"You may come greet her." Afrodite stepped aside as the hosts stepped forward one by one to introduce themselves to Melissa.

The first was a delicately beautiful petite woman dressed in a white bralette and matching thong with thick straight hair flowing down her back past her buttocks. "Hello. I'm Lily." Her voice was as soft and sweet as her smile.

Next was Rose, a statuesque, tattoo-covered dark-haired beauty wearing nothing but a thong, her perky pierced nipples catching Melissa's attention before she quickly gazed up at Rose's grin. Then Hyacinth, a tall willowy figure with elegant feminine features, a bald head, softly rounded breasts, and a jockstrap with a very large bulge, informed Melissa of their nonbinary pronouns, took her hand and narrowed their gaze at her. They stared intensely at her for a full minute then smiled brightly and nodded before walking away. Melissa was wondering if they were all named after flowers until a handsome, chiseled jawed, muscled God stepped forward, bowed at the waist, placed a kiss on the back of her hand and introduced himself as Brutus in a French accent. After Brutus was Ginger, Lola, Ava, Lourdes, and a set of fraternal twins named Luna and Venus. They were a diverse group in physical appearances, ethnicities, and gender. And, if their friendly smiles and jovial personalities were any indication, were excited to get their day started.

"What should we call you?" Lily asked softly.

Melissa gazed at her in confusion. "Melissa."

Lily giggled girlishly. "No, silly, your Red Dahlia name."

Melissa still didn't understand.

"When you come to work at the Red Dahlia, Vivienne encourages you to choose a name that will only be used within these walls. Something that will keep your experiences here separate from your life outside," Afrodite explained.

"So, your real name isn't Afrodite?" Melissa realized how foolish that question was as soon as she asked. Fortunately, no one laughed at her.

"As cool as it is, no, it's not my real name, which is Grace. I chose Afrodite because it reminded me of those badass women from the seventies Blaxploitation films. This is my real hair though." Afrodite patted her bloom of hair proudly.

"Well, since I'm only going to be here for a couple of weeks, a name probably isn't necessary," Melissa said.

Hyacinth stepped toward her. "Hun, whether you are at Red Dahlia for two weeks or two years, a name you shall have. I can choose one for you."

"Hyacinth is not only a beast with the bullwhip but our resident psychic. If they say you should have a name, you shall have a name," Rose said with a very serious expression.

Melissa gazed around the room. All the hosts looked reverently at Hyacinth. She looked back at Hyacinth to find them smiling knowingly down at her. "May I?" They held their hands out to Melissa.

She hesitantly laid hers on their palm. Hyacinth closed their eyes, and the room grew eerily quiet. A moment later, their eyes slowly opened as a happy smile spread across their face. "Mistress of the Heart but I think Mistress Heart will do just fine. It's a name that will be whispered throughout these walls for years to come." They released Melissa's hand, bowed again at the waist, and stepped back.

She turned to find everyone grinning at her as if they were in on a secret that she wasn't privy to.

"All right, children, doors open in an hour," Afrodite said.

They all scrambled to a dressing table, the music clicked back on exactly where it had been paused, and Afrodite took Melissa's hand to lead her out of the room.

"That wasn't weird at all," Melissa said as they exited through the secret door.

Afrodite chuckled. "Hyacinth is a bit eccentric but as sweet as they come. Vivienne found them working as a submissive in an underground sex club in Los Angeles about five years ago. She saw how miserable they were and waited for them after the club closed. She took them to get something to eat and learned that they were basically a slave to the owner of the club and was being abused because they owed the guy money. The next day Vivienne paid Hyacinth's debt and brought them back here that night. She brought them to me, and I showed Hyacinth how to take their power back by becoming a domme."

"And the psychic thing?"

Afrodite shrugged. "Hyacinth said it's always been there. It was just beaten into submission like them during their time at the club in LA. We don't take what they tell us lightly because they're usually right."

"Usually?"

"Hyacinth believes that we all have the power to change our paths. One decision could completely reroute what was predicted to happen. Now, Mistress Heart, shall we give you a tour of the playrooms?" Afrodite grinned.

Hearing the name that she was given by Hyacinth being used gave Melissa a shiver of pleasure. "Yes, and what would I need to do to attend your demonstration on Sunday?"

CHAPTER ELEVEN

Golden stood in the middle of one of her dance studios filled with pride. The grand opening for the Legacy Dance Academy was scheduled for tomorrow and she was doing a final walk-through to make sure everything was ready for the big day. She still couldn't believe it was happening. A year ago, when she began to realize that her day job no longer gave her the satisfaction it once did because her love of dance had her more eager to leave work at the end of the day to practice a routine or get ready for a performance, Golden knew a decision had to be made. She had to choose between the steady dependable income of her day job or the passion and joy of her first love, dance. Once again, she had leaned on her friends and family to talk it through, and just as they had when she was deciding whether to start a side career as a burlesque performer, they all told her to choose what was in her heart and that they would support her.

Golden left her prestigious six-figure salary job, took fifty thousand dollars from her nest egg, which barely made a dent in what she'd been saving and investing since she was eighteen years old, bought a warehouse space near her home in Jersey City, converted it to a dance studio, and started on the road to entrepreneurship. The first floor had two large studios and a locker room for training young dancers in various styles including ballroom, ballet, and hip hop. The second floor was dedicated to Satin and Lace Burlesque, the location for Golden's burlesque school and home of her burlesque performance troupe. There was a large dance studio, dressing room, conference room, break room, and her office. She turned and gazed up at a picture of her father during his hip hop dance days hanging just inside the door of the studio. The second studio had a picture her mother had taken of her and her father as he helped her lace up her shoes for a ballet performance. The Satin and Lace studio had various performance pictures of her aunt Dinah hanging throughout the room. They were her inspirations and she hoped they were proud of how she was carrying on their legacy in her own way.

"Hello!" she heard someone shout. "Is this where we sign up for striptease classes?"

Golden chuckled and made her way out to the lobby where Melissa and Zoe greeted her with flowers and balloons. "I'd pay for your lessons myself if it meant getting you into one of my burlesque classes," she said to Melissa who had been the one to ask the question.

Melissa handed her a vase filled with a huge bouquet of orange roses, Golden's favorite color. "I'll leave that talent to you, thank you very much."

"If you're not booked up already, you can sign me up." Zoe handed her a bouquet of orange and red balloons with a few silver ones that said *Congratulations* and *Good Luck* that were kept from floating up into the ceiling lights by a glittery weight.

Golden set the flowers on the desk then the balloons next to it. "You know I'll always have a spot for you guys. How about a tour?"

"Yes. We haven't seen the place since it was an empty rodent condo," Melissa teased her.

Golden rolled her eyes. "Would you lock the door, please? Wouldn't want anyone wandering in while we're walking around."

After the tour ended in the break room, Zoe pulled a bottle of champagne from her bag. "You can't have a celebration without champagne."

"No, you can't." Golden grabbed paper cups from a cabinet.

Zoe popped the cork and filled them.

Melissa held hers. "To living our best lives."

"Cheers to that," Golden said.

They tapped their cups together and took a drink.

"Look how far we've come since that day you two walked into my salon for our first Sunday appointments. Who would've believed those three young women would be the boss bitches we are today?" Zoe said.

Golden looked at her two best friends and grinned. "I knew. You two just needed to catch up."

Zoe and Melissa laughed. Golden was so proud of all that they had accomplished. She was living the dream she never knew she had. Zoe's salon and recently opened spa had been listed on several *Best Of* lists and her hair product line was flying off store shelves. Melissa, her dear sweet sister from another mother, had finally come into her own power and confidence and was being groomed to manage the gallery whenever Vivienne decided to retire. There was only one thing missing in each of their lives...romance.

"So, ladies, I was thinking for this year's getaway we could do one of those Olivia cruises. Imagine that instead of spending another week at some resort with mostly hetero folks, we could spend our vacay partying with like-minded women," Golden suggested.

"One of my stylists took an Olivia cruise once and said she loved it. She said even the onboard entertainment is done by queer performers," Zoe said.

Melissa frowned. "Cruises always make me think of old people and germs."

Zoe laughed. "Why those particular things?"

"I don't know. On TV whenever an old person talks about going on vacation, they always pick a cruise. Then there's all those news reports about whole ships of people getting sick from some strain of virus. I'm not trying to be quarantined in some tiny stateroom because people don't know how to wash their hands or cover their mouths when they sneeze."

Golden shook her head. "Girl, you really need to stop watching so much TV. Cruises have become whole ass destinations now with amusement park-like rides, private islands, and enough shit to keep you so busy you forget you're on a ship. All that and a ship full of women like us, how could you say no to that?"

Melissa shrugged. "I guess I can think about it."

"Well, the other option is the St. Kitts music festival. We've always talked about going and now we have the means to afford it," Zoe said.

Melissa nodded. "Now that I could get with."

"Okay, I like that idea also." Golden pulled out her phone and searched for information on the festival. "Wow, Sean Paul, Maxi Priest, Keyshia Cole..." Golden frowned.

"What's wrong?" Melissa asked.

"The Rhythm Twins are listed as performers." After all this time she didn't believe that it would still hurt to think about them.

"Maybe we could look at the cruises after all," Melissa said.

Golden shook off the regret that she began feeling. "No, Zoe's right. We've talked about going to St. Kitts for years. Now is as good a time as any. I'll explore getting a rental instead of staying at a resort. I know we've got about eight months, but it's better to book something sooner rather than later."

Zoe looked at her with concern. "Are you sure?"

Golden waved dismissively. "It's a huge concert. What are the chances that I would even run into the Twins while we're there. It's fine, really."

Golden was trying to convince herself more than her friends. She hadn't spoken to Jade and Kendra since the night the harassment story broke. Including ignoring their calls when the woman recanted her story after Jade and Kendra's manager released the bank statements for the payoff she had asked for as proof that she had extorted money from them. Then several other artists that she had sung backup for released their own statements that she had done the same to them. For Golden, it wasn't the accusations that had caused her to end whatever it was between her, Jade, and Kendra. It was them not being forthright with her. They were telling her she was the only one they were thinking about but sleeping with someone else. Golden had been hurt and completely cut off all communication with them. She even removed them from her social media feeds and contacts. That didn't stop the radio interviews or the stories popping up on her newsfeed from reminding her of them as their popularity grew.

She suddenly remembered an email she'd received from Jade a few months back that she hadn't even opened. There had been a video attachment which she had assumed was probably a message from them since she wouldn't answer their calls. If she didn't take their calls, why would they think that she'd watch any recording of what they had to say? She archived the message and didn't think about it again. After Melissa and Zoe left, Golden sat in her office with Jade and Kendra still on her mind. She opened her emails and searched the archive. She had never set it for a period to delete anything so there were emails from years ago. When she located Jade's email, she noticed the subject line for the first time. It simply read *For Golden*. She opened the email then clicked on the video attachment. Jade's face popped up as she was setting up the phone to record. Golden could hear Kendra in the background teasing Jade about her lack of camera skills. To prove Kendra correct, the camera view switched from pointing to Jade to pointing toward the window of a recording booth, then back to Jade's face.

"I think I got it." Jade slowly backed away from the camera.

"Yeah, you did. I can see us," Kendra said.

Seeing them both sent Golden's heart skipping. She missed their long conversations, daily text messages, how they made her feel so special with weekly flower deliveries, and just how talking to them on the phone could make her whole day. Kendra sat on a stool tuning a guitar as Jade sat on one beside her.

"Hit it, Lamar," Jade said.

"Okay, we're recording," a disembodied voice responded.

Kendra began playing an upbeat jazz tempo on the guitar as Jade closed her eyes and nodded to the music. A moment later, the sound of other instruments joined her, and Jade began to sing. Her melodic tone always reminded Golden of honeyed whiskey—smooth, rich, and deep. She sang a song about the regret of losing a love, losing her golden girl. The song was obviously about her and was being performed in a bluesy jazz tempo like the type of music Golden enjoyed performing to.

I had a notion
To find the one who's Golden
And have a love begin
That just won't ever end
But suddenly you were gone
Now my rainy days
Come with the dawn
But the sun can't leave me now
You're my Golden Girl, yeah
In this crazy world...

She closed her eyes and could imagine herself choreographing a routine to the song. It ended with the other instruments fading out, leaving Kendra finishing with a guitar solo. Golden glanced at the screen, wiping a tear from her eye. As if they knew she was watching, Jade and Kendra looked right at the camera with such tenderness that Golden was flooded with all the feelings for them that she had tried so hard to tuck away.

"Golden, we don't know if you're going to watch this or not," Kendra said, "but please know that Jade and I will always regret not being straightforward with you."

"We had no intention of hurting you," Jade said. "As much as we regret what happened, it did make us realize how much we care about you which is why we wrote this song."

"We don't know if you'll ever have it in your heart to forgive us, but if you do, we will do whatever it takes to make it up to you," Kendra said.

"However, if you'll allow us to bask in your golden light, we'll be happy to accept it. Even if it means staying in the friendzone," Jade said with a grin.

Kendra smiled and shook her head. "All this is to tell you that we miss you and have never once stopped thinking about you. You know where to find us if you have it in your heart to take pity on us. Take care, Golden Girl."

They both threw a kiss to the camera before Jade stood to turn it off and accidentally switched the view toward the booth again. "Shit, I think I did something wrong."

"Dude, seriously? How do you not know how to work your own phone?"

The camera was jostled and then Kendra's amused grin came into frame before it went black. Golden couldn't help but laugh. She placed the email back in her inbox and hit reply.

Jade and Kendra,

Apologies for the delayed response. I've had a lot going on and am just getting a chance to sit and watch your video. Thank you for the beautiful song. It's touching to know that you still think of me so affectionately after all this time.

Golden wasn't sure how to continue. Should she tell them that she missed them? That she regretted cutting them out of her life the way she did? That something has been missing from her life ever since? Not that she was unhappy. On the contrary, she was thrilled with her life. But Jade and Kendra had given her something that she didn't even know was missing, companionship on a deeper level than her family and friendships provided. Because Golden had never experienced the feelings that she had for the Twins with anyone before, she didn't know how to handle being hurt by them, so she walked away to avoid dealing with it at all. She looked at what she'd written so far. Should she open the door to allow those feelings in once again by admitting she still cared for them, or should she play it safe and end the email where it was with a polite sign-off? Golden decided to open the door just enough for them to peek through and offer a hand of friendship.

Feel free to give me a call sometime so that we can catch up.

Have a good night,

Golden

Simple, succinct, nothing to misinterpret as an overture of anything more than friendship. She clicked *Send* before she could change her mind, then shut her computer down as if that would keep any response from coming through.

❖

"You know you're starting to make me feel like you don't trust me," Jay, Zoe's spa manager, said in greeting as she walked into his office.

"Why would you feel like that? I trust you implicitly."

He quirked a brow. "Prove it. Don't come up here to check on things for at least two days."

Zoe frowned. "Am I that bad?"

"Girl!" He looked at her as if she said something truly ridiculous.

Zoe frowned. "I'm sorry, I just figured since I'm right downstairs it wouldn't hurt to check on things up here occasionally."

"If it were occasionally then there would be no issue, but you're up here every day. Hell, I live with my mother, and I don't even see her every day."

Zoe chuckled. "So, you're saying I'm micromanaging you."

"No, I'm saying you're a control freak and need to let go of the reigns. You hired me to run the spa for you. Let me do that. If you want to stop in once or twice a week, I'll be fine with that. If there are any issues, I'll either come downstairs to tell you or we can discuss them during our weekly meetings with Nadine, who, by the way, warned me you were like this. Look at it this way, you trusted Nadine and I enough to hire us. Let us do our job and trust that we'll do it just as well as you would."

Nadine managed Hair For You's distribution center and had been with Zoe since the day it was originally located above the salon where her spa, the Lotus Wellness Sanctuary, was currently located. Zoe had insisted on being hands-on with both the salon and distribution center despite knowing that Nadine had twenty years of experience in warehouse and distribution management under her belt while Zoe had only taken a few months' worth of classes in distribution management. She felt like these businesses were her second child, and as her first child no longer needed her constant mothering, she had poured that attention into her businesses. Since the distribution center had been moved to larger facilities on the other side of Brooklyn, she no longer had the ease of being able to just pop in daily, which was probably why Nadine no longer rolled her eyes when Zoe came by the distribution center every other week.

Zoe sighed in resignation. "You're right. It's just difficult. Up until Alex decided to invest, all of this had just been ideas on a vision board for so long that it's still unbelievable that it has all become a reality. I feel like I need to keep touching everything to make sure it doesn't just disappear."

Jay nodded. "I can understand that, but I'm here to tell you that it's real and you've done everything you needed to make it happen. Now let us take some of the pressure off your hands so that you can breathe and reap the benefits of all your hard work."

"You're good."

Jay gave her a smug grin. "That's why you hired me. Now shoo."

Zoe shook her head with a smile. "I'll see you on Monday for our managers' meeting."

She left Jay's office, tamping down the urge to do a quick walk-through to see how things were going, and made her way back down to the salon. Despite it being very busy Zoe had no bookings of her own and the other stylists didn't seem to need any assistance, which was why she had ventured upstairs to the spa. As she re-entered the salon, she caught the tail end of her receptionist telling a woman that there were no stylists available for walk-ins today. The woman had her back to Zoe, but she could hear the desperation in her voice as she practically begged to see someone today and even offered to sit and wait all afternoon if she had to. She looked to be about Zoe's height, dressed in a baggy sweatsuit, and an oversized sleeping bonnet on her head.

"What's going on, Erica?"

"Miss Zoe, this woman is a walk-in and is insisting on seeing someone today. I tried to tell her that we're all booked up, but…" Erica looked at the woman in exasperation.

"I've got it." Zoe turned to the woman with a smile and was completely caught off guard by her beauty.

She had a warm golden complexion, wide set almond-shaped amber-colored eyes that were brimming with tears, and a straight nose and full lips that were trembling slightly. Zoe could tell that the woman was doing her best not to break down.

She gave her a friendly smile as she offered her hand in greeting. "Hi, I'm Zoe. This is my salon. What can we do for you today?"

She took Zoe's hand with a tremulous smile. "Hi. I'm Danice. I'd like to get a haircut, but it has to be done today." The desperation still tinged her voice.

"Okay, Danice. I can help you with that. If you'll just have a seat in the first station when you walk in, I'll be right with you."

"Thank you." She was still on the verge of tears.

Zoe watched her walk to the entrance of the main salon area. Even with the oversized sweatsuit, she could tell Danice had a generous figure underneath. She turned back to Erica.

"We don't turn people away without checking with either me or the other stylists to see if they can squeeze them in. Understood?"

"Yes, ma'am. She just looked a little crazy, so I wasn't sure what to do."

Zoe shook her head. Erica had started working there just a few weeks ago after Zoe's former receptionist finished beauty school and was given her own chair in the salon. She was young and eager, but she could also be a bit of a space cadet.

"It's fine. Next time just check, okay?"

Erica nodded. Zoe walked into the salon area to Danice waiting in her chair dabbing at her eyes. She placed a hand on her shoulder.

"Are you all right?"

She gave Zoe a sad smile. "I'll be fine. Thank you."

Zoe wouldn't push. This was obviously not going to be a standard hair appointment. She reached for the bonnet then stopped.

"Do you mind if I take this off?"

Danice shook her head.

Zoe eased it off and realized why she was wearing such a large bonnet. Danice's hair fell out in one long sweep. By the time the midnight black mass settled, it was down past the back of the chair. Zoe determined it must reach just past Danice's behind. It was straight, thick, and heavy.

"Are you looking to get a trim?"

"No. I want it all off."

Zoe looked up to meet her gaze in the mirror. "All of it?"

Danice's expression had turned from sadness to angry determination. "All of it."

Zoe had seen this before. Whether it was a bad breakup, needing a major life change, or just wanting something easier, the first drastic thing most women would do in response was a big chop or major hairstyle change. She called it the Bernadine Effect after Angela Basset's character in *Waiting to Exhale*, but she had never done a chop this drastic.

"Are you sure? I can give you a nice, layered cut that will be easier to manage."

Zoe normally wouldn't try to talk a woman out of her big chop because if she'd gotten to that point, she wasn't looking to turn back, but Danice's hair was so gorgeous and healthy. There were clients who would kill for even a wig that looked this good.

Danice's eyes began to water again, but her angry expression was still there. "No."

"Okay. I have one request in return. You have such beautiful hair, and we partner with Locks of Love, have you heard of them?"

Danice nodded.

"Well, if you don't want all this hair, then I'm sure they could use the donation."

"Okay. At least something good will come out of this."

Zoe wasn't one to pry into a client's business unless they chose to talk. Despite instinct telling her that Danice could use someone to talk to, she wouldn't be the one to broach the subject. She handed Danice her bonnet, then went and grabbed a cape and placed it around her. Next, she combed and brushed Danice's hair until it was free of any tangles, separated it into four ponytails with nylon bands, braided them, and placed another band at the bottom then picked up the scissors. She met Danice's gaze in the mirror again and knew by the look in her eyes that there was no need for Zoe to ask again if she was sure. As Zoe looked away, she caught half the salon's occupants staring in wide-eyed disbelief in their direction. She looked back down at Danice's hair and began cutting a few inches above the band of the first ponytail. There was no turning back now and a collective gasp filled the room. She even heard "Uh-uh, no she didn't" from someone. Zoe laid each braid on her supply cart. When she cut through the last lock of hair she gazed up and saw tears streaming down Danice's cheeks.

Zoe stepped away to wrap the braids in tissue paper then placed them in a Ziploc bag to prepare them for shipping later. She stepped back over to Danice and fluffed out what was left of her hair, which without all that weight pulling it straight had a soft natural wave to it.

"Should I continue?" she asked.

Danice took a deep breath and her lips curved into a small smile. "Yes."

"Are we talking pixie cut, fade?"

"No, bald."

Zoe opened her mouth then shut it again. This woman was obviously shedding some serious baggage. She pulled out her clippers and gave Danice what she wanted. Clients finished with their appointments would slowly walk by looking and shaking their heads. One older woman walked up, patted Danice on the shoulder, and said, "I feel you, girl. Shave that man right out of your hair." Danice fully smiled in response, making Zoe's heart skip.

When she finished, Danice's head was smooth with a small round birthmark just above her right ear. She stared at her reflection with a mix of awe and curiosity on her face. The cut enhanced her beauty making her eyes seem bigger and brighter. Zoe turned and asked the young woman who had been shampooing clients to bring her a warm towel, which they kept a supply of in a warmer for their male clients who came in for a cut and shave. A moment later, she placed the towel on Danice's scalp and gently pressed and massaged. Danice's eyes closed as she sighed with pleasure. Zoe had to force herself not to shudder with the desire that clenched between her legs.

She set the towel aside, picked up a dropper bottle of Hair For You chamomile scalp oil, and placed a couple of drops in the palm of her hand. She gently rubbed her hands together to develop some warmth then smoothed and massaged the oil into Danice's scalp as she watched her in the mirror. Danice's eyes were still closed, and her face was relaxed as she bit on her bottom lip. The desire that began between Zoe's thighs spread throughout her body. She had to force herself to remove her hands from Danice's head and clear her throat as she picked up the now cooled towel to wipe the oil from her hands.

"You're all set."

Danice's eyes fluttered open, catching Zoe's gaze in the mirror before quickly looking at her own reflection. She turned her head left to right, lifted her hand, and smoothed it over her scalp, smiling broadly.

"It feels so weird. I've carried that heaviness for so long that I feel light enough to practically float out of here."

"Well, you look great."

Danice stood, dropped her bonnet in the trash can at Zoe's station, and turned to her with a soft smile. "Thank you so much. You don't know what this means to me."

Zoe smiled. "I think I have a pretty good idea."

Her eyes glistened once again, but Zoe had a feeling that these were happier tears than when she arrived.

"What do I owe you?"

"Thirty-five."

"That's all?"

"For just a haircut, yes. Oh, and this." Zoe picked up the bottle of hair oil and handed it to her. "It's on the house. After you shower, place a warm towel on your head just as I did, then massage a couple drops of the oil to keep your scalp moisturized. And don't forget to wear a hat if you're going to be out in the sun for an extended period to avoid sunburn."

Danice took the bottle, placed it in her purse, then opened her wallet and offered Zoe a twenty-dollar bill.

Zoe shook her head. "As the owner I don't accept tips." That wasn't true, but for some reason she didn't feel comfortable taking a tip for this big chop.

"Thank you again."

"My pleasure."

Zoe watched Danice walk away until she turned into the reception area and was no longer in sight. When she turned back, her neighboring stylists were grinning knowingly. She ignored them and went about cleaning her station.

CHAPTER TWELVE

Melissa took a waterproof eyebrow pencil and carefully made an outline of a heart just above the right corner of her lip, then filled it in. With her faux beauty mark complete, she picked up her favorite black matte liquid twenty-four-hour lip color by MAC. Once she finished with her makeup, she unpinned her locs from the haphazard updo she wore them in while she was getting dressed and shook them out to hang freely. The next item she put on was a smaller, lightweight black leather version of a Maleficent-style headpiece and matching leather Venetian mask that covered the entire top half of her face.

"Do you need help tightening your corset?" Rose asked.

"Yes, thank you."

Melissa walked over to one of the full-length mirrors in the Red Dahlia dressing room. Rose came up behind her, and Melissa pulled on a pair of elbow-length leather gloves with silver steel pointed fingertips, then she felt a slight tug around her waist.

Rose rested her hands on Melissa's waist and caught her gaze in the mirror. "Have I told you how badass you always look in this costume? Angelina Jolie ain't got nothing on our Mistress Heart."

Melissa smiled and reached back to softly stroke her metal fingertips along Rose's butt cheek bared from the thong she wore. "Thank you. Are you ready for the show?"

"So ready." She fluffed her blond wig then placed a kiss on Melissa's cheek before walking away.

Melissa gazed back at her own image. What a difference a year made. Well, technically a year and a half. If anyone had told her on the first day that she had covered for the Red Dahlia Social Club's receptionist that in over a year's time she would be one of their top tier Dommes, she would have laughed in their face. She had no idea what an eye-opening experience those two weeks would be for her. The first surprising thing she learned was that Red Dahlia's members were some of the most prominent people in New York. Celebrities, politicians, CEOs of Fortune 500 companies, and wealthy socialites. She had also learned that there was a Red Dahlia in both Paris and London where it was rumored some of the Royal family frequented. All members had free access to any of the other social clubs.

Her second surprise was getting to know Afrodite and the hosts. Other than Hyacinth, whose heartbreaking story of being thrown out of their home at fourteen when they came out to their parents and had been homeless for most of their teen years, they all had fairly well-adjusted childhoods. There was no abuse or emotional trauma that led her fellow hosts to a life of fetish sex work. They found something they enjoyed and chose to make money doing it. That was her next realization. Being a sex worker didn't always mean you had to have sex. There were clubs that did provide such services in addition to kink, but Red Dahlia was not one of them. Vivienne strictly forbade hosts from engaging in sexual intercourse with any client within the confines of the club. If she found out that they had they were immediately fired. If a member even offered to pay extra for such services, they were escorted from the premises and their membership was revoked. On the other hand, whatever arrangement was garnered between a member and host outside of the club was their own business. If Vivienne didn't know about it, it wasn't happening.

All the questions Melissa had been too afraid to ask Afrodite that first day covering for Shari she was encouraged by the hosts to ask after her first couple of days working there. At the end of the night, after the members had left, the place was locked tight and the cleaning crew were preparing the playrooms for the next day, Melissa would sit in the dressing room with the hosts listening with rapt attention like an eager child listening to bedtime stories. When Shari, the receptionist, returned and Melissa's time at Red Dahlia had come to an end she found that she couldn't just go back to her everyday life like she hadn't finally discovered where she belonged. She had grown melancholy and did her best to hide it, but she hadn't been able to hide it from Vivienne.

❖

Melissa had locked up the gallery for the night and was heading back to Vivienne's office to see if she needed anything else before she went home.

"Yes, I'd like you to sit. We need to have a chat." Vivienne looked concerned.

Melissa had taken a seat in one of the chairs across from Vivienne's desk. "Is everything okay?"

"I was going to ask you the same question."

"Me? Why? I'm fine."

"I think we've known each other long enough to tell when we're not fine. You haven't been yourself since you finished covering for Shari next door. Are you mad at me? Did I overstep our relationship by asking you to cover?"

"No, not at all. I agreed to do it and I'm glad I did."

"Then why the moping and long face these past few weeks?"

"Well…" Melissa hadn't been sure what she wanted or how to ask for it even if she did.

Vivienne had smiled knowingly. "You've been bit by the bug and want more."

Melissa had gazed down at her lap, too embarrassed to look at Vivienne who came over and sat in the chair beside her.

"My sweet Melissa, there is no need to be embarrassed about discovering something new and wonderful about yourself, even if it's something society doesn't consider polite or normal. You're a gay Black woman, so you're already being looked down upon as unacceptable, yet you found a way to accept yourself for who you are. Enjoying kink is just a bonus to who Melissa Hart is."

It was at those moments that Melissa wished Vivienne had been her mother. "But what do I do with it now that I've discovered it?"

"Explore it, silly. I own a kink club, for Pete's sake."

Melissa had smiled. "You do realize you don't pay me enough to become a member."

"Who said anything about being a member? I've been looking to add a couple more hosts. I can't think of anyone better than you to be one of them." Vivienne had given her an encouraging smile.

"Me, a host?" Melissa had shaken her head at such an idea.

"Why not?"

"I love being your assistant and working at the gallery. Also, spending two weeks as a receptionist and listening to Afrodite and the others talking about what they do doesn't make me qualified to do it."

"First, no one said you had to quit your day job. I wouldn't let you anyway. My kids have no interest in running my gallery after I retire, or kick the bucket, whichever comes first, so who else would I leave the gallery too?"

Melissa had looked at Vivienne in surprise. "Seriously?"

"Yes. If you're interested."

"Hell yes, I'm interested!"

"Phew, that's one worry to take off my plate. Now, knowing that your job with me is safe, would you also be interested in becoming a host at Red Dahlia?"

Melissa had chewed her bottom lip in contemplation. Knowing what she'd learned of her own pleasure while exploring with Riley, how it played into what the Red Dahlia offered not only to their members but their hosts, and hearing Riley's voice in her head telling her she'd be crazy to turn down such a tempting opportunity, Melissa had known there was only one answer to Vivienne's question.

❖

Now here she was, manager of Life is Art Gallery by day and dominatrix Mistress Heart by night like some kink superhero with a secret identity, mask and all. Vivienne, Riley and the other hosts at Red Dahlia were the only people who knew who she really was without the mask. It was the only way she could keep her life outside of the club separate from who she was at the club. She was so determined to keep her life as Mistress Heart separate from her life as Melissa Hart, that she hadn't even told her best friends what she was doing. She didn't think she would be able to keep this secret forever. She planned to tell them eventually, but until then, Melissa enjoyed not having to explain to anyone why she chose and enjoyed her new career in kink.

She ran her hands down her waist cinched in by a black strapless leather corset with an ankle-length train attached, then over her hips which were covered in skintight leather pants that zipped from front to back over her crotch, then she gazed down at the black ankle boots with a solid brass six-inch heel. Satisfied with her dark villainous inspired attire, Melissa closed her eyes and cleared her mind of her everyday life. When she gazed at her refection once again, Melissa was gone, and a mischievous grinning Mistress Heart was ready for a night of fun and games.

❖

Since Kiara would be out on a date tonight, Zoe decided to treat herself to dinner at the diner around the corner from the salon. She settled into the booth that she'd been seated in and looked at the menu trying to decide if she would go with her usual or order something different for once.

"Zoe?"

She looked up to find Danice standing before her looking totally different from the woman who had entered the salon earlier that afternoon. She was dressed in a multi-colored snake print, wide leg jumpsuit that complemented her generous figure much better than the oversized sweatsuit she had worn, and a crop denim jacket. She accessorized her look with large iridescent teardrop earrings with a matching necklace. She even wore makeup. Not a lot, just a soft cranberry eyeshadow and lipstick to match one of the colors in her jumpsuit.

"Wow, Danice, if I hadn't been the one to cut your hair, I would never have recognized you. You look great."

Danice gave her a shy smile. "Thank you. This is all because of what you did for me."

Zoe waved dismissively. "I just did what you asked."

"Which was more than I could've imagined." She looked as if she were going to cry then shook it off and smiled again. "Well, I saw you and just wanted to thank you, again. I'll let you get back to your evening."

"Wait, are you meeting anyone?"

"I'm here alone. I was just going to order something and take it back home."

"Well, if you're not in a hurry, would you like to join me?"

Danice's smile broadened. "Yes, I'd like that." She sat in the seat across from Zoe.

"Would you like to see the menu?" Zoe offered.

"No. I already know what I want. My sister and I used to come here all the time and I always ordered the same thing. The crabcake burger. I haven't been here in years, but I saw online that they still have it."

Zoe chuckled. "Yes, they do. Despite my best intentions to change it up, it's what I always order."

"Really? What does it for you? The frizzled onions or the chipotle sauce?"

"Without a doubt the chipotle sauce, but I'll let you in on a little secret." Zoe leaned in toward her and whispered, "I always order extra frizzled onions on the side instead of fries."

Danice looked amazed. "I never thought to do that."

"Only two other people know my secret so consider yourself lucky." She gave Danice a wink.

Danice grinned. "I think my luck started when I walked into your salon today."

"Mine too."

Their gazes held for a moment before they were interrupted by their server.

He placed two glasses of ice water on the table. "Are you ready to order?" Zoe recognized him from the many times she came here to eat.

"Yes, may we get two crab cake burgers with extra frizzled onions instead of fries on the side?"

He must have recognized her because he smiled. "Yes. Anything to drink?"

"Allow me," Danice said. "Two boozy chocolate shakes, please."

Their server nodded. "You got it."

"Wow, I usually save the boozy shakes for a special occasion."

"Well, I consider this a special occasion."

"What are we celebrating?"

Danice took a sip of water and continued looking down into her glass. "My divorce."

Zoe wasn't surprised. "Oh. Was that the reason for the visit to the salon today as well?"

Danice gave her a small smile. "Yes, but I think I'm going to need my shake before I can talk about that."

"I understand. You don't have to talk about it at all if you don't feel like it. No pressure."

"No, I do, but I'll understand if you don't want to hear it. You don't know me from Eve."

"True, but sometimes talking to someone who doesn't know you can give you a clearer perspective than someone who's too close to the situation and can muddy the waters with their lack of objectivity. I find it's why so many people will sit in a salon or barber chair and tell their whole life story as they're getting their hair done."

Danice nodded. "Now that I think about it, I can see that."

Their server arrived with their shakes. "Enjoy," he said in parting.

Zoe picked up her frosted glass and raised it toward Danice. "Here's to new beginnings."

Danice touched hers to Zoe's. "To new beginnings and friends."

Zoe took a healthy sip. "Woo! If the brain freeze doesn't get you the rum will. Now I remember why I only order this when I'm hanging with my girls."

Danice laughed. "Yeah, I've forgotten how strong they are."

Zoe set her shake aside and took a sip of water. "So, tell me what led you to make such a drastic change?"

Danice sat quietly in her own thoughts for a moment then sighed heavily. "Pressured by my parents, I married someone I barely knew and spent the past eight years having little pieces of myself slowly and methodically whittled away until there was nothing left but his image of the perfect wife."

Looking anxious, she picked up her napkin and distractedly began tearing little pieces off as if she were trying to show what happened to her. Zoe reached across the table to still Danice's hands. Danice blinked rapidly then looked at Zoe as if she'd just remembered she was there.

"Why don't we save this conversation for another time," Zoe said gently.

Danice gave her a sad smile. "I'd rather just get it over with and never talk about it again."

Their server arrived with their food, so Zoe slowly released Danice's hand. Danice pushed the shredded bits of napkin aside as their plates were set in front of them.

"Can I get you ladies anything else?" their server asked.

"No, I think we're good for now," Zoe answered.

He walked away and she turned back to Danice who was taking a big gulp of her boozy shake directly from the glass instead using the straw. When she set the glass back down it was half empty and she gazed up at Zoe with an adorable milkshake mustache above her lip.

Zoe chuckled. "You've got a little something…" She pointed to her own lip.

With an embarrassed smile, Danice picked up a napkin from the extras their server had brought with their food and wiped her lips. "Can't take me anywhere."

Although it was probably meant as a joke, Zoe found the way she said it held that same bitterness in her tone that she had talking about her marriage. Danice had a lot of baggage to unpack, and as attractive as Zoe thought she was, that and the fact that she was probably straight tamped down any attraction she felt toward her. It was obvious Danice could use a friend more than a lover, which Zoe was happy to provide.

Danice picked up her crab burger, took a bite, and moaned with pleasure as she slowly chewed. The look on her face had Zoe's body calling her a liar for thinking that she could ignore her attraction. She chose to focus her attention on her own food instead of the way Danice's tongue snaked out to lick a drop of chipotle sauce from the corner of her mouth. They ate quietly together for some time before Danice sighed happily.

"I can't eat another bite. This was just what I needed to finish out the day," Danice said.

Zoe noticed that she'd barely eaten half her sandwich but had picked off most of the onions. "Lightweight," she teased her.

Danice pointed to the empty glass next to her plate. "I blame the shake."

"Yeah, they're so thick and rich it's pretty much like having dessert first. Looks like you'll have a delicious midnight snack though."

Danice gazed down at what was left of her food. "I sure will. And no one there to nag or stop me from eating it."

"If you don't mind my asking, what made you stay so long in a marriage that you obviously weren't happy in and what was the final straw that made you leave?"

"My parents' marriage was arranged by their parents and a matchmaker in India. My mother had been a nurse but gave up her career to move here with my father and take care of our family. For as long as I can remember, our mother drilled it into my and my sister's heads that no matter what our career goals were, our main purpose in life was to find a good man to marry, have children, and devote our lives to them. I finished college and became a special needs teacher while my sister escaped by joining the Peace Corps as soon as she had her degree in hand. All my mother's focus was on me, especially since I was the oldest. What she didn't know was that I was dating men and women and had no interest in marrying anyone any time soon."

Danice smiled sadly. "By the time I was thirty she was despairing over never seeing her daughters wed or giving her grandchildren. My sister was immune to the guilt because for years while she was traipsing around the globe saving the world, she had been able to avoid the daily guilt trip my mother was laying down, especially since I was still living at home because I couldn't afford an apartment on my own. So, my father suggested hiring a matchmaker to find a husband for me. That's when I told them I was bisexual."

"I'm assuming that didn't go over well."

"Ha, that's the understatement of the year. My father left it up to my mother to express their outrage. My mother wailed and accused me of bringing shame to our family and breaking her heart after everything she'd sacrificed for us. The guilt trip worked, and I gave in to the matchmaker idea. On paper, Malik was everything my parents, mostly my mother, approved of. He even appealed to me after we met because he came across as a more contemporary Indian man than the ones the matchmaker had been setting me up with. He said all the right things, he had no interest in having me leave my career or rush into having children. He also claimed he was cool with me being bisexual, which I felt was important to be upfront about."

"But that wasn't the case."

Denise frowned. "No. Everything was good in the beginning, but a year into our marriage he started getting jealous of me spending time with friends, suspicious of co-workers or if I had to work late, pushing me to be home more and hinting at wanting to start a family sooner rather than later. Then came the comments about how I dress too provocatively and that my short hair looked too masculine."

Zoe knew too well what Danice was describing. Her husband was sounding very much like what Ray ultimately would have become if she'd stayed with him. "I've been in a similar situation."

Danice gazed at her curiously. "Really? That's surprising."

"Why?"

Danice shrugged. "You just seem so confident and self-assured. I can't see you allowing anyone to control you."

Zoe quirked a brow. "Well, you're right on that. That's why I'm not with him."

Danice's expression turned sad. "That's where we differ. I was weak. I stayed and turned into my mother. It took two miscarriages and finding out that he was not only having an affair but had a child with the woman, for me to finally leave."

"You are not weak. It doesn't matter how long it took, what matters is that you finally did it."

Tears gathered in Danice's eyes. "You think so?"

"I know so. I also understand now why you cut your hair. Like that customer said earlier, you really were cutting that man out of your hair."

Danice chuckled. "Yeah, I guess so. My hair seemed to be more his crowning glory than mine."

"I guess it worked considering the wreck of a woman who walked into my salon compared to the bright confident one sitting across from me."

Danice looked shyly away. "I'm not quite confident yet. Haircut and new clothes are just the tip of the iceberg of the work I need to do to get back to who I was before Malik."

"How about becoming who you want to be now, because I have a feeling that the Danice you were before Malik wasn't as confident either."

"No, she wasn't."

Their server stopped by asking if they needed anything else. Zoe asked for a to-go box for Danice and the check. When he returned, Zoe handed him her credit card. Danice took out her wallet.

"Put that away. It's on me in celebration of your new beginning."

"Then you'll have to let me treat you the next time in appreciation for getting me started on my new beginning and listening to my story."

"Sounds like a plan." Zoe took a business card from her wallet. "This has the salon and my cell on it. Call or text me. Even if you just need an ear to listen."

Danice took the card. "You're probably sick of hearing it, but thank you, again."

"My pleasure. It was nice not to have to eat alone."

They stood and left the diner together.

Zoe gazed at Danice admiringly. "That cut really suits you. Brings more attention to your gorgeous face."

"Thank you." Danice's face darkened with a blush. "I hope to see you again soon, Zoe."

"Me too."

As Danice walked away, Zoe watched the sway of her generous hips appreciatively.

Chapter Thirteen

"L adies and gent, you are looking fabulous!" Golden said, addressing three of the dancers from her six-performer burlesque troupe who had just performed their final routines for Golden in preparation for an event hosted by the Burlesque Hall of Fame in Las Vegas.

Lexi, whose stage name was Lotta Chocolate, was a former dancer for a well-known entertainer who featured plus-sized dancers in her shows and videos. JoJo and Kyle, known as Fire and Ice, were a married couple that performed burlesque together. The three were the best acts in her troupe so when Golden was offered an opportunity to showcase Satin and Lace at the event, she knew they would be the perfect performers to take with her. She was performing her aerial act to make sure that the audience saw the diversity and talent of Black burlesque performers.

"I'll see you guys bright and early at the airport. Our flight departs at seven twenty in the morning."

Lexi frowned. "I don't understand why we couldn't get a later flight at a more reasonable hour."

"I told you it was the only flight I could get all of us a seat in business class and I want us to get to Vegas and registered as early as possible so that we can chill the rest of the day. It's going to be a busy weekend," Golden explained.

"Don't worry, Lexi, you can still party tonight. Just take your luggage with you, go straight to the airport from the club, then sleep on the plane," JoJo suggested with a teasing grin.

Lexi nodded. "I might just do that."

Golden laughed. "I don't care how you get there, just get there before the flight leaves."

Golden walked with them downstairs to where her mother manned the reception desk.

"Are you ready to head home?" she asked.

Carlin nodded. "Just one more thing. You got a call from the Rhythm Twins' manager asking if you could call her back about a collaboration." She handed Golden a note from her message pad.

Golden frowned down at it.

"I may not understand what happened between you three or how it would've worked if you had pursued it, but I do know that you haven't really been happy since you stopped talking to Jade and Kendra. What would it hurt to find out what they want?"

Golden sighed. "I hate it when you're reasonable and right."

Carlin chuckled. "I'm always right. You should be used to it by now. Go make the call while I lock up."

Golden trudged back up to her office and called the number.

"Hey, Golden, I'm so glad you called. How've you been?" Trish Parker, the Twins' manager, greeted her.

"Hey, Trish. I'm good. You wanted to talk about a collaboration?"

"Yeah, Jade and Kendra have been asked to perform their new song "Golden Girl" at a festival in February in Montmartre Paris honoring the Black entertainers that made it their home back in the day and they'd like you to perform with them."

"Golden Girl" was the song Jade and Kendra had said they wrote for her. Golden didn't realize they had released it on their new album until Zoe sent her the YouTube link for the song. It wasn't really played on the radio stations because it wasn't the Twins' usual dance party vibe, so she never heard it unless she chose to listen to it, which had been a lot these past few weeks.

"Since I don't sing, I don't know what kind of performance you're looking for."

"Well, as you know, the number is a bluesy ballad that they were hoping you could perform a burlesque number to. See, there's going to be jazz bands and singers, a few select R&B artists, swing dance performers, showgirls, and vaudeville acts. Jade and Kendra thought a burlesque performance would fit perfectly."

"I don't know. I have a business to run. I don't have the time or money to just jet off to Paris. The airfare alone would be a small fortune." Golden knew she had enough in her savings to afford the trip.

"All your expenses would be taken care of, and you'd also be paid for the performance. I understand if you need to think about it. Give me a call by the end of the week and let me know your decision. And, Golden, I personally think this would be an awesome opportunity for a performer of your status."

"Thanks, Trish. I'll let you know."

Golden knew she was just making excuses. The school practically ran itself as long as her mother was there to keep things in check, and she could afford the airfare; she was just a chicken. She could hear her mother, brother, and best friends all in her head asking her if she'd lost her mind. A trip to Paris to perform at an international event, in the very town her Aunt

Dinah had called home, was reason enough to say yes. But to perform with Jade and Kendra singing the song they wrote for her was like the icing on the cake. She went back downstairs to meet her mom.

"So?" her mother asked in anticipation.

Golden told her about the call.

"And you said yes."

"Not yet."

Carlin looked at her with exasperation. "Golden, c'mon. If romantic feelings weren't involved, what would you have answered?"

"I would've said yes, of course, but romantic feelings are involved. Hell, the song is proof of that. I don't know if I can keep it strictly professional."

"Look, it sounds to me like Jade and Kendra are trying to repair whatever was broken while also giving you the opportunity of a lifetime. You only find that special person, or persons in your case, once in a lifetime. Don't let pride keep you from doing what you love or connecting with who you love."

Golden looked at her mother with amusement. "I can't believe my mother is actually encouraging me to date TWO women."

Carlin placed a hand on Golden's cheek. "Look, I may not always agree with or understand the fluidity you young folks relate to, but I do know that as long as my children are happy and it's not hurting anyone, I'm cool."

Golden pulled her mother in for an embrace. "I love you, Mommy."

"I love you too, honey."

After Golden got home, she went down to her private studio in the basement, pulled up "Golden Girl" on her music app, and played it through the studio's Bluetooth. She stood in the middle of the room, closed her eyes, and let the music envelop her and Jade's voice and words stroke her. She normally listened to the song while she was doing something else, never allowing herself to stand still and really listen to it since the first time she heard it on the video they sent. She could see Jade standing on a stage in a 1920s jazz lounge crooning this song as a dancer stepped onto the floor. Golden began to sway, then to move, sensual and free. By the time Kendra played the final note on the guitar, Golden was stepping into her final pose. The music trailed off, she opened her eyes, gazed at herself in the mirror, and noticed what she thought had been sweat running down her cheeks while she was dancing turned out to be tears. She walked over, disconnected her phone from Bluetooth, and dialed.

"Hey, Trish, I'll do it. Send me the details and I'll have a booking contract sent to you first thing tomorrow."

❖

Melissa heard the opening refrain of Janet Jackson's "Velvet Rope" and walked out of the hidden door in Red Dahlia's party room. She slowly strolled out from behind the curtain that concealed the door to a room full of people all dressed in black cocktail attire and wearing masks. Tonight was the Red Dahlia Social Club's annual masquerade fundraiser to help raise funds for a public school art program that the Art is Life Gallery sponsored. She slowly walked through the guests surrounding the platform in the center of the room where Rose, dressed as a very sexy version of Sleeping Beauty in a long blond wig with a tiara, white lace peekaboo bra, matching thong panties, and a white satin and lace mask, was standing spread-eagle with her arms raised above her head, wrists handcuffed to a spreader bar, and her ankles cuffed to restraints attached to the platform. Her head lay against her raised arm, her eyes were closed, and a sweet smile was on her face as if she were pleasantly sleeping and dreaming.

As Melissa walked, she reached out to graze the faces, arms, and bare legs of the guests she passed with her steel-tipped fingers. When she reached the platform, she paused at a table placed next to it with various floggers, ticklers, spanking paddles, and riding crops. Melissa chose a riding crop with a heart-shaped silicon tip. The music faded and Melissa stepped onto the platform, walked to the edge, and faced the audience. There were still people talking in the crowd, so she stood in a wide-legged stance, her eyes slowly peering out, slapping the riding crop against her leather gloves which gave a loud pop. She continued doing that until it was quiet enough to hear a pin drop. Power was her addiction.

Once she knew she had the full attention of her audience she gave them a sexy smile. "Shall we awaken Sleeping Beauty?" She turned and walked back to Rose.

Slow seductive music played softly in the background. Melissa circled Rose until she was behind her and grazed the riding crop over her butt cheek before raising it and bringing it down with a pop leaving a heart-shaped red imprint behind. Rose whimpered and stuck her behind out for more. Melissa did the same to the other cheek in the same spot giving Rose matching heart imprints against her pale flesh. Rose avoided tanning so that her skin would stay pale for any marks placed on her body to show prominently.

"Does that feel good?" Melissa asked.

"Yes, Mistress," Rose said breathlessly.

Melissa raised the crop and left three more marks on each cheek. She felt a clenching between her own legs, something that occurred frequently during exhibitions like this and sessions with her clients. Despite that reaction, it never led to anything more than arousal until after she got home at the end of the night and pleasured herself using memories of those moments to bring on her own release. That was the only time kink merged into her personal life because she was afraid of how addictive having such power over someone felt. Melissa still enjoyed regular sex but rarely sought out partners for it because she was still a bit of a prude when it came to finding casual sex partners. Riley had been the first and was still one of only two when she came to town. The other, which had been going on for the past few months, was Lily from Red Dahlia.

Lily had recently ended a relationship and, just like Riley, wasn't looking for anything serious. With all that Melissa had going on with the gallery and working at Red Dahlia, she wasn't interested in anything serious either, so it worked out for both. Like Melissa, Lily didn't mix kink with her life outside the club because she considered it more work than pleasure.

Melissa walked around Rose again until she stood in front of her. She then placed the riding crop between Rose's spread legs, tapped her sex with the head of the crop from front to back, then stroked it from back to front. She repeated this action until Rose was moaning and squirming against her restraints then stopped and strolled back to the table with the floggers and paddles. She ran her fingers over the options before her, then gazed up at the audience who watched her eagerly.

"What do you all think I should choose?" she asked, holding up a feathered tickler. "Something soft and sweet?"

"No!" they answered almost in unison.

Melissa picked up a leather paddle next and cocked her head at the audience. There were more *nos* than *yeses,* so she placed it back on the table. The next item she chose was a leather bull-hide flogger. She hadn't even fully picked it up before the audience excitedly cried *yes.*

Melissa grinned. "Lovely choice."

She stepped back over behind Rose and heard shuffling as it seemed most of the audience had followed to get a better view of the action from the back. Melissa lifted the flogger and started with slow steady strokes over each of Rose's butt cheeks. She steadily picked up the rhythm and intensity of each slap until the marks from the tails blotted out the hearts left from the riding crop and Rose was bucking in the restraints shouting, "Yes, Mistress…Harder, Mistress…More, Mistress!" Melissa also heard gasps and moans of pleasure from the audience surrounding the platform. Just as Rose cried out with her orgasm, various other feminine cries were heard as well.

Melissa lowered the flogger and gently stroked Rose's red-marked behind with her leather gloves. "Are you awake now, my beauty?"

"Yes, Mistress," Rose said, sounding very satisfied.

The volume of the background music was raised, and Melissa nodded to Hyacinth and Brutus who stood nearby. They stepped up onto the platform to remove Rose's restraints. Once she was free, Melissa took her hand, and they stepped off the platform together to walk through the crowd. Rose proudly showed off her marks and Melissa received praise and admiration for her handiwork. As they mingled with the guests, several times Melissa caught sight of a tall, elegant figure wearing a black tuxedo, black shirt, and a black domino mask that covered the entire top part of their face, but their smile was broad and sexy as they gazed at her. Because of the distance between them and their slicked back, parted on the side, fade haircut, Melissa couldn't tell if they were a man or a woman. Just as she decided to approach them out of curiosity, someone asked her a question. She turned to respond and by the time she looked back in the direction of her mysterious admirer, they were gone.

After the party as Melissa and her fellow hosts were preparing to leave for the night, she found herself wondering about the person in black watching her most of the night. She had searched for them shortly after she missed an opportunity to speak with them, but they must have left because she didn't find them anywhere throughout the party. A few days later as Melissa checked her appointments calendar, there was a note to see Afrodite about a new client, which wasn't out of the ordinary. The hosts were briefed prior to any new client appointments on the profile they filled out and their requested service. She stopped by Afrodite's office as soon as she arrived at the club. The door was open, but she knocked anyway.

"Good evening, Mother Afrodite," Melissa said respectfully as was the required greeting by all the hosts, no matter what their position or seniority was.

Afrodite looked up with a smile. "Good evening, Mistress Heart. You may sit."

Melissa sat in a guest chair across from Afrodite.

"I'm sure you already know that the fundraiser was a huge success. Mistress Vivienne was thrilled with the money raised."

"Yes, I'm so glad it went well. I know how important that art program is to her."

"The fundraiser wasn't the only success from that night. We had several prospective members attending and they all joined the club. One was particularly interested in Mistress Heart and already booked an appointment with you for this evening." Afrodite grinned.

"Was that the one I saw for my last appointment of the night?"

Afrodite nodded then placed a client profile form on the desk in front of Melissa. "This is a voyeur fantasy. The client prefers to remain anonymous, so they'll be wearing a mask, which I guess makes you the perfect pair." Afrodite smiled in amusement. "Pronouns are they/them and they simply go by the pseudonym Black."

Melissa quirked a brow. "Just Black, as in hello, Black, nice to meet you?"

Afrodite chuckled. "Yep, that's it.

Melissa shrugged. "Okay. I'm assuming this first session will just be a consultation to discuss details since they didn't give much on the form."

"Yes, they preferred discussing their requests with you only. Of course, they've been made aware of the rules, and you know that you don't have to do anything you aren't comfortable with."

"I know."

"Good. That's all I have. You may leave."

"Thank you, Mother Afrodite." Melissa stood to leave.

"Oh, one other thing."

Melissa turned back toward her. "Yes?"

Afrodite gave her a broad smile. "I'm so happy you found a place with us and truly proud of the dynamic host you've become. I feel like a mother bird watching her baby spread her wings and soar."

Melissa felt her face flush. "Thank you. I'm just trying to follow in the footsteps of Red Dahlia's Mighty Afrodite."

"Flattery will get you everywhere. Now go." Afrodite winked and shooed Melissa away.

Chapter Fourteen

Zoe found herself thinking about Danice a lot since their impromptu dinner last week. Even now, as she sat waiting for Golden at the airport, she was beating herself up for not getting Danice's number. She was so caught up in her thoughts that she jumped at the sound of tapping on her passenger window. She looked over to find Golden grinning and waving. Zoe pressed the button to open the trunk, then got out of the car.

"Hey, girl!" She embraced Golden before grabbing one of her two suitcases.

"Hey, what had you all lost in thought?"

It took two lifts to get the heavy bag into the trunk. "What do you have in here?"

Golden chuckled. "That's my costume, wig, and makeup bag."

"Jeez, feels like a whole ass body." Zoe closed the trunk after Golden put her other suitcase in the trunk as well.

"Judging from your social media posts, it looks like your trip went well."

"It did. I spoke briefly with the manager at 1923 Prohibition Bar about my Harlem Noir Showcase idea, and he seemed genuinely receptive. We've got a call scheduled tomorrow to discuss it further."

"That's great! A showcase of Black burlesque dancers in Vegas? I'm there!"

Golden laughed. "Thanks. Now, back to you. What's going on?"

"Nothing. I was just thinking about all the stuff I have to do for the bridal showcase next month."

"Yeah, okay," Golden said skeptically. "I feel like we've all got so much going on that we're drifting apart. Everybody seems to have their own little secrets."

Zoe frowned. "What do you mean? You know I'm an open book and I can't imagine Mel keeping secrets, especially from you. Also, are you including yourself in that secret keeping category?"

"I guess I'm not used to seeing you distracted. You're always so laser focused. Mel, on the other hand, has canceled dinner and brunch plans with us too many times to count in the past several months and when I ask her about it, she hems and haws and blames work at the gallery. And yes, I'm including myself, but only because I agreed to do something that I'm now second-guessing."

"I'll tell you why I'm distracted if you tell me what you're second guessing."

"Okay. Well, the Twins' manager contacted me about booking me to do a burlesque performance during a show that they're doing in Paris, and I said yes."

Zoe glanced over at Golden in surprise and then back at the road. "Wow, my secret's got nothing on yours. When did this happen and why didn't you tell us?"

"It happened just before my Vegas trip. I didn't say anything because I needed to sit with the decision for a bit before I told you guys, especially since you both think that I shouldn't have broken it off with them. I wanted to make the decision based on my feelings, not what everyone thinks I should be feeling."

Zoe nodded. "I understand. I never said you shouldn't have broken it off, I said you should have given them the opportunity to earn your forgiveness. If you found that you couldn't get past what they had done, you could at least say you tried, but it just wasn't meant to be. Is that why you're having second thoughts about doing the show?"

"Kind of. I don't know if I can separate the business aspect from the emotional."

"So don't. Go to Paris, show the world how fabulous you are, and let whatever happens happen. Or not happen." Zoe shrugged.

"You make it sound so simple."

"It sounds simple because it is. If anything, you'll get some good marketing from it."

Golden laughed. "There's that laser-focus boss bitch I'm used to. Your turn."

Zoe grinned. "I feel silly after hearing about your situation."

"C'mon, spill it."

Zoe told Golden about Danice coming into the salon then running into her at the diner later that evening.

"You're feeling her," Golden said.

"She literally just got divorced that very day and has a lot of emotional baggage that she needs to shed. I'm sure she is not in the headspace to be dating. Besides, I think she could use a friend more than a girlfriend."

"Some of the best relationships start as friendships. Be her friend and let whatever happens, happen."

Zoe laughed. "So, you're just going to throw my advice back at me like that?"

"Hey, if it applies, why not?"

She had a point, Zoe thought. Just because she was attracted to Danice didn't mean she couldn't be her friend. You didn't always have to act on physical attraction. There were plenty of hookups where she had realized that she would've been better off just leaving it alone and keeping the person as a friend. Maybe, in time, being friends with Danice would override what she was currently feeling. Zoe's phone rang, but she didn't recognize the number. Thinking it could be a client, she pressed the Bluetooth button to answer it.

"Hello."

"Hi, Zoe, it's Danice."

Golden playfully punched her in the arm. Zoe mouthed "Stop."

"Hi, Danice. I was just thinking about you." She mentally slapped herself because it sounded like she was thinking about her in a romantic way. "And wondering how your new look is going over," she quickly added.

Golden smothered a snicker.

"It's nice to know you're thinking about me. It's going as well as I expected. My sister loves it, my mother accused me of trying to kill her and that I'll never be able to find another husband now, and my father just said it was an interesting look, so…" She sounded amused.

Zoe smiled. "Well, technically, no one said they hated it."

Danice laughed. "True. I know it's the last minute, but I called to see if you had plans tonight. I owe you a dinner, remember?"

"Yes, I do, but I'm in Jersey right now getting ready to spend the evening with my girls."

"Oh, my apologies. It was silly of me to assume you would just be free at a moment's notice."

"There's no need to apologize. How about Friday?"

"Friday works for me."

"Great, now that I have your number, I'll call you tomorrow to discuss logistics."

"Okay, I look forward to it. Enjoy your evening with your friends."

"Thanks. Talk to you tomorrow."

"She sounds cute and very flirty. I think she likes you," Golden teased her after Zoe disconnected the call.

"Stop. I'm not trying to be someone's rebound or emotional bandage."

"From what you told me about her marriage, it doesn't sound like there was any love left in the end. Maybe what she needs is to be shown that she's worthy of being loved and you, my friend, have a lot of love to give but you're just pouring it all into being a workaholic."

"Ha! Look who's calling the kettle black?"

"Touché," Golden said, grinning. Her phone buzzed. "Speaking of workaholic." She held up her phone so that Zoe could see that it was Melissa calling.

"I'm with Zoe and have you on speaker. You better not be calling to say you can't make it."

"Weeell…"

Golden groaned in exasperation. "C'mon, Mel. Can't Vivienne do without you for one night? What are you doing, sleeping with the woman?"

"Ew, no! She's old enough to be my grandmother. She asked me to attend a meeting about the art program she's sponsoring. I promise I'll be there on Sunday for brunch. It'll be on me for standing you guys up so much."

Golden sighed. "You better or I'll come to that damn gallery and drag you out by your locs."

"Wow, okay. Well, I've gotta go. I love you guys."

"Love you too," Zoe said.

"Yeah, yeah, whatever," Golden said before hanging up.

"That was pretty bitchy."

Golden angrily tossed her phone into her purse. "I'm allowed to be a bitch every now and then. Especially when my best friend of twenty years is lying to me and I can't figure out why."

❖

Melissa gazed guiltily down at her phone. She hated lying to her friends, especially Golden who was more like a sister than a friend, but she just wasn't ready to tell them what was going on. Vivienne had given her more responsibilities since promoting her to gallery manager and curator and was further grooming her to eventually take full reins of the gallery, but none of that were the reasons she had been canceling with her friends so often these past months. Mistress Heart's popularity was growing, so she was taking on more clients which meant longer weeknights and weekend days. Melissa was going to have to either figure out how to balance her life better or admit to her friends that the Gallery wasn't her only work. This morning she was all set to go to Golden's for dinner, but then the new client was scheduled, and her plans changed.

She placed her phone back in her bag and gazed at herself in the mirror. Today's attire was more sedate than what she'd worn for the fundraiser since she was simply meeting with her new client and not actively in a session. Lola, another of the hosts, who was also a talented makeup and hair artist, had braided and twisted Melissa's locs into several ropelike loops hanging at the back of her head. She wore her usual mask that hid most of her face, a sheer blouse, a waist cincher, fitted knee-length leather skirt with a slit up to her right hip that provided a generous glimpse of the garters holding up her silk stockings, and six-inch heeled platform pumps all in her signature color of black. She chose deep burgundy lipstick as her only makeup. The intercom buzzed and Shari's voice came over letting Mistress Heart know that her client had arrived and been escorted to Playroom Eight which was one of the two voyeur and exhibition rooms on the second floor.

Melissa walked the short distance from the dressing room to Playroom Eight and was given quite a surprise when she entered to find her admirer from the fundraiser sitting on the sofa. Black looked quite sexy wearing the same mask they had worn at the event, their hair no longer slicked back but in soft waves. They were dressed in a black button-down shirt tucked into fitted black slacks and black shoes and socks. It was as if they and Melissa had purposely matched their attire. They stood when Melissa entered, and she could tell that beneath the masculine attire was a slim, athletic, feminine body.

They offered Melissa their hand in greeting. "Mistress Heart, thank you for taking my appointment on such short notice." Their voice was low and sexy. Their broad, friendly smile reminded Melissa of someone, but she couldn't place who it was.

"You're quite welcome, Black. Please, sit." She joined them on the sofa. "What can I do to make your visits to the Red Dahlia enjoyable."

"First, I have to admit that I'm not much into submissive and dominant play. I've dabbled in some soft bondage but nothing to the level of what you so wonderfully exhibited at the fundraiser."

Melissa gazed at them curiously. "Then what brought you to us that night?"

"A friend told me about the event, and I thought it might be an interesting way to spend the evening while supporting a worthy cause."

"Is that why you disappeared halfway through the party?" Melissa gave them a mischievous smile.

They chuckled. "No. I had a flight to catch early the next morning so I couldn't stay. As a matter of fact, I just returned yesterday and immediately scheduled this appointment."

"Which brings us back to why you're here. As I'm sure you know, we do offer other services besides BDSM play. I was told you're interested in voyeuristic play."

"Yes, but I honestly have not done anything like this before."

Melissa laughed. "Black, I'm a bit confused. You're not really into kink yet you've paid a very high fee to join a club whose sole membership benefit is offering kink and fetish services to our members."

Black smiled sheepishly. "Okay, full disclosure, and I'll completely understand if you walk out right now and have my membership revoked, but I joined for the opportunity to see you again. And before you freak out, I'm not some weird stalker. You just fascinated me."

Melissa didn't know how to respond. It was one thing for a client to say they joined due to a referral from one of her clients but another just because they saw her at an event and were fascinated with her.

Melissa stood. "While I'm flattered, you're paying for services that we offer. If none of those services appeal to you, then I'd be happy to see if it's possible to get you a refund."

"Mistress Heart, I didn't say I wasn't interested in the services offered, I would just like to discuss which service would best fit my desire to spend time with you."

Melissa was torn between walking out and telling Afrodite that she didn't believe Black was a good fit for the Red Dahlia and learning what this charming and, from what she could tell even with the mask on, attractive person wanted. Their patient smile won her over. She sat back down.

"Now, Afrodite gave me a brief description of the voyeur service offered, but I would appreciate if you could provide me with more detail as it did interest me."

"Of course. We offer what is considered consensual voyeurism. It's basically when a member and host consensually agree to a voyeuristic behavior, then that service is performed as agreed. For example, if a member enjoys watching someone masturbate then the host will perform masturbation as they watch from within the room or from behind that two-way mirror." Melissa directed Black's attention to a full-length mirror that faced the king-size bed in the center of the room. "That room also gives access to a two-way mirror in the bathroom if a member enjoys watching activities from there."

Black walked over to the mirror, found the latch that opened it, and peered into the small nine-by-six room with a comfortable chair, a small wicker laundry basket, a small trash bin, wall shelves with lube, various vibrators and dildos, hand towels, and moist wipes and a view of the bedroom through the mirror door they had opened and the bathroom through another full-length two-way mirror on the adjacent wall.

"Interesting." Black closed the door and returned to sit with Melissa.

"As the voyeur, you're welcome to encourage me to do whatever pleases you, within my comfort and reason."

Black nodded in understanding. "And what would not be within reason for you?"

"I will shower, bathe, or perform any other bathroom tasks for your enjoyment with the exception of urination and scatting."

Black scowled distastefully. "I don't blame you and would never ask that of you or anyone. I can't imagine who would find that to be a turn on?"

"If you only knew," Melissa said to herself, containing a grin. "I'll perform masturbation, but I will not perform a sex act with any other host for you." Although she had provided a member's voyeur fantasy with her spanking Lily, she had never masturbated for anyone so that request would be a new one for her. "Also, I will not remove my mask."

Black nodded. "Understood."

"That about covers it. Do you have any questions?"

"Just one. Are you available at this same time on Friday? I know that's soon, but I'm traveling again next week."

Melissa stood and offered Black her hand. "I believe I am, but Shari at reception can confirm it when you make the appointment with her. It was a pleasure to meet you, Black."

Black stood and grasped her hand. "The pleasure was all mine, Mistress Heart. I look forward to our time together." Their lips turned up into a sexy grin and their eyes held such an intense look that she almost believed they could see past the mask to who she really was.

Melissa felt her body flush with desire, something that had never happened when meeting a client before. The only desire she felt during sessions was from the rush she got from being the one in control of their pleasure and had nothing to do with any attraction toward them.

"Yes, so do I. I'll escort you back downstairs."

She eased her hand from Black's warm grasp and turned to lead them from the room. They walked in silence and Melissa once again sensed a familiarity with Black. Despite the size of New York City, it wouldn't be unusual to run into people you knew or hadn't seen in years. Big city, small world was how Melissa thought of it. Black could be someone she'd seen at the gallery or lived in her building. Whoever they were, they obviously wished to remain just as anonymous as Melissa, so it didn't matter. Melissa walked with them as far as the exit back to reception.

"I will see you on Friday."

Black smiled charmingly. "Yes, Mistress." They gave her a slight bow of deference then turned and walked out the door.

Melissa raised her hands to cool her flushed cheeks, but her hands were just as warm. In fact, her whole body felt like someone had turned on a furnace inside her.

"This is going to be interesting," she said to herself.

❖

Golden stood on her doorstep waving to Zoe as she pulled out of the driveway. They had ordered Thai, turned on a movie, then they both fell asleep not even fifteen minutes into the opening scene. It was halfway over when Zoe shook Golden awake to tell her she was leaving. She turned back into the foyer, dragged herself back up to her apartment, locked up, turned everything off, and headed straight to bed. She considered, just for a second, taking a shower but was so tired that she would probably fall asleep standing up. Golden was just drifting off when her phone buzzed on the nightstand. Who would be calling her this late? Then she looked at the screen and noticed that it was only nine o'clock. She swiped to answer, then put it on speaker.

"Hello," Golden said sleepily.

"Hey, Golden, it's Trish. Did I wake you?"

"Yes and no. What's so important that it can't wait until morning?"

"Sorry, it's only six p.m. here so I thought you'd still be up. I'll make it quick. Jade and Kendra want to have a video call this Friday to discuss Paris. They asked me to schedule it based on your availability."

Golden sat up in bed. "I have a show Friday night, but I'm available until four."

"Great. Why don't we try for noon your time. Jade and Kendra should be finishing up with their trainer by then."

"That's fine."

"All set. I just sent you the invitation link. Talk to you then. Sorry again for waking you. Good night."

"Good night, Trish."

Golden placed her phone back on the nightstand but knew she wasn't falling back to sleep anytime soon. She wavered between thinking about what both her mother and Zoe said about just doing the show and seeing what happened from there and calling Trish to tell her she couldn't do it. For most of her adult life, Golden had made it a point to limit who she allowed into the close circle of her loved ones that included her mother, her brother Drew and his family, and Mel and Zoe. She knew it was to avoid the pain and hurt caused by her father's death. The fewer people she allowed in, the less heartbreak she had to endure. But somehow, Jade and Kendra had found their way in and at the first sign of possible heartbreak, Golden had run.

Now she had to try to find a way to keep them at a distance while working with them for at least a week. After that, with Jade and Kendra now living full time on the West Coast, it would be easier to maintain that distance once they returned to their regular lives. They could remain friends but for it to work she would have to put restrictions on that friendship so that it didn't straddle that fine line between friendship and romance. No sexy late-night chats, no impromptu flowers and gifts, and no talk of the possibility of becoming more than friends. When she was ready to settle down, Golden decided it would need to be with ONE special person. Not the complicated, albeit tempting, version of a relationship that Jade and Kendra offered. Satisfied with that final thought, Golden lay back down and practically willed herself to sleep only to be betrayed by her conscience with sexy dreams of Jade and Kendra.

The rest of the week, Golden's calendar was busy enough to help keep her anxiety down about the call with Jade and Kendra on Friday. She had interviews to add two more dancers to her troupe. Then she was teaching all the burlesque classes this week instead of just the two she usually taught because Lexi, who was her usual instructor, had stayed in Vegas for an extended vacation. Lastly, she had a show this Friday and the dance school's recital this weekend to plan for. By the time the reminder popped up on Golden's phone about the call, her mind was filled with checklists of what she needed to do once she finished the call.

She closed her office door and logged into the meeting link. When she dropped in, Jade and Kendra were already on screen. Golden left her camera and microphone off while she allowed herself to just admire the two women who had completely stolen her heart. Although she still wore it with an undercut, Jade had let her hair grow to shoulder-length and had dyed it a deep auburn. Kendra still wore her faded cut, but she looked like she'd put on some muscle the way her T-shirt hugged her biceps.

"Hellooo…are you there?" Kendra said.

Golden remembered that despite her camera not being on they could still see her profile pic and know that she had logged on. She quickly rummaged through her desk for a compact to check her appearance, fluffed her curls, then took a deep breath and turned her camera and mic on.

"Hey, sorry, I got interrupted shortly after I logged on. How are you guys doing?"

They were both smiling happily. "We're doing great now that you're here," Kendra said.

"More than great," Jade commented.

Golden felt a blush, but she promised herself that she would not fall for their charm. "Will Trish be joining the call?"

"Yeah, she'll be on in a minute. We're so glad you agreed to this. When Jade came up with the idea, I wasn't so sure you'd want to do it after everything that happened," Kendra said.

Golden waved dismissively. "Let's leave the past in the past. I would be crazy to turn down such a great opportunity to perform on an international stage."

"I knew you'd like the idea, especially since you told us that Montmartre was where your great-aunt lived," Jade said.

Golden's heart warmed. "You remembered that?"

"We remember everything," Kendra said.

There was something in their eyes that Golden didn't want to believe was there. If she ignored it, then maybe it would go away.

"Golden, we—" Jade began to say.

"Hey, folks, sorry I'm late, had a client emergency. Did I miss anything?" Trish said as she dropped in just in time.

"No, we were just catching up." Golden looked directly at Trish's image trying to avoid looking at Jade and Kendra.

"Great. So, let's go over travel logistics first, then we'll get into the performance."

Trish kept the meeting moving with an efficient professionalism that didn't give any room for flirting, apologies or confessions from Jade and Kendra.

"Any questions?" Trish asked.

"No," Jade and Kendra said in unison.

"Me either," Golden said.

"I guess that's it then. We'll do another call in December and one last one in January. After that the next time we all see each other will be in Paris. Thanks for taking time for the call, Golden," Trish said.

"You're welcome. I'll get a video recording of the performance I choreographed with the adjustments Jade and Kendra mentioned to you all before our next call. I have to get ready for a show tonight so I've gotta run. It was good seeing you guys again." Golden hoped she didn't sound as anxious to get off the call as she felt.

Jade and Kendra smiled. "You too," Kendra said.

"We'll talk again soon," Jade said.

"Okay, bye."

Golden gave an awkward wave and disconnected. She laid her head back over the top of her chair with a sigh of relief. If she could make it through the rest of the calls like that, then she'd be fine. She just had to avoid being on with Jade and Kendra alone, try not to look at them during the call, and ignore the feelings that welled up whenever she couldn't avoid looking at them. Easy as climbing Mt. Everest during a blizzard wearing ballerina slippers.

CHAPTER FIFTEEN

"H ot date tonight?" Kiara asked as she walked into Zoe's room. "No," Zoe said unconvincingly. "Just going out to dinner with a friend."

"Uh-huh. It's obviously not Aunts Mel and Golden because you just said *a friend* instead of their names and you're never this indecisive about what to wear when you go out with them. There are at least three discarded outfits on the bed here." Kiara picked up a dress Zoe had just tossed aside and held it up against her herself.

"That doesn't make it a date."

"Then who is this mystery woman?" Kiara set the dress back on the bed then walked over to stand beside Zoe looking in her closet.

"She's just a woman who came into the salon. We became acquainted, and now we're just going to dinner." Zoe was beginning to reconsider going now because Kiara was right, she was acting as if this dinner with Danice was a date.

"Okay." Kiara stepped forward and began grabbing things out of Zoe's closet, moved the small pile already on the bed aside, then set what she had chosen out in their place. "Here you go."

Kiara had chosen a red mock turtleneck long-sleeved sweater dress with a hem that hit just above her knees and burgundy block-heeled ankle boots.

"It's subtle and sexy without looking like you tried too hard. I would suggest gold hoop earrings and a low hanging necklace."

Zoe looked at her daughter in wonder and shook her head. "Don't you have a date or something tonight?"

"No. My friend Amber is coming over to hang out. Can I order dinner for us?"

"Yes."

"Thanks." Kiara leaned over and kissed Zoe on the cheek. "Have fun on your not-date," she said as she left the room.

Zoe chuckled. That child was a pain in her ass, but she was going to miss her when she left for college. She hung up her discarded outfits and put on the one Kiara had chosen. Turning to the left and right, she grinned as she looked in the mirror. Her daughter had chosen well. She didn't have Golden's curves, but the dress enhanced what she did have. As Kiara suggested, Zoe chose large gold hoop earrings and a gold double chain, low-hanging necklace.

"This is not a date," she reminded her reflection who was smiling a little too broadly about how good she looked.

She grabbed a jacket then headed out to meet Danice in front of the salon. It turned out that Danice's sister, who she was living with, lived just a couple of blocks from it, so they decided to meet there and go to the restaurant together. Danice was already standing out front when Zoe arrived and she looked bright and beautiful in a multicolored scarf-print wrap dress and black platform pumps with gold chain anklets, orange beaded and gold dangle earrings, and matching necklace. Even the lightweight jacket she wore was a bright orange, matching one of the colors in her dress. Zoe had a feeling that, like her haircut, Danice's colorful attire was another physical way she was trying to break free from what her ex-husband had done to her. Danice's smile when she spotted Zoe lit up her face and gave Zoe butterflies.

"This is not a date," she repeated in her head, but her body wasn't listening as it warmed to the thought of being on a date with this gorgeous, sweet woman.

"Hey, you look great," Zoe said.

"Thank you. So do you. I wish I had the figure to pull off a dress like that."

"What are you talking about? You could rock a dress like this and look damn good doing it."

Danice's smile dimmed. "Maybe back in the day, but I can't be squeezing all of this into something body hugging like that. I'd look like an overstuffed sausage."

Zoe hated that she saw herself so negatively. "Have you not seen what plus-size celebrities Amber Riley, Danielle Brooks, and Michelle Buteau, just to name a few, are wearing? And we can't forget the *Big Grrl* queen herself, Lizzo. It's not what you wear but the confidence you need to wear it."

Danice chuckled. "Well, I definitely don't have Lizzo-level confidence."

"I guess we'll have to work on that." Zoe winked then looped her arm around Danice's. "We can discuss it over dinner."

They took a short subway ride to their destination, Masalawa & Sons, an Indian cuisine restaurant in Brooklyn.

"Oh my God, it smells wonderful in here. My mouth is watering already," Zoe said.

"Wait until you actually taste the food. This is authentic, old world Indian cooking at its finest."

"I can't wait, although I'm ashamed to admit that as long as I've lived in New York I have not dipped into the melting pot for traditional Indian cuisine before."

"Really? Don't worry, I've got you. Do you have any food restrictions or allergies?"

"No."

"Good. Since you ordered for us at the diner, allow me to order tonight."

Zoe bowed her head. "I defer to your expertise."

Danice smiled happily and didn't even look at the menu when their server came to take their order. "May we have two glasses of lemon water and two moon moon sen, then we'll be sharing an order of dahi vada and sabudana vada to start. After that we'll have morog boti, daab chingri, khichuri and a side of chapati. Thank you."

Zoe looked at Danice skeptically. "That sounds like a lot of food."

Danice laughed. "It's a good amount for sharing and gives you a good taste of the cuisine without stepping too far outside of your comfort zone."

"Do you come here often?"

"I've been here at least once a week since they opened last month, but I used to be a regular at their first location on the Lower East Side. Malik travels a lot for work, and I would take advantage of the time alone to do little things that I enjoyed. Activities that if anyone we knew happened to see me wouldn't cause him to get jealous if it got back to him. Treating myself to dinner at their original location, spending time at the Brooklyn Botanical Gardens, the Audubon Center at Prospect Park, and going roller skating at the Brooklyn Bridge skate park, if the weather permitted."

"Roller skating? I'm impressed. I haven't been on a pair of skates since I was in middle school."

"I guess I'll have to get you back in the rink while you're working on my confidence."

Zoe laughed. "We'll see. I'll ride any roller coaster you put in front of me, zip line through a South American rain forest, and even parachute out of a plane, but zooming out of control on a pair of roller skates could be a deal-breaker."

Danice laughed. "Are you serious? What if I offer to hold your hand the whole time?"

Zoe looked thoughtful. "Hm, that could possibly tempt me. Throw in not cursing me out when I pull you down with me as I fall and it's a deal."

Danice smiled. "You got it."

The cocktails Danice ordered arrived. Zoe took a sip and looked down at her glass in surprise. "This is REALLY good. It's like a spiked lemonade but better."

"Yes, this is my favorite. It has vodka, lemon verbena, aloe vera, guava, and cucumber. Next time you'll have to try Tagore's Lyric. It's made with smoked bhuk jolokia, a type of ghost chili pepper."

Zoe liked the idea of a next time. "Sounds like a liquid version of that ghost pepper chip challenge folks are doing."

"Not quite, but it does have a nice kick and goes well with the dahi vada that I ordered because the yogurt helps to temper the heat if you can't handle it."

"Oh, I can handle it, believe me," Zoe said suggestively.

Danice rested her chin on her hand, giving Zoe a sexy grin. "Are you sure? It can get intense if you try to consume it too fast, but if you take your time to savor and enjoy it, it can be a very pleasant experience."

Zoe had a feeling their not-date was quickly turning into a date-date and she didn't mind. Danice was giving her a peek of what she was like before Malik dimmed her light, and Zoe was enjoying it. Their moment was interrupted by their server delivering their first course. Zoe assumed the dish covered in white cream was the yogurt dish Danice had mentioned.

"This is the dahi vada which is lentil dumplings in a seasoned yogurt sauce," Danice explained as she scooped one of the dumplings onto a plate. Next to that she placed what looked like a fritter. "This is sabudana vada, basically a fried fritter made with tapioca, peanuts, and spiced potatoes. There's a chili yogurt dip, but I'll let you decide if you'd like to try it." She placed the plate in front of Zoe then made one for herself.

Zoe placed a scoop of the yogurt dip on her plate. She was not afraid of trying new foods and enjoyed spice as long as it wasn't burning her taste buds from her tongue. Neither vadas was spicy until she dipped the fritter into the yogurt dip, but it wasn't an overpowering heat because of the yogurt.

"Well?" Danice said expectantly.

Zoe licked her fingers and reached for another fritter. "It's so good. Just enough heat, wonderful spices, and flavors. I'm officially a fan of Indian food."

Danice smiled proudly as if she had been the one to prepare it. "I'm so glad you like it."

"What's there not to like? Sauce on the dumplings is a littler richer than I'm used to, but it's so good." As if to prove her point, Zoe scooped another dumpling onto her plate as well.

Danice laughed. "Remember, this is just the starters. Save room for the main course."

"Good idea." She placed the dumpling back in the dish but finished the fritter. "I'll just have to take the rest home for lunch tomorrow."

Their server returned with the main course. The dishes were served in clay pots and platters. Zoe guessed they must have come straight out of the oven from the heat rising off and the still bubbling and scorched sauce around the edge of the dish. The last item they set on the table was a raw coconut shell with huge prawns, heads still attached, peeking above the rim. It was an aromatic and mouthwatering display.

"This isn't a dinner, it's a feast. I don't know where to begin."

"Allow me." Danice picked up one of the two fresh plates that the server brought, placed a scoop of rice, a scoop of the shrimp dish over the rice, then some of a chicken and rice dish and a slice of flatbread. She placed the plate before Zoe. "So, the shrimp is daab chingri, a curry dish, the rice is khichuri, a vegetable and rice mixture, and the chicken with basmati rice is morog boti. My other recommendation, if you like fried fish, is the biye barir fish fry. Once you have that you'll never want fish fried any other way."

Zoe loved how Danice's face lit up when she spoke about the food of her culture. "Do you cook in the traditional way?"

"I try. My mother gave me copies of recipes handed down in our family for generations as a wedding gift. In the beginning, I was too busy with work to take the time to prepare such complicated dishes. Then I had my first miscarriage, which Malik blamed on me working too much. I was working as a full-time special education teacher and volunteering with an organization for individuals with autism. It was basically two full-time jobs. I guess I was so focused on all of that I didn't take care of myself like I probably should have with missing doctor appointments, missing meals, and then when I did eat it wasn't very healthy." Danice picked up a prawn and distractedly peeled the shell off.

"I gained more weight from eating like crap than baby weight. After I lost the baby, I left my job, stopped volunteering, and became a substitute teacher to give me more flexibility and time to take care of myself when we decided to try for another baby. Since I had more time, I started cooking more rather than ordering takeout or fixing quick-fix meals. I wasn't working so much, I was taking better care of our home, and making traditional meals, Malik was thrilled. When Malik was happy, he wasn't criticizing me. So, cooking became my safe space. Unfortunately, so did eating." Danice gazed briefly down at her body and back at Zoe with a sad smile.

Zoe shook her head. "Looks like we're going to have to start working on that confidence sooner rather than later. Until then, I'd like to enjoy this wonderfully prepared meal with the beautiful woman sitting across from me."

Danice's smile turned shy. "Yes, we should eat before it gets cold."

Zoe's heart was softening to Danice with each story she told about her asshole ex. Golden was right, Danice needed to be shown that she was worthy of love. Zoe was still wavering between romantic involvement and just being a supportive friend, but either way, she was drawn to being in Danice's life. They spent the rest of the main course chatting about everyday life. Zoe was glad to hear that Danice was looking to return to work full-time at the organization she had originally been volunteering for and had begun therapy to help her move past her marriage into a new life on her own terms.

"I also need to find a place to live so that I can get off my sister's sofa. I suggested getting an apartment together, but she likes her place and doesn't want to move," Danice was saying as their server cleared their table.

"Are you looking to stay in Brooklyn?"

"Yes, I'd like to. It's where most of my family is, but I don't know if I'll be able to afford to live alone and I feel like, unless they're family, I'm too old to be trying to find roommates."

A little voice of warning in the back of Zoe's mind told her not to say what she was about to, but sympathy for Danice's situation overrode it. "If you're interested, I have a small studio apartment on the third floor of my house. I haven't had to rent it out since I don't need the money so my daughter has been pretty much using it as a hangout with her friends. You're welcome to take look at it and if you're interested, we can work out a number that will best suit your situation."

Danice's eyes went wide as she shook her head. "I can't possibly impose on your family, and you barely know me."

Zoe chuckled. "I know you better than I would a stranger I would be renting it out to. You need a place to live, I have a place for you, it works out. Besides, you haven't seen it yet, you may hate it."

"I can't imagine that. Okay, I'll look at it then we can go from there. If you keep doing things for me, I'm going to be owing you more dinners."

Zoe quirked a brow teasingly. "If you take the apartment I'll just have to come up and have one of your traditional family meals every now and then."

Danice gave her a soft smile. "You won't even need an invitation."

Danice went from shy to flirtatious without missing a beat. Zoe didn't know if it was purposely or that she was so used to being put down by her ex that compliments made her self-conscious while a flirty part of her that still held on from before her marriage made an occasional appearance to respond to Zoe's flirting. Zoe realized that although Danice had revealed that she was bisexual, Zoe hadn't mentioned her sexuality. She assumed that since she flirted back, Danice had figured out that she was at least interested in women. Until she could figure out what she wanted and what it meant to what was happening between her and Danice, she wouldn't bring it up unless Danice did.

They finished their dinner with Indian filter coffee and the only dessert on the menu, bhapa doi. Danice described it as a cheesecake-like dessert made with steamed yogurt, which didn't sound appetizing to Zoe but, to her relief, tasted delicious.

"Thank you. That was a wonderful dinner," Zoe said as they left the restaurant.

"You're welcome. I'm so glad you enjoyed it."

"I did, and I'll enjoy these leftovers tomorrow as well." Zoe held up the bag filled with takeout containers of what they hadn't finished as well as an order of the biye barir fish fry.

"I hope you plan on sharing with your daughter."

Zoe snorted. "It'll be gone before she even knew it was there."

Danice laughed. "I guess I'll just have to bring her a sampling of her own. When I come by to look at the apartment."

"It's still early, you could always look at it now. Unless you have other plans."

Danice sighed. "Yes, and I don't know if I can change them. I've got a date to binge-watch the first season of *Harlem* with a big bowl of homemade kettle corn."

Zoe laughed. "Well, I'm sure we can get you home in time for your hot date."

"I don't know. Even after our dinner that warm bowl of kettle corn is whispering sweet nothings in my ear." Danice smiled.

"Look at that, she's beautiful and funny." Zoe playfully bumped Danice with her shoulder as they walked.

They took the subway back to the salon since there wasn't a station closer to Zoe's house, then walked the three blocks it took to get there. Zoe had grown up in the house, moved into the attic apartment after she had Kiara until she finished school and got her own place. Then when her mother decided to downsize to an apartment at the same adult community Zoe's grandmother had moved to, she signed the house over to Zoe. The attic apartment hadn't been rented since Zoe and Kiara moved in. When they arrived at the house, Zoe noticed the lights in the studio were off which meant Kiara either went out for the night or was in her room. She wouldn't be too happy about losing her little hangout spot, but Zoe knew she would understand.

She led Danice straight up to the third floor and into the apartment. She turned the lights on and found Kiara hadn't left too much of a mess. There was a blanket tossed haphazardly over the sofa and a couple of fashion magazines left open on the table. Other than that, it was neat and clean. The apartment was a true studio with everything in one space. Upon entering was the living area with a sofa, two side chairs, a fireplace, and a television above it. Past the living area was the bathroom with a sink, toilet, and shower, the kitchenette with all the necessary appliances, and an island with three stools that doubled as the dining area. At the back of the apartment was the sleeping area with enough room for a queen-size bed, nightstand, and small desk.

"It's cute," Danice said.

"And comes fully furnished. There are even dishes and cooking utensils."

"It's perfect. How much rent are you asking?"

Zoe gave her a number that was much lower than the going rent in the area and the look on Danice's face told her that she knew it.

"I may not have gotten the condo since it was Malik's before we got married but I did get a bit of a settlement to tide me over for some time. I can afford a little more that."

"Well, that's what I'm asking. Would you like it?"

Danice gazed around the apartment, her brows furrowed in contemplation. "I can't believe this is happening, but yes, I'll take it. As long as it's not inconveniencing you and your daughter."

"Not at all. I can have a rental agreement drawn up by tomorrow and have the place clean and ready for you to move in by the end of next week. Can you do a deposit and first month's rent by then?"

Danice turned back to Zoe grinning happily. "Yes. This is crazy. Just last week I was walking past your salon feeling like my life was a complete mess, then I saw these women walk out looking confident and beautiful in their natural glow and I wanted some of that confidence." She reached out and took Zoe's hand, tears pooling in her bright eyes. "You walked in and literally changed my life with a pair of clippers and now this. I don't think I'll ever be able to repay you."

Her heart aching with emotion, Zoe reached up to wipe away a tear that escaped with the pad of her thumb then rested her palm against Danice's rounded cheek. "You don't have to repay me. If we can't, as Women of Color, lift each other up when we need it, who will? Just do whatever you need to find your peace and happiness."

It took Zoe a moment to realize that Danice's face was moving tentatively toward hers. Despite the voice in her head telling her it wasn't a good idea, Zoe closed the distance, pressing her lips to Danice's. Their kiss began tentatively. Danice's lips were full and soft. Zoe eased her tongue past them and tasted the cool, sweet flavor of the mints Danice had eaten after dinner. Danice's tongue eagerly chased Zoe's as she stepped close enough for their bodies to graze. Zoe wrapped her arms around Danice's waist to pull her closer. Danice wrapped her arms around Zoe's neck as their passion intensified. The voice of reason in Zoe's head was drowned out by the desire coursing through her body. She lowered her hands to cup Danice's voluptuous behind and received a whimper of pleasure in response. That whimper was like an alarm, waking up Zoe's common sense. She slowly ended the kiss and put some distance between them.

Zoe ran her hand through her locs. "I shouldn't have done that. I'm so sorry."

Danice was still breathing a little heavily looking at Zoe with a dreamy smile. "I'm not." She took a step toward Zoe who raised her hand to stop her and took a step back, bumping into the arm of the sofa.

"You're fresh from a divorce and still feeling vulnerable. I'm not the type of person to take advantage of that despite how attracted I am to you."

Zoe wondered if Danice knew what a tempting picture she made with her kiss-swollen lips, generous breasts rising and falling with her heavy breathing, and a look in her eyes that said she would say yes to anything Zoe wanted to do to her.

She closed the distance between them, grasped Zoe's hands, and raised them toward her lips, placing a kiss on the knuckles of one hand. "Do you know how long it's been since anyone, including my husband, touched me in a sexual way?" She kissed the knuckles of Zoe's other hand. "Three years." Danice placed Zoe's hands back on her hips. "So, if I have to beg you to touch me. To make me feel something other than fat and unworthy, I will."

Zoe believed her. There was a determined gleam in her eyes. She raised her hands and gently grasped Danice's face. "You don't have to beg for anything. Just ask and I'll do whatever you need to prove that you are beautiful and very worthy of being touched."

Danice smiled appreciatively. "Zoe, please touch me."

Zoe placed a soft kiss on Danice's lips then took her hand to lead her over to the bed. Once there, she reached up to remove Danice's jacket, lay it on a trunk at the end of the bed, then continued undressing her. Danice watched her with a mix of wonder and arousal as she removed each item of clothing. Zoe placed a soft kiss atop each full breast as she reached behind to undo the strap of her bra. Danice's breaths were coming out in steady pants by the time Zoe knelt before her and reached for the waistband of her panties to slide them down her legs. Danice used the bedpost to balance herself as she stepped out of them. Zoe set them aside with the rest of her clothes as she continued to kneel before Danice, admiring her. Danice's self-consciousness kicked in and she attempted to cover herself with her arms. Zoe reached up to stop her.

"You are a powerful, beautiful, sexy woman that Ruben himself would be honored to paint. You don't ever have to hide yourself from me."

As she stood, Zoe placed soft kisses on Danice's belly, each breast, her neck, and ending at her lips for a kiss that left them both breathing heavily. She stepped away from Danice to undress. Danice lay down on the bed watching her. The intensity in her gaze made the walls of Zoe's sex clench excitedly. She was once again seeing a glimpse of the woman that she was before her marriage. There was a passionate woman locked away under all that insecurity and Zoe was determined to set her free. She joined Danice on the bed, pulled her into her arms and returned to kissing her lush lips.

Feeling Danice's warmth and softness against her own, hearing her whimper and moan just from kissing, sent Zoe into a red haze of desire, but knowing Danice hadn't been touched like this for so long made Zoe want to take her time to show her how sexy and desirable she was. She rolled so that Danice was beneath her then shifted to kneel between her legs and simply gazed down to admire her. Danice met her gaze, her expressive eyes filled with anticipation, her lips were moist and slightly parted, and her chest rose and fell with her excited pants. Zoe lowered her gaze to Danice's full and generous breasts with her dark mahogany areolas looking like tempting treats against her warm complexion. Danice thought she was fat, Zoe disagreed. She thought Danice's ample full figure was sexy. She mentioned that she hiked and roller-skated which showed in her muscle tone, her hourglass figure, and shapely legs.

Zoe gazed back at Danice with a smile. "You are so sexy." She leaned down to mute any response Danice would have with a kiss that she hoped would drown out any negative thoughts Danice had about herself, at least for a little while.

From there, Zoe kissed and nipped her way down to Danice's breast, taking one hardened nipple into her mouth while massaging the other. Danice moaned loudly and arched her back in response. She also began thrusting her hips against Zoe's thigh. She could feel Danice's whole body heating up as if she had a fever. Zoe released the breast she was massaging and slid her hand down between Danice's legs. She was so wet Zoe's fingers were coated with moisture before she even slid one inside. When she did, Danice's inner walls practically sucked Zoe's finger in deeper as she began grounding her sex against Zoe's hand. Zoe slid another finger in and continued sucking Danice's nipple as she slowly slid her fingers in and out of Danice's now dripping sex. Danice tangled her fingers in Zoe's locs, her pants growing more breathless, and her walls contracting with each thrust of Zoe's fingers.

Danice sucked in a quick breath, then released a loud moan before shouting, "OH GOD...ZZZOOOEE..." Then her body tensed just before a rush of fluid flowed over Zoe's fingers and pooled in the palm of her hand as Danice's body convulsed with her orgasm.

After a moment, Danice's body went slack, and Zoe gazed up to find her with her eyes closed trying to steady her breath and a dreamy smile on her face. Zoe felt a bit of pride at having been the cause of that smile. She gently slid her fingers from between Danice's legs then slid up next to her.

"I'll be right back."

Zoe gave Danice a quick peck on the lips then left the bed and went to the bathroom. She grabbed a washcloth, wet it with warm water then headed back out to Danice who hadn't moved an inch since Zoe left her. She sat on the side of the bed and tenderly cleaned away the moisture on the inside of Danice's thighs then lifted the cloth to clean her sex.

Danice whimpered and reached down to place her hand over Zoe's. "I'm supersensitive once I come," she said in a breathy voice."

"Really?"

With a mischievous grin, Zoe set the washcloth aside then moved back between Danice's thighs, lowering her whole body for better access. Danice gazed down at her as if she wasn't sure if she should stop her or not. Zoe dipped her head and ran the tip of her tongue up and down along the folds of her sex. Danice must have given up the thought of fighting it because Zoe felt her relax then her body shudder with each stroke of her tongue. She nudged Danice's legs wider and up, then grabbed her hips as she took Danice's erect clit into her mouth, alternating between suckling and stroking it with her tongue. Danice's whimpers quickly turned to passionate moans as her hips began bucking, which was why Zoe held them to keep her in place. Then she dipped her tongue into Danice, was rewarded with another flow from her orgasm and stayed there until she had personally licked away every drop.

Zoe moved up, lying on her side next to Danice, watching her trying to steady her breath once again. She was even more beautiful in the afterglow of her pleasure. She looked more relaxed than Zoe had seen her in the short time they'd spent together, and her skin glowed with a light sheen of perspiration. Zoe reached over and smoothed a hand over Danice's head where soft sprouts of new growth prickled her palm.

Danice smiled. "I never knew you could get turned on by someone touching your head until you massaged that oil into it after you cut my hair. I guess it had been so long since I'd been touched so intimately that as innocent as that was, I would've probably come in that chair if you hadn't stopped when you did."

Zoe chuckled. "That would've made for quite an interesting appointment. The scalp is considered an erogenous zone because it's covered with nerve endings. That's why scalp massages feel so good."

"Well, that was my first ever scalp massage." Danice sighed contentedly as Zoe continued running her hand lightly across her head. "You might want to stop though unless you want me to be a puddle of goo that won't be able to walk out of here after."

Zoe did as she asked but moved her fingers to explore the space between her breasts. "That sounds very tempting. Besides, this is your place now, so you don't have to leave."

"Are you sure, that after this, that would be a good idea?" Danice asked.

Zoe shrugged. "I don't see why not. You need a place to live, I've already offered it to you. I'm not going to kick you back to your sister's sofa because of this. Even if you decide that you don't want it to happen again, you have a place to live with no repercussions."

Danice turned to her side and ran her fingers across Zoe's cheek gazing at her in bewilderment. "How did I get so lucky to find someone as kind as you?"

Zoe placed a kiss on her nose. "I guess someone thought you could use some good in your life."

Danice laughed. "I guess so and I think I know just how to thank you."

By the time Danice left an hour later, Zoe felt extremely appreciated.

CHAPTER SIXTEEN

M elissa paced nervously.

"Okay, if you don't sit down and relax, I'm going to tie you to a chair," Rose said with an annoyed gaze directed at Melissa from her dressing table mirror.

"I haven't seen you this nervous about an appointment since your first week here. Is this some celebrity or someone you know?" Lily asked.

"No. It's a new member who joined the night of the fundraiser. They're intent on keeping their anonymity by wearing a mask and being addressed simply as Black for our appointments. They chose a voyeur fantasy which you know I haven't done many of."

Rose grinned. "Both of you in masks trying to keep your secret identities. Sounds very Batman and Catwoman to me."

Hyacinth turned to her, their head cocked to the side and eyes narrowed as if they were listening intently to someone speaking.

Melissa shook her head. "I don't want to know."

Hyacinth quirked a brow knowingly. "Are you sure? It's pretty good."

"If she doesn't want to know, tell us," Rose said excitedly.

Lily playfully punched Rose's shoulder. "No. Anything Hyacinth sees for Heart is for her to decide to hear."

Rose pouted prettily. "You're no fun." She turned back to finish her makeup.

Melissa had no idea why she was so nervous. There was something about Black that gave her feelings that she hadn't felt in a long time. Anticipation. She didn't know if it was the familiarity of their gaze when they looked at her, the casual confidence about them, or the fact that they had been so intrigued by her at the fundraiser that they were willing to drop a thousand dollars a month for membership at a club they would normally not have any interest in to spend time with her. They didn't even know her other than what she presented as Mistress Heart. That last thought made her stop. Black was interested in Mistress Heart, not her so she was being anxious over nothing. This was her job, not a date. She didn't need to do anything but what they were paying for her to do. Be Mistress Heart.

Melissa took a deep calming breath and walked over to a mirror to check her appearance one last time. Black had emailed a request for her to dress in a similar fashion to what she had worn to meet them. She wore the same skirt with a lace sheer blouse, a satin bustier bra, garters with stockings, and six-inch stiletto heel pumps.

"Mistress Heart, your client has arrived," Shari said pleasantly over the intercom.

Melissa turned to find Hyacinth walking toward her. "Hyacinth, I love you but—"

She was cut off by Hyacinth pulling her into a hug. "I just want you to know that I'm happy for you." They placed an affectionate kiss on Melissa's forehead then turned back the way they came.

Melissa watched in bewilderment. "Oookay." She would like to believe that after all this time that she had gotten used to Hyacinth's quirkiness, but she'd only be lying to herself.

Melissa left the dressing room to make her way downstairs to collect Black. When she arrived, they stood gazing at one of the landscape paintings on the wall. It was of the London Eye, but it always reminded Melissa of the Ferris wheel at Coney Island. Melissa stood in the doorway to take a moment to admire Black's expensive black tailored suit, the white shirt unbuttoned down to just between their breasts, the way the slim fitting slacks complemented their long muscular legs. She gazed back up toward their face, secretly wishing she could see it.

"Good evening, Black," Melissa said, forcing her attention back to the task at hand.

They turned and gave her a soft smile. "Good evening, Mistress Heart."

She got tingles from the intimate way they said her name. "Shall we begin the evening?"

Black walked smoothly toward her. Even their walk was full of casual confidence. "Yes. Please, lead the way." They held the door, gazing down at her tenderly.

Melissa was momentarily lost in that look before she shook it off and turned away. They walked along the hall toward the stairs to the second level.

"I'm sure Shari asked already, but would you like a refreshment before we get started?"

"No, thank you."

They continued the rest of the way in silence. As Black walked closely beside her, Melissa could feel their eyes on her every now and then. She reached for the doorknob to their playroom when the warmth of Black's hand gently covered hers.

"Allow me."

Melissa slid her hand from the doorknob trying to keep herself from rubbing where Black's smooth fingers had touched hers. They opened the door and Melissa entered, stepping aside to allow them to enter as well.

"I hadn't really looked at this room the last time we were here. It's nice." Black strolled around looking things over.

The room resembled a plush, luxurious bedroom with cream and gold furniture and accents. A king-size bed with a quilted headboard was the focal point of the room. Above the bed hung a steel suspension bar while hidden underneath the mattress were bed restraints. Other furnishings included a large wingback chair, a plush sofa, and a curvy chaise lounge. While the chair and sofa were regular furniture, the chaise doubled as a bondage lounge with hidden restraints stored underneath. Melissa always felt like this room represented her. It looked chic and normal on the surface, but there was more than met the eye if you looked beneath the pretty cover.

"Yes, it's different from our other playrooms in that other than the suspension bar hanging from the ceiling, the kink paraphernalia isn't obvious."

Melissa walked around to show them the hidden restraints on the chaise and the bed, the padded bench at the end of the bed that doubled as a storage box filled with bondage gear, spanking tools, and blindfolds. Then the walk-in closet where cuffs, collars, harnesses, ropes, hoods, and muzzles were set up like a store display along with a whole shelf of cleaning and sterilizing supplies.

"Of course, you already know about the peekaboo closet." Melissa pointed to the floor to ceiling mirror that was the entrance to the voyeur room.

Even with half their face covered with their mask, Melissa could tell that Black was a little overwhelmed with these new discoveries.

They gazed from the closet to Melissa curiously. "You use all of this?"

"Not all of it. Since I'm a domme I may use the restraints and spanking toys on my clients who are predominantly submissives. I have used this room for couples where one enjoys watching the other be restrained and spanked or single clients who enjoy seeing others in that situation as well."

Black walked over to the bench that Melissa had left open and picked up a flogger. "Is it presumptuous of me to assume that as a domme you aren't usually on the other end of one of these?"

"You are correct. My services are primarily for submissives looking to be dominated. The voyeur services I've provided have been within that same service." Melissa held her hand out for the flogger, Black handed it to her, and she turned to place it back in the bench. "This is my first voyeur session solo," she hesitantly added. She didn't know why she felt the need to tell them that.

"Well, I guess this will be a new experience for both of us." There was a gentleness in Black's tone that made Melissa warm.

Girl, get back into character, she silently reprimanded herself. "So, Black," she turned back to them, back in Mistress Heart mode. "What are we doing this evening? I'm sure you don't want to waste your session chatting."

Black grinned. "What if I did?"

"Then I would say you were in the wrong place. If that's all you're looking for I would suggest a dating app or an escort service."

Black laughed out loud. "They should be calling you Mistress Heartbreaker."

Melissa smiled, enjoying the way their deep husky laugh stroked over her. "I'll have to consider a name change."

"May we sit?" Black asked, indicating the sofa nearby.

"Of course."

Black folded their long frame on the sofa, crossed an ankle over their knee, and placed an arm along the back of the sofa, their long fingers just inches from touching Melissa's shoulder when she sat. The images those long fingers suggested almost made her sigh aloud. She tore her gaze from their fingers back to their face and was greeted by a knowing smile that she ignored.

"What can I do for you?"

"First, thank you for dressing as I requested. You look stunning."

Melissa was glad she wore a mask as she felt her face flush hotly from the compliment. "I'm glad it's to your liking."

Black's gaze went to the expanse of thigh showing from Melissa's crossed legs through the hip-high slit of her skirt, they looked back up at her with a sexy smirk.

"I thought long and hard about what I wanted since we last spoke and I think I've figured it out. I don't know if it's too tame for what you normally do, but if I understand the rules correctly from the research I did, voyeur fantasies have some flexibility to incorporate role play."

"Yes."

"So, here's what I'm thinking." Black reached into the inside pocket of their jacket and pulled out a small stack of index cards. "I'd like you to be the character in a series of scenes I'll be narrating, like a director. You mentioned that there's a way for me to tell you what I like from inside the voyeur room, correct?"

"Yes. There's a microphone in the room connected to a speaker out here and in the bathroom." Melissa gazed curiously at the cards in Black's hand. She was genuinely intrigued.

"Great!"

Black smiled eagerly as they stood, gazing around the room again. They turned back to Melissa. "Mistress Heart, for our first scene, I would like you to re-enter the room as if you're just getting home from work. You've had a stressful day and all that you can think about is getting out of your clothes and relaxing with a hot shower and curling up in bed. We'll start there and I'll direct you with more details as we go along. Is that acceptable to you?"

Melissa smiled with a shrug. "This is your fantasy. Whatever you'd like is fine with me."

"Within means," they said with a wink.

Melissa nodded. "Exactly."

Melissa walked toward the door. She'd done some role-play, mostly teacher-student, nurse-patient, boss-secretary scenarios, but nothing like this.

"Wait for about a minute before walking back in," Black directed her in a strong tone that told Melissa they were used to being in charge.

She nodded in response, then walked out and started counting to sixty. While she was doing that a thought occurred to her that gave her pause. She was the submissive in this session, Black was in control. When Melissa began her training as a host for Red Dahlia, Afrodite asked what her preferred role was, submissive or dominatrix. Melissa knew right away being a domme was what she wanted, especially since she'd spent most of her life as a submissive person allowing others to have more control over her than they should. But she did decide to try some training in submissive work and didn't like the negative emotional space it put her in. Afrodite agreed and promised to only provide her work as a domme. Since Black hadn't provided many details there was no way for Afrodite to know exactly what Black's voyeur fantasy would include which was why she told Melissa that she didn't need to do anything she wasn't comfortable with.

Melissa reached the one-minute mark and stared at the door. Black didn't seem to be someone who would want to degrade or control her, but Melissa had gotten so used to being the one in control that even giving over this small bit made her nervous.

"C'mon, shake it off. You still have control. You can walk right back out of that room if something doesn't feel right," she said to herself, then took a breath to get back into Mistress Heart mindset.

Melissa walked into the room and Black was nowhere in sight. It was a bit off-putting to walk into an empty room. She usually worked in this room with a couple. They all entered together, and the voyeur would take their place behind the two-way mirror while she and the sub would get set up to do their thing.

"Mistress," Black's voice came over the speaker, startling Melissa who hadn't realized she was still standing at the door gripping the handle tightly. "Just breathe. I wouldn't ask you to do anything you're uncomfortable with and you can say no to any request. I want this to be enjoyable for both of us."

Melissa gazed toward the two-way mirror.

"Should I come out?" Black asked.

Their tone was so gentle and comforting. She loosened her death grip on the door handle and closed the door. "No. Thank you. I'm fine. You may continue."

"After a long and stressful day at work, all Mistress Heart wants to do is wash away the day and relax. She's barely through the door when she starts shedding her clothing."

Black went silent again, which Melissa took as her cue to do as they directed. She gave a tired sigh then leaned against the door for support as she took off each shoe, casually tossing them aside. As she walked toward the bed, Melissa slowly unbuttoned her blouse then stationed herself between the bed and mirror as she began to undress. She imagined herself doing a sexy striptease performance like Golden, except without the dancing. She slowly took the blouse off her shoulders then slid each arm out individually before letting it fall to the floor. Her skirt was next. Melissa turned her back to the mirror, reached around, and slowly slid the zipper down her skirt. She shimmied her hips, then bent over to give a generous view of her backside as she slid the skirt down her legs and stepped out of it to walk over to the bench at the end of the bed. She sat down and took her time unhooking her garters and sliding her stockings off.

With Black not speaking but knowing they were watching, Melissa found herself getting caught up and, dare she say it, turned on putting on a show for them. Was this what Golden felt during her performance? She would have to ask her. She continued her performance with slow, graceful movements until she was left with nothing but her mask on, something she'd never done with a client, but she pushed that thought aside to continue to enjoy the moment. Melissa stood, turned toward the bench, opened it, and pulled out a silk scarf that was usually used for restraining or blindfolding someone, then walked directly up to the mirror. Gazing at her reflection, she could swear she felt Black's eyes watching her and her nerves began getting the best of her so, after gathering her locs into a twist atop her head and tying them with the scarf, Melissa did something she did on almost a daily basis that her therapist had encouraged her to do to build her self-confidence.

She took a moment to study herself naked in the mirror while trying to ignore the fact that Black was on the other side. They were wanting to "direct" a scene as if Melissa had come home from work and just wanted to shower and relax, well, this was part of what she did before taking a shower. She ran her hands from her head, down her face, over her breasts, along her waist, over hips, down her thighs and back up to glide over her behind, around to her belly, then sliding slowly down over her groin area. Cupping her sex, Melissa closed her eyes and silently repeated to herself, "I am power, I am beauty, I am love." Then she opened her eyes and gave herself, and Black, a sexy smile. As she walked to the bathroom, she thought to herself that she would have to remember to bring her clips to pin her hair up next time like she did when she took a shower at home. The thought of doing this again gave her a thrill of excitement. She wondered what could be going through Black's mind at that moment and if they were satisfied with what she had done so far. The quiet and lack of direction was a little disconcerting in that it tended to put Melissa in her own thoughts.

As if they had read those thoughts, the soft click of the microphone came through just before Black's voice said, "That was nice," in a low, husky tone.

Melissa gave a quick nod toward the bathroom's two-way mirror then turned away to hide her proud grin from Black's praise. She opened the shower door to turn on the water and set it to a comfortable temperature then adjusted the shower head so that the spray would be directed mostly toward her body. In the shower was a soft sponge that was replaced daily by the cleaning staff and bottles of moisturizing body wash, shampoo, conditioner, and even shaving cream and disposable razors because some voyeurs truly want the genuine experience of watching someone shower with all the tasks that went along with it. The shower door was made with fog resistant glass so that the voyeur could clearly see what was going on inside without water spraying everywhere.

Black's voice came through again. "Mistress Heart steps into the shower and lets the water flow over her body to ease the pressures of the day away."

Before stepping into the shower, Melissa reached up to readjust the setting to a massage pulse then stepped in with her back to the spray of water. She'd never used this shower before but had heard that the massaging shower head was so good that a couple of the hosts had bought one for their own showers after experiencing it. Melissa could see why. She had no idea how tense she was until the pulsing rhythm of water gently hammered her lower neck, shoulders, and upper back. For a moment she forgot where she was, closed her eyes, and moaned with pleasure. As soon as the sound escaped her, she quickly blinked her eyes open and turned to face the spray of water, which turned out to be a bad idea as the pulsing massaged her breasts, causing her nipples to harden in pleasure.

"As her stress falls away with each drip of water from her body, Mistress Heart reaches for the sponge and squeezes soap onto it," Black said, drawing Melissa back to where she was.

She followed Black's instructions, getting the sponge good and soapy. Lily had told her voyeurs loved a good soapy shower show.

"She takes her time lathering her body, taking pleasure in washing away all that's happened today."

Black's voice was low and soothing. Closing her eyes, Melissa relaxed and gave herself permission to let go, just for a little while, and found herself becoming aroused.

"As the sponge outlines the contours of her breasts…her waist…her hips…she follows along with her other hand, but her fingers don't stop at her hips. They slide toward her inner thigh until she's mere inches away from intimately touching herself."

Melissa's breath was coming faster, and it took her a moment to realize that she had followed Black's directions to the letter. She could feel the pressure of her hand resting at the juncture of her thighs, her fingertips hovering just above her clit.

"But she stops herself, wanting to save that pleasure for after."

There was a teasing tone in Black's voice that made Melissa smile. She finished her shower, wrapped herself in the plush oversize towels provided, then grabbed a bottle of lotion before heading back out to the bedroom. Just because she was role playing it didn't mean she had to have dry skin while doing it. Melissa stood by the bench at the end of the bed in the same location that gave Black an unhindered view of what she was doing and once again thought to herself, *what would Golden do*? She let the towel slide off her body, squeezed lotion onto her palm, and took her time moisturizing her body from her face to her toes, making sure to position herself in seductive and teasing poses as she did. Then she strolled up to the mirror, reached up and released her locs, arranging them around her shoulders in a way that resembled Lady Godiva with her waist-length hair covering her upper torso.

Melissa directed a mischievous smile at the mirror. "Any further direction?"

"How far are you willing to go?" Black asked.

Melissa had a pretty good idea what length they were referring to. "You're the narrator of this story, you tell me."

A sexy chuckle came through the speaker and gave Melissa a shiver of desire.

"Still basking in the glow of relaxation from her shower, Mistress Heart retires to bed to pick up where she'd left off."

Melissa climbed up onto the bed, propped herself up with pillows, and lay directly in the middle so that Black would see her clearly, then waited with anticipation for the sexy timbre of their voice to give the next instruction.

"Mistress Heart knew that there was only one way to shed the last bit of stress from her day. Will you touch yourself for me, Mistress Heart?"

Realizing Black had directed the question directly to her gave Melissa pause. They were giving her a choice whether to decide to participate further and she found that at this point she would do almost anything.

"Yes," Melissa answered breathlessly.

"Touch your breasts for me," Black requested.

Melissa grasped her breasts, massaging each, then grasped her nipples with a gentle squeeze just the way she liked. She moaned as a feeling like an electrical spark shot from her nipples directly to her clit.

"Are you enjoying that, Mistress Heart?"

"Yes," Melissa moaned.

"Show me what else you enjoy. Show me where to touch you if I were making love to you."

Melissa felt as if she might come just by listening to Black speak. She did as they asked, moving one of her hands down her torso to the juncture of her thighs and cupped her sex as she pinched her nipple just a little harder than she normally did. She felt her fingers become wet with moisture and sunk the first three inside with a long groan.

"Show me that clit, Mistress Heart."

Melissa slid her fingers from her vagina and spread her lips to bare her clit.

"So beautiful. I want to see you come, Mistress Heart. Will you please come for me?"

Melissa was lost in wanting to please Black as well as to release the fire of desire burning within her for this mysterious person. She released her breasts, slid her fingers down to pinch her clit and stroked in and out of her pussy with her other hand until she was riding the edge of orgasm, then slowed down to prolong it. She wanted to give Black their money's worth and wasn't ready to end their time together.

"Are you touching yourself as well, Black?" Melissa asked between pants.

"Is that what you want, Mistress Heart?" Black sounded just as breathless, which told Melissa that they were probably masturbating also.

"Yes."

"Yes, I'm touching myself also."

Melissa felt a cocky sense of satisfaction that she may have chipped at the control Black had of the session. She focused back on her pleasure and gave Black what they were looking for. Just as she felt her orgasm quake through her body, she heard a muffled groan coming from the direction of the voyeur room. Melissa lay in the bed for a few moments to calm her breath then slowly rose. Black walked out of the voyeur room with a satisfied smile and their shirt no longer tucked into their slacks.

"Well done, Mistress Heart."

Melissa smiled as she gathered her clothes. "Why thank you. Did I get the part?"

Black sat on the sofa. "I think I can find an ongoing role for you."

Melissa laughed. "I look forward to seeing how this story unfolds."

"Me too." Despite their grin, there was something serious and intense in Black's eyes as they watched her dress.

Melissa liked the way they looked at her, it made her feel truly seen.

She dressed in everything but her stockings and garter, slipping her shoes on her bare feet. She left her remaining items on the bench to pick up on her way back to the dressing room. "You still have a half hour left in your session."

"It's not the quantity, but the quality of time," Black said with a wink as they stood.

Melissa nodded in agreement. "I'll walk you out."

"Thank you."

Black held the door open for her and followed behind as Melissa walked down the stairs.

"That truly was a fascinating and enjoyable experience," Black said as they stepped up to walk at her side.

"Yes, it was. There were several firsts for me," Melissa admitted.

"Thank you for allowing me to be the one to experience them with. I wish I didn't have to travel for the next couple of weeks. Do you think you could make time for me again when I return?"

"Of course. Just check my schedule with Shari to see what fits your schedule. If you have any requests for our next session, just contact me directly. Shari can provide you with my email information."

"A direct line to Mistress Heart. You may regret giving me that," Black said.

Melissa laughed. "Don't go getting yourself banned before you even get to enjoy your membership."

"Definitely not going to let that happen. I've just discovered I'm kinky after all. I have so much more to learn."

They reached the reception area where Shari greeted them with a friendly smile. "I hope you had an enjoyable experience."

Black smiled charmingly at Shari. "Very enjoyable. I'd like to make my next appointment now if that's possible."

Shari nodded. "Of course."

Black turned back to Melissa, taking both her hands in theirs. "Mistress Heart, it's been a wonderful pleasure to share some time with you. I look forward to the next time." They raised Melissa's hands and placed a soft kiss on the back of each.

Melissa felt her body flush. "The pleasure was mine as well. Until next time."

Nodding, Black released her hands. She turned and could feel their eyes on her as she walked away. As soon as the door closed behind her Melissa placed her hand on the wall for support as she was overcome with an almost girlish excitement over what just occurred. The first thing she wanted to do was call Golden and tell her about it, but she hadn't even told Golden what she was doing so that was out of the question. She took a few steadying breaths to calm her racing heart then made her way back up to the room to collect her stockings and garter. Melissa gazed at the two-way mirror and couldn't wipe the grin from her face at just the thought of her next session with Black.

CHAPTER SEVENTEEN

Melissa walked toward the diner where she was meeting Golden and Zoe for brunch with one task in mind. To finally admit to her friends what was going on. After she had gotten home from work on Friday, she couldn't shake the need to want to talk to her friends about what happened with Black and how it was making her feel. Rose and Hyacinth had been in the dressing room when she had finished her appointment and she considered talking to them but didn't feel that they were close enough, or understood her enough, to talk about it. When they asked how her session had gone, she simply told them it was good. Hyacinth had grinned at her like she knew that it was far more than that, but Melissa had ignored her, quickly changed into her street clothes, and headed out the back door that connected with the gallery's second floor storage room.

She, Vivienne, and Afrodite were the only people with keys to that door. She never entered or left the club from the front entrance to keep her anonymity in case there were members in the halls or reception area. Once Melissa entered the storage space, she made her way downstairs to the main entrance of the gallery. She realized that night that she no longer wanted to keep her anonymity and secret life from her best friends. She just hoped they weren't too shocked to learn the truth.

"You look just like this chick we used to know," Golden said as Melissa reached their favorite corner booth where she and Zoe had been waiting.

Melissa rolled her eyes. "Yeah, yeah, I know. I'm a bad friend."

Golden stood and pulled her into a hug. "I didn't say that. We just never see you anymore now that you're a big-time gallery manager and art curator."

Zoe stood and hugged her as well. "Yeah, we thought it would be Golden who got too famous for us, but it looks like it's you."

Melissa laughed. "Both of you can kiss my ass."

They all sat down. It felt good to be with her girls again.

"I took the initiative of ordering mimosas for all of us right before you arrived," Zoe said.

"Good, I could use a pick-me-up," Melissa said.

Golden quirked a brow in question. "Another late work night?"

Melissa turned her focus to the breadbasket in the middle of the table. "Yes."

Golden snorted. "I don't believe you one bit. Who is she?"

Melissa gazed up in confusion. "Who's who?"

"The woman that's obviously got you so wrapped up that you can't even talk to your girls about it." Golden looked a little offended.

Melissa sighed. She never meant for her decision to do what she was doing to cause her to ostracize her friends, especially Golden. "I'll tell you everything, but first I need a drink and to hear what's been going on in your lives."

"The Twins booked me to perform at a show they're doing in Paris in February," Golden said nonchalantly.

"I broke my own rule and went on a date with a salon client and now she's moving into the studio apartment at my house," Zoe said, just as nonchalantly.

"Are you serious! How and when did this all come about?" Melissa asked.

As they caught her up on what had been going on in their lives while she was so caught up in her own, Melissa felt an immense amount of guilt. Golden and Zoe always had her back, supported her without question, and she'd been blowing them off to fulfill her need for control in her life. Once they ordered their food and were enjoying their mimosas, Melissa decided now was the time.

"Okay, here's what's been going on. Yes, the gallery keeps me busy, mostly during the day. Of course, there are the showings and private events that happen as well. I'm also not seeing anyone. Most of the nights when I've regretfully canceled or just couldn't plan to hang with you guys, I was working a second job."

Golden looked surprised. "You've got a second job? I thought Vivienne was paying you very well, especially since being promoted to manager."

"She is. I didn't take a second job for the money, although it doesn't hurt. Especially since I use it to fund the investment portfolio you helped me put together."

"If you're not doing it for the money then this must be what I call a passion gig. A side gig that you enjoy doing but wouldn't want to make a career of," Zoe said.

Melissa smiled. "Yeah, that's pretty much it."

"What's this side gig?"

Melissa gazed nervously around at the tables nearby, then leaned in and whispered, "I'm a dominatrix at a fetish club."

There was a moment of stunned silence from her friends who first looked at her in disbelief then confusion.

Golden leaned in the same way Melissa had. "You mean the tie people up and whip their asses for pleasure kind of dominatrix?"

Zoe chuckled. "Is there any other kind?"

Golden rolled her eyes at Zoe. "So, you've been blowing us off all this time to get your freak on and instead of just being up-front about it you've been lying. Why? Did you honestly think we...I...would judge you?"

Golden's voice was filled with so much hurt it broke Melissa's heart. "Yes and no. It all happened so unexpectedly, and I didn't know how to tell you guys because I didn't understand it myself, but I felt it was something I needed to keep as my own for a little while before sharing it."

Golden looked at her in disappointment. "Mel, c'mon, we know more shit about each other than our future wives will probably ever know. You know damn well you can talk to me about anything, and I won't judge you."

"Golden, that isn't fair, especially after you said that we all deserve to have our little secrets every now and then," Zoe reasonably pointed out.

Golden didn't look happy to have her own words thrown back at her. "What Mel did isn't the same and you know it. She's got a whole ass secret life going on."

"You're taking this too personally. This isn't about us, it's about Mel and something she needed to figure out on her own," Zoe said.

Golden looked truly annoyed. She hated it when Melissa and Zoe called her out on her shit despite her doing the same to them.

Melissa reached across the table and grasped Golden's hand. "I'm sorry I didn't tell you about what was going on, but Zoe is right. I know you would've been supportive and encouraging because that's the kind of friend you are and what I've relied on to get me through pretty much every difficult thing that happened in my life, but this time I needed to figure out what was best for me on my own."

Golden sighed then gave Melissa's hand a gentle squeeze. "I understand and I'm sorry for being such a bitch about it. You're my sis, I love you, and I'm very protective of you. I don't ever want you to feel like you have to go through anything alone or that you can't at least talk to me about it."

"I know and I love you too." Melissa scooted closer and pulled Golden into a hug.

Zoe applauded. "Yaaay, now that you've kissed and made up, we need the full story. How the hell did our sweet, shy Mel become a dominatrix?"

Melissa realized she was going to have to reveal another secret. She knew there was no way of explaining how she came to the realization that she had a penchant for being a domme without telling them about her relationship with Riley, which meant she was going to have to admit to Golden that she lied about something else. Melissa first told them about the Cat Lady exhibit in the gallery and how it made her feel. Then she explained how she met Riley, which Golden just shook her head and smiled in response, and how their friendship with benefits led to her figuring out that she enjoyed being in control and learning about the dominant and submissive fetish. She then went on to tell them about finding out Vivienne was the Cat Lady and that she owned the Red Dahlia Social Club. Melissa held back a chuckle at the rapt look of attention on her friends' faces as she described how she ended up working at Red Dahlia and about her secret domme identity. Their server appeared with their order, giving Melissa time to think about how she would approach the topic of her appointment with Black.

Golden didn't even look down at the plate set in front of her. She turned back to Melissa with an eager expression. "Can we see what Mistress Heart looks like?"

Melissa hesitated then picked up her phone, pulled up the Red Dahlia member page, logged in and chose the *hosts* tab that listed profiles of the hosts. She located her profile and opened it. It was a picture of her sitting on a black and gold throne wearing a leather and Swarovski crystal branch-like crown, a half face mask lined with the same crystals in the crown, an evening gown with a leather patchwork bustier that laced up the back, and a tulle handkerchief skirt with a slit up the side that revealed thigh-high leather pointed toe boots with a six-inch heel, all in her signature black color. She held an oversized riding crop with a large, red crystal heart at the tip in her hands like a scepter. She looked like an evil queen from some fantasy novel. She had taken several photos during that shoot, but she, Afrodite, and Vivienne all agreed that this picture was the perfect representation of Mistress Heart. As Melissa passed her phone to Golden her face flushed hotly with embarrassment.

"Holy shit!" Golden looked up at Melissa in amazement then back down to the phone again. "If you didn't tell me that this was you, I wouldn't have even known. The only thing I recognize about this woman as you is your hair, and even that seems different because you rarely wear it loose. Very sexy." Golden passed the phone to Zoe.

"Damn, girl, you are HOT." Zoe scrolled down the screen. "You do all of this stuff listed?"

Golden slid closer to Zoe to look at the phone with her. Melissa was regretting showing them the picture through her profile page, but she didn't have any pictures on her phone of her in her Mistress attire. "Uh, I can but I haven't done all of them."

"Who in the world gets turned on by tickling?" Golden said.

Melissa grinned. "You'd be surprised."

"Do you have celebrity members?" Zoe asked.

"Celebrities, politicians, well-known business moguls, and the not so famous but rich."

Zoe handed the phone back and Golden slid back over to her seat to drizzle her chicken and waffles with syrup. "So, you really enjoy this work?" Golden asked just before taking a bite of her chicken.

Melissa was cutting her blueberry waffles. "I do. Although not in a sexual way. I don't get off on whipping folks or commanding someone to suck on the heel of my shoe—"

"Wait, what? People actually do that?" Golden said.

Melissa nodded. "Foot fetish and degradation are actually two of the most commonly requested services."

Zoe scooped a spoonful of her shrimp and grits. "Let me guess, by rich men who spend their day wallowing in power."

"Exactly. It's an opportunity for them to drop their guard and not have to think. They allow someone else to be in control for once," Melissa explained.

Golden gazed up at her, smiled and shook her head. "It's funny, I still find it hard to believe that the Melissa I've known practically my whole life is a dominatrix, but then it's not so hard to believe knowing about how you spent so much of your life being hampered from controlling your own life. I'm proud of you for finding a way to be the you that I always knew was in there."

"Yeah, you are a true Boss Bitch," Zoe said.

Melissa smiled. She knew that she should've probably told her friends sooner about what she was doing, but better later than never. "Thanks, guys. I'm so glad you understand because there's something I want to get your thoughts on."

"Let me guess, you want to start your own fetish club," Zoe said.

Melissa shook her head. "No, absolutely not. It's a situation with a client."

Golden quirked a brow. "Oooh, this sounds like it's going to be juicy."

Melissa knew her friends well enough to be prepared for any teasing that would follow what she was about to tell them. "I took on a new client this week and we had our first session on Friday."

Melissa went on to tell them about Black and describe their session, avoiding looking directly at Golden or Zoe as she did. Once she finished her story, she gazed up to find them both looking at her in amazement.

"That was so surprising and hot. I am truly impressed," Golden said.

Zoe nodded. "Me too. What do they always say about church girls?"

Golden chuckled. "That they're usually the biggest freaks."

Melissa shook her head, grinning. "This is why I hate telling you guys anything."

"We tease because we love you. Now, besides that being the hottest thing I've heard happening to anyone ever, what's the problem?" Zoe said.

Melissa stabbed at her pancakes distractedly. "Well, I enjoy what I do, but not in a sexual way. I've never felt any sexual connection with my clients until now and I don't know what to do about it."

Golden shrugged. "How about just enjoying it. That sounds like what Black wants you to do. At least that's what I got from their fantasy request. It was all about you and your comfort and enjoyment."

"I agree. Maybe they're one of those busy executives that doesn't have time to date and is supplementing what's missing in their life through their voyeur fantasy," Zoe said.

Melissa chewed her food in contemplation. She hadn't thought of that. Black getting off on Melissa's, rather Mistress Heart's, pleasure.

"Do any of the other dommes there enjoy their work that way?" Golden asked.

"Two of them have mentioned that they do. The rest look at it as just a job. They come in and leave it all there when they finish at the end of their shift."

Melissa knew that's why Rose was so popular as a sub because nine times out of ten, she had a genuine orgasm during her sessions. When she didn't, she faked it well. Like Meg Ryan in *When Harry Met Sally* level. Brutus was the other person who got turned on but only during wrestle play, but he never had an orgasm while doing it.

"Then I repeat what I said. Just enjoy it. I get aroused when performing sometimes. It's usually when it's a more intimate show and audience where I can slow it down and take my time performing. There's no rush to finish in time for the next act to hit the stage," Golden said.

"And I have a little fetish I never told anyone about. Bald heads. Everyone's head is shaped and feels different, and I love the way it feels to run my hands over a bald head," Zoe admitted.

Melissa looked at them in surprise. "So basically, we're all freaks."

Golden and Zoe laughed.

"Guess so," Golden said.

"So, what are you going to do?" Zoe asked.

"I guess enjoy it, like you guys suggest."

Melissa felt so much better having talked to them. Part of the reason she chose to work at Red Dahlia was to experience something new and exciting. What she was experiencing with Black was definitely new and exciting.

❖

Golden had been proud and a bit envious of Melissa taking charge of her needs and desires the way she had. She was a far cry from the insecure, meek girl Golden had befriended back in high school. Golden had put her personal needs and desire on the back burner to put all her focus on her business. It was the same thing she had done while pursuing her career in finance, but at least then she'd made time for hookups every now and then. Now, between shows, traveling, and running the school, she barely had time to spend a day just relaxing at home, let alone go on dates or find someone to hook up with. She arrived home at the same time as her mother who was wearing the same clothes that she had worn for her date last night.

"Hey there. Don't tell me you're just getting home."

Her mother blushed. "Yes."

Golden couldn't help but chuckle. Damn, even her mother had a better love life than her. "I guess moms have to get some too."

Her mother playfully swatted Golden on the arm. "Don't be so vulgar. We spent most of the night talking."

Golden quirked a brow. "And what about the rest of the night?"

Her mother's complexion darkened even more. "You're a mess."

They walked into the house together then went their separate ways as Golden headed upstairs to her apartment.

"Dinner tonight?" her mother asked.

"Does six work for you?"

"Yes. Drew might also come by. Keisha and the kids are out of town visiting her mom."

"Okay, cool. It'll be just like old times with the three of us."

"That'll be nice. See you then."

Her mother entered her apartment and Golden continued her way up to hers. If it weren't for her mother being downstairs, Golden would spend a lot of time alone, something she wasn't used to. She knew that if her mother decided to remarry, which she saw happening, she was going to have to learn how to live without the convenience of having her right there whenever she was feeling lonely. She knew she wanted a relationship, but what she wanted she was too afraid to seek out. She wanted Jade and Kendra and what they had been hinting around offering her. She never imagined she would ever be part of a throuple and it more than likely would never have crossed her mind if she hadn't met them.

Ever since Golden lost her father, she'd never allowed anyone to get too close except for the small group already around her. It frightened her to let anyone else in that close circle because she didn't want to add to the people she could lose. The pain of losing her father still affected her after all these years. She couldn't control the family growing around her, but she could control the people outside of the family that she allowed close. Somehow, Jade and Kendra had found their way in, and Golden was determined to keep them at a distance for her own sense of well-being. Her feelings for the Twins were so intense and out of her control that it scared her. One thing she knew she needed to do before she left for Paris was to make sure Jade and Kendra knew that this was strictly business. She wouldn't allow herself to be tempted again by their attempts to sweep her off her feet. She would stand strong and steady in her conviction to avoid any romantic entanglement with them. To prove her determination to herself, Golden decided to take advantage of her free Sunday afternoon to work on her routine for the Paris show. She changed into a pair of dance tights and a sports bra and headed down to her studio in the basement.

She had just pulled up the Twins song on her phone when it dinged with a text message notification. She looked at her messages in surprise, wondering if the they were psychic and knew she had been thinking about them. The message was from Jade.

We just wanted to thank you again for agreeing to do our show. You don't know how much this means to us. We sent you a little something in appreciation. Enjoy!

As if on cue, another notification popped up for Golden's doorbell camera letting her know someone was ringing her bell. Sure enough, it looked to be a delivery person with a large package. Golden jogged back upstairs to answer the door.

"I have a delivery for," he gazed down at the tablet in his hand, "Golden Hughes."

"Yes, I'm Golden Hughes."

"I hate to ask, but do you mind if I see some identification? I was told to make sure I was delivering directly to Ms. Hughes."

Golden put her hands on her hips with a sigh. "Do I look like I have ID on me right now? It says G. Hughes on the doorbell you rang, and I answered so I'm sure you can take a wild guess who I am."

He seemed to contemplate the sense in what she said, then offered her the tablet and a stylus. "Please sign here."

Golden signed the screen and gave the tablet back to him. In exchange, he handed her a small box, then pointed toward the large one that he had propped against building. "You have two packages."

Golden looked at the larger one that was a rectangular shape that stood hip high. It looked like something a large, framed picture would be shipped in. There were openings on the sides for her to be able to carry it. "Thank you."

The delivery guy nodded then jogged back down the driveway to his truck. Golden placed the smaller box atop the larger one, slid her hands into the openings, and hobbled back into the house. It was easier just to go back down into the basement than upstairs so that's where she went. She propped the boxes along the wall just inside the door, then picked up the smaller of the two. She didn't have scissors in her studio, so she grabbed her keys, sat in the chair she used for her choreography, and used her car key to tear along the tape sealing the box. Inside were three gift boxes in signature Tiffany blue and a white envelope with her name written in Jade's flourishing script that Golden would recognize anywhere. When it came to acknowledging appreciation or a special occasion, Jade preferred sending handwritten cards and notes to people rather than emails or text messages. They were never simple one-liners or corny phrases. Jade wrote as if she channeled some flowery poet from the past. She had even taken classes in American and Japanese calligraphy. Golden opened the envelope to find the handwritten note she had expected.

To Our Golden Treasure,

Kendra and I can't express enough for how grateful we are for the gift that you have given us with not only your forgiveness for our idiocy but also allowing us to share the stage with your mesmerizing presence, tremendous talent, and flawless beauty. These gifts, which we each chose

for you ourselves (this one is from me), are just a small token of our
appreciation and affection for you. We hope you enjoy them.
With love,
Jade

Golden gazed at the note for a moment, her heart doing just what she didn't want it to do. Filling with emotions for these women that she didn't know if she could handle. With a shuddering sigh, she reached for the largest of the three Tiffany boxes and opened it to find a pearl wrap necklace long enough to wear as two to three strands. This wasn't a piece of inexpensive costume jewelry that she wore for her shows, it was the real thing. She looked at the tag hanging from a string around the sterling silver clasp. It read Ziegfeld Collection. Golden shook her head in disbelief. She was familiar with Tiffany's Ziegfeld Collection. It was inspired by the 1920s Jazz Age era and Golden had considered purchasing a necklace and earrings from the set until she saw the price tag. The shorter sixteen-inch pearl necklace was over seven hundred dollars. She couldn't imagine how much this longer strand was.

Golden carefully laid the necklace back on its satiny bed, set the box aside, and pulled out the other two boxes. One was a pearl bracelet and the last was a pair of sterling silver and pearl drop earrings. With the necklace there had to be at least two thousand dollars' worth of jewelry. She gazed over at the box sitting unopened against the wall and couldn't imagine what it was. She carefully placed all the jewelry back into the box they had arrived in and walked over to the other package. Once again, she used her keys to break the seal of the tape along the top. Once she opened the top flap, she noticed the edge of a black frame showing through bubble wrap. She had been right; it was a picture. For a moment, Golden grinned at the thought of Kendra sending her a picture of herself but knew that despite her vanity in her appearance, Kendra wasn't so vain to send someone a portrait of herself unless it was a joke.

Golden carefully eased the picture out of the box, then set it on the chair so that she could unwrap it. She gasped at the site of one of her favorite portraits of Josephine Baker taken by George Hoyningen-Huene, an iconic fashion photographer from the 1920s and 1930s. Josephine stood nude on a draped pedestal holding a long strand of pearls, similar to the ones Golden had been gifted with, and using some of the material draped over the pedestal to cover just enough of her body for modesty, but the look she gave the camera was the epitome of a come-hither stare. Golden had only seen poster reprints until she visited the Staley-Wise Gallery in New York and saw the original Hoyningen-Huene's portrait collection. To see Josephine's portrait in person almost ranked up there with discovering two similar portraits Golden's grandmother had of her aunt Dinah, painted by an artist friend, that she promised to leave to Golden in her will. Gazing down at the box of pearls from Jade, Golden decided that she might just have to re-create the image during her next photo shoot to update her portfolio.

Golden looked for a note and found it tucked into the back of the frame. When she removed it, she had another surprise. A small silver sticker with embossed print that read:

Josephine Baker, 1920
George Hoyningen-Huene
Staley-Wise Gallery

It was the very portrait she had seen at the gallery. The pearls, the portrait, this was all too much for a simple thank you. Her hands trembled so she carefully set the portrait against the back of the chair and sat on the floor to read the note written in Kendra's neat, compact print. Golden grinned. She knew it probably took a lot for Jade to convince Kendra to handwrite her note. Even when she wrote songs, Kendra used a digital notebook rather than writing it down.

To Golden,

I'm not going to try to top what Jade said in her note because she said everything that needed to be said. When I found out that we were being offered an opportunity to perform in your aunt's old stomping ground, I agreed with Jade that we had to figure out some way to get you there also. I know how important your aunt's legacy is to you and your family, and I hope this opportunity will bring you a little closer to her. As you see from my gift to you, I also listened to your stories about your aunt's friendship with Josephine Baker and your admiration for her and the portrait as well. Maybe one day we'll come visit to see it gracing the walls of your dance studio inspiring future performers. Until then, we can't wait to see you and be able to share in such a wonderful experience.

Much love,

Kendra

Golden wiped a tear away. Jade and Kendra knew her like no one except maybe Melissa did. They were so in tune with what was in her heart, listening to not only what she said but what she didn't need to say. She couldn't imagine finding any one person who could compare to what both Jade and Kendra meant to her. That frightened her more than the thought of spending her life without them.

CHAPTER EIGHTEEN

Zoe placed two drops of oil into her hand and rubbed her palms together. The aromatic scent of frankincense and myrrh drifted on the air as she smoothed, then massaged the oil into Danice's freshly shaved head. Danice sighed with contentment and Zoe's sex clenched with desire. She smoothed her hands down the back of Danice's head to the nape of her neck then slid the top of her robe from her shoulders, continuing to massage and knead the tightness and kinks away.

Danice moaned pleasurably. "You keep this up we're going to be late for dinner, and I don't want to show up to meet your mother and grandmother late, looking like we just rolled out of bed."

Zoe laughed. "They're only fifteen minutes from here. We have plenty of time." She bent and placed a kiss between Danice's shoulder blades in a spot that she knew was a pleasure point for her.

Danice moaned again. Zoe began sliding Danice's robe off when her phone rang with her mother's personalized ring tone.

"Saved by the bell," Danice said breathily.

With an annoyed sigh, Zoe placed Danice's robe back on her shoulders and walked over to the kitchen island to answer her phone.

"Hey, Mommy…No, I don't have any, but we can stop and pick some up on the way…Okay. See you then." Zoe turned back to find Danice grinning.

"That can't be a coincidence."

"Well, it was." Zoe walked back to Danice and reached for her robe.

Danice swatted her hands away. "Nope. Go downstairs and get dressed. I'll be down as soon as I'm ready."

Zoe poked her lips out petulantly. "Fine. I can't believe I got blocked by my mom." She walked out with the sound of Danice's laughter following her out the door.

She moped all they back down to the lower level of the house to find Kiara lounging on the sofa still in her pajamas with a bowl of popcorn watching television.

"Did you forget we're going to Grandma Letty's for dinner?"

"No. I skipped lunch and just needed something to hold me over."

"I'm not talking about the popcorn. Shouldn't you be dressed?"

"I didn't know how long you'd be upstairs, so I figured I had time."

"You know I just went up there to cut Danice's hair."

Kiara gave her a side-eyed glance that said, "Yeah, right."

"Do you have something to say?"

"Nope. As you're so fond of saying, you're a grown woman. You don't need a teenager telling you how to live your life."

Zoe looked at Kiara with surprise. "That never stopped you before." She walked over to sit beside her. "Kiki, talk to me."

Kiara sighed then placed her popcorn on the table, turned the television off, and faced Zoe. "I like Danice, I really do, but don't you think you guys are moving way too fast? In a matter of a few months, you went from renting an apartment to a woman in need to practically living together. I never imagined my Mom was a U-Haul lesbian."

This wasn't the first time someone had suggested Zoe had moved too fast with Danice. Golden and Melissa had also expressed some concern about Zoe getting so serious with a woman she barely knew who had a lot of baggage piled in her past. They didn't understand that the connection Zoe felt for Danice at the start of their relationship had only grown over the past months. Even when they both decided shortly after Danice moved in to slow down and spend some time apart from each other, or as apart as basically living in the same house would allow, to figure out if what was happening between them was a result of Zoe's unintentional celibacy and Danice finally receiving the affection and passion she had been denied during her marriage or genuine feelings developing between them. They lasted a few weeks before a clogged sink in Danice's apartment sent Zoe up to try to fix it before deciding whether to call a plumber. She fixed the sink and somehow managed to end up in bed with Danice. They decided to stop trying to fight what was happening between them and see where it went.

Zoe had made sure to talk to Kiara about it since there was no way of hiding what was going on and she was determined that she wasn't going to be sneaking up and down stairs in the middle of the night in her own house. Kiara had been fine with it in the beginning, but as Danice began spending more time in their place than hers, it was obvious that they were no longer just sleeping together. That's when Zoe began noticing Kiara would make it a point to hide in her room when Danice came down for dinner or to watch a movie. Zoe had thought she was just trying to give them their space, but now she realized that wasn't the case.

"I know it seems fast, but sometimes you meet people, and you just know that they're the person for you. Danice and I had the same concerns in the beginning, but the two of us haven't really had someone like this in our life for a very long time, so we know when it's casual and when it's a little more serious."

"But she has had someone in her life. She's barely divorced. How do you know you're not just a rebound and that she won't end up breaking your heart when she gets her life together?"

The worry in Kiara's tone and on her face clenched Zoe's heart. She opened her arms. "Come here."

Kiara didn't hesitate to move into Zoe's embrace. She gave her a squeeze and placed a kiss atop her head. "I'm not going to lie and say that I know that's not the case, because I had those same concerns. All I can do is trust that Danice is being as honest with herself about her feelings toward me as I am about how I feel about her. If I worried about getting my heart broken, I would never love anyone."

"Do you love her?"

"I have strong feelings for her, but I can't say that it's love."

Kiara was quiet for a moment, then sighed and extricated herself from Zoe's arms. "I believe that you're being honest with yourself, but I'm still wary that Danice is. I'll hold my acceptance of her back a little longer if that's okay with you."

Zoe smiled in understanding. "It's fine with me." She grasped Kiara's hand. "I'm lucky to have you helping to guard my heart. Now, let's go get dressed."

She stood and pulled Kiara up with her. They walked together to Kiara's bedroom where she leaned in and placed a kiss on Zoe's cheek before entering her room and closing the door. When Zoe arrived at her room, she sat on the edge of her bed thinking over what Kiara said. Was her daughter seeing something in Danice that she wasn't? When Zoe and Danice had a similar conversation, Danice assured her that she wasn't a rebound, but how could she know that for sure? Danice had been unhappy for so long that all this could be a result of her experiencing a good relationship for the first time in years. Now that she knew it was possible, she could end up leaving Zoe heartbroken just like Kiara said.

The doubt planted in her mind slowly took root in her heart as she got dressed. When Danice came down so that they could all go over to Zoe's grandmother's together she found herself feeling withdrawn and quiet.

"Are you okay?" Danice asked as they exited the subway for the remaining walk to the apartment.

Zoe attempted a half-hearted smile. "Yeah, I'm good."

Danice frowned. Zoe took her hand. "I'm fine. We need to make a quick stop to pick up some coco bread."

Danice nodded, but Zoe could see she didn't believe her. They stopped at a Caribbean grocer that her grandmother and mother frequented and picked up the coco bread her mother had requested. They arrived right on time, and basking in the light, joy, and love of her family made Zoe forget her doubts and just enjoy sharing her family with Danice, who seemed to soak up the experience like a dry sponge in water. It reminded Zoe that Danice's husband wasn't the only person who left her bereft of love and affection. Danice told her that she knew her parents loved her and her sister, but they were never demonstrative about it. Not even with each other. She couldn't remember ever seeing her parents hold hands, let alone kiss, or show any affection toward each other. When it came to her and her sister, there was praise, a pat on the head, maybe even a very brief hug when something good happened, but that was about it. There was a sense of contentment in her home growing up. Teasing, laughter, and joy was reserved for the larger family gatherings not for their little family.

Zoe grew up in a happy, affectionate, and boisterous family so she tended to forget not every family was like hers. Melissa and Danice and the issues they carried with them were proof of that. Zoe loved seeing the happiness on Danice's face as she was gently teased by Zoe's grandmother for the small amount of food she'd placed on her plate. Or when Zoe's mother asked about her work with autistic children, listened intently, and asked questions. It was obvious no one took the time to really talk to Danice and genuinely be interested in what she had to say. Whether she ended up being a rebound for Danice or not, Zoe was glad to have at least helped her to see that she mattered.

As they left her grandmother's place with a grocery bag holding several plastic containers filled with jerk chicken, rice and beans, and callaloo with saltfish and were heading back to the subway, someone called Danice's name. She slid her hand from Zoe's grasp and slowly turned. Zoe and Kiara turned as well to find a man jogging toward them. He was tall, attractive, with the same complexion as Danice, thick medium-length hair that stopped just at the nape of his neck, a goatee, and was well dressed in a sports jacket, sweater, jeans, and loafers.

"I thought that was you," he said happily as he pulled Danice into a hug.

Zoe noticed she didn't hug him back. As a matter of fact, Danice didn't look the least bit happy to see him.

He must have noticed her lack of response because he released her with an embarrassed smile. "I almost didn't recognize you. Your mom told me you cut your hair, but she didn't say it was such a drastic cut."

Danice shrugged. "It was just too much work to maintain it. I figured there was no longer any reason to keep it, so I shed it with the rest of my baggage."

The man flinched as if her words had made physical contact. That's when Zoe realized who he was.

He gave Danice a nervous smile. "Well, you look great. I guess life is treating you well."

Danice sighed. "Malik, you really don't have to do this. You could've just kept walking. You paid me little attention while we were married, why go out of your way to start now?"

He quickly glanced at Zoe and Kiara, then back at Danice. "Can we go somewhere and talk? I've been trying to reach you, but you haven't returned my calls."

"Because there's nothing for us to talk about. You made it quite obvious that you wanted something I couldn't give you, so I freed both of us. You got what you wanted, and I'm finally happy with myself and my life."

While Zoe wondered why Danice hadn't mentioned Malik had been calling her, she was proud at how she was handling the encounter.

"Now, if you don't have anything else to say we're on our way home." Danice turned toward Zoe.

"I made a mistake. It wasn't my kid and we're not together anymore," Malik blurted.

"Not my problem."

Danice grasped Zoe's hand again and started walking. Zoe had to go along or be pulled.

"Wow, if words could physically cut, I think he'd be shredded."

Zoe gave Kiara a pointed look and got a smirk in response, then she gently tugged Danice's hand to get her attention. "Uh, Danice, can we slow down? He's not following us."

Danice slowed her pace but kept her gaze straight ahead. "I'm sorry."

"No need to apologize. He pretty much ambushed you on the street. I think you handled it well."

Danice gazed over at Zoe with a soft smile. "I did, didn't I. That felt really good."

Zoe smiled in return. "I bet it did. He's probably still standing there in shock."

"And a pool of blood," Kiara added, taking Danice's other hand.

Danice gazed over at her and laughed. It bothered Zoe that Danice didn't tell her about Malik reaching out to her, but it wasn't worth bringing up now.

❖

"Mistress Heart, your client has arrived and gone to Playroom Eight," Shari announced over the dressing room intercom.

Melissa was glad she was there alone because she couldn't contain her excitement at seeing Black. They'd had only a few sessions since Black became her client three months ago, and each session had been different, exciting, and intimate. The first had been with her showering then masturbating for Black. The second had begun with Black having props pre-set in the room which were a beribboned box on the bed and a small tray of chocolate-covered strawberries, a bottle of champagne and a champagne glass on the side table next to the sofa. Black would already be in the room behind the two-way mirror. When Melissa entered, she was given direction just as before, beginning with a slow undress and shower, which she had gotten tips from Golden on how to maximize the tease, then Black had instructed her to open the gift box on the bed where she found sexy sheer lingerie.

Beneath the lingerie was a book titled *Iridescence: Sensuous Shades of Lesbian Erotica*. She had seen this book before, many years ago. Golden had a copy and offered to let Melissa borrow it, but she hadn't wanted to chance her stepfather finding it. She would only read it when she spent the night at Golden's and promised herself that she would get her own copy when she finally moved out on her own. She'd forgotten about that until seeing the book now. She ran her fingers over the sexy image on the cover, a topless woman with her back to the reader wearing a pair of loose white pants sitting low on her waist. Melissa always loved the sight of her rich brown complexion and the dimples on her lower back just above the waistband of the pants. She was drawn to the anonymity of the woman, curious to know what she might have been thinking and ached for her to turn around and look at her.

"Do you like your gifts?" Black had asked.

"Yes, thank you."

Melissa had refused to turn around, not wanting them to see how much it affected her. That book had been one of many symbols of freedom to Melissa that she had never obtained. Now she finally had both her freedom and the book, and it meant more to her than anyone would ever realize. She had managed to hold back the tears that had blurred her vision for a moment to get back into character. She had put on the slip, walked to the mirror, did a little pose and given Black a teasing wink. Black then instructed Melissa to choose a few stories from the anthology and read them aloud while enjoying the strawberries and champagne.

The next two sessions followed a similar pattern, striptease, shower, opening a gift of soft, lacey lingerie, much different from her usual boned corset and leather outfits, with a book of lesbian erotic short stories or poetry. The sessions were always the last of her day, so Melissa would go home feeling relaxed, sexy, and like she'd spent an hour at the spa rather than in a client session. Black was always attentive, complimentary, and more focused on what pleased her than what their pleasure was. One other difference from the last three sessions than the first was that Black had not directed Melissa to masturbate, although she had wanted to after reading so much erotica and knowing Black would be watching while she did it. Would tonight be the night they asked her to touch herself again? If not, would she really be that disappointed? In a strange way, Melissa was enjoying the vulnerability of her sessions with Black. She had spent so much time these past years focusing on gaining and maintaining control of her life that she never thought to just relax occasionally and let someone else take control. It was somewhat freeing to not have to plan every moment to a safe and predictable outcome.

As she always did before a session, Melissa stood before the full-length mirror, checked her attire which, for her sessions with Black, was always what she called the Domme Boss Bitch uniform of sheer blouse, bustier, pencil skirt with a high slit, thongs, garters, stockings, stiletto pumps, and of course her mask. She closed her eyes, took a deep breath and sought her Mistress Heart persona, but found herself not able to connect with it. Melissa opened her eyes, went through the process of physically seeing herself as Mistress Heart, then closed them again to seek the attitude for her, but once again felt disconnected. She'd had several clients prior to this and had no problem getting into character so she didn't know why it wasn't working now. With a frustrated sigh, she left the dressing room hoping she would be in the right mindset once the session began.

She entered the playroom and noticed a gift box on the bed, but in place of chocolate-covered strawberries and champagne, on the side table was a vintage rotary phone that belonged to the 1940s.

"Good evening, Mistress Heart," Black's sexy voice came through the speaker giving Melissa a shiver of pleasure.

"Good evening, Black." It was weird. Despite still not connecting to Mistress Heart, she heard the tone in her voice that she shifted to as her other persona. She also was no longer bothered by not connecting to it either.

"We'll begin as usual, but I thought we might try a little something different after your shower," Black said.

"All right."

As Melissa performed her striptease, she noticed something different. She wasn't performing as Mistress Heart wanting to please a client. She was Melissa wanting to please her lover. She wanted Black to see her as herself, not a paid entertainer. Once she stood nude before the mirror, Melissa gazed directly where she assumed Black's eyes were then reached up to touch her mask. She wanted so much to snatch it off. To reveal her true self to the sexy, intriguing, and mysterious Black. To open the mirror and step through to remove theirs as well, but just as she lifted the edge of the mask, common sense thankfully intervened and the moment was lost. Melissa quickly turned away from the mirror and went into the bathroom. In the shower Mistress Heart finally came through as if she knew Melissa was about to make a huge mistake and needed to be reeled in.

She went through the motions of her sexy shower scene, her teasingly slow body moisturizing, then opened the box on the bed. Inside wasn't the usual overtly sexy lingerie. Today's gift was a pink babydoll nightie with adjustable spaghetti straps, sheer V-neckline top with lightly embroidered floral appliques over the breast and lace trim, an empire waist with a satin bow, pleated skirt, and matching sheer and floral thong panties. It was a softer, sweeter look than what she even wore at home. It was also the only thing in the box. There was no book of erotica. Melissa didn't question it. She put on the nightie, walked to the mirror, and did her usual twist and turn to check out how she looked. Suddenly, the sound of a phone ringing startled her. She was confused for a moment because she hadn't brought her phone with her, then she realized it was coming from the speaker. Had Black forgotten to turn their phone off? It rang again.

"The phone rings and Mistress Heart wonders who could be calling this late," Black said.

Melissa smiled as she remembered the phone on the side table. She walked over to "answer" it.

"Hello."

"Hello," Black said, as if they were on the other line.

Melissa sent a quick glance toward the mirror then sat on the sofa in a sexy pose as if she was a sexy starlet in a movie scene from the same era as the telephone. She gazed back toward the mirror, winding the phone cord on and off her finger.

"Who do I have the pleasure of speaking with?" she asked.

"A secret admirer."

"Are you the one that has been leaving me the gifts?"

"Only if you've enjoyed them."

"Yes, I have. Thank you."

"My pleasure. I hope I'm not disturbing you."

"Not at all. You called just in time. I was just winding down from my day."

"And how was your day?"

"Long and busy. I look forward to these opportunities for me to just relax and not worry about anything but enjoying the evening."

Melissa noticed her Mistress Heart facade was slipping away again and she didn't mind. She had had a long day with working in the gallery from eight this morning until three this afternoon then three client sessions starting at four thirty that included working with Lily for a ninety-minute bondage session with a married couple, another ninety-minute session alone for a couple's combined voyeur and spanking session, and then an hour foot fetish and trampling session. Her session with Black began at ten and was fortunately her last one of the day.

"So, you're saying you look forward to our time together?" Melissa could tell Black was smiling by the tone in their voice.

"I'm not sure what you mean. After all, you're my secret admirer, how have we spent time together?" Melissa teased them.

Black laughed and it made Melissa's sex clench with desire.

"How was your day?" she asked.

"Long as well. Lots of meetings and several projects to oversee."

"Then I guess we both need some time to decompress and relax."

"I guess so. Why don't we try to do that now? Are you wearing what I left you?"

Melissa grinned that they knew very well what she was wearing but they were staying in character. "Yes. It's very lovely."

"Like you."

Melissa's face flushed. "Thank you."

There was a moment of silence, then soft music began to play. A sexy female voice began to sing, and Black let the song continue for another moment. Melissa listened to the words and knew Black had chosen this song specifically for her. The artist spoke to someone about giving up control, stepping away from what they'd always done, and not being afraid. That they would be safe in her hands.

"So, Mistress Heart, are you ready to decompress?"

"Yes."

With the sexy voice of the singer serenading them in the background, Black engaged in another first for Melissa, phone sex. Well, simulated phone sex since they technically weren't on the phone, but hearing Black describe touching themselves in the same way Melissa was touching herself, hearing their heavy breath of arousal, and then the moan of their orgasm just before Melissa's rushed through her body with such intensity that she dropped the phone and had to cover her own mouth to keep from crying out too loud. Lying in a daze of desire, it took Melissa a moment to realize Black was speaking to her.

"Hello, Mistress Heart, are you still with me?" they said breathily, as if they were still on the phone.

Melissa had just enough energy to move her arm to search for the receiver lying on the floor beside the sofa.

"Yes," she said, just as breathily.

"I'd say that was a very successful decompression. What about you?"

Melissa grinned. "I agree."

"You can hang up now." Black's voice came from right beside her.

Melissa blinked her eyes open to find Black kneeling beside the sofa, their clothes a bit disheveled, gracing her with a sexy smile. She slowly sat up and hung up the phone.

"Hello."

Black chuckled. "Hello." They sat beside her.

"So, this was a little something different?"

"Yes. Was it within reason?"

"Very."

Black turned to face Melissa. "By the way, I look forward to our sessions also. I think about them when I'm not here."

"Really?" Melissa shyly avoided their gaze.

"Yes. I was hoping to schedule them more frequently. Of course, that's if your schedule allows for it."

Melissa's heart skipped from the thought of being able to spend more time like this with Black. "How often were you thinking?"

"Every other week rather than once a month. I won't be traveling as much over the next few months, so my schedule is more flexible."

"If we keep your sessions as the last one of the evening, I'm sure we can work something out." Melissa dared to look up and meet Black's gaze. Their eyes held a dark intensity that made her want to promise them anything.

They smiled happily. "That works for me."

They stood and offered Melissa a hand. Melissa took it and stood.

"No need to walk me out, I know the way. I look forward to enjoying your company again in two weeks, Mistress Heart."

Black brought Melissa's hand to their lips and pressed a soft kiss on her knuckles then left her standing alone in the room holding her hand against her chest as if their kiss was a far more treasured gift than any of the actual gifts that they had brought her.

CHAPTER NINETEEN

Golden arrived at Charles de Gaulle Airport at six in the morning surprisingly rested. She purposely booked an overnight flight so that she could sleep and avoid jet lag trying to get adjusted to the time difference. Trish said she would be sending someone to pick her up so Golden headed to the baggage claim area for her luggage, then made her way to customs. Fortunately, she managed to breeze through customs after which she located the passenger pickup area and, among a group of drivers holding signs with names, found her ride. Pulling her two suitcases along behind her, Golden walked up to a young Black woman holding a sign with her name.

"Hello, I'm Golden Hughes."

The young woman's eyes widened in surprise. "Wow, you are gorgeous," she said with a soft French accent.

Golden smiled. "Thank you. What's your name?"

She smiled broadly, lowered the sign she was holding, and offered Golden her hand. "Camille. I will be your assistant and translator during your stay."

It was Golden's turn to be surprised. "Assistant? I didn't ask for one."

"Ms. Parker thought you would appreciate having someone to assist you and show you around. I was told that you once had family here and I've done some research so that I may be able to answer any questions you may have about the area in which she lived."

Golden was impressed. "That's very kind of you."

"It is my pleasure. I have family that came over from America during World War I that settled in Montmartre, so I've become a big history buff on the African American expats from that time."

"Well, I look forward to having your assistance."

Camille blushed prettily. Back in the day Golden would've leaned into her reaction with flirting, but she wasn't that same woman driven by the need for money and casual sex.

"I'll take one of your suitcases," Camille offered.

"Thank you." Golden handed over the smaller of the two that held her costumes, shoes and makeup. She had brought a few options to choose from wanting to get Jade's and Kendra's opinions on what look they would like for the show.

As they exited the terminal and made their way toward parking, Camille gave Golden a brief rundown of her schedule for the day.

"I'll be taking you to where your group is staying, Hôtel des Arts which is located right in the heart of Montmartre, so that you have an opportunity to freshen up and rest if you need to. At eleven I will collect you to escort you to Al Caratello for lunch with your group. After that your afternoon is free and I will be available to take you anywhere you'd like to go."

"Are you sure? I don't want to take up all your time unnecessarily. I traveled often with my previous job. I'm sure I can get around fine on my own."

Camille's expression became very serious. "No, I will not hear of it. I've been hired to assist you and be your guide and that is what I will do."

Golden chuckled. "Okay. Thank you."

Camille nodded in satisfaction. They arrived at the car, loaded her luggage into the trunk, then Camille walked to the back-passenger door and opened it for Golden.

"No, I will not have you driving me around like a chauffeur." She walked to the front passenger door, opened it, and climbed in.

Camille got in on the driver's side a moment later with an smile. "Americans are so laid-back."

Golden chuckled. "Oh, there are plenty that would've hopped into the back seat with no problem."

During the drive, Golden asked and learned quite a bit about Camille's family. One very interesting piece of information to Golden was that the American relative she spoke of, her great-grandmother, was an artist whose family moved to Montmartre from New Orleans to support their daughter's budding artistic career and escape the violence of the south. Golden thought it was too much of a coincidence to hope that the same artist that had painted her aunt Dinah's portrait would be Camille's great-grandmother. She decided to save that inquiry for later. As they reached the village of Montmartre, Golden fell in love with the ivy-covered buildings, cobbled streets, cafes, and street vendors.

"I feel like I've traveled back in time."

"It pretty much still looks the same way it did in our ancestors' time."

Golden opened the window, gazing eagerly out like she did when she was a little girl, and her family took their first trip to Disney World. "I can see why they chose to stay. It's utterly charming."

"It's even better when you tour it on foot. I look forward to showing you around."

"Do you live in Montmartre?"

Camille smiled. "I moved here over six months ago. The cottage that my great-grandmother owned while she lived here is still in the family. It's been a rental property for decades, but when the last tenant moved out, I asked my uncle, who was managing the property, if I could buy it. He sold it to me for two euros. Because of his kindness I was able to take the money I had planned to buy it with and renovate it. It still has the charm of the original cottage."

"It sounds nice."

They pulled up in front of a three-story building with front-facing windows on the upper levels, each with a shutter-framed-window balcony with a decorative wrought iron rail and overhanging basket of flowers. Like everything else she'd seen, the only way to describe it was charming. Other than the Sacre Coeur, one of Paris's major religious sites which sat atop a hill, there didn't seem to be any buildings taller than eight stories in the town. Camille assisted Golden with getting checked in, then left her on her own until lunch because she was double-parked.

Golden was told that she was on the same floor as Jade, Kendra, Trish, their band, and backup singers. As she made her way up to her room, she hoped that she didn't run into either Jade or Kendra since she was looking a bit disheveled after her flight. Fortunately, she didn't run into anyone and was very happy with her accommodation. The room was one with a balcony that faced the front of the hotel and larger than she expected with a large double bed, a marble top desk, a small café table with chairs, and a well-appointed bathroom with a comfortable-sized shower. Set on the little café table next to the balcony door was a bouquet of pink peonies in a vase, a bottle of champagne on ice, a champagne flute, and a box of macaroons. She would save the champagne for later after she had something to eat. Golden hadn't eaten since the dinner served on the flight, so she enjoyed a few of the cookies then unpacked. She hated the idea of digging through a suitcase every day to find something to wear so when she was going to stay somewhere for more than a few days Golden liked to make herself at home. After she chose a pair of jeans, a gold cashmere V-neck sweater, and a pair of denim walking shoes as her outfit for the day, she hung her costumes in the closet along with a few cocktail dresses she brought just in case she went someplace fancy, then placed the rest of her clothes in the dresser and her toiletries in the bathroom. Once that was complete, she stripped, took a long hot shower, moisturized, tied up her hair, and set her alarm for a quick nap.

❖

Golden heard ringing in the distance and couldn't figure out why there would be a bell ringing while she was cuddling in bed with Jade and Kendra. She didn't know how she ended up there, but one minute, she was at home getting ready for bed after practicing her routine for the show, and when she came out of the bathroom Jade and Kendra were waiting for her.

They didn't say a word, just pulled her between them and wrapped her in their arms. It was the most loved and safest she'd felt since her father had hugged her the day that she'd been accepted into AMDA, but that damn ringing wouldn't stop. Golden realized that it was her phone alarm, then she was no longer enclosed in the warmth of the Twins' bodies and awakened with a start.

Looking in confusion at her unfamiliar surroundings, it took Golden a moment to remember where she was. As her confusion cleared, she reached toward the nightstand for her phone and looked bleary-eyed toward the screen. She had a couple of hours before Camille would be back to take her to lunch. Golden felt more tired after her nap than she did when she arrived. Instead of napping she should've pulled out her laptop and done bookkeeping for Satin and Lace that she'd been putting off. She went to the bathroom, washed her face again, got dressed, and went downstairs to grab some coffee from the cart that had been set up in the lobby when she arrived. The coffee had been replaced with lemon water and juices, but the clerk gave her directions to a patisserie a short walk from the hotel.

When Golden arrived, she texted Camille to let her know where she was so that she could meet her there instead of the hotel. She did her best to ignore the tempting displays of pastries and ordered a café crème, an espresso with steamed milk and topped with a lot of foam. Golden considered sitting outside at one of the café tables, but since it was February there was still a nip in the air so she found a seat inside by the window so that she could people watch, one of her favorite things to do when she traveled. A half hour later she saw Camille crossing the street toward the patisserie and waved to get her attention when she entered. Camille's smile was bright and happy when she spotted Golden and hurried to her table.

Camille gave her an appreciative glance as she sat down across from her. "You look rested. The color of your sweater is beautiful against your skin tone and brings out the gold in your eyes."

"Thank you. You look as if you've had some good news."

"Oh, I have, for you. I found something very interesting, but I want to save it for after the lunch so that I can show it to you."

Golden's curiosity was piqued. "Okay. I can't wait to find out what it is."

"How were you able to resist the pastries?" Camille indicated Golden's empty coffee cup.

"You said we were going to an Italian restaurant, so I wanted to be sure to save room for pasta and dessert."

Camille chuckled. "Wise decision. Their panna cotta and tiramisu are decadent. If you prefer something a little lighter, they have refreshing fluted limoncello."

"I will keep all of those in mind."

"Wonderful. We can walk over now. It's nearby."

Camille wasn't exaggerating. The patisserie was just a little over a block up from the restaurant. Trish was already there, but Jade and Kendra hadn't arrived yet, which Golden was a little relieved as it gave her a moment to gather herself in preparation for seeing them in person after all this time.

Trish stood and pulled Golden into a bear hug. "It's good to finally meet you in person. I've heard so much about you from the Twins that I feel like I already know you."

"Is that good or bad?" Golden joked.

Trish laughed. "Oh, it's all good. They should be here any minute." She turned to Camille, greeting her with a handshake. "I see you got the schedule I sent. We'll go over the schedule for the rest of the week when Jade and Kendra get here which is why I asked that you join us since you'll be assisting Golden."

"I appreciate the thought and Camille is wonderful." Golden gave Camille a smile. "But I didn't need an assistant."

"Let's sit," Trish said. Once they were seated, she continued. "Jade and Kendra insisted that it would be helpful if you had someone familiar with the area and the history to guide you in finding information about your relative that lived here. Camille comes from a very reputable agency in Paris that offers translators, area guides, and administrative assistance to business travelers. I know you mentioned that you speak enough French to get by, but they wanted to make sure you didn't have any issues."

"You didn't mention you spoke French," Camille said.

"Not fluently. I learned because my friends and I traveled to St. Martin several times for vacation, and I thought it would be nice if at least one of us was able to communicate on the basic level if needed. Of course, I brushed up in the months leading to coming here so I was a little more fluent."

Camille nodded. "That's a good idea. I've noticed a lot more tourists have been doing that over the past few years. Not so much that translators like me aren't needed but enough to be appreciated by the locals."

Trish raised her hand to get the attention of a server. "How about we start with some wine. I don't know much about it except that I prefer something on the sweet side, so I'll leave it up to Miss Camille to order."

When their server arrived, Camille ordered a bottle each of pinot grigio, pinot grigio rosato, and Moscato D'asti Canelli moelleux which covered anyone who enjoyed a white, a red, and a sweet wine. As their server left, Golden saw Jade and Kendra enter, and she had butterflies in her belly. Jade was dressed in black jeans, a pink button-down shirt, and a black tank top. Two huge pink diamond studs sparkled in her lobes, and she had her bobbed hair pulled back into a ponytail. Kendra wore blue jeans with a baby blue crew neck sweater and a pair of blue sapphire studs. They looked casual but put together and even more attractive than she remembered, especially when they smiled broadly at her as they walked toward the table. Trish stood first, offering each a hand and a half hug. Trish then introduced them to Camille. All the while, Golden avoided looking at either of them, intently staring at the menu until a shadow darkened the page. She gazed up to find Jade standing beside her looking unsure. To see the usually cocky and confident woman appear as if she were afraid to even speak to Golden saddened her. She stood and opened her arms and Jade gently wrapped hers around Golden in an embrace that said more than words ever could.

"It's so good to see you," Jade whispered in her ear.

Golden smiled. "You too."

"Yo! You aren't the only one happy to see her," Kendra said impatiently.

Jade stepped out of Golden's embrace to give Kendra a chance to greet her. Golden barely had time to look at Kendra before she was wrapped up in her arms and lifted a few inches off the ground.

"Girl, you don't know how much you've been missed."

Golden grunted. "I think I have a good idea."

"Bro, you're gonna squeeze the life out of her before we even get to spend five minutes with her," Jade teased Kendra.

Golden's feet touched the ground, but Kendra's arms stayed around her waist for another moment before releasing her. There was some maneuvering of seating at their round table, but in the end, Golden was seated between Jade and Kendra with Trish and Camille grinning knowingly across from them. The wine was brought over shortly after everyone was settled and preferences were poured for each by their server. A basket of bread and a bottle of olive oil were next, then the server disappeared until they were ready to order.

"How was your flight?" Jade asked Golden.

"It was good. I slept through most of it." Golden grinned.

"Yeah, it was smart of you to take an overnight. That's what we do. Lessens the jet lag. What about your room?" Kendra asked.

"Very comfortable and the view is amazing. Thank you."

They both nodded with satisfaction.

"Now that we've got the small talk over, we should order and get down to business. We've got a lot to cover," Trish said.

Camille translated the menu for Trish, Jade, and Kendra, but Golden was able to read enough to figure out that she wanted risotto gamberoni which was risotto with shrimp. Once everyone decided what they wanted, Trish signaled their server, their orders were given, and Trish pulled her tablet from her backpack.

"Okay, here's the schedule. Today you're free to relax, be a tourist, and even sleep in tomorrow morning, but we have a walk-through at the venue in the afternoon at two, then the stage crew will meet us there to go over setup. We'll have our first rehearsal as a group after that, then break for the day at six. After that, we have two more full days before the concert to work any kinks out. The last day of rehearsals we'll meet with wardrobe, do a dress rehearsal, and call it a day around three so you guys are well rested for performance day. I'll send a more detailed schedule to you all this afternoon. Does that timing work for everyone?"

Golden nodded. "I'm good."

"So are we," Kendra said.

Trish smiled and stored her tablet back into her backpack then picked up her glass of wine. "To a successful show and hoping those entertainers that came before us to this beautiful town are blessing us with their pride and talent."

Everyone raised their glasses and touched them to Trish's with cheers of agreement. The food arrived shortly after, and Golden's stomach growled loudly as her entrée was placed in front of her.

"Someone's hungry," Jade teased her.

"I haven't eaten since dinner on the flight."

Kendra bumped her with her shoulder. "Ignore her. Bon appetit." She raised her fork, which already had a mouthful of linguine twirled around it, in salute and shoved it in her mouth, moaning with pleasure as she chewed.

Golden chuckled and dug into her own entrée. It was moan-worthy. As hungry as she was, she managed to take her time eating to enjoy the rich flavors.

"What are your plans for the rest of the afternoon?" Jade asked.

"I believe Camille is taking me on a tour based on my aunt Dinah's time living here."

"Oh, cool, mind if we tag along?"

"Dude, let Golden have her time. We're going to be seeing each other all day every day for the rest of the week, she doesn't need us invading her alone time," Kendra said.

If it weren't for Jade and Kendra, Golden wouldn't even be here so she didn't see any reason not to invite them. "If Camille doesn't mind the extra people, I'd be happy to have you tag along."

"The more the merrier," Camille said.

"Are you sure?" Kendra's sexy smile had Golden wishing they were doing something more private after lunch.

She gazed back down at her plate to slice a large shrimp. "Positive. Trish, you're also welcome to join us."

"Thanks, but a friend of mine back home connected me to a friend of theirs that lives in the Marais area who's going to meet me."

They chatted throughout their lunch about the show as well as the other performances taking place at different locations throughout Montmartre celebrating its rich African American expat history. The whole time, Golden somehow managed to barely focus on the conversation as Jade's and Kendra's nearness played havoc with her senses. Their legs rubbing alongside hers. Their arms or hands brushing hers on the table. The way they gazed at her when she spoke, like they hung on to her every word. She almost sighed with relief when lunch came to an end. After saying their good-byes to Trish, she, Jade, and Kendra turned their attention to Camille.

"We're all yours," Golden said.

Camille looked at the three of them with a wistful sigh. "If only."

The three of them chuckled, but Golden noticed Jade and Kendra both sounded a bit nervous, which amused her.

"The first stop on our Dinah Hampton History Tour is my place where I found something very interesting in my great-grandmother's archive of work."

"Really? How exciting." Maybe Camille's great-grandmother was connected to Golden's aunt Dinah. She tamped down the hope that it was true so that she wouldn't be disappointed if there was no connection.

Camille said her home was a twenty-minute walk from where they were. As they strolled along the cobblestone streets, Camille pointed out historical landmarks and buildings as well as its African American history.

"After the Great War, lower Montmartre was known as Harlem-on-the-Seine. African American soldiers chose to stay in Paris after the war to escape the ongoing racist violence in America. They introduced Paris to jazz music, and war-weary Parisians dove headfirst into the free-spirited music. When the soldiers in Paris wrote back to America about the freedom and acceptance they experienced in Paris as well as Parisians' love of jazz, African American musicians, artists, writers, and dancers flocked to Paris in what was known as the Jazz Migration. Lower Montmartre was home to jazz greats like Arthur Briggs, Maceo Jefferson, Adelaide Hall, and of course, Josephine Baker's club Chez Josephine." Camille stopped in front of a dress shop gazing at them with a sad smile.

"For sixteen years, Montmartre was the Harlem of Paris, the mecca of Black and Afro-Caribbean culture and jazz music, then it all ended with the Great Depression in America which affected American tourism, in turn, affecting the Parisian entertainment industry. There was also the arrival of Germans in Paris. I'm sure you can guess how that affected African Americans living here."

Golden's grandmother had given her a few boxes of letters that her mother had kept, written by her sister Dinah. "My aunt and her partner, Celine, stayed in Paris for as long as they could until the Nazis began banning African Americans from hotels, restaurants, and theaters and throwing Blacks into prison camps. It also didn't help that they were gay, which if word had gotten out, they would have been captured as well. She had to close her dance school and she and Celine followed their friend Ada Smith, who had once owned the nightclub Chez Bricktop to Cannes. They stayed there until the war was over and moved back to Montmartre, but she said it was never the same after that."

Camille nodded. "Sadly, other than the stories passed down, there is no trace of the African American community that had lived here. It's why my family was so determined to keep my great-grandmother's house in the family. Our roots are just as much here in Montmartre as they are in New Orleans." She gazed pointedly at Golden. "Just as with your aunt Dinah. I know I said the first stop was my home, but I have a little surprise for you."

Camille grinned and indicated the store they stood before with a quick head tilt. "This was where your aunt's dance studio used to be."

Golden looked from Camille to the shop and back with surprise. "Seriously?"

Camille chuckled. "Seriously. I spoke with the shop owner yesterday and she was thrilled to know that you would be stopping by."

Golden's heartbeat quickened. She was going to be walking through the same door that her aunt walked through every day over eighty years ago to teach her students to dance.

Camille held the door open for her. "After you."

Golden took a tentative step forward then stopped. She felt a warm hand grasp hers and turned to find Jade standing beside her.

"I think Dinah is thrilled to know that one of her descendants is here to walk in her footsteps. To see her life through their eyes."

With tears blurring her vision, Golden gave Jade a grateful smile. Jade gave her hand a quick squeeze then released it and stepped back. Dinah looked at the large picture window with a display of three mannequins dressed in soft pastel colors looking as if they stood in a field of spring blooms. For a second, she wondered if during the time Dinah's school was here, if the window had been left free of displays so that passersby could see what was going on inside. She took a deep breath and continued forward, walking up the steps and through the door Camille still held open for her. It was a very nice shop, but there was nothing about it that told of its history as a dance studio.

"Bonjour."

Golden turned to meet the smiling face of a tall willowy young woman with a lavender pixie haircut, lavender floral overalls, a yellow tank top, a nose ring, and earrings from her lobe up the entire outer area of both ears.

"Bonjour," Golden said.

The woman's face lit up even brighter when Camille entered behind Golden. They greeted each other affectionately and chattered away in French. They spoke so quickly Golden only managed to pick up a few words including her name. They walked toward Golden.

"Golden, this is Felice. Her mother owns the shop. Felice helps every now and then. Felice, this is Golden, Jade, and Kendra."

"Hello, welcome to Montmartre," Felice said in heavily accented English.

Handshakes were given all around, then Felice grasped Golden's hand and pulled her toward the counter. "My mother and I found these things in the basement when we bought the shop five years ago." She pulled a hat box from underneath, set it on the counter, and slid it toward Golden. "There are other things down there as well. A trunk full of costumes, a dozen hat boxes, show posters, and a rack of dresses. We asked the previous owner about it, and she'd said she had no idea they were down there."

"From what I could find out, the shop had been in your aunt's name until the Nazi invasion. After that it was seized by them and never returned to her. The next owner converted it from the dance studio to a shop and that's what it's been since then. Felice and her mother found everything she described by accident in a hidden room downstairs during renovation. They held onto everything hoping someone would claim them someday," Camille further explained.

"And here you are," Felice said happily.

"Have you been down there to look at it all?" Golden asked Camille.

Camille shook her head. "I wanted you to be the first."

Golden's hands trembled as she reached to open the hat box. Inside were two small stacks of black-and-white photographs tied with a satin ribbon, a rolled yellowing paper, and two pairs of ballet slippers. She carefully unrolled the paper first. It was a sketch of what must have been the inspiration for plans for the dance studio. It even showed people walking past the large picture window just as she imagined it. She passed the drawing to Camille who shared it with the others and picked up one of the stacks of photos. There were pictures of young girls dressed in leotards and tutus stretching along the ballet bar, caught in a dance pose, or just laughing and being silly. These were her aunt's students, many of them young girls of color. There were even similar photos of adult women that her aunt must have taught as well.

Golden passed those along and picked up the other stack. This was when she was given the gift of her aunt Dinah just the way she'd always imagined her. Smiling, bold and happy amid a group of people, but these weren't just any people. Golden recognized Josephine Baker, Ella Fitzgerald, Langston Hughes, and many other famous faces of that time. There were photographs of her on stage, instructing a class, and the last few of Dinah sitting and looking as if she held the worry of the world on her shoulders as she gazed contemplatively out the studio's picture window. In all the photographs there wasn't one with Celine, which was probably because she was the one behind the camera. Dinah had mentioned in one of her letters of Celine receiving the gift of a camera from a fashion photographer she worked with while she mentored with Coco Chanel and how photography had become a hobby for her.

"These are awesome," Jade said in wonder.

"This is more than I would've ever wished to find while I'm here." Golden set aside the photo of her aunt in the window from the second stack and placed the rest back in the box.

"Would you like to see the rest?" Felice asked.

"Yes, if it's not too much trouble."

"No trouble at all. Camille can take you down."

"Thank you."

Golden, Jade, and Kendra followed Camille to the back of the shop then down a flight of stairs. The basement was well lit with shelving and racks filled with inventory for the store. Camille walked to the far wall to a rack on wheels with plastic covered dresses hanging from them.

"Jade and Kendra, would you mind assisting me?" Camille asked.

Jade and Kendra stepped forward to help Camille move the rack. After it was set aside, she pressed the wall and a hidden door popped open.

"Now that is cool," Jade said.

"Many Parisians helped to hide their Jewish neighbors by building hidden rooms in their homes and businesses. This may have been what this was used for," Camille explained.

Jade frowned. "Wow. Kinda like Europe's version of the Underground Railroad."

"Exactly." Camille opened the hidden door wider, and Golden was surprised to see a room the size of a large walk-in closet.

Along the back wall was a clothing rack with eight garment bags hanging from it, two stacks of hat boxes, a large steamer trunk, and what looked to be a few framed posters. Golden got a chill up her spine that had nothing to do with the cool temperature of the room as she slowly walked toward the treasure trove of her aunt's life. She unzipped one of the garment bags to find a beautifully beaded gown.

"Wow. Did your aunt make this?" Camille asked.

Golden smiled. "No. It was more than likely Celine, her partner. She was a very talented designer. I'm sure the hat boxes are full of hats that she made as well. She had a little boutique here and designed and created fashions for many of the rich and famous of Paris."

"What was her full name?" Camille asked.

"Celine Montre."

Camille gazed at her in confusion. "I wonder why I have never heard of her?" She pulled her phone out of her pocket.

"You probably won't find anything about her. From what I was told and gauged from my aunt's letters to my great-grandmother, Celine wasn't much for the spotlight. Coco Chanel herself attempted to sway her to work for her once her mentorship was complete, but after spending her entire life living the way her family and society thought she should live it, Celine was determined to do what she wanted to do however she chose to do it." Golden walked past the clothing rack and hat boxes toward the trunk.

"That was very brave of her for such a time in history. Do you mind if I look through the others?" Camille asked.

"Not at all."

Golden wasn't ignoring Celine's part in her aunt's life, but something was pulling her toward the trunk. She unhooked the latch and carefully opened the lid. There were what looked to be stacks of satin parcels. She unwrapped one of the top ones to find a beaded bra top, matching tap shorts and a scented sachet. She turned it over to find the embroidered CM that she knew would be there. This was also Celine's contribution to Dinah's history. She had custom-made all of Dinah's performance costumes. Golden lifted the top to her nose, closed her eyes, and inhaled a hint of lavender. She felt tears roll down her cheeks even before she opened her eyes to find her vision a watery blur. She felt, rather than saw Jade and Kendra sit on either side of her.

Kendra rubbed slow circles in the center of her back. "Are you okay?"

Jade gently wiped away a tear with a knuckle. "We can leave you alone for a bit if you need it."

Golden was so grateful to them for bringing her to Paris. "I'm fine. It's just that I've felt a connection to Dinah for so long that to finally hold an actual piece of her life in my hands like this is overwhelming. Thank you so much for inviting me to be a part of your show. I had always dreamed of coming to Paris. Of walking in my aunt's footsteps through her letters, but it just didn't seem right without my father who had encouraged my connection to her."

"These dresses and hats are fabulous. How do I look?" Camille said excitedly.

Golden looked up to find her wearing a coral linen cloche style hat with a chocolate brown band, and a rhinestone and pheasant feather brooch. It complemented her heart-shaped face. "I like it and insist you take it in appreciation for helping me discover this treasure trove."

Camille's eyes widened with surprise. "This is far too priceless to just give away."

"Consider it a tip for your services. Besides, I think Celine would love it on you and insist you take it."

Camille opened the camera app on her phone, posed and took a selfie, then reviewed it with a happy smile. "I do look good in it."

Golden chuckled. "I also insist you find a dress as well."

"You are too generous."

"Or I just can't afford the cost of shipping all this back home," Golden said, partly joking.

"What about giving them to a consignment shop to sell?" Kendra suggested.

"I'm sure Felice or her mother would know someone," Camille said.

"It's amazing how well all of this has stood the test of time," Golden said.

"It's probably because it's fairly cool down here and with it being sealed up behind the hidden door it's been stored in its own little preservation chamber." Jade surprised even Kendra with her observation.

She noticed all their amazed expressions and rolled her eyes. "I read."

Golden gazed back down at the trunk. She could spend all afternoon going through what was in there, but she wanted to see what Camille had found with her great-grandmother's things. She rewrapped the costume, and as she placed it back in the trunk, she noticed the edge of an envelope peeking out from a pocket underneath the lid. She pulled it out, then closed the lid and the clasp.

"What's that?" Jade asked.

"Give her a chance to open it," Kendra said.

Golden held back a grin. They seemed to live for picking at each other. "I think I'll wait until I get back to the hotel. Right now, I want to see what you found, Camille."

"Oh, yes, that's right. I was so caught up in what was found here that I completely forgot. Yes, let's go."

They headed back upstairs, Camille carrying her hat box in her arms as if she were afraid someone would snatch it back.

"Did you find everything okay?" Felice asked.

"Yes. Thank you so much. I'll be here for the week, but at the end I would like to come back to arrange to have the trunk, posters, and box of photographs shipped home. Would that be okay?"

"Of course! You can meet my mother then. I called her while you were downstairs, and she was very excited to hear that we found the rightful owners."

"I hope it's not too much to ask, but I was wondering if you knew of a consignment shop that we could sell the dresses and hats through? I think the designer would want them to stay here and go to homes of people who would appreciate them."

"I know the perfect shop. It's Sissi's Corner on Rue des Tournelles. It is a Black-owned business. She loves period clothing, and I think she would be honored to be the caretaker of such historical items. I will call her and see if she can come by the shop to meet you on your return."

Golden offered Felice her hand. "Thank you so much."

Felice took her hand, but instead of shaking it she pulled Golden toward her and placed a kiss on each cheek. "You are very welcome. I will see you soon."

As they left the shop Golden placed her hand atop her bag where the photograph of Dinah and the envelope lay within. She half listened as Camille, Jade, and Kendra chatted excitedly about their findings at the shop, injecting comments when appropriate but all the while wondering what was in the envelope. They arrived at Camille's less than a ten-minute walk later.

"This is a great space," Golden said as they walked into the cozy open space.

Camille smiled proudly. "Thank you. It was originally a single story. I added a bedroom, closet, and bathroom on the second floor, kept the open layout of the first floor and turned the main bath that was down here to a half bath and extra storage. Why don't you have a seat in the garden while I make some tea and grab what we came here for."

Golden, Jade, and Kendra went out the French doors Camille indicated. It was a cute garden with a small seating area and a three-level raised planter with a mixture of flowers and vegetables.

"So, how are you feeling about all of this?" Jade asked Golden.

Golden sat down with a sigh. She didn't know if she was weary or just overwhelmed. "It's a lot all at once, but it's good. I went from only seeing Aunt Dinah in videos and reading about her life in letters or through stories handed down in the family to practically walking in her path and holding real objects from that life in my hand. I just wish my father had lived long enough to experience it."

Kendra reached over and took her hand. "He's with you now. He and your aunt. They probably had a hand in getting you here and connecting you with Camille."

Golden gave Kendra's hand a squeeze. "With a little help from you two. I'll never be able to thank you enough."

"Seeing you happy is all the thanks we need," Jade said with an affectionate pat on her shoulder.

They sat quietly enjoying the peace of Camille's little garden haven. When she finally joined them, Camille rolled out a tea cart then stepped back inside and returned with a medium-sized canvas. She gazed at Golden with a big smile, but her eyes sparkled with unshed tears.

"When I was hired to help you and learned that you had family here, I would have never guessed that there would be any connection between us. Then after I dropped you off at the hotel yesterday, I went to see my uncle who is our family archivist to see if he had anything that I could use to help locate any more information on your aunt. I told him her name and found out that Dinah and my great-grandmother Bridgette were friends."

Had her intuition been correct that Camille's aunt was the artist who painted Dinah's portraits that her grandmother had promised to leave to her? She looked at the canvas Camille was holding in front of her.

"It turns out that Dinah posed for many of my great-grandmother's paintings. This," Camille offered the painting to Golden, "is just one of a dozen featuring your aunt stored away in a storage unit full of paintings she never showed or sold."

Golden stood and accepted the canvas from Camille and her breath caught at the image of a nude Dinah and Celine. Dinah lay with her head in Celine's lap. They were gazing so lovingly at each other she felt as if she were intruding on a very intimate moment. Bridgette had captured the love between them perfectly, as if it were one of the photographs found at the former dance studio.

"Wow," Jade and Kendra said in unison.

Golden gazed up at Camille who no longer held back her tears. She looked toward the painting with pride. "My family has two of Bridgette's portraits of my aunt. We never knew who the artist was. Dinah had sent her aunt and her sister the portraits as a gift."

Camille covered her mouth with a gasp. "My great-grandmother kept meticulous records of her paintings in a journal. She wrote the name of the model, the title of the painting, if it sold, and how much it sold for. There are a few missing from her inventory that we assumed she gave as gifts because there's no record of them ever having been sold. There are two missing titled *Dancer one* and *Dancer two*. Your aunt is listed as the model for both. I had never seen this journal until today or I would've made the connection sooner. There's also a third missing titled *Sadness* with just *C* under the model's name. Do you think that could be Celine?"

"It must be. My grandmother was sent my great-aunt's belongings upon her death, but there was nothing of Celine's there. She didn't have any family to leave anything to. Her parents had cut her off when she declared her love for Dinah and the only other family she had, an aunt, passed on long before Celine did. Since she was an only child there were no nieces or nephews to leaving anything to."

"So many families were torn apart by bias toward their sexuality back then. It may not happen as often but it's still that way today. My great-grandmother was bisexual, which is probably the only reason I'm here today, but she never wanted to marry, she just wanted children," Camille said.

Golden gazed back down at the painting of Dinah and her lifelong love Celine and remembered that Dinah was about her age when she met Celine. It gave her hope that if her aunt could find love during a time where their love was illegal, then she could too.

CHAPTER TWENTY

Melissa raised the flogger in her hand and brought it down with a loud *thwack* across her client's already reddened butt cheek. "Have you had enough?"

The woman gave a vigorous shake of her head, the only part of her body that she could move as she was face-down with all her limbs strapped to a spanking bench.

"No, Mistress, just a few more please," she whined.

Melissa gave the clock on the wall a quick glance and realized that her client still had ten minutes left in her session. She had never been so ready to end a session early before. She always made sure to give her clients every second they paid for, but today was different because all she kept thinking about was her next and last appointment of the day. Tonight was her third bi-weekly appointment with Black and she was anxious to see them, but rushing her current client out wouldn't make the time go by any faster so she focused on her task at hand. When the red light above the door flashed signifying the end of the session, Melissa held back a sigh of relief as she assisted the woman out of her restraints.

"Thank you, Mistress," she said happily.

Melissa impatiently waited to give the woman enough time to walk to the member locker rooms then peeked out the playroom door and hurried down the hall and upstairs. She had a half hour until Black's appointment and wanted to quickly shower since they no longer requested the showers from Melissa. Their sessions had become less kinky voyeurism and more like dates. Black would still arrive in the room before her to get settled in the voyeur room, still left gifts for her as her secret admirer, but instead of Melissa putting on a sexy performance, she would strip down to her bra and panties, curl up in the bed, her secret admirer would "call" her, ask her about her day and ask her to read whatever book of poetry, erotica, or even romance they gifted her with. They were always sapphic books, something

Melissa had very little of in her library until Black introduced her to the genre.

When she arrived at the dressing room, Hyacinth was packing up their bag for the night.

"Heading out?" Melissa asked as she began shedding the corset and leather gear she wore.

"Yes. Meeting with Black tonight?" Hyacinth asked.

Melissa couldn't hide her smile. "Yes."

"Are you sure you don't want to know what I see?"

Melissa grasped Hyacinth's hand as she walked past them to the showers. "Positive. Have a good night, Hyacinth."

Melissa believed in Hyacinth's visions, but that didn't mean she wanted to know what was in store for herself or her time with Black. She wanted to just enjoy whatever was happening for as long as she could. She wasn't foolish enough to think that anything could come of these sessions that could continue outside of the Red Dahlia. Despite how Vivienne's romance with her husband began, Melissa didn't see that happening to her. What happened in the Red Dahlia stayed in the Red Dahlia. After a quick shower and changing into her usual attire for her sessions with Black, Melissa reapplied her lipstick and was checking her appearance in the mirror when Shari's voice came over the intercom. Melissa smiled at her reflection, no longer needing to tap into Mistress Heart for her time with Black. They kept their masks on and maintained their host and client appearances, but Melissa found herself being more herself than Mistress Heart during their sessions.

She stepped into Playroom Eight and found Black not waiting for her in the voyeur room but sitting on the sofa looking sexy as hell in a black deep V-neck tee, black jeans, and biker boots. They stood as she walked into the room and closed the door.

"Good evening, Mistress Heart."

"Good evening, Black. Is everything all right?"

Black smiled charmingly. "Everything is perfect. You're perfect. Unfortunately, I won't be able to stay for our entire session. I have a business emergency that I need to fly out on a red-eye for tonight, but I didn't want to leave without seeing you and giving you this." They offered her an envelope.

Melissa was disappointed about not being able to have their time together, but she smiled and accepted the envelope. She opened it to find a reservation for a villa in St. Kitts.

She gazed at Black in confusion. "What's this?"

"You mentioned that you and your friends were planning to go to the St. Kitts Music Festival, and I have a vacation home there so I'm gifting use of it to you and your friends to stay."

Melissa shook her head. "I can't accept this. It's too much."

What she didn't say was that it was also too personal of a gift. The books, lingerie, champagne, and chocolates were all gifts that Melissa could accept as Mistress Heart without it spilling into her personal life, but this, luxury accommodations for a vacation with her girls, crossed the line for her.

"With everything you've been sharing with me during this experience, I don't think it's enough. Besides, it didn't cost me anything since I own it. You'd be doing me a favor because it would be sitting there empty anyway as I usually don't go to St. Kitts during the music festival. The peace and serenity that I seek when I do go to escape is pretty much gone that weekend."

A thought occurred to her. Rose had once been offered an all-expense paid vacation from a client in exchange for sexual favors. She had walked out in the middle of the session, and he was banned from the Red Dahlia for life. She hoped this wasn't what Black was doing. "And what more are you expecting in exchange for this gift?"

Black shook their head. "I don't expect anything other than what we've been doing. I'm not here looking for sex. Not to brag, but I could get that anywhere. I'm only here for your company, that's all. The house is there, you can choose to use it or not. There will be no repercussions if you don't. It's totally up to you."

She gazed down at the envelope, seriously considering giving it back to them because despite the sincerity she heard in their tone, she felt as if this gift was leading to something more intimate between them that she honestly wasn't as averse to happening as she should be.

Melissa gave them a hesitant smile. "Thank you."

Black looked pleased that she'd accepted the gift. "Well, I have to go, but I'll be back in time for our next appointment."

"Have a safe trip."

Black lifted their hand, their gaze soft as they tenderly cupped Melissa's cheek. "I'll be thinking of you the whole time."

Melissa was caught up in the spell of Black's dark gaze, willing them to kiss her while also hoping that they didn't because she knew that she wouldn't have the strength or desire stop them.

"Good night, Mistress Heart." Black brushed their fingers along Melissa's cheek as they stepped away and left her standing alone and aching in the middle of the room.

❖

"Girl, this shit sounds like something straight out of a romance novel," Zoe said.

"I thought my situation was complicated, but it's a kiddie ride compared to the roller coaster you're on," Golden said.

It was six in the morning New York time and noon in Paris, and Melissa was on a video call with Zoe and Golden that they had scheduled the previous day to hear about Golden's Parisian adventures. Instead, it turned into Melissa story hour when Zoe remembered that she'd had her appointment with Black and asked how it had gone.

Melissa sighed dejectedly. "After the way they looked at me before they left, I can't possibly accept their gift."

"Uh, yes you can. They said it was for your girls' trip, which meant it was a gift for all of us, and Zoe and I will gladly accept it if you don't want it. We'll find a nice hotel for you to stay."

Melissa couldn't help but laugh. She loved Golden so much. She always knew how to keep Melissa from going off the deep end.

"What she said," Zoe said in agreement.

"Well, since I have the reservation and the house info, y'all won't get far without me so I guess I'll have to accept it now."

Golden clapped happily. "Nice! Now that we have a place to stay for free, we'll have more money for the necessities like food and alcohol."

"Don't forget spa services," Zoe added.

Melissa shook her head. "Are we planning on going to any of the performances? We still need to buy tickets."

Golden waved dismissively. "I got that covered. I'm getting VIP Experience Passes for each of us. We won't have to do a damn thing but enjoy the shows, eat good food, and drink ourselves stupid for all three nights."

"Melissa, how long do we get the villa?"

"For that whole week and weekend."

"Okay, if you don't want Black, I'll take them," Zoe said.

"Excuse me?" Danice said in the background.

Melissa snickered. "Doh! Busted!"

Zoe gazed away from the camera attempting to look all innocent. "Babe, you know I was just joking. Black's money couldn't hold a candle to your cooking."

Next Zoe's eyes widened just before she ducked out of the way of a pillow that flew over her head.

Melissa laughed out loud. "That's what you get."

Golden was cracking up as well. Zoe looked back at the camera with amusement.

"You're messed up for laughing at my misery."

Melissa snorted. "Misery. You have a beautiful, wonderful woman who simply adores you that cooks like a Michelin Star chef living upstairs and you're miserable? I must be doing something wrong."

Zoe chuckled. "Yeah, she does adore me, doesn't she."

Golden rolled her eyes. "Bragging doesn't look good on you."

"Anyway, Golden, how are things going with the Twins?"

"It's actually going well. They're all business when it comes to their shows so that's where their focus has been. Today is the dress rehearsal and working out a few kinks on staging, but I think it's going to be such a great show. I told you they're livestreaming it, right?"

"Yes. Ms. Carlin is having a watch party at the school but only for family, friends, and students eighteen and older. Anyone younger than that has to come with a parent or guardian because of your sexy content," Melissa told her.

"Yeah, she told me about it yesterday."

"What about the search for more information on your aunt?" Zoe asked.

"Nothing new since finding out Camille's great-grandmother was the artist of the portraits of Dinah. Along with that and finding the location of her former dance studio, all the pictures, costumes, and Celine's dresses and hats, there isn't much more to really find. I've got her whole story from those things and the items and stories from my family. The big mystery now is where Celine's personal effects were sent and what's in the letter I found in the trunk."

Melissa gazed at Golden in surprise. "Girl, you still haven't opened it?"

"What's holding you back?" Zoe asked.

Golden shrugged, with such a sad look on her face. "I feel like once I do that chapter will be closed. After all these years of envisioning Dinah's life and my and my father's mutual connection to her, I don't want it to be over."

Melissa felt for her. She knew Golden still felt the loss of her father just as strongly as the day he died. She couldn't imagine such a loss, but she also knew that Golden was keeping his spirit alive in how she lived her life. Nothing could break that connection.

"Golden, as long as you continue to carry the love you have for both your father and Dinah, nothing will be closed. You carrying on their legacy is keeping them alive and I'm sure they're smiling down on you with enough love and pride to last beyond a lifetime." Melissa hoped that would make her feel better.

Golden smiled. "Thanks, Mel. I always told you that you should've been a therapist."

Melissa chuckled. "What kind of therapist would I be with all the issues I got going on."

"Like all these therapists out there got their shit together. Most of them are probably going to therapy also," Zoe said.

Melissa laughed. "You're probably right."

"Well, ladies, I've gotta go. I have an appointment at the dress shop to make arrangements for shipping Dinah's belongings and meet with the woman from the consignment shop about Celine's dresses and hats."

"Okay. We can't wait to see the show. Break a leg," Melissa said.

"Yeah. Show them that they may have the Moulin Rouge, but we've got the famous Dinah Hampton's niece ready to blow them all out of the water," Zoe said.

Golden laughed. "Thanks, guys. Talk to you soon."

After their call, Melissa walked over to her work bag and pulled out the reservation from Black. There was nothing on it to tell her who their real identity was. She made herself a cup of coffee, looked up the resort where the villa was located, and almost spit out the sip she had taken.

The resort wasn't like a typical resort, it was more like a neighborhood with cookie-cutter but gorgeous two-story homes sitting within walking distance from the beach. The house had a formal living room, dining room, entertainment room and a home chef's dream kitchen. The back patio ran the length of the house with an outdoor kitchen, dining area, pool, and a studio style pool house. On the second floor were three bedrooms with ensuite baths and access to a second-floor deck with views of the ocean and surrounding mountains. This wasn't a villa; it was a damn mansion in paradise. It made Melissa even more curious about who Black really was.

❖

Zoe walked up behind Danice, wrapped her arms around her waist, and kissed the nape of her neck. "Come back to bed."

"Nope. You know I need to be at the center by eight for the cooking class. Unless you could get the mysterious Black to teach it instead." Danice smirked at Zoe over her shoulder.

Zoe chuckled. "Even if I was interested in Black, which I absolutely am not, they're obviously obsessed with Mel. Hell, they're paying a thousand dollars a month just to spend a few hours with her."

Danice passed a cinnamon roll she'd been frosting back to Zoe. "Do you think they'll ever reveal themselves to each other? Maybe even fall in love?"

Zoe took the roll, stepped away from Danice to grab a napkin, then leaned against the island licking gooey frosting from her fingers. "I don't think Mel would know what to do if Black revealed themselves and their undying love for her. She'd probably run for the hills."

Danice turned, holding her own cinnamon roll. "I don't know. From how she talks about Black, I think she's falling for them as much as they're falling for her."

"You're such a romantic." That was one of the many endearing things about Danice. Despite what Malik had put her through and her devastating losses from her miscarriages, she still managed to put a positive spin on almost every situation.

Danice set her roll down and stepped toward Zoe. "No." She plucked Zoe's half-eaten roll from her fingers and set it on the counter. "I just want to see your friends as happy as us." She grabbed Zoe's hands and placed them on her hips.

Zoe quirked at brow. "I thought you had to go to work."

Danice plucked a bit of frosting from the corner of Zoe's lips and licked it off her finger. "I think I can spare another fifteen minutes," she said seductively.

Zoe loved how bold she'd become over the past few months. "Well, in that case, we better hurry." She kept her hands on Danice's hips as she walked her backwards out of the kitchenette toward the bed.

Well after Danice had left, Zoe sat downstairs in her apartment looking in awe at the link Melissa had sent to her and Golden for the resort home they were staying in.

"Wow, that looks awesome. Is that your next trip with Aunt Mel and Aunt Golden?" Kiara said, coming up behind her and looking over her shoulder.

"Yes, but a friend is loaning it to us because I can't imagine, even with Golden's small fortune that we could afford to get something like this ourselves. It may be a resort, but these homes are individually owned vacation homes for the rich and famous. Danice made cinnamon buns. They're on the counter."

"Nice!"

Kiara kissed Zoe on the cheek then hurried to the kitchen. A few moments later, she sat beside Zoe on the sofa.

"Mom."

"Yes."

"I owe you an apology."

Zoe closed her laptop and gazed curiously at Kiara. "For what?"

"Last month I kinda went off on you about dating Danice. I was wrong to do that. I was acting like a spoiled kid and should just trust that you know what you're doing. Besides, the way she told her ex off was enough proof for me that she was over him."

Zoe wrapped an arm around Kiara's shoulder. "Thank you for that, honey. That was very mature of you."

Kiara peeked over at her. "Mature enough to go to the music festival with you guys?"

Zoe gave her a pat on the shoulder. "Nope, but nice try." She grinned and stood. "What you can do since you don't have school today is clean your room. I'm going down to the salon. Come by when you finish, so we can pick up some groceries."

Kiara sighed with exasperation. "Yes, ma'am."

Zoe placed her laptop in her backpack, then left to walk to the salon. Technically, she was supposed to be taking the day off, so she didn't have any clients, but she noticed the stock of Hair For You inventory was getting low which meant Erica, the receptionist, hadn't placed the order with the warehouse last week like Zoe had asked her to do. She was already interviewing candidates to replace her because as personable as the girl was, Zoe didn't have the patience to walk her through practically every administrative thing she asked Erica to do. She turned the corner onto the block where the salon was and was surprised to see Malik standing out in front. For a moment she considered turning around and going back home, but he spotted her and waved. Zoe slowed her pace, walking toward him cautiously. He looked tired with dark circles beneath his eyes. His hair was lackluster compared to when she'd last seen him a month ago, and his clothes hung loosely from him.

"What can I do for you, Malik?"

He gave her a tentative smile. "So, you do know who I am."

"Yes, and I assume since you're here that you know who I am. Now, what can I do for you?"

"Danice won't return my calls. Her mother wouldn't give me her new address, but she suggested I try here since you're friends with her."

Friends? Is that what Danice was telling her family she was? She'd met Danice's sister who was aware that they were dating, but it was obvious that she was the only person in her family that knew.

"What makes you think I'm going to tell you where she lives?"

"I don't, but I was hoping you could get a message to her." He sounded desperate.

Zoe sighed. "Malik, did you ever think that she's not returning your calls for a reason? You hurt her. Broke her spirit. What makes you think that she's going to want to associate with you."

Malik glared at her. "What do you know about us?"

"I know enough to know that she's happier now than when she was married to you. That she's a strong, confident, and beautiful woman who has finally accepted herself for who she is, not what others expect her to be."

Malik continued silently glaring at her for a moment before laughing bitterly. "You're not just her *friend,* are you?"

"That's none of your business."

"She's my wife."

"She's your EX-wife."

Malik flinched in reaction to Zoe's emphasis on ex.

They were at a stand-off in the middle of the sidewalk, with people having to walk around them to get past.

"Look, Malik, if Danice wants to call you back, I'm sure she will. If not, it might be best for both of you if you moved on."

Malik looked her up and down with a sneer. "She's done this before. Thought she wanted to be with someone like you, then eventually realized it's not the life for her."

Malik didn't even wait for Zoe to reply. He just walked away without a glance back. Zoe entered the salon hot with anger, barely acknowledging the greetings sent her way as she walked to her office in back and slammed the door shut. She tossed her backpack on her chair and paced back and forth in front of her desk, wanting to scream and curse but not wanting anyone out in the salon to hear her. What the fuck did he mean Danice had done this before? Zoe knew that Danice used to date women before Malik, but she'd never mentioned having done so since then. Were women just something to pass the time with until the right guy came along? Zoe stopped and shook her head. No, Danice wasn't like that. She wasn't necessarily out, but she also wasn't in the closet. She didn't shy away from

PDA with Zoe in public and had even taken Zoe with her to work events, so Malik had to be wrong. He was just bitter and angry over losing Danice and trying to mess up what she and Zoe had.

Zoe took a deep breath to calm herself, then dug her phone out of her backpack.

She typed, *We need to talk*, then deleted it and typed instead, *Hey, I know you're busy. Just wanted to let you know that I'm going to the store later. Let me know if I can pick anything up for you. Or I can wait until you get home, and we can go together. Let me know.*

That was less foreboding than *We need to talk*. Zoe sat at her desk with her head in her hands. She refused to cry because there was nothing to cry about. At least not until she could talk to Danice to find out what Malik meant. She took her laptop out of her bag and pulled up the inventory for the salon. Work would distract her. Work was dependable. Work didn't break her heart.

CHAPTER TWENTY-ONE

Golden lifted her leg and placed it on a bar along the wall and stretched. She slowly breathed in and out. She usually didn't get jitters before a performance, but tonight was different. She'd had flutters in her belly all day and so much nervous excitement coursing through her that she was afraid to even have a cup of coffee. She switched legs on the bar and repeated the stretch and breathing. She wasn't concerned about the show because everything that could go wrong went wrong during the first couple of days of rehearsals. They managed to work the kinks out well enough for the dress rehearsal yesterday to go smoothly. At one point Golden had been working through the final move where she had decided to use the center aisle for her exit at the point in the song when "Golden Girl" has decided to leave her love. As she stepped off the stage and began her slow walk up the aisle, Golden spotted a man sitting in the back of the theater with his feet up on the back of the seat in front of him.

It was still partially dark in the theater as they were only using the stage lights for now, but as Golden drew closer to him, she saw that he wore an outfit straight out of the eighties. It looked exactly like something her father wore in a picture her mother had of him with his dance troupe. A red Kangol bucket hat, red Adidas track suit with the signature three white stripes down the arm and side of the pant leg and a pair of white Adidas sneakers with red laces. Even in the shadows she recognized that wide toothy grin and stopped to stare in disbelief. Someone called her name and she turned away for just a second to tell them she'd be right there and when she turned back, the man was gone.

She hadn't told anyone about what she saw because she wasn't sure if it had been real or just wishful thinking on her part. Either way, it made her feel as if her father was with her, just as excited as he always was to watch her performance. Tonight's performance would be for her father and for Dinah.

"How are you doing?" Jade asked.

Golden smiled. "Nervous but in a good way. Would it sound weird if I told you I saw my father in the audience during our rehearsal yesterday?"

"Not at all. Kendra sees her grandfather sometimes while she's performing. He sang and encouraged her when she started singing. He was our biggest fan. She was devastated when he passed away five years ago, but she says she always feels him close. I think that's why she was so keen on you finding your ancestry here."

"I had no idea. She's never mentioned him when we've all talked."

"Kendra holds him close to heart. When she's ready to share him with you, you won't be able to shut her up."

Golden grasped Jade's hand and gave it a quick squeeze. "Thank you for not treating me like I was crazy for saying that."

Jade shrugged and grinned. "As long as you don't come to me on a regular saying you see dead people then we're cool."

Golden laughed.

"Okay, folks, we've got a full house!" Trish announced, rubbing her hands together gleefully.

"She's like the evil scientist of music," Kendra said as she joined Golden and Jade. She grasped Golden's hand. "Are you ready for this?"

Jade still held her other hand and Golden felt safe within their circle. "As ready as I'll ever be."

Golden and the Twins weren't the only performances of the night. There was a jazz quartet, a tap crew, then they would be closing the show. The twins would be performing two of their more popular songs before performing "Golden Girl" so she had plenty of time to work through her nervousness.

Trish joined them with a huge grin on her face. "The livestream is already blowing up. I don't think I was even this excited while we were on tour. It feels different tonight."

"Yeah, I feel Pop-Pop here," Kendra said, then gazed at Golden. "I'm sure your aunt Dinah and Celine are here as well. We're here to honor our ancestors and they're returning the favor by honoring us in spirit with their presence."

Trish nodded, kissed her finger, then pointed it up. "Let's link up with the band for our pre-show ritual."

Golden didn't mind that Jade and Kendra still held her hand as they walked further backstage to where their band members were gathered in a circle. Golden, the Twins, and Trish joined the circle, and everyone clasped hands. Trish said a prayer. Then Kendra began chanting softly, "Together we stand…Together we fall…Together we rise." The rest of the group joined in a moment later and Golden could feel the energy rising off them. So much so she chanted right along with them. The chant ended with hugs and high fives all around.

"I wanted to tell you guys that I love the outfits and how you chose to match them to what Golden is wearing. The look brings it all together," Trish told them.

Jade gave Golden's hand a squeeze. "That was Golden's idea."

Golden had brought several costume options to best match what Jade and Kendra's stylist was choosing for them, but the only outfits the stylist brought were fashionable contemporary attire that would be great if they weren't honoring the entertainers of the past. She had suggested something contemporary but with a jazz-era flair. As soon as they finished rehearsal the other day Camille took them to a men's store where they found vintage 1920s-style black suits. Golden also found champagne brocade vests that were almost a perfect match to a champagne satin and brocade corset she'd brought with her. They finished the look with black button-down shirts, champagne satin ties, and black felt Panama hats. Golden's attire wasn't as complicated as it usually was because she was performing more of a choreographed burlesque routine rather than a striptease. She wore the corset that matched Jade's and Kendra's suits with champagne satin dance briefs, garters, shimmering thigh-high stockings and a pair of gold low-heeled dance shoes.

As Golden looked between the three of them, she wondered what a life with Jade and Kendra would be like, and the intensity of her emotions overwhelmed her.

"I forgot something in the dressing room." Golden snatched her hands from Jade's and Kendra's and practically ran back to the dressing room they had been assigned. She dug her phone out of her bag and called Melissa.

When Melissa answered it sounded as if she were at a party. Then Golden remembered she would be at the dance studio for the watch party. "Hey, hold on, let me try and get someplace quiet."

A moment later, the background noise was gone. "Okay, I hope you don't mind but I'm using your office. What are you doing calling me? Shouldn't you be stretching or going over your routine for the twentieth time as you're in the habit of doing right before a performance?"

"Mel, I don't know if I can do this." Golden began gasping as she felt a panic attack coming. The same type of attack she would get when she attempted to dance right after her father died.

"Golden, breathe."

Golden took a deep breath, held it for a moment and slowly blew it out. The pressure in her chest subsided, but her heart still beat quicker than usual.

"Talk to me," Melissa said.

Golden sighed. "I don't know why I called. You're right, I should be prepping for the performance."

"Nope, I'm not letting you escape that easily. Obviously, something happened because you haven't had a panic attack like that in over ten years. Like I said, talk to me."

There was the no-nonsense Melissa that she loved. She might have helped Melissa escape from her family when needed, to get her to loosen up her conservative style and to step out of her comfort zone when it came to enjoying life, but Melissa had been her rock through the worst time of her life and the voice of reason during times she doubted herself.

"This isn't like before where I couldn't perform. It's performing with Jade and Kendra. I shouldn't have agreed to do this because the emotional part is starting to get mixed up with the business part."

"Have you even talked to them about what happened or did you just decide the past is the past and no need to dwell on it."

Melissa knew her too well. Golden couldn't even bring herself to lie so she didn't say anything.

"Judging by your silence I'm assuming it's the latter. I don't know how someone who's such a boss in life and gives such great advice on relationships can be such a chicken with her own love life."

"What do they say about those who can't?"

Melissa chuckled. "Look, I'm the last person to be trying to give romantic advice to, so I'm going to tell you what you would probably tell me or Zoe in this situation. Put your big girl panties on and talk to Jade and Kendra about how you feel. You already know how they feel about you. The ball is now in your court."

Golden frowned. "I hate when you use my own logic against me."

"If you just followed your own advice then I wouldn't need to."

"You're such a bitch."

"I love you too. Now go show Paris who you are."

Golden hung up feeling much better, but as good as Melissa's advice was, she wasn't going to take it. Sharing a life with Jade and Kendra both frightened and intrigued her. If she couldn't get past being afraid of the intensity of such a relationship, then she didn't need to be in it. But what she could do was focus on what she was here for. To entertain. That's what she did best and that's what she was going to do tonight, then take her ass straight home tomorrow afternoon.

❖

The curtain was drawn. The Rhythm Orchestra, the name of the Twins' band for the night, were all set up just like a jazz orchestra back in the day. Jade and Kendra stood on stage looking like they also came from the jazz era. It suddenly felt so surreal especially when the curtain came up, the crowd cheered loudly, and then they sang their first two songs not in the original style they were released but in an upbeat jazz tone that Kendra had composed. When Golden first heard the reimagined version of the first song about a night at the club, she thought it was a new song until she recognized the verses when Jade began singing. Where many artists today took old songs and made them new, Jade and Kendra reversed the process showing the world the range of their talent. During rehearsal earlier, the small audience of Golden and the theater crew absolutely loved the switch-up. Tonight's crowd also went wild. Some even stood up in the aisle and the open space before the stage and began Lindy hopping and jitterbugging looking just like the old film reels that had been shown in her dance class when she was younger in preparation for a Black History Month showcase.

Then came the first strains for "Golden Girl" and as Golden stepped onto the stage, the butterflies she'd been feeling all day dissipated. As usual, the music enveloped her within its warm and comforting cocoon. Within the music there was no heartache or judgment, just the joy of movement. Golden completely let go and felt a presence as if someone was dancing with her, in perfect sync. They weren't controlling her movements but were enhancing them, adding steps she hadn't choreographed but still worked with her routine. When the instrumental moment came for Golden Girl to walk out of the Twins' lives, Golden did something else unplanned. She walked seductively toward Jade and Kendra, took Jade's face in her hands, gave her a soft lingering kiss, did the same to Kendra, then made her way off the stage and into the audience for her exit. As she walked, Kendra sang the last refrains of the song with the final notes from a saxophone trailing behind Golden as she walked out of the back of the theater.

Before the door closed cheers and applause filled the air.

Golden gazed up with a tearful smile. "Thank you, Aunt Dinah."

Then she re-entered the theater. As she jogged to the stage, the applause grew louder. Golden didn't realize it was for her until she arrived on stage and joined Jade and Kendra who stepped back, but the applause continued. Golden covered her face, laughing and crying all at once, overwhelmed with joy. It wasn't like she never received applause for her performances, but this felt different. Jade and Kendra rejoined her, took her hands, and all three gave a bow to the audience then walked off stage together where they were met with more applause backstage. After taking a moment to soak it all in, Jade and Kendra led Golden to the dressing room.

"Oh my God, did you feel that energy?" Jade excitedly pulled Golden into an embrace then did the same with Kendra.

"That was hype to the nth degree. I felt all the ancestors that came to Montmartre for a better life and freedom to be the performers that they always wanted to be lift us up. And, Golden." Kendra looked at her with a gaze full of love. "Damn, girl, you been holding back during rehearsals? That was incredible!"

"I agree. You had the audience riveted. I don't even think they were paying me and Kendra any mind, which is understandable since you were the most beautiful woman out there." Jade's gaze matched Kendra's.

Golden, still high from the energy of the performance, stepped toward Jade, took her face in her hands, and kissed her. Not like the sweet kiss during her performance, but one with everything she wasn't brave enough to say. Jade placed her hands on Golden's waist and kissed her back just as passionately. A moment later, Golden ended the kiss then turned to Kendra and kissed her with equal fervor. By the end all three were panting as if they had just finished a full dance. Jade was just about to speak when the door opened, and Trish walked in whooping and pumping her fist.

"Y'all! You blew that shit all the way up! I know I had my worries about you changing up your songs like that, but I'm not afraid to admit when I'm wrong and I wouldn't be surprised if we got home to find 'Golden Girl' playing on the R&B stations now. As you know this was livestreamed throughout Paris and the US, but the highest numbers came from the US at fifty thousand. Once word gets around, I'm sure the folks that missed the livestream will be watching the replay to bring the viewer numbers up even higher." Trish was so excited she was practically vibrating. "It's time to party!" She clapped and rubbed her hands together then almost bounced out of the room.

Golden smiled at Jade and Kendra then shyly looked away. "I better get changed."

Kendra gave her a knowing grin. "Of course. We'll meet you out there to drive over to the after-party together."

"Okay. I should only be about fifteen minutes."

Jade reached up to stroke Golden's cheek with her thumb. "Take your time. We'll always wait for you."

Then they left the dressing room and Golden took a shuddering breath as she sat down at the vanity. She wasn't alone for long as the tap dancers from the first performance entered the room, saw Golden, and began showering her with praise for her performance. It took her a little longer to get ready than she had planned, but she appreciated the distraction they provided from where her thoughts were heading after that moment with Jade and Kendra, then Jade's parting comment about how they'd always wait for her.

As Golden walked out of the dressing room, Jade and Kendra stood nearby chatting with Camille. They all turned with smiles as she drew near the group.

Camille pulled her into an embrace. "That was just...wow. There's no other way to describe it. I felt like I had been transported back to the Jazz Age and could've been watching your aunt up there. You were breathtaking."

"Aaww, thank you. That's sweet of you to say," Golden said.

Camille shook her head. "And still so humble. Come, we have a party to get to. We'll be making a grand entrance as I believe everyone is probably there already."

Camille took the garment bag that held her costume from Golden, handed it over to Jade, then looped her arm through Golden's and started walking. Golden smiled at Jade and Kendra as they followed along looking as if Camille had taken their candy away. Golden sat up front with Camille as she drove to Coeur Sacré Basilica where the after-party was being held in their rooftop restaurant. As they drove, Golden's phone began buzzing with text messages popping up on the screen from her family, friends, and fellow burlesque performers giving her praise for her performance. Golden could easily let her head get filled with it all, but she knew that moments like this could be fleeting and to just enjoy them. As Camille chatted away,

Golden gazed back at Jade and Kendra. Jade blew her a kiss and Kendra gave her a wink. She gave them a smile and as she turned to face forward, Camille was grinning knowingly.

"Eyes on the road."

Camille chuckled. "Oui, mademoiselle."

❖

Zoe collected paper plates still lying around after the watch party at Golden's dance studio.

"Have you spoken to her yet?" Melissa asked as she held a garbage bag open for her.

"No. I think Malik realizes he fucked up and that Danice has moved on without him and he's bitter about it. There's no need to even bring it up."

Melissa gazed at her skeptically. Zoe ignored her.

A giggling Kiara and her friend Amber hurried over toward them. "Hey, Mom, can Amber spend the night?"

"Is Amber's mom okay with it?"

"Yes," they answered in unison.

Zoe smiled indulgently. "Okay, then yes, but only if you finish helping us clean up."

"Okay," Kiara said before they dashed off toward another group of girls clearing away the food.

"You know, Kiara might have been right about Danice," Melissa said.

Zoe sighed. "Can we just let it go?"

Melissa shrugged. "For now."

As they finished their task, Zoe gazed around the room for Danice and didn't see her. She walked over to Kiara. "Have you seen Danice?"

"Yeah, she was in Auntie Golden's office on what looked like a pretty intense call."

"Okay. We'll be leaving in fifteen minutes."

Kiara nodded and turned back to chatting with her friends. Zoe walked to Golden's office, started to turn the doorknob, then decided to knock. Danice opened the door with her phone still to her ear looking extremely annoyed and waved Zoe in.

"Mother, what do you want me to do? I'm not his wife anymore," she was saying as Zoe entered and closed the door behind her.

"No, I did everything he and you expected me to do as his wife and it wasn't enough. I won't allow you to guilt me over not being there now. I have to go. Bye." Danice hung up and leaned against the edge of the desk with a heavy sigh.

"What's going on?"

Danice ran her hand over the peach fuzz on her head. She had decided to start letting it grow back but only long enough to have a pixie-style cut. "If you hadn't guessed, that was my mother. It seems Malik is sick. Prostate cancer. He's in treatment right now but it's aggressive and there's no one to help him. His parents won't be back from India for another month, and he hasn't told them yet, so he called my parents because I've been ignoring his calls and text messages."

That explained why Malik appeared so haggard when he approached Zoe. "Your mother thinks you should help him."

"Yes. She says as his wife it's my duty to care for him in his time of need."

"But you're not his wife anymore."

"It doesn't matter. He has no one else and, in her eyes, I will always be his wife until I decide to marry someone else. A piece of paper saying we're not married doesn't change the vows we made to each other. She thinks I should forgive him because he realizes his mistake and has suffered enough for it."

Zoe stood beside her. "He has no other family here?"

Danice shook her head. "Malik's parents brought him and his brother to the US when they were just toddlers. Kareem lives in Los Angeles with his wife and kids and isn't going to fly out here to take care of his brother."

Zoe was very tempted to tell Danice about her run-in with Malik, but that would be like kicking a horse when he's already down. "I don't exactly agree with your mother about you still being Malik's wife, but I do see her point in asking you to help." Danice began to protest, but Zoe stopped her. "I know he did you dirty and you coming to his rescue is probably more than he would ever deserve, but this is different. My father had prostate cancer, which they caught early enough for him not to need aggressive treatment, but the treatment he did receive had him weak and sick for some time. My mom took time off from the salon to take care of him. If Malik has no one else and you're the closest to family he has, I can't see you allowing him to suffer out of anger over what he did. At least until his parents return."

Zoe couldn't believe what she was saying, but after watching her father's battle with cancer, she wouldn't wish that on anyone. Not even an asshole like Malik.

Danice gazed at her in disbelief. "You're actually suggesting I help him?"

Zoe moved to stand before Danice and wrapped her arms around her waist. "I'm not saying you move back and become his full-time caretaker. I'm suggesting you at least check in on him and see if there's anything, within reason, that you could do for him. Sometimes something as simple as bringing a homecooked meal for someone in that situation could make all the difference in the world."

Danice embraced Zoe then laid her hand on her shoulder with a sigh of resignation. "I know you're right. I guess I'm not as over everything as I thought."

Zoe placed a kiss on Danice's temple. "Let me know if I can also help."

Danice lifted her head to meet Zoe's gaze. "Zoe Grant, have I told you how wonderful you are?"

Zoe cocked her head to the side as if she were thinking. "Not recently." She gave Danice a teasing grin then lowered her head to kiss her.

A knock at the door interrupted them.

"Unless you two plan to stay the night I suggest you finish up whatever you're doing and come on. Janice is ready to lock up," they heard Melissa say from the other side of the door.

Zoe grinned. "We'll be out in a minute."

"Okay. You don't want her coming to get you."

Danice chuckled. "Uh-oh, we better go. Wouldn't want you getting in trouble with Janice."

Zoe took Danice's face in hers and gave her another brief kiss. "Okay, now we can go."

A few hours later, they lay cuddled on Zoe's sofa watching a movie. Zoe could hear music and laughter coming from Kiara's room and smiled to herself. From Zoe, Kiara inherited her bull-headed stubbornness and a work ethic that sometimes had her stressing herself out to get a task, an assignment, or a competition perfect. From Ray, she only inherited good qualities, his height, athletic ability, and smile. Somehow, despite not having her father in her life and her mother spending more time in a classroom and the salon, Kiara turned out well-adjusted. Honor roll student, star athlete in track and soccer, president of the debate club, and she designed and made most of her own clothes. She understood people in a way that was far wiser than anyone her age, which Zoe's mother deemed was because she had an old soul. It was that understanding of people that had Zoe wondering if Kiara had been right about her being a rebound for Danice. Especially after what Malik intimated about Danice having done this before and came back.

She gazed down at Danice and wanted so much to ask her about that but was too afraid of ruining what they had. She also worried that encouraging Danice to extend help to Malik would be like pushing her back into his arms. She had to remind herself what brought Danice into her salon and how that was reason enough not to worry about her going back to Malik, but because it had been a long time since she'd been in a serious relationship, doubt and insecurity pricked at her like an annoying mosquito that she couldn't get rid of.

Danice shifted in Zoe arms, gazing up at her with a sleepy smile. "I'm ready to call it a night. Are we staying here or heading up to my place?"

"Might as well stay here since this is where we are now. You go back while I lock up."

Danice gave her a peck on the cheek. "Okay." She got up and left the room.

Zoe took her time shutting off the TV and lights, making sure everything was locked and secured and setting the alarm. She was in no rush to go to bed knowing what the evening would eventually lead to and not being in the right frame of mind for it because all she could think about was Malik. On her way back to her bedroom, she stopped at Kiara's door and knocked.

"Come in."

Zoe opened the door to find Amber sitting on the bed and Kiara sitting at her feet painting her toenails.

"Are you girls good? You need anything before I turn in?"

"We're all good. G'nite," Kiara said distractedly as she focused on painting Amber's toe.

"Good night, Miss Grant," Amber said with a happy grin.

"Good night."

Zoe closed the door and continued to her room where she found Danice already asleep. She completed her bedtime tasks as quietly as possible, using the dim lighting from the nightlight in the bathroom rather than turning on the full light as she washed her face and brushed her teeth. As she settled into bed, Danice cuddled against her.

"I texted Malik and told him I'll stop by after work on Monday," she said sleepily.

"That's good," Zoe managed to say past the sudden lump in her throat.

"Thank you for being so understanding. I love you." Danice punctuated her last declaration with a soft kiss below Zoe's ear before snuggling her head in the crook of her neck.

Zoe waited until she heard Danice's soft snores before whispering, "I love you too."

Chapter Twenty-two

Golden unsuccessfully tried to hide a yawn that she'd been holding back for the past half hour. It was only just past eleven at night and she was ready to sneak out and head back to the hotel. It had been a long, nerve-wracking and exciting day, and it was starting to catch up with her.

"I saw that," Kendra teased her.

Golden laughed. "There'll be more where that came from if I don't find someplace to crash soon."

"I say we've earned the right to leave early. What do you say I grab Jade and we head back to the hotel."

Golden yawned again, not bothering to hide it this time. "Sounds like a plan to me."

"Cool. We'll meet you at the entrance."

Golden went in search of Camille who she found on the dance floor. She looked as if she were having such a good time that she didn't want to disturb her. Golden waved to get her attention and Camille bounced happily toward her.

"This is such a great party!"

Golden smiled. "Yes, it is but the Twins and I are going to head back to the hotel."

"Oh, okay. I'll grab my coat and we can go."

"No, you stay and have fun. It's a nice night. We'll walk."

"Are you sure?"

"Positive. You deserve it for being such a wonderful assistant. I'll see you tomorrow for my ride to the airport."

"Okay. Thank you for being so wonderful!" Camille pulled her into a warm embrace then bounced back onto the dance floor.

Golden watched her for a moment then went to the coat check to grab her things. Jade and Kendra were already there. Jade had her backpack and garment bag, and Kendra had her jacket.

Kendra assisted Golden with putting her jacket on. "Where's Camille?"

"I thought I'd give her the rest of the night off. I figured you guys wouldn't mind an evening stroll."

"Not at all." Jade handed Golden's garment bag to Kendra.

"I can carry something." Golden reached for the backpack.

Jade shifted it out her reach. "Nope. We got you."

Kendra walked to the door and held it open for her. When they arrived outside, both Kendra and Jade offered Golden a hand. She didn't hesitate in placing hers in their grasps. The streets were quiet, there was a hint of spring warmth in the air and the skies were clear enough to see several constellations twinkling above. There didn't seem to be a need to fill the silence as they strolled along holding hands. It was a rare occasion to have both Jade and Kendra quiet, but Golden enjoyed just being in their company after the wonderful night they had. It wasn't until they reached the hotel that they released her hands, but it was only long enough to walk through the entrance since they couldn't all fit in at once. They grasped them again as they rode up the elevator to their floor. Jade exited first, tugging Golden and Kendra along toward Golden's room. They stopped outside the door where Golden swiped her card key to open it then took her garment and backpack from the Twins.

"Thanks for walking back with me," Golden said.

Jade brushed her fingers along Golden's arm. "It's the least we could do after the performance you gave tonight."

Kendra did the same to her other arm. "You stole the show, and we didn't mind one bit."

Golden fought the tremble of desire she felt from their touch. "You guys were just as good. Paris loves you."

Jade cocked her head to the side, giving Golden a soft smile. "That's great but Paris's love isn't the one we've been hoping for."

Golden wasn't sure what to say to that. She gave a nervous smile, slowly backed into her room, said, "Good night," then shut the door in their faces.

She stood at the door, her feet unwilling to cooperate with her brain to move. "Well, you probably scared her off for good now. I thought we were going to take it slow," she heard Kendra say.

Jade's response was muffled as they walked away. Golden released a shuddering sigh as she leaned her forehead against the door. What the hell was she so afraid of? Feeling too much? Being overwhelmed by Jade and Kendra? As she dropped her bags in the middle of the floor and made her way over to the mini fridge, she realized the answer was both. Golden took out the champagne that had been left for her when she arrived, carefully popped it open, then poured herself a healthy glass of the sparkling beverage. Sitting in the chaise by the patio doors, she gazed out at the twinkling lights of Paris in the distance, once again finding it amazing that she was even here. Here to live a dream and find a connection with family because Jade and Kendra knew what a chance like this would mean to her. They had been perfect gentlewomen while she had spent more time worrying about them pressuring her to pursue a romantic relationship than just enjoying their companionship.

Golden finished off her glass and poured another. Halfway through the second glass, her head began to feel fuzzy, and she realized she hadn't really eaten and should probably slow down. The pre-show jitters and the post show excitement had her stomach all in knots, so she had only nibbled on a few hors d'oeuvres at the afterparty. Not wanting to waste good French champagne, she finished the glass then placed the bottle back in the fridge. Tipsy thoughts of Jade and Kendra ran through her mind as a hungry growl rumbled in her belly. Golden decided to make a trip to the lobby hoping the short walk would help clear her head and to see if they could assist her with finding a late-night snack to help absorb the alcohol that would keep her awake for another hour. She walked out of the room and as soon as the door clicked shut Golden realized she had forgotten her key.

"Shit." So now her errand included getting another room key.

"Golden?"

She turned to find Kendra coming out of their room. She had shed her jacket and tie, and her shirt was pulled out of her pants and partially unbuttoned. She looked sexy as hell.

Golden's whole body flushed with heat. "Oh, hey. I've locked myself out."

"Where were you going this late?"

"To find food. I didn't eat much at the party. What about you?"

Kendra held up an empty ice bucket. "I like my coffee iced in the morning."

"Oh. Well, I won't keep you." Golden headed toward the elevators.

"We have some leftover quiche from dinner tonight if you'd like some. No need to go all the way downstairs."

"I still need to get another key."

"You can call the desk from our room."

Golden chewed her lip in contemplation then decided it would be easier just to go with Kendra's offer. There was probably nothing really open this late that would deliver. Besides, she was beginning to feel a little nauseous.

"Okay."

Kendra smiled and swiped her key card to reopen the door to her room.

"Back already?" Jade's voice came from the direction of the bathroom.

"No, I picked up a hungry visitor out in the hall," Kendra responded.

Jade popped her head out of the door, her eyes widening in surprise at seeing Golden. "Hey there."

"Sorry to interrupt. I was hungry and Kendra offered food."

"No need to apologize. There are a couple slices of spinach quiche in the fridge and a box of lemon lavender cookies on the table. Help yourself.

I'll be out in a minute." She gave Golden a quick smile before shutting the bathroom door.

"You heard the lady. I'm going to get the ice. There are also bottles of fruit juice and soda in the fridge if you'd like something to drink," Kendra offered.

Golden nodded. "Thank you."

"You're welcome. I'll be right back."

Golden was left standing alone in the middle of their room. It was the same style as her room and surprisingly neat considering there were two people staying in it. She wasn't surprised to see that there was only one bed. She knew that Jade and Kendra sometimes shared a bed, not just for intimacy but comfort and companionship. She tore her gaze from the bed as other thoughts came to mind that she didn't want to think about now. Golden focused on what she was there for, free food. She opened the fridge, found two carryout containers, and grabbed one. There were no utensils available, so she just sat at the bistro table and ate the slice of quiche with her hand. Of course, it was delicious, they were in France, after all. She was almost finished when Kendra returned.

"Good, isn't it. I'm not usually a fan of quiche, but I figured I had to try it since we were here."

"Yes. So much better than I've had at home." Golden licked her fingers.

Kendra pulled a few tissues from a box on the end table and offered them to her.

"Thanks."

Jade exited the bathroom followed by a cloud of steam dressed in basketball shorts and a tank top, her hair damp and curly. Golden no longer craved the quiche as she salivated over how sexy the pair looked.

"All yours," Jade told Kendra.

"Did you at least save some hot water for me?" Kendra teased her.

"Maybe a drop or two." Jade gave Kendra a playful wink.

Kendra chuckled. "Golden is also locked out of her room, so she needs to call the front desk to get another key." She picked up her own pair of basketball shorts and tank top off the bed then headed into bathroom.

Jade sat across from Golden, opened the box of cookies, took one for herself, then offered the box to Golden. She took a cookie and set it on the unused side of the quiche container.

"Golden, I need to apologize for what I said earlier when we dropped you off at your room. I shouldn't have said something like that, especially since we promised to keep this whole trip about business."

Golden tried to play like she had no idea what Jade was referring to. "What did you say that wasn't business-like?"

Jade's expression was hurt, then she pasted on a smile that didn't reach her eyes. "So, um, what time is your flight tomorrow?"

Golden wanted to reach out and tell Jade that she knew exactly what she was referring to and that she thought she did love them, but she couldn't bring herself to do it. "It's at noon. What about yours?"

"We're not flying out until the day after tomorrow. We're taking the train into London for a small, intimate show at She Soho."

"Sounds like a cool name."

"It's a cool spot. They do drag and burlesque shows as well. Maybe you'll perform there someday."

"Maybe."

They sat silently munching on their cookies for a moment, then Jade stood and walked over to the nightstand where the phone sat. "I'll call downstairs to ask them to bring up a key."

"Thank you." Golden finished her cookie, barely tasting it, then went about cleaning up her small mess as she listened to Jade explaining about her locking herself out of her room.

Jade hung up a moment later. "They'll send someone up right away."

"Okay. Maybe I'll just go wait by my room."

"No need. I asked them to drop it off here. It's late so there's no telling how soon they'll be able to get someone up. You might as well get comfortable."

"No, I've imposed on you guys enough for the night."

"Nonsense. We don't mind."

"We don't mind what?" Kendra asked, exiting the bathroom but with less steam following her than Jade.

"Golden imposing on us."

"Not at all. Gives us more time to spend with you before we're whisked back to our regular lives." Kendra hung her pants and shirt up in the closet then placed her other items in one of the plastic laundry bags the hotel supplied. "Come, let's sit and talk. We haven't really had an opportunity to do that since we've been here. I want to hear everything about the school and how well it's doing." She hopped onto the bed, sitting cross-legged at the end of it.

"I have an idea," Jade said excitedly. "Her flight isn't until noon, which means you probably won't be leaving for the airport until nine, we could have a little slumber party. Sit and catch up the way we used to except instead of via video chat, it's in person."

"Awesome idea!" Kendra said.

They both gazed eagerly at her, looking like two kids waiting to be told they could stay up all night. It was very appealing, especially since they touted it as catching up and she probably wouldn't be able to fall asleep anytime soon.

"How about a compromise. Instead of a slumber party, I'll stay and talk for a couple of hours. I'd rather not be up ALL night," Golden offered.

Jade pouted playfully. "Okay," she said with mock dejection.

Golden frowned down at her dress and heels. "I feel a little overdressed."

Kendra scrambled off the bed and opened a dresser drawer. She pulled out a pair of basketball shorts and a tank top, then offered them to

Golden. "You can change in the bathroom. It might still be a little steamy but clear enough to do what you need to do."

Golden chuckled. "Okay. I'll be right back."

She walked into the bathroom to find it damp but not steamy. The mirror was just beginning to clear, so she picked up a dry hand towel and wiped the moisture away. She gazed at her blurred reflection wondering what she was doing. This could lead to trouble, but she wanted so much to be with Jade and Kendra while she could that she would be willing to risk the compromising position this could put their friendship in. Golden decided that no matter what happened she would keep things strictly platonic, after all, she was only going to stay for a short time then go right to her room to bed ALONE. Golden spotted a package of makeup remover cloths and took one to clean her face then changed into the shorts and tank top, leaving her undergarments on. The lacy, feminine undergarments under the boyish top and shorts made her feel strangely sexy.

She walked back out to find Jade and Kendra sitting back in bed against the headboard. They gazed at her with a mixture of amusement and desire.

Jade shook her head as if awakening from a trance. "There's a hanger in the wardrobe there if you want to hang up your dress. Also, they dropped your key off. It's on the credenza."

"Oh, okay, thanks." Golden walked over to the wardrobe and hung up her dress next to the suits Jade and Kendra had worn. There was a sense of rightness in her clothes sharing space with theirs. She quickly shook it off and turned back toward them.

Kendra patted the empty space between them on the bed. "Join us. We promise to keep our hands to ourselves."

Golden quirked a brow in skepticism but joined them on the bed anyway. She had to laugh when she looked between the three of them and their matching attire. "Is this what it was like when your mothers dressed you alike as kids?"

Kendra chuckled. "Pretty much. Even our pajamas matched when we had sleepovers. Our outfits may not exactly match daily, but we still dress similarly without even intending to."

"Now we can be the Rhythm Triplets," Jade quipped.

Golden chuckled.

"So, things are going well with your businesses?" Kendra asked.

"Satin and Lace Burlesque and Legacy Dance Academy are doing great. I'm happy where we are with both businesses."

"That's great. I'm going to have to admit I've become a huge fan of your burlesque troupe. To watch the videos of a group of talented performers, in all our diverse, brown-skinned glory and shapes, being so graceful, beautiful, and sexy is amazing. You are doing the damn thing, Miss Golden." Jade gazed at Golden with a look of admiration that made her heart swell with pride.

Golden shyly gazed away. "Thank you. My goal was to bring attention to the talent of burlesque performers of Color. It's good to hear that it's working. I want to help promote women like my aunt Dinah, Madeline Sahji Jackson, Eleanor Joiner, and Jean Idelle, who weren't fortunate enough to get the international attention and billing that Josephine Baker received. I want today's Black burlesque performers, no matter what their style of burlesque may be, to feel and be seen just as much as their White counterparts."

Kendra grasped her hand, giving it a gentle squeeze. "We've got our own Burlesque Freedom Fighter here."

"Whatever," Golden said with a smile.

Jade took her other hand. "Well, whatever we can do to help, let us know. I already share the videos with any and everybody I can, but I'm happy to do more to support you and your fellow performers."

Golden looked from Kendra to Jade. "You two are too good to me."

Jade opened her mouth to speak.

"How about a movie," Kendra interrupted her, grabbing the remote off her side table with her free hand and turning the television on.

Jade tore her gaze from Golden's but not before Golden saw the depth of her emotion in her eyes. "Yeah, a movie. Good idea."

Golden stared blankly at the television screen as Kendra flipped through the channels to stop at a black-and-white film in English but with French subtitles. They sat quietly watching together, Golden's hands still softly grasped in Jade's and Kendra's. Wanting to hold onto this moment, this time with the two women she was too afraid to love, Golden made a decision that she knew she would probably regret in the morning. She released their hands, sat up on her knees and turned to face Jade and Kendra. She leaned toward Jade and kissed her tenderly, did the same to Kendra then sat back on her heels awaiting their response.

"Are you sure about this?" Kendra asked.

Golden didn't hesitate to answer, "Yes."

Kendra looked toward Jade, their gazes holding as if they were silently communicating, then they both looked back at her as Kendra turned the television off and set the remote back on the nightstand. Jade slid off the bed and offered Golden a hand. She took it and allowed Jade to assist her.

"If at any point it's too much and you want to stop, just tell us. This has to be your decision just as much as ours," Jade said gently.

Golden nodded, her heart beating frantically in her chest. "Okay."

Jade grasped Golden's face and lowered her head to settle on Golden's lips for a slow, sensual kiss. While that was happening Golden could feel the heat of Kendra's body against her back before her hands rested on her waist and her lips pressed against the nape of her neck. While Jade's lips moved from Golden's to kiss along her jawline to the right side of her neck, Kendra's traveled from her nape to the left and just as they had done when making out with her in the car, they moved in unison. Before she even realized it, Jade was now behind her, and Kendra was grasping her face and kissing her passionately.

They stepped away from her just enough to undress her. Once what little clothing she wore was set aside, there were hands and lips all over her, she felt disoriented by the onslaught. Suddenly, Kendra's lips and hands left her body and Golden was turned and pulled into Jade's arms for her to pick up where Kendra had left off. A moment later, Jade turned her toward a now nude Kendra. She was all hard muscle. Even her full breasts sat high and firm on her chest. The intensity of her gaze filled Golden with fear and desire. She didn't fear what Kendra and Jade would do to her. She feared the way it would make her feel. For just a moment she considered putting a stop to what was happening and running back to her room like a frightened rabbit being chased by two hungry foxes but her desire for them quickly overcame it.

"It's not too late to stop," Kendra said, as if she'd known what Golden had been thinking.

Golden gave her a sexy smile. "Yes, it is."

Kendra gave a low chuckle and a quick glance over Golden's shoulder. Jade's slim nude body pressed against the back of Golden, her hands coming around and lifting Golden's breast as if in offering to Kendra. Kendra held Golden's gaze as she licked her lips then lowered her head to take an offered nipple into her mouth. Golden moaned as electricity shot from her nipple straight to her clit making it throb painfully. Jade massaged her breasts as Kendra suckled her nipples, Jade lowered her lips to Golden's neck, grazing her teeth along the column of her throat. Golden sucked in a breath as her head fell back against Jade's shoulder. Before she could even catch her breath, she felt fingers slide over her hardened clit and into the slickness of her vagina. She whimpered as her legs weakened. They would've buckled if Jade hadn't been holding her up around her waist. As Kendra slowly stroked Golden's sex with long, nimble fingers, Golden's hips seemed to move of their own accord, grinding against Jade's pelvis.

Jade moaned. Golden turned her head toward Jade's and was rewarded with Jade's soft lips devouring hers. Golden felt her orgasm coming fast and strong.

"Cum for us, Golden," Kendra said huskily before taking Golden's other nipple into her mouth while she sped up her fingers, driving in and out of Golden's sex.

Jade released her lips. "We've waited so long for this," she whispered in Golden's ear.

It was the tipping point to send Golden over the edge. She grasped the back of Kendra's head with one hand and reached up to grasp Jade's with the other as her body exploded in an orgasm like she'd never experienced before. It just kept coming in waves of mind-blowing pleasure that had her body turning into a mass of jelly as she collapsed back against Jade who tenderly wrapped her arms around Golden's waist as she nuzzled her neck. Kendra wrapped her arms around both Golden and Jade as she brushed her lips along Golden's.

"Why don't we take this to the bed," Jade suggested.

All Golden could manage to do was nod in response. Kendra released them then surprised Golden by scooping her up into her arms, then walking the few steps it took to get back to the bed to lay her gently in the middle of it. Proving that all those muscles weren't for show because Golden was not a dainty woman.

"Show off," Jade said knowingly as she walked to the other side of the bed.

Kendra chuckled, gazing down at Golden with mischief twinkling in her eyes. "Maybe a little."

Golden smiled. She absolutely loved being a part of their teasing banter. They joined her on the bed, kneeling on either side of her. Golden didn't know who to touch first, so she reached up to run her fingers down Jade's smooth flat abs and Kendra's sculpted four-pack. They both worked out regularly, but while Jade did so to keep her slim figure toned for health reasons, Kendra was more dedicated to sculpting her stocky build into a muscular show piece. They couldn't be any more different yet still be so similar. Her feelings for them were even equal. She didn't care for one more than the other, she couldn't see being with one over the other, or being with one without the other. They told her they were a package deal, and it wasn't until this moment that she realized how true that was. Even their tender gazes were twins of each other's.

"What do you want, Golden?" Jade asked.

"Tell us and we'll do whatever we can to please you," Kendra added.

Golden's heart felt as if it would burst in her chest. "Right now, this moment, is all I want."

Golden could tell by their hesitancy that they were hoping she'd ask for something more. Something that would tell them their feelings for her were requited, but she couldn't do it. Not yet. Then they descended on her to give her a night filled with more passion than she could ever have imagined.

As the dawn light peeked in through the curtains, Golden tried to carefully untangle herself from Jade's and Kendra's limbs. Kendra's arm tightened around her waist.

Golden softly stroked her arm. "I'm just going to the bathroom."

"Okay," Kendra mumbled, lifting her arm from around Golden's waist.

"What's going on?" Jade said sleepily.

"Golden has to go to the bathroom," Kendra answered.

"Oh." Jade lifted her hand from Golden's belly and moved her leg from atop Golden's thigh.

She scooted to the bottom of the bed then hurried to the bathroom, quietly shutting the door behind her. She gazed at her reflection in the mirror, her hair lay in a wild halo around her head, her lips were swollen from their kisses, her body still tingled and throbbed from their lips and hands. Jade and Kendra hadn't left any part of her untouched, including her heart.

"I have to go," she said desperately to herself.

Golden walked to the door, opened it just enough to peek out to see Jade and Kendra still asleep, the empty spot she'd left between them still there as if they were just waiting for her refill it. As quietly as possible, she collected her clothes, eased her room key off the credenza and silently left the room without bothering to check to see if anyone was out in the hall before she raced to her room, completely naked, carrying her clothes and shoes. Fortunately, Golden didn't encounter anyone. She picked up her phone, barely a charge left since she had unexpectedly gotten locked out of her room and spent the night with Jade and Kendra. She had several missed calls from her mother, Melissa and Zoe, and a text from Camille sent just a few minutes ago letting her know she was up and available whenever Golden was ready to go to the airport.

Ignoring the voicemails from her mother and friends, Golden texted Camille to let her know she would be downstairs in about twenty minutes. Camille responded with *So early?* Golden simply answered *Yes.* She had already packed most of her things yesterday before leaving for the theater since she knew she would be back late and didn't want to be up all night packing, so she only had to pack what she'd worn last night and her toiletries. After a hasty freshening up and tying her hair up in a headwrap, she quickly dressed in the loose pants, top, and slip-on sneakers that she'd left out to wear for the flight, then headed down to the lobby to check out and wait for Camille. She pulled up moments later and Golden was dragging her stuff outside before Camille could even get out of the vehicle.

The trunk opened and Golden threw her smaller suitcase in with no issues but struggled to pick up the larger one.

"Here, let me help you." Camille grabbed part of the suitcase and assisted Golden with lifting it into the truck.

"Thank you."

Camille gazed at her with concern. "Are you all right?"

Golden smiled but avoided meeting Camille's gaze. "I'm fine." She turned to walk around to the passenger side, then climbed in.

"I'm a very good listener if you'd like to talk, but also understand if you prefer not to."

"Thank you but there's nothing to talk about." Golden gazed longingly at the hotel wondering what she would say if Jade and Kendra ever spoke to her again.

CHAPTER TWENTY-THREE

"You just left!" Melissa was looking at Golden as if she'd completely lost her mind.

"What was I supposed to do? Tell them I'm just as in love with them as I think they are with me?" Golden said defensively.

"Uh, yeah," Zoe said, not blaming Melissa for her reaction.

Golden had returned from Paris a week ago and had decided to cook instead of them meeting up at their favorite diner for brunch. Golden's eyes were brimming with unshed tears.

"I wanted to, but every time I thought about it, I was overwhelmed with fear. I can't bring myself to give so much of my heart to anyone else. You guys and my family are all I have left to give."

Zoe sighed then reached across the table to offer her hand to Golden. "I understand. Danice told me she loved me, and I never responded. She was half asleep when she said it, but still, I waited until she was fully asleep to say it back."

Melissa shook her head, looking exasperated at Zoe and Golden. "I don't understand you two. You're both always telling me I need to find love yet you both have it sitting right in front of you and you're too chicken shit to do anything about it."

Zoe looked guiltily down at her plate of food. "Mel, it's easier said than done."

"Bullshit. The closest I've gotten to a relationship since Leah is Riley and that was more friendship than romance, but if it had become more, I would've happily accepted it."

"I'm calling bullshit now," Zoe said. "What about Black?"

Melissa took a sip of her Bellini. "What about them?"

"You too aren't fooling anyone. Trying to keep up this guise of kinky games, but you might as well be dating," Zoe said.

"But we're not and I would never cross that line with a client. It would never work."

"It worked out for Vivienne, the woman who got you into this life in the first place. Why wouldn't it work for you?" Golden said.

"This isn't about me and Black. It's about you two being afraid of commitment. I love you, Golden, which is why I need to say that you have to stop using the loss of your father as an excuse for why you can't commit to not one, but two women, who would love you like no one else could. He would be so upset to know that you were denying yourself that because of him." Melissa turned to Zoe. "And you. I don't understand what's holding you back. You've raised a wonderful child who is going to set this world on fire with her brains and talent, and now that she's practically grown you can take some of that time you've devoted to raising her to make yourself happy. Unless you're still hung up on that idiot Ray leaving, which you shouldn't be because, honestly, I think he did you and Kiara a favor. In other words, both of you need to get your shit together, unpack your baggage, and grab up these women before you lose them."

With that, Melissa went back to eating as if she hadn't just read Zoe and Golden to filth. Zoe gazed over at Golden, her knowing smirk matching Golden's as neither missed how expertly Melissa steered them away from her own love life.

❖

After she returned home, Zoe thought about what Melissa said and why she seemed hesitant to accept her love for Danice. If she was honest with herself, it had nothing to do with Kiara or Ray. Not directly. She had spent so long guarding her heart from any romantic relationships so that she could focus on Kiara and her business that she was now afraid to allow herself to take that step. It had been so long that the thought of giving herself over to love only to have her heart broken was something she didn't have time, or the desire, to deal with.

When Zoe had arrived home Danice hadn't been there. She had texted Zoe to let her know she and her mother were picking up groceries for Malik so that they could prepare his meals for the week. This was Danice's third visit to Malik's since she decided that she was going to assist him while he was going through his cancer treatments. She and her mother had come up with a plan to share the caretaking duties until his parents returned from India, which wouldn't be for another two months since Malik was insistent on not telling them about his illness because he didn't want them cutting their visit home short for him. Zoe knew it was just an excuse to get Danice where he could try to convince, or guilt her, into going back to him. Once again, Zoe didn't express her concern because she felt it made her seem insecure. She had to trust Danice wouldn't fall so easily for such obvious manipulation, but then again, she had stayed with Malik for all those years, allowing him to slowly manipulate her into being what he wanted her to be. Who was to say that it couldn't happen again?

Zoe shook her head as if to shake the negative thoughts from it. Danice told her that she loved her, and Zoe didn't think she took saying such a thing lightly after what she'd been through while married. Zoe knew that should be enough to embrace what she and Danice had, but she felt as if she were waiting for the other shoe to drop. To distract herself from her worries, she decided that with everyone out of the house it was the perfect opportunity to take care of the tasks that she'd been putting off. She grabbed her toolbox from the hall closet and went about the apartment clearing clogged drains in the bathroom and kitchen, hanging the double mailbox she'd bought a month ago and never hung, then came the housework. Emptying and cleaning out the refrigerator, dusting and mopping from the kitchen through to the living room, and changing the sheets for her, Kiara's, and the guest room beds.

By the time she was finished and about to sit down to watch a movie, Zoe heard the front door to the house open, then the sound of someone walking upstairs to Danice's apartment. Zoe stared at her door in confusion wondering why Danice hadn't come to her place first. She considered going up to check on her, but it was obvious that she needed a minute before seeing Zoe, which had her worrying. She hit play on the movie, paying little attention to what was on the screen. She kept gazing up at the ceiling, willing Danice to come down, but it was another hour before Zoe heard footsteps coming down the stairs then keys jingling outside her door. She turned back toward the television as if she was absorbed by what she was watching as Danice walked in.

"Oh, hey," she said, a little too chipper.

Danice gave her a small smile as she walked over to the sofa to flop down beside Zoe. Then she laid her head on her shoulder with a heavy sigh. "Hey."

Zoe placed a kiss on her head. "Everything okay?"

"Not really. My mother is bugging me about getting back together with Malik, even if it's just until he gets past this, and Malik is refusing to tell his parents that he's even sick. Only our family knows, and he's sworn my parents to secrecy." Danice sounded extremely annoyed. Zoe didn't blame her.

"He hasn't even told his brother?"

"No, but I haven't sworn to his little secret pact. He and my mother are not going to guilt me into falling back into that life again. I'm about to call his mother. I'm sure she'll be on the first flight back to care for her baby."

Zoe slipped an arm around Danice's shoulders. "Are you sure you want to do that? To be the one to break that news to them? It should come from Malik."

She hated pointing that out because she would love Malik's parents to come back so that Danice could walk away from the situation before she got any more entangled.

Danice sighed again then snuggled closer to Zoe. "Sorry I didn't come right over. I needed to change my clothes. Malik got sick and I was in the line of fire. What are you watching? Haven't we seen this one before?"

Zoe gazed up at the television. She had forgotten she'd been watching anything. "Oh yeah. I couldn't remember so I just figured I'd watch it anyway."

Danice tilted her head to look at her. "Then you won't mind turning it off so we can talk?"

"No, not at all." Here it comes, Zoe thought as she clicked the television off.

Danice sat up to face her fully. Zoe did the same, smiling to hide her worry.

"Earlier this week I said something that I've felt for a while but hadn't meant to say yet. I'm sure you know what I'm referring to. I just want you to know that I don't expect you to feel the same way, nor do I want you to feel obligated to say it if you don't mean it. I think I was just a little tipsy and half asleep which, as you know, is when my filter is usually turned off." She smiled sheepishly.

Zoe hadn't known where the conversation was going, but she hadn't expected it to go this way, especially since Danice hadn't brought it up sooner. She also wasn't sure if she was more relieved or disappointed that Danice hadn't heard her response. Zoe carefully considered what her next words would be, keeping in mind what Melissa said about accepting the love Danice was offering and not being afraid to return it.

"So, you meant it when you told me you loved me? You weren't just casually throwing it out there?"

Danice shifted closer to her and took her hands. "I would never casually throw something like that around. I love you. I think I've loved you since our first few weeks together. I know that sounds crazy considering how we'd barely been dating at the time. I don't believe in love at first sight. I even tried convincing myself that it probably had to do with spending so long being starved of love and affection with Malik that I was rushing into things with you because it felt so good to be desired and touched again, but I was just fooling myself. I love you, Zoe Grant." With a broad smile, Danice lifted Zoe's hands and placed a kiss on the back of each.

Hearing Danice's declaration and seeing the love and sincerity in her eyes, Zoe figured it was time to stop denying the truth. "I guess there's nothing for me to say but I love you too."

Danice's eyes widened. "Really? You're not just saying it so that I don't feel like a fool?"

Smiling so hard that her cheeks ached, Zoe pulled Danice toward her. "I guess we're both fools."

As she pressed her lips to Danice's for a kiss that made sure that she knew Zoe meant what she'd said, She pushed the last of her worries about Malik's bitter words to the back of her mind. He was obviously attempting to sow doubt into their relationship, and she had almost allowed him to do it.

❖

Golden nervously paced back and forth in front of her desk. She had just returned to her office to find she had a missed call from Jade. Although the Twins had texted in the two weeks since Golden returned from Paris, all three had been too busy to speak on the phone or via video so there had been no conversation regarding what happened that last night. Golden had received a text from Kendra wishing her a safe flight and asked her to let them know when she made it home. That text was followed by one from Jade telling her they had a wonderful time and missed her already. Golden had said she enjoyed it as well and would text them when she landed, which she did. Then she went straight from the airport to the dance academy where her mother told her that she had been fielding calls all day with people requesting to sign up for burlesque classes as well as booking inquiries for Golden and her troupe.

Livestreaming the show had done just what Trish had said it would, draw more attention to Golden. What Golden hadn't known was that Trish had streamed a video highlight and bio about the Twins and Golden. Golden's video had featured clips of some of Satin and Lace's performances and an interview Golden had done for a local news channel when she opened the academy where she talked about wanting to encourage young dancers of Color to practice in classical ballet and ballroom as well as the more popular fields of hip hop, jazz, contemporary, Broadway, and tap. She also spoke of diverse representation in burlesque and how she wanted Satin and Lace to carry on the work of Black burlesque revues such as Brown Sugar Burlesque, Yamms Burlesque, and Jeezy's Juke Joint. That interview in combination with her Paris performance had the academy's phone ringing off the hook, leaving her little free time for a call with Jade and Kendra when they returned from Europe.

Now Golden had the rest of her evening free which meant she had no excuses not to return Jade's call. She texted Jade back asking if she and Kendra would like to do a video call in an hour. Jade agreed and Golden went about doing what she needed to close for the night. When she arrived home she showered, took ten minutes trying to figure out what she was going to wear before settling on an oversize, off-the-shoulder sweatshirt with the Satin and Lace logo, a sports bra, and dance shorts. She pulled her mass of hair up into a curly puff, then nodded in satisfaction at her comfy casual appearance. Golden had just enough time before her call with the Twins to fix a cup of tea and set up her tablet on a stand at her dining table because she didn't want to be anywhere near a bed when she spoke with them. They called right on schedule. Golden took a deep calming breath, smiled, and answered. She didn't expect the onslaught of emotions that overwhelmed her at seeing their equally smiling faces for the first time in two weeks.

"Hey, beautiful," Kendra said.

"Hey, Kendra. Hey, Jade."

"See, this is how I like to see you. As your natural beautiful self. I mean, don't get me wrong, you're gorgeous when you're all dolled up, but there's something about you looking fresh and natural that's sexy as hell," Jade said.

Golden felt her face flush with heat. These were the only women that had ever been able to make her feel shy and blush. "Thank you. How did your private show in London go?"

They both smiled knowingly at her changing the subject.

"It was great, although much of the crowd was asking for you when we began singing 'Golden Girl.' It turns out most of them had watched the livestream and hoped you would be there," Jade said.

"Wow, really? I'm flattered."

"You're a hit. Now everyone is going to be expecting to see you every time we perform that song." Kendra smiled.

"Well, that might be tough since Trish's promotion efforts prior to the livestream have given me more business than I can handle. Satin and Lace performers are booked for the next four months, and we've had an influx of new students at the dance academy and burlesque school."

"Nice! We have some more good news. 'Golden Girl' is currently topping the Billboard Music charts at number three. It moved up from ten since the show. If it continues in that direction, we're hoping that gets us a nomination for a Billboard Award. We were already asked to perform, but it'll be the extra cherry on top if we get nominated." Kendra smiled proudly.

"Congratulations! Is it too soon to hope for a Grammy as well?" Golden said.

Jade made a show of crossing her fingers. "From your mouth to the Recording Academy's ears."

Kendra quirked a brow. "Do you think we could convince you to perform with us at either or both?"

Golden chuckled. "Let's not get that far ahead of ourselves."

"Just putting it out in the universe," Kendra said.

"Well, we know it's a little late there and we're sure you've had a full day, so we'll get to the other reason for our call." Jade's face suddenly darkened with a blush.

She hesitated for a moment until Kendra elbowed her in the side. Jade flinched then smiled nervously at the camera.

"Despite what happened between us in Paris, Kendra and I don't want you to feel pressured into anything. We understand that we shared something intimate for the moment and that it doesn't mean that we expect you to give up your freedom to be exclusive with us, especially with residing on opposite coasts."

"Yeah. We hope that we can remain friends," Kendra picked up where Jade left off. "Maybe even spend time together when we happen to be on the same coast. We're leaving the ball in your court. We just wanted to get that out in the open so that there wasn't any awkwardness between us after Paris."

Jade nodded. "We lo—enjoy having you in our lives and hope we didn't scare you off."

Golden didn't miss Jade's slip with the word love and had a feeling Kendra might have had something to do with this whole conversation. Kendra was all about logic and reason while Jade was the more emotional and expressive of the two. She probably noticed Golden's hesitancy when Jade became more expressive with her feelings toward Golden and pointed it out to her. Golden felt bad that she might have indirectly been a part of having Jade hold back what made her the beautiful person and artist that she was.

"I enjoy being a part of your lives and appreciate you thinking of my feelings with all of this. You haven't scared me off. What happened between us is something I wanted. Just like that night, let's just let whatever this," Golden pointed between herself and the monitor, "is to happen naturally."

They both smiled, but Jade's was broader as she also looked relieved. Golden was glad that she was able to take away the guilt she saw in her face.

"Great! So, we're going to be in New York next month for some radio and talk show interviews Trish set up for us. We were wondering if you have any availability in your growing schedule if you'd be interested in doing some of the shows with us? You know, for more promotion," Kendra said.

"And if you're not available for that, then maybe coming to the Long Island house for dinner," Jade offered, a hopeful expression on her face.

Kendra smiled. "Or we can come to you for dinner. No need for you to traipse all the way out there."

"Let me know the dates and times and I'll see what I can do. I can't make any promises," Golden said, secretly wishing she wasn't so busy, even though that was what she'd been hoping for since starting on her business endeavor.

Jade's face split into a broad smile. "We understand. I'll have Trish send you the details. Whatever you can make, even if it's just to grab a quick cup of coffee, we'll be happy."

Kendra rolled her eyes. "Okay, we'll let you go. It was good seeing you, Golden. Take care."

"Same here. G'night, guys."

"Good night," they said in unison before dropping the call.

Golden felt a sense of relief, but whether it was because they hadn't put any pressure on her or because that night hadn't caused the awkwardness between her and the Twins that she had been expecting, it didn't matter. What mattered was that she hadn't lost them and still had time to figure out what she was going to do about being in love with them.

❖

Melissa carefully applied her makeup, giving herself a more natural glow and replacing her usual black lipstick with a sexy red that made her lips appear fuller. She plaited her locs into three sections then intertwined them into one long plait that she bound at the end with a red leather cord. She even replaced her black sexy business domme attire that she usually wore for her sessions with Black with a similar look but all in red. This would be the first time Melissa would be seeing them since their last session. She wanted to feel less foreboding and dark around Black.

"Red suits you," Lily said as she entered the dressing room.

"Thank you. I felt like I needed a change." Melissa didn't know why she felt the need to explain.

Lily set her bag on the dressing table next to hers. "Sometimes change is necessary for us to grow," she said sagely as she sat down facing Melissa.

Melissa picked up a plain red satin mask that she'd just bought the other day. "Or just a way to break up the monotony."

"Is that what's happening with Black? You're just breaking up the monotony?"

She glanced at Lily who watched her curiously, then shrugged. "Maybe. They're not like my other clients."

"And is that a good thing? You seem excited when you're scheduled for appointments with them."

"Do I? I never noticed." Melissa placed the mask over her eyes and tied the ribbons at the back of her head.

Lily chuckled. "Liar." She turned away from Melissa to unpack her bag.

Melissa grinned. Lily might not have Hyacinth's gift of foresight, but she was very observant. She also didn't push the conversation further than pointing out the obvious, which Melissa was grateful for. She'd had enough questions and ribbing about her relationship with Black from her friends, she didn't want to have to deal with it here as well. Red Dahlia had become her safe space to just be whatever it was she chose to be without having to explain why to anyone. After one last look in the mirror, she checked the time and decided she would meet Black in their room. They were very punctual so she knew they would arrive any minute now. Before heading out of the dressing room, she picked up the phone and called Shari at the reception desk to let her know so that she didn't have to use the intercom to let Melissa know when Black arrived.

"Enjoy your session," Lily said in a teasing tone.

Melissa grinned. "Thank you."

❖

Black was walking up the stairs as Melissa walked toward their playroom. She couldn't hold back a broad smile when she saw them. They were dressed more casually than usual in a V-neck, beige, fitted sweater that stretched across their broad shoulders, hugged their muscular arms, and tapered down to their small waist. A pair of straight leg jeans enhanced their long legs and cupped their softly rounded hips and behind attractively. A pair of tan leather oxford boots and a suede face mask completed the look.

Black's lips spread into a broad smile as well. "Well, hello. I didn't expect to see you so soon. I thought I'd have time to set up."

Melissa stopped then began to turn back toward the dressing room. "I could always go back."

"No, no, I was just pleasantly surprised."

They met just at the start of the hallway leading to the playrooms.

Black gave Melissa an admiring glance. "Red is definitely your color."

Melissa felt her face flush. She gazed down and smoothed her hands over her waist to hide it. "Thank you."

Black opened the door for her, then stepped aside to let her walk ahead. This was new for them. Melissa realized she was at a loss as to what to do next. She was used to walking in and getting right to their routine or having Black direct her next move. This seemed more like a date rather than a session.

"How was your trip?" Melissa asked.

"Very productive, but I'm glad to be back here with you." Black smiled tenderly, making Melissa's heart skip.

As much as she wanted to tell them how happy she was to see them, she held back from doing so. "So, what will we be doing today?" she asked, going to her safe space of business before heart.

Black grinned knowingly. "Well, Mistress Heart, I thought I would venture into your domain today. I'd like you to teach me about dominance and spanking."

As surprised as she was, Melissa kept her face neutral. "Oh…um… are you wanting to be dominated and spanked or are you wanting to be the dominator? I usually have one of the other hosts that are experienced at being a submissive assist me, but that's only if I have advance notice so that we may plan accordingly."

"So, you don't perform as a submissive?"

Melissa smiled nervously. "Not for quite some time. Most of my work here is as a domme."

"Oh, well, never mind. I was just curious to see things from Mistress Heart's perspective, but we can go back to our usual play." Black walked toward the two-way mirror.

Despite their mask, Melissa hadn't missed the disappointment in their face. "Wait, I'm sure we can figure out a way to do this with just the two of us."

Butterflies took flight in her belly as Black turned and smiled at her. "Great. I'm not looking to do anything crazy like the performance you put on the night of the fundraiser. Just some light play to appease my curiosity."

"I see." Melissa hadn't done submissive work since her training days at Dahlia and she hadn't been a fan of it which was why Afrodite suggested she stick with domme work. She never said she wouldn't play submissive roles, but she was also never given domme clients. "You sound as if you know what you want to do. This is your session, where would you like to begin?"

Black chuckled. "I may have done a little internet research to prepare. The first thing I'd like to do is ask what your limits and safe word are."

Melissa smiled. "I guess you have been doing your research. My limits are light restraint and bondage. No rope bondage, impact play or cuckolding, and as you have known since our first session, no bodily fluids or penetration."

Black nodded. "Got it. Since I remember where everything is kept after your tour of the room during our consultation, why don't I choose some items and you tell me whether they're a yea or nay."

"Okay."

Black's sexy lips spread into a smile like a kid on a shopping spree at their favorite store. They went to the bench at the end of the bed and opened it. After perusing the contents, Black reached in, picked out a few items, and eagerly turned back to Melissa.

"Will any of these be acceptable?" They held out a spanking paddle with black fox fur covering one side and leather covering the other, a twelve-inch leather flogger, and a riding crop.

"Whichever you choose will be fine with me."

Black nodded then closed the bench and laid the spanking tools on top. "Now, regarding restraint. You mentioned the leather chaise there could be used for what we need?"

"Yes. You'll need cuffs."

"I guess that would be helpful," Black said in amusement as they reopened the bench and chose a pair of leather wrist cuffs.

"There are ankle cuffs as well," Melissa pointed out.

"I don't think those will be necessary."

Melissa almost sighed aloud with relief. She removed her skirt, walked to the chaise, straddled it, then lay on her stomach and placed her hands near the D-ring that the cuffs would latch to. She gazed expectantly up at Black. The intensity in their eyes made Melissa's sex clench with desire. Black knelt beside the chaise to clasp the cuffs to the D-ring, then around Melissa's wrists.

"Let me know if they're too tight," they said as they adjusted the buckle around her wrists.

"That's good."

"What's your safe word?" Black gazed at her again then raised their hand to softly graze their knuckles along her cheek.

"Red."

"Red. Got it."

Their faces were mere inches from each other's. Melissa wanted so much for them to kiss her, and for a moment, she thought Black would, but they gave her a soft smile then shifted to stand. Melissa was both disappointed and relieved. Today's session was already making her feel as if she had no control over her emotions, now she was willingly giving over control of her body, neither of which was a common occurrence for her.

"If you're not comfortable with this, we don't have to do it."

"I'm fine."

"The tense way you're holding yourself says that you're not."

Melissa closed her eyes, unclenched her fists, then took a deep breath to relax. She could stop this at any time. Black had never done anything that she wasn't comfortable with and she doubted they would start now.

"You may begin." She was still wary but not tense.

Black stood beside her for another moment then moved toward the bench where they picked up the leather and fur paddle. With a playful grin, they tapped the leather side against their palm.

"Are you ready, Mistress Heart?"

Melissa felt some of her anxiety dissipate at Black's teasing smile. "Whenever you are, Domme Black."

Black frowned petulantly. "Not Master?"

Melissa quirked a brow. "You haven't earned that title."

Black nodded. "I see. Domme sounds better anyway. Being called Master isn't very appealing." They walked out of Melissa's line of site to the foot of the chaise. "Remember, we can stop any time you're feeling uncomfortable."

Melissa nodded. Words suddenly stuck behind the nervous lump in her throat as she anticipated the feel of the paddle against her bare ass displayed from the thong panties she wore. After what seemed like several agonizing minutes later, she felt a light tap against her right butt cheek. As light as it was, the surprise of it still made her jerk in surprise.

"Did I hurt you?" Black's voice was tinged with concern.

"No, I was just surprised. You may continue."

A moment later, there was another tap on Melissa's other cheek followed by several more between each butt cheek. Although they began to sting a little, Melissa didn't find them as unpleasant as expected, especially when Black took the fur side and gently stroked it along the stinging areas.

"I read that following up with a soft touch made spankings more pleasurable. Is this true?"

It took Melissa a moment to respond as she was surprised by the pleasurable warmth spreading throughout her body. "Yes. For some subs, especially beginners, a soft touch can literally take the sting away from the spanking." Why did her voice sound so breathy?

"Interesting." Black brought the leather side of the paddle back against her behind with a touch more pressure than before.

Melissa gasped, but not due to surprise or pain.

"Is this pleasurable as well, Mistress Heart?" Black's voice had taken on a husky tone. The same tone Melissa recognized from their "phone" sex during their sessions.

She arched her back so that her ass was raised a little higher. "Yes," she said breathily.

To Melissa's surprise, none of the fear and anxiety of not being in control that she had felt during her submissive training appeared. Even the small bit of anxiety that she'd felt just after Black had secured her cuffs was replaced by desire. Black once again smoothed the fur side of the paddle across Melissa's butt and her inner walls clenched again. Her ass was more sensitive after the paddling. She bit her lip to hold back a moan threatening to escape. Relief and disappointment warred with each other when Black removed the paddle.

"Let's try something different."

Melissa gazed up to see them walking back with the leather flogger then quickly looked away as she realized that she was feeling an excited anticipation at what was to come. Was this what Rose felt when she was performing sub play? She had said that with the right partner, maybe even Melissa could find enjoyment in being a sub occasionally. Melissa had vehemently disagreed, but Black seemed to be proving Rose's theory correct.

Black lightly grazed the flogger back and forth across Melissa's cheeks, slowly building the momentum until it was a steady rhythm of light to medium slaps. Melissa's breath began coming out in quick pants then Black slowed down the flogger to a soft graze once again then changed direction bringing the flogger down the crack of her butt and back up between her spread thighs. Melissa couldn't stop the moan of pleasure as the soft leather straps of the flogger brushed her sex through the thin layer of her panties.

"Ah, I think we've found just the right rhythm to please my Mistress," Black said as they alternated between the side-to-side flogging of her butt and the up and down of her slit.

To Melissa's further amazement, she felt an orgasm building. She shifted as much as her position on the chaise would allow to feel the flogger along her now wet crotch. It felt so good that she no longer cared about being in control or that she was getting off on something that had once triggered feelings she would rather not deal with while working at Dahlia's. When Melissa's orgasm hit her, it was like an internal pleasure bomb exploding and sending shockwaves throughout her entire body. She buried her face in the pillow to muffle her shout as her body stiffened then trembled with pleasure. When Melissa became aware of her surroundings again, she felt the softness of fur smoothing across her behind. A moment later, Black knelt beside her to unbuckle her cuffs.

"How'd I do, Mistress?"

"I think you did a little more than research."

Once Melissa was uncuffed, Black offered her a hand to assist her up into a sitting position, then gave her a sheepish grin.

"I might have watched several YouTube videos and practiced with a couple of pillows placed next to each other to represent an ass and a feather duster and ruler as a flogger and paddle."

Melissa laughed. "I hope this was done at home and not your office."

Black laughed as well. "Oh, that would've made quite a scene for my assistant to walk into. It was in the privacy of my home. Although, with the amount of feathers missing, I'm probably going to need to buy my cleaning lady a new duster before her next visit."

Black's expression softened as they gazed at Melissa. "Thank you for stepping out of your norm to do this."

Melissa found herself lost in their gaze for a moment, feeling a sense of familiarity with it. "As I've said before. I'm here for your pleasure." She tore her gaze from theirs, stood and walked over to collect her skirt where she left it at the end of the bed.

"Is that all you're here for? You don't get any pleasure out of this as well?"

Melissa turned to find Black walking toward her. "I enjoy my work."

"That's not what I asked." Black stood directly before her, gazing down at her as if waiting to glean the truth from her response.

The sound of buzzing interrupted them, saving Melissa from having to admit something that she wasn't sure she was ready to. Black hesitantly walked past Melissa to pick up their phone from the end table near the sofa.

"Hello," they answered with an annoyed tone. "I asked not to be interrupted for the next two hours...Can't Karina take care of it?" Black sighed heavily. "Okay. I'll need to grab some things from my place and can be there first thing in the morning...No problem, see you soon." They hung up, gazing dejectedly at Melissa.

"You have to go?"

Black nodded. "Work emergency. I need to go out of town, but I'll be back in time for our next appointment."

"I'll be here."

Black smiled, walked over to Melissa and placed a soft kiss on her cheek. "Until next time, Mistress Heart." Then walked past her.

"Black," Melissa called just as she heard the door open.

"Yes."

"In response to your question, yes, I do." She kept her back to them, not ready to admit any truths face-to-face.

"That's good to know," Black said before Melissa heard the door close softly behind them.

She sat on the bed with a heavy sigh. This was so unlike her. She made it a point to keep her relationships with her clients strictly business, but what she shared with Black was crossing the line into dangerous territory. She thought about how Vivienne met her husband and wondered if a relationship with Black outside of Dahlia's could work as well as theirs did. Was she even willing to find out?

CHAPTER TWENTY-FOUR

W ow, so you actually said the words?" Golden asked.
Zoe fluffed Golden's hair to distribute the big curls cascading over her shoulders. Golden normally wore her hair in its naturally curly state, but she was switching it up with a blowout and curl for a burlesque show that she was working double duty as host and MC.

"Yeah. I figured it made more sense to stop fighting what I was feeling."

Golden sighed. "I wish I could do that."

"I'm assuming you're referring to you and the Twins."

"Of course. We haven't seen each other since Paris, but we're back to weekly video calls when our schedules allow. We mostly talk about work and how our week went. They never pressure me about where our relationship is going, yet, despite the casualness of it all I'm finding myself thinking about us in a romantic relationship more every day."

"Have you tried dating other people? Maybe use one of those apps you're always getting Melissa to try. I think it would give you the opportunity to see if the Twins are who you want or if it's just a matter of you haven't been seeing anyone else romantically."

"I thought about that. I've had other performers ask me out, but I don't like to mix business with pleasure. I haven't been in any kind of real relationship since high school. After that were brief affairs and hookups. I wouldn't even know what to say that I'm looking for."

Zoe chuckled. "Combine the best parts of the Twins into one person and you'll have your perfect match."

Golden rolled her eyes. "Yeah, that helps. What do I owe you?"

Zoe waved dismissively. "Don't worry about it."

"Girl, you keep doing these freebies you're going to go out of business."

"I have too many businesses to be going out of business. I think I'm good. I'll see you later."

After giving Zoe a sisterly hug, Golden was on her way. Tonight was going to be a big night for Satin and Lace. She had wanted to host a burlesque review featuring BIPOC performers since she began performing. Golden had finally reached the status and respect within the industry to be able to pull it off with some of the top Black and Brown burlesque performers participating. She was more nervous about the show than she was when she performed. Her mom, Drew and his wife, Melissa, Zoe, Zoe's mother, Danice, and all the Satin and Lace's students would be attending. If she pulled this off, Golden hoped it would become a regular event like Sugar Brown Burlesque's Bad and Bougie or maybe even get featured in Vegas like the Black Girl Magic Burlesque Show. Golden didn't see herself as competition for those shows. She only saw it as working together to promote performers of color in the industry.

When Golden arrived at the theater that she had booked in New York's Times Square theater district, she headed straight to the rehearsal hall where the performers were doing their run-throughs.

Char, her stage director, greeted her with a beaming smile. "Girl, I don't know what strings you pulled to get us in this theater, but this is fucking awesome!"

Golden chuckled. "Thanks. Keeping my contacts from my financial days pays off every now and then. How are things going?"

"Pretty good. We had a couple of heads butting over the lineup, but Opal nipped it in the bud before I even needed to step in. She's thankfully keeping the performers in line so I can do my job without playing mediator."

"Great. I'd like to do one final run-through on stage if that's okay with you."

"Works for me. I'll get the theater crew together and meet you out there."

Golden watched Char walk, or rather bounce, away. She was full of excited energy but somehow very focused. Kendra recommended her and she had been a lifesaver because Golden had no experience arranging anything on this grand scale with so many moving parts. Golden spotted Opal speaking with a performer out of Atlanta who didn't look happy.

"Hey, Opal, Trinity, is there an issue?"

Opal began to speak, but Trinity beat her to it. "Yes, how are you going to put me after some chick who's barely busted her cherry in this business?"

Golden could see Opal was ready to curse Trinity out. She had the patience of a saint, but Trinity was pushing her past her saintliness.

"Trinity, you're the first act for the neo burlesque performers. Jackie is the last for the classical performers which is why we placed you after her. We discussed this during the Zoom call with the other performers last week and you had no issue with the order then so what's the problem now?"

Golden had heard rumors that Trinity was a diva and difficult to work with, but she always tried to give people the benefit of the doubt when it came to rumors because you didn't know their source. Obviously, the source in this case was correct. Trinity had been butting heads with not only the newer performers but with a couple of Satin and Lace's performers as well. She and Lotta had almost come to blows yesterday during rehearsals when Trinity had made a derogatory comment about Lotta's size. Golden had taken her aside, doing her best not to seem as if she were talking down to Trinity who had been performing just as long as Opal, and reminded her that this show was about showing the diversity of BIPOC performers so there was no judgment about size, sexuality, or identity allowed. Trinity had sucked her teeth, said "Yeah, whatever," and walked away. Golden then had to smooth Lotta's feathers because if she had to choose between the two, Trinity would be on the first plane back to Atlanta.

"I just assumed you would come to your senses and change the lineup once you saw run-throughs, but you obviously don't know what you're doing and need some direction."

Trinity had spoken loud enough for others around them to hear her. There was a collective gasp and a *"Oh no she didn't"* from the others in the room. Golden had dealt with bullies like Trinity throughout her early years in dance. She couldn't do much about it then, but she could now.

"Trinity, I don't think you'll be a good fit for this showcase. We are an inclusive group who support each other. We have enough people outside putting us down without doing it here so I'm going to have to ask you to leave. I'll still pay you, but you will not be performing this evening."

Trinity stared at Golden as if she hadn't heard her correctly. "You're not serious?"

"Very. Please collect your things and leave. I'm happy to have security assist you if needed." Golden gave her a pleasant smile.

"You're actually kicking me out of the show hours before curtain?" Trinity said in disbelief.

"Yes, which means we have some lineup adjustments to make so if you would please remove yourself from the premises so that we can get to work we would all appreciate it."

"You bitch!"

Before the hand Trinity raised to slap Golden made it anywhere near her face, Golden's years of self-defense training from her father kicked in and she had Trinity's wrist held tightly in her grip. Still holding her wrist, Golden took a step toward Trinity and met her now frightened gaze.

"Don't mistake my kindness for weakness. You have five minutes to gather your shit and get out of this theater on your own or I'll personally escort you out and I won't be gentle." Golden gave her wrist a squeeze before releasing her.

Trinity winced as she held her wrist against her chest. "I didn't want to be in your weak ass revue anyway. I only accepted because it was easy money."

"Girl, if you don't get to steppin'…" Lotta said threateningly as she stepped forward.

Trinity saw her and practically ran from the room with no further comment.

Opal was grinning. "I'll make sure security escorts her out."

"Thank you." Golden turned to the group of performers also smiling. "Okay, folks. The show is over. Let's meet on stage for a final rehearsal, then hair and makeup will meet you in the dressing room."

Once the room was cleared, Golden breathed a sigh of relief. She hated having to do that. She couldn't understand why, with the world the way it was today, she still had to deal with crabs in a barrel mentality from within the Black burlesque community. They should be trying to uplift each other rather than dragging each other down. There were so few of them given opportunities to compete with their White counterparts in the upper ranks of burlesque.

"You handled that like a true professional."

Golden turned in surprise to find Jade leaning against the doorframe smiling. Everything within her wanted her to run over and throw herself in Jade's arms, but she somehow kept her cool.

"Hey, you didn't tell me you were coming to the show." She strode over, Jade opened her arms, and Golden happily accepted a hug and brief but affectionate kiss from her.

"We wanted to surprise you. Kendra is assisting security with making sure your troublemaker is escorted off the property."

"Mission accomplished." Kendra walked in, went straight to Golden, and pulled her into her arms, lifting her several inches off the floor. "Mmm…It's good to see you."

Golden wrapped her arms around Kendra's neck. "You too."

"Hey, you're gonna break a rib squeezing her like that," Jade teased her.

Kendra gently lowered and released her. "Sorry about that."

Golden grasped her face and gave her a kiss. "It's okay. I'm a lot tougher than I look."

"Yeah, we saw. We walked in just before she was about to lay hands on you. I haven't seen anyone move that fast since I saw the Wonder Woman movie," Kendra teased her.

Golden rolled her eyes. "Shut up. I have a rehearsal to do. Can you two occupy yourselves until I'm finished?"

"I think we can find something to do," Jade said.

"Good."

Golden gave both another kiss then left feeling like she was walking on air.

❖

Zoe spritzed loc oil on her hair then massaged it into her scalp. As she washed the extra oil off her hands, her phone rang in the other room with Danice's ringtone. She didn't make it in time to answer so she called her right back.

"Hey."

Zoe didn't like the tone in Danice's voice. "Hey, what's up? I thought you'd be back by now."

"Yeah, so did I. I'm at the hospital with Malik. I found him unresponsive on the bathroom floor just before I was going to leave. My mom had already left so I couldn't send him to the hospital in the ambulance by himself. They're running some tests and will probably keep him overnight for observation, but it'll probably be another hour before that's determined."

Zoe sat dejectedly on the bed. If she didn't know any better, she'd swear Malik was faking his illness to get Danice back. "You're not going to make it in time to go to the show, are you?"

"Probably not. I'm sorry, babe. I told Malik that he needed to tell his parents or I would. I didn't sign up to become his full-time nursemaid."

Zoe knew that if she was frustrated with this whole situation then Danice was doubly so. That's why she tried not to complain when Danice would cancel plans because Malik needed her for one emergency or another. "Do what you need to do. Maybe you can still make it to the reception after."

"I'll do my best. Give Golden my love."

"Will do." Zoe tried to sound chipper than she felt.

There was a knock on her bedroom door. "Mind if I borrow some hair pins," her mother said from the other side.

"Hey, Mommy. Of course. Come in."

Zoe's mother walked in holding her carefully wound chignon in place. "I thought I put in enough pins."

Zoe followed her to the bathroom. "Here, let me help you."

Sandra had styled her long hair into two-strand twists then intertwined the twists into a chignon at the back of her head. Several twists were springing free from the knot.

"The pins you used were too small for your heavy hair."

"I don't know why I thought I could do this with my arthritis." Her mother flexed her stiff fingers in and out of a fist.

"Because you're stubborn." Zoe took a container of large hair pins from a drawer in her vanity. She retwisted the hair that was unraveling and pinned it back into place.

"The apple doesn't fall far from the tree." Her mother grinned at her in the mirror.

Zoe barely cracked a smile.

"What's wrong?"

After pinning the last escapee, Zoe checked to make sure the rest were secure then patted her mother's hair. "There you go. Nothing's wrong." She walked back into her bedroom.

"Child, I know you almost as well as I know myself. Something is bothering you. Is it Danice? I notice she's not here and we're supposed to be leaving soon."

Zoe opened her jewelry cabinet to avoid looking at her mother. "Malik had to be rushed to the hospital. Danice is there now. She may not make the show, but she'll probably make it for the cocktail reception."

"Zoe, look at me."

Zoe sighed then hesitantly turned toward her mother. She hated seeing the pity in her dark gaze.

"Have you talked to Danice about how her helping Malik is making you feel?"

"What am I supposed to say? I hate you being a good person and helping your sick ex-husband as he fights cancer?"

"Well, not in those exact words."

Zoe sat beside her mother on the end of her bed. "All I can think about is what Dad would have done without you when he was sick. I can't imagine wanting anyone to go through something like that alone. Even an asshole like Malik."

"The difference is I was married to your father. Danice and Malik ended their marriage."

"Technically, it hasn't even been a year since their divorce. Can you honestly say that if you and Dad had been divorced when he got sick and he didn't have anyone to help him that you wouldn't have stepped in?"

Sandra shrugged. "I can honestly say I don't know. I guess it would depend on why we were divorced and where we stood with each other. It's obvious Danice still cares for Malik, despite what their relationship was at the time of their divorce, or she wouldn't be there now. That's not to say it's enough to want to go back to him, but it's enough for her to make his well-being a priority over your relationship. Is that something you really want to be a part of?"

Zoe thought about it. She knew Danice loved her but was it enough to overcome the obligation she felt toward Malik? He had eight years to manipulate her into completely losing herself into his image of a perfect wife. Could Danice really have gotten over that and changed in a matter of months? It wasn't like Malik didn't have the money to hire a home health aide to do all the tasks Danice and her parents were doing for him. These were all concerns that Zoe had avoided thinking about because it made her question why she and Danice were even together or if she was just a rebound for Danice that had gone too far to end without Zoe getting hurt.

Sandra grasped her hand. "Zoe, I like Danice. I think that if you two had met after she'd had more time to get over Malik, you would still be good for each other. I just don't know if now is the right time."

Zoe's phone rang beside her on the bed with a notification. She gazed down then sighed. "Our car will be here in ten minutes. I better finish getting dressed."

Her mother gave her hand a squeeze and placed a kiss on her cheek. "You know I love you."

Zoe smiled. This time it was genuine. "Yes. I love you too, Mommy." She just wished she didn't know her so well.

❖

Melissa entered the theater and made her way toward the front. She spotted Zoe waving, lifted her hand to wave back then froze mid-wave when she saw the back of a tall familiar figure a few rows over. She only had a few moments to stare before a woman behind her cleared her throat followed by an annoyed "Excuse me." Melissa tore her gaze away just as the person was about to turn around and hurried toward the front rows. She greeted Zoe, Sandra, and Golden's family. As they shifted so that Zoe and Melissa could sit together, she tried to find the seat where she could have sworn she had seen Black.

"You're gonna give yourself whiplash. Who are you looking for?" Zoe asked.

"I thought I saw someone I knew."

"I wouldn't be surprised. Golden said tickets sold out within a week. The Twins are even here."

That drew Melissa's attention as Zoe pointed over to another front row of seats located to the left of the stage. The theater was set up amphitheater style with five rows of seats in front and on the left and right of the stage. "Wow. Does Golden know?"

"I assume she does. They walked from backstage a few minutes ago."

"Where's Danice?"

Zoe frowned. "Take a wild guess."

"Again? I thought today was her night off from babysitting her ex."

Zoe explained why Danice couldn't make it and Melissa felt a little bad. "Sorry to hear that. My mom had similar chemo treatment and it made her anemic which caused her to almost black out a couple of times. Hopefully, they'll get his red blood cell count up and he'll be able to go home soon."

"Oh man, I forgot your mom had cancer also."

"I'm sure she would like to forget as well since she hates how the treatment has affected her ability to get around like she used to."

"Now I feel like shit getting jealous of Danice spending so much time with Malik."

"There's no need for you to feel like shit. Malik is a manipulative asshole who is using his illness to keep Danice in his life. I'd be jealous too if I were you."

Zoe gave Melissa's hand a quick squeeze. "Thanks. That makes me feel better."

Melissa smiled. "You know I'll be your cheerleader anytime you need it."

Zoe leaned closer to her. "Enough about my love life. Have you seen Black since your last session?"

Melissa felt her cheeks flush. "Yes."

"And?"

Melissa quickly glanced over her shoulder, but there were too many people to attempt to find anyone unless she stood up and walked out to the aisle. "And I'm not going to talk about it here, but I will say it was very interesting."

Zoe chuckled. "I expect details during brunch tomorrow."

As the lights lowered and everyone took their seats, Melissa was tempted to use the excuse that she had to go to the bathroom so that she could make her way back up the aisle to see if she could spot that person again. If it was Black, how would she know for sure? They had never seen each other's face so she wouldn't even recognize them. If she did, what would she say? "Hi, I'm Melissa. I've been your kinky masked playmate for the past several months. Wanna get a drink?" Melissa had to laugh at herself for that thought. No, it was better that she didn't know. As tempted as she was, there's no way she was mixing her personal life with what went on at Dahlia's.

Moments later, a spotlight shone on the stage, Nina Simone's seductive voice sang "I Put a Spell on You," and an arm with a gold serpent bracelet wrapped around it with red crystal eyes snaked through the curtain, followed by a long leg with a matching snake around the ankle. Golden slinked through the curtain looking spellbinding in a gold belly-dance outfit with a bralette covered in iridescent stones and crystals fringed with gold beads, a gold chain around her waist attached to a belly ring, and a layered chiffon skirt that sat low on her hips with slits beginning just below her hip. She moved seductively to the music, bringing Nina's voice and words to life with her choreography. Melissa had always loved watching Golden dance and tonight was no exception as she combined jazz, belly dance, and burlesque into one mesmerizing routine. She moved around the stage bringing everyone into her seductive lair as if she actually were putting a spell on the audience. Melissa gazed over at Kendra and Jade and knew that they were fully and completely caught within Golden's magic. The crowd whooped loudly as Golden made her way over to them, and just as Nina crooned the last phrase of the song declaring that the listener was hers, Golden gave the Twins a sexy smile and with a fluidity that made Melissa think she had no bones, lowered herself to her knees, beckoning Jade and Kendra to her as she shimmied into a partial back bend.

Golden finished her routine in that pose, her full breasts pushing against the bralette as she breathed heavily, looking spent and satisfied. The audience was on its feet, with Jade and Kendra whistling loudly. Golden slowly unfolded herself, beaming at the audience as she stood and was handed a microphone. Melissa was so proud and happy to see her oldest and dearest sister-friend finally living her dream. No one deserved it more than Golden. She and Zoe blew her kisses and Golden winked at them in return before quieting the applause with a humble thank you and beginning her master of ceremony duties for the revue. After the show, Melissa couldn't get backstage fast enough to tell Golden how proud she was. They all gushed over her and the talented and diverse cast of performers, then headed out to the lobby for the cocktail reception.

"You're doing it again. Girl, who are you looking for?" Zoe asked as they waited in line at one of the three bars set up.

"I thought I saw Black."

Zoe's eyes widened in surprise. "Here? Do you know what they look like without the mask?"

"No, which is why I'm probably wrong. I saw someone from the back whose height and frame resembled Black's and just assumed it couldn't be anyone but them."

Zoe smirked. "Damn. They got your nose wide open. Do you want to casually cruise the room and look for them?"

"No! Let's drop it. It probably wasn't even them."

"Okay, but if it was, what would you have done?"

"Probably stare like an idiot then run in the opposite direction if they spoke to me." Melissa's shyness wasn't as bad as it used to be, but in certain situations, like the prospect of running into a client she found herself thinking about often, it reared its awkward head.

The sound of applause interrupted their conversation. Zoe and Melissa turned to see Golden walking into the room dressed in a shiny satin gold snake print corset with matching pants that accentuated her full shapely figure, and gold open-toe stilettos. She wore smoky golden eye makeup with small jewels lining the corners and a metallic bronze lip color. Her hair looked just as fresh as it did at the start of the show.

"How much hold gel did you have to use on her hair for it to still look that good?" Melissa asked.

"I used my new Hair For You extra hold set lotion. It's not as heavy as the other stuff so all she needs to do is put a little heat to the curl to freshen it up and she's good to go."

Melissa gave Zoe an appraising look. "I see you trying to put Tracee and Taraji out of business."

"Psh, there's enough room for all of us. Let's get our drinks and give time for Golden's adoring fans to worship her."

Melissa made sure to grab a white wine for Golden, then she and Zoe shouldered their way through the throng of people around her. She looked relieved to see them. Melissa handed her the glass of wine, then they each took an arm.

"We just want to steal her for a moment, folks. We promise to bring her back," Zoe said as they steered her away from the crowd toward a cocktail table nearby. "You don't mind if we steal your table to give our star a rest, do you?"

The two women who were sitting there saw Golden, gushed over her performance, promised they would be signing up for classes at Satin and Lace soon, then left.

"You didn't need to kick them away from their table," Golden said.

Zoe sucked her teeth. "Girl, please. They just sat through a two-hour show, they can stand for a little bit. Besides, we don't need prying ears while you tell us about the Twins' surprise appearance."

Melissa gazed around the room. "Speaking of them, where are they? I haven't seen them since the show ended."

Golden smiled wistfully. "They left right after. They said that they didn't want to steal my thunder. I'm meeting them at their hotel later."

"Oh okay, so you're trying to do a repeat of Paris?" Zoe teased her.

Golden looked down at her wine glass. "Shut up."

"Wait, are you blushing?" Melissa was surprised to see her confident friend reacting like a schoolgirl with a crush.

"Yes, she is. I guess that settles the matter we discussed earlier. I can't imagine you finding anyone else who makes our Golden giddy like Jade and Kendra," Zoe said.

Golden rolled her eyes. "Okay, we're changing the subject. Melissa, did you see Alex?"

Melissa's brow furrowed in confusion. "Alex who?"

"Prince."

"She's here?" Melissa gazed around the room again, but there were too many people now crowding the small space.

"Yes, and Alex identifies as non-binary now so it's they/them. They came backstage after the show shortly after you guys left. I'm surprised you didn't run into each other."

Alarm bells rang in Melissa's head. She hadn't seen or spoken to Alex since their date to Coney Island all those years ago.

"I haven't seen them."

"Maybe that's who you thought you recognized earlier and thought it might have been Black," Zoe said.

It was Golden's turn to look confused. "Hold on, you saw someone you thought may have been Black, who happens to go by they/them, and Alex was here, who also goes by they/them."

Zoe gasped. "You don't think Black and Alex are the same person?"

Melissa gazed at both like they were crazy. "Of course, they're not. First, I haven't spoken to Alex in eighteen years. Second, they have no idea that I work at Dahlia and even if they did, why would they keep their identity a secret?"

"What did the person look like that you thought you recognized?" Zoe asked.

Melissa shrugged. "I only saw them from the back. Tall, athletic, short naturally curly hair wearing a dark jacket and pants."

Golden grinned like she had a secret. "That sounds like Alex and what they were wearing."

"It also sounds like how you described Black," Zoe pointed out.

"There are hundreds of people that could fit that description." Melissa didn't want to accept the possibility of what they were saying.

"C'mon, Mel, what are the chances of this being a coincidence?" Golden said.

What were the chances? But if Alex and Black were the same person, why were they playing these games? There was only one way to find out. She had an appointment with Black next week, her last one before she, Golden, and Zoe left for St. Kitts. Due to Black's requests to stay anonymous in the agreement for their membership to Red Dahlia, Melissa couldn't ask Afrodite to reveal their identity. Maybe she could ask Black questions that would give her a clue as to who they really are. Not to call Alex out if it really was them, but for her own peace of mind.

CHAPTER TWENTY-FIVE

Danice still hadn't returned by the time Zoe got home. Her apartment was dark, and Danice wasn't waiting for her in her apartment either. She checked her phone to make sure she hadn't missed a message, but the last one came during the reception when Danice told her that they would be releasing Malik shortly and that she was so sorry she'd missed everything. That was two hours ago. Zoe checked in on Kiara who was working on the design for her prom dress, changed into her pajamas, warmed up some leftover pizza, then planted herself in front of the television hoping to distract herself from the hurt building up in her heart. She woke up to the clatter of her empty plate hitting the floor. She hadn't even realized she'd fallen asleep. One of the late-night talk shows was on and the sound of music no longer came from Kiara's room. Zoe considered waiting for Danice in her apartment then thought better of it. She turned off the television and lights, put her dishes in the sink, and was just about to turn the alarm on when she heard keys and someone entering the outer door. Shortly after, her door opened with Danice jumping in surprise.

"Jeez! You scared me. Why are you just standing at the door?"

"I was just about to turn the alarm on."

"Oh, I guess that was good timing." Zoe didn't move to allow Danice to enter.

"Maybe you should sleep up at your place tonight."

"Is everything okay?"

"No, but it's not something I want to get into tonight. We can talk in the morning."

Danice looked disappointed. "Okay. Good night." She leaned in to give Zoe a kiss.

Zoe brushed her lips across Danice's. "Good night."

Danice looked as if she were about to say something more, but then turned to go up to her apartment. Zoe closed the door, leaned her head against it, and allowed tears of frustration to roll down her cheeks.

Danice came downstairs late the next morning.

"Good morning."

Zoe continued loading the dishwasher without looking up at her. "Good morning. There's still some coffee and a cinnamon roll left if you haven't had breakfast."

"Thanks. I ate already. Zoe, what's going on? Are you mad at me for missing Golden's show?"

Zoe closed the dishwasher with a sigh then leaned against the counter as she went over in her head what she'd planned to say, which had kept her up for most of the night.

"I'm disappointed you weren't there, but I understand why you couldn't make it. What upsets me is the hold Malik still seems to have over you."

"What are you talking about? Malik has no hold over me."

"I understand what he's going through. I watched my father battle cancer and the effects of the treatment after. I wouldn't wish anyone to have to suffer through that alone, but it's not like Malik has no family to help him. I know he couldn't help getting cancer, but I feel like he saw an opportunity to bring you back into his life when he realized he fucked up and he's taking full advantage of it."

"Zoe, you can't be serious."

"I can only go by what you've told me about him, and it sounds like something he would do. He's been sick for months and still hasn't told his parents and made you and your parents promise not to tell them. If that isn't manipulative, then I must be missing something. C'mon, Danice, tell me you don't see it."

"Malik has always been a needy person when he's sick. He whines when he has a simple cold. As far as his parents, he just doesn't want to worry them. They don't get back home to see their family as often as they like and he doesn't want to take that away from them."

"Do you hear yourself? Last night you said that if he didn't call his parents soon you would do it. Now you're making excuses for him. Do you still love him?"

Danice looked offended. "I can't believe you're asking me that. You do recall what he put me through."

"It's a simple question. Do you still love him?"

Danice sighed with frustration and ran her hand through her hair, now long enough to wear a pixie cut that framed her full face beautifully. "Why do we have to repeatedly go through this conversation? I don't want to be with Malik. I left him for a reason and I don't ever plan on going back."

"Do. You. Love. Malik?"

Danice sat on a stool at the counter, gazing at Zoe pleadingly. "Don't do this."

Zoe didn't say anything. She just waited for the question to be answered, although she felt like it already had been.

"We were married for eight years. He was my best friend until he turned into an asshole. There were rare moments of the old Malik that cared about me more than his familial duty and reputation. Those rare moments and that same sense of duty instilled in me by my mother kept me there for all those years. I don't love him like I did in the beginning, but I do care for him and I can't just sit by and watch him suffer, no matter what he did. I told you that in the beginning and you encouraged me to follow my heart. Now you're twisting it into something it isn't. Despite the shitty husband that he turned out to be, Malik is genuinely a good person. He wouldn't use his illness to manipulate me or anyone."

Zoe walked over and sat beside her. "Maybe it's that twisted sense of duty that's keeping you from seeing the truth. Malik may not be taking advantage of the situation to be cruel but to try to get back what he knows he lost. Maybe losing you made him realize his mistakes. As the saying goes, you don't know what you have until you lose it. I just don't want to see you manipulated back into a situation that, from what I saw when you walked into my salon, had taken you to the lowest point of your life. I love you too much not to express my concern."

"Is it concern or jealousy? If it is, you have nothing to be jealous of. I know I've been spending more and more time over at Malik's, but my mother has also been there at times. Even if Malik wanted to try something, he's too sick and weak most of the time to do it."

"I'm not jealous, especially of Malik. I'm worried that now that you've experienced your first positive and loving relationship after Malik that I'm going to end up being the jump off for someone else that may come along and turn out to be the one you decide to rebuild a life with. I don't think my heart could take something like that happening."

Danice grasped Zoe's hands. "You are not a rebound or jump off from my marriage. I'm with you because I know you're the one for me. I've known it since the beginning."

"I want to believe that, but I don't know."

"I don't understand where these doubts are coming from. I thought we had settled this. Do you want me to spend less time at Malik's? Other than today's hospitalization, he's been getting stronger, his treatment will be ending soon, and his parents are due to be home in a couple of weeks. We can get back to where we were."

Zoe shook her head and slid her hands from Danice's. "There's something about Malik that I should've told you when it first happened, but then you told me he was sick and I didn't think it would've been right to tell you then."

"What are you talking about?"

"When we first began seeing each other, Malik came by the salon hoping I could get a message to you. He made a comment that you had done something like this before. Thought you wanted to be with someone like me then realized being with a woman isn't what you want. Is this true? Have you been with other women then gone back to Malik?"

Danice stood and began pacing. "I can't believe he told you that. Although most of the issues in our marriage had to do with Malik's treatment of me, I made mistakes as well. I met a woman, a fellow volunteer at the organization, and we became friends. After a while, our friendship became something more. I told Malik about the affair and that I wanted a divorce, then I found out I was pregnant." Danice stopped pacing and gazed pleadingly at Zoe.

"After the loss of our first baby, I was told it would be difficult to get pregnant again. I had to make a choice, the baby I had been wanting, or the woman I'd been seeing for less than a year. I hadn't gone out looking for an affair, it just happened, and yes, I thought being with her was what I wanted, but I wanted our baby more. More than my own happiness and freedom. But in the end, I still ended up not getting what I wanted." Her eyes filled with tears.

Zoe stood and took Danice in her arms. Holding her as she grieved for the loss she still felt. Moments later, she stepped from Zoe's embrace, wiping her eyes and nose with her sleeve. Zoe grabbed a napkin from the counter and offered it to her.

"Was that the only one?" Zoe hated having to ask while Danice was still so emotional, but she needed to know.

Danice wouldn't meet her gaze. "No. there were a few others after that. Casual affairs that served as nothing but an escape from the grief and loneliness of my situation. There were many times when I was determined to leave Malik, but then he or my mother would lay some guilt trip on me and I'd stay. I was more relieved than hurt when I found out he had been having an affair and was about to have a baby with her. I finally had my escape, but I was still wallowing so deep in self-pity and doubt that it didn't give me the freedom I thought I wanted."

She finally looked up at Zoe with a soft smile. "Until I met you. You showed me what was possible and how to accept the right kind of love."

Zoe's smile in return was sad. "And here we are. Back to where it all began, with your obligation to Malik. You may not be married to him anymore, but you're still jeopardizing your own happiness for him. I can't…I won't compete with that, Danice."

Danice frowned in confusion. "What are you saying?"

"I'm saying I think you need some time to figure out what your priorities are. What if Malik's cancer doesn't go into remission or comes back? Do you think you could just be an objective observer with his care? Especially if your family pressures or guilts you into wifely duties that you legally signed away with your divorce."

"If you're asking me to choose between you and Malik, I choose you."

Zoe shook her head. "I'm asking you to choose between YOU and Malik. Can you look me in the eye right now and say that you can totally cut him out of your life and no longer accept the obligation and guilt that he and your mother lay on you if you do?"

Zoe's heart was breaking as she watched Danice's internal struggle play out in the doubt and indecision on her face. She didn't think Danice even realized what was going on until Zoe just brought it to her attention. Danice had thought she was fine. She had, despite Zoe suggesting she not do so, stopped going to therapy shortly after their relationship had become more serious because she thought she was good. She probably would have been if Malik had stayed out of her life, but it was obvious life had other ideas.

Zoe sighed tiredly. "I have to get dressed and go pick up some things before meeting Melissa so we can go to Golden's for brunch. If you like, we can have dinner later and finish talking."

Danice nodded then rushed from the room. Zoe heard her door close and footsteps hurrying upstairs. She leaned against the counter suddenly feeling numb.

"Mom?"

She gazed up to find Kiara standing in the kitchen doorway.

"Hey, baby girl. How much of that did you hear?"

"All of it. Are you okay?"

Zoe tried to speak but instead of words, a whimper of despair came out. She covered her mouth, but she couldn't stop the tears that followed. Kiara wrapped her arms around her waist. Zoe wrapped hers around her daughter and cried. She could count three constants in her life, her family, her business, and her friends. Zoe decided that everything outside of those things was unnecessary.

❖

Golden awakened to the feeling of warmth and contentment with visions of last night's sexscapade flittering through her mind making her body flush with desire. She blinked her eyes open to find herself cocooned between Jade and Kendra. Kendra's nose was buried in the crook of her neck, her arm resting across her hips, and a leg tangled with one of Golden's. Jade's head lay on Golden's chest, an arm thrown across her waist and her leg tangled with Golden's other leg. After the reception, Melissa and Zoe insisted on walking Golden to the hotel where Jade and Kendra were staying near the theater. Golden knew it was because she was considering not meeting the Twins and they wanted to make sure she didn't chicken out. They even stood in the lobby to make sure she got on the elevator. It was funny that even with their own complicated love lives, her friends were still butting into hers and she loved them for it. She wouldn't have been surprised if they had decided to sit there a little longer just to make sure she didn't turn around and come back down. Which she had considered until she realized how much she missed Jade and Kendra and loved how they had dropped whatever they were doing to come out and support her.

Golden ran one hand through Jade's straight hair and smoothed the other over Kendra's smooth waves. As if connected by some invisible force, they both moaned, shifted, then turned sleepy gazes and sexy smiles up at her.

"Good morning, beautiful," Kendra said.

"You're still here," Jade said.

Golden smiled at them. "Good morning. Yes, I'm still here."

Golden knew they were both hurt by her abrupt departure in Paris, but it seemed to have affected Jade the most, judging by the look in her eyes the few times they discussed it.

"What do you say we order room service and laze about the rest of the morning?" Kendra nibbled at Golden's ear.

"Sounds like a plan to me." Jade took one of Golden's nipples into her mouth.

"Mmm…as tempting as that sounds, I have plans with Melissa and Zoe today. I need to go home and get ready." Desire throbbed between her legs.

"Oh, in that case, let's help you." Golden almost whimpered in disappointment as Kendra rolled off the bed followed by Jade who offered her a hand.

Golden looked from one to the other in confusion then took Jade's hand. They led her to the bathroom where Kendra turned on the water.

"What are you doing?" Golden asked.

"We're helping you get ready. Figured we could save you some time by taking a shower before you go." She stepped in, now offering her hand.

"It's just a shower. We promise," Jade said.

Golden knew better than to trust Jade's feigned innocent expression, but she stepped into the shower anyway. Jade followed holding two thick wash cloths. Fortunately, it was a good-sized walk-in shower so there was enough room for the three of them as long as they adjusted the shower head, which Jade did. She also wet and soaped up the washcloths, then handed one to Kendra.

"I'll take care of the front if you can handle the back." Jade gave Kendra a mischievous grin.

"Oh, I think I can handle that," Kendra said from behind Golden.

They both began at her neck and worked the soapy cloths down her body. Jade spent a little extra time gently washing her sex while Kendra decided two hands worked better than a cloth over her ass. Golden moaned with pleasure thinking she'd never be able to take another shower without thinking of this one. She was panting when Jade knelt to wash her legs and feet. Golden opened her eyes just enough to see the water raining down her back as she gazed up at Golden with a look of pure adoration. Not only did it make her heart skip, but it also filled her with panic. Jade quickly looked away and stood to adjust the showerhead so that they could rinse Golden off. Kendra took over, using her hands once again to finish the job, making sure to reach around to pay particular attention to Golden's breasts as the water cascaded over her.

As Kendra massaged her breasts, Golden leaned back against her and felt her move to lean against the shower wall. She heard the squeak of the shower being turned off, and before she could open her eyes, she felt Jade's body flush against her own, pressing her further against Kendra. Golden's lips parted to moan, but Jade covered her mouth with her own, catching the sound before it escaped. Their wet bodies slid against each other's sensuously as Jade kissed Golden's breath away and one of Kendra's hands slid down from her breasts to slide over her clit and into her slick vagina. Golden thrust her behind against Kendra's pelvis, rotating her hips seductively, making Kendra moan in response. Not wanting to leave Jade out, Golden slid her hand between her and Jade's body, down her hardened abs, and slid her fingers into Jade's sex. Golden didn't know how they managed to stay upright as she felt Jade's walls contracting around her fingers, triggering her own orgasm, which also seemed to trigger Kendra's and they all cried out in a harmonic symphony of pleasure.

All three stood panting from exertion. Kendra held onto the towel rack with an arm around Golden's waist. Golden's head lay back against Kendra's shoulder and Jade held Golden's hips with her head in the crook of her neck. Golden's legs felt like rubber and she was afraid that if Kendra released her she would collapse into a puddle on the floor. Then, just barely above a whisper, Golden heard Jade say something that both thrilled and frightened her.

"I love you, Golden."

❖

To The Beautiful Mistress Heart,

I hope your weekend is going well. Unfortunately, I'm going to have to cancel our session this week as I need to travel out of the country to handle a personal matter. As I know you are traveling next week, I will contact you when you return to see about rescheduling. Have a wonderful time and I hope that your accommodation is satisfactory (wink emoji).

Your willing servant,

Black

Melissa read Black's email that she'd received through her Mistress Heart account to Golden and Zoe. Last night, she'd read it over several times foolishly trying to read between the lines for something that would give away Black's real identity. She'd tossed and turned all night thinking about her friends' crazy theory that Black was really Alex Prince.

"They sent it last night? What time?" Zoe asked.

Melissa gazed back down at her phone. "A little after seven."

"Unless they were emailing during the show, then it must not be Alex," Golden said.

Melissa hadn't thought of that. She didn't know why that gave her a sense of relief. Maybe because it gave her back the anonymity that she needed to continue with her work at Red Dahlia objectively. She never took a client whose name or face she recognized from her work or personal life.

Zoe took Melissa's phone from her. "You know, you could easily solve the mystery by looking up Alex on social media."

"You know I only do social media for the gallery. I have a Facebook account, but I haven't used it in years and deleted the app off my phone." Melissa held her hand out for Zoe to return it to her.

"That's all right. I'll look her up. I haven't seen her since she sold me back her percentage of Hair For You several years back, but we still follow each other on Insta. I'll just pull up a recent pic and you can compare it to what you know of Black's features."

"No," Melissa said.

"Aw, c'mon." Zoe continued tapping away on her phone. "Here we go."

As Zoe began to turn the phone toward her, Melissa swung, knocking it out of Zoe's hand and sending it flying across the dining table. She looked up to find Zoe and Golden looking at her as if she'd lost her mind. Melissa felt her face grow hot with embarrassment.

"I'm sorry." She picked up the phone as it teetered on the edge of the table, making sure to keep the screen facing away from her as she handed it back to Zoe.

"Okay, message received." She closed whatever app she had open and handed it back to Melissa.

"Why are you so afraid to find out who Black is?" Golden asked.

Melissa knew she needed to talk about what she felt was happening between her and Black before it got out of hand because after their last session, she was seriously considering offering to see them outside of Dahlia's like Rose did some of her clients who she was willing to enjoy a more intimate arrangement with.

"My sessions with Black are starting to feel less like work and more like something I'd like to pursue in the real world." Saying it out loud seemed to give it a life she wasn't ready to deal with.

"Do you mean as in dating or extra services for pay?" Golden asked.

"I honestly don't know. You know my sessions with Black haven't been like any with my other clients. They want straightforward kink with Mistress Heart and nothing more. I feel like Black has been looking for a girlfriend experience without the real-life commitment and found a loophole on how to get it with the varied services the Red Dahlia offers."

"And they've got your nose wide open because you haven't had a girlfriend in real life in forever," Zoe said.

"Subtle," Golden said.

Zoe snorted. "Have you ever known me to be subtle?"

Melissa shook her head. This was why she loved these women. "She's probably right."

"Do you want to be Black's girlfriend? Do you think that's what their goal is, to seduce you into making your business arrangement more personal, because that's what it sounds like to me. They saw you at the fundraiser, found themselves attracted to you, and realized the only way they were going to be able to get at you was booking an appointment," Golden said.

"Pretty ingenious if you ask me," Zoe said, looking impressed.

Melissa remembered something Black said during their consultation. *"I joined for the opportunity to see you again. And before you freak out, I'm not some weird stalker. You just fascinated me."*

She repeated it to Golden and Zoe.

Golden nodded. "Maybe Zoe is right. The focus on your pleasure instead of theirs, the gifts, the concern for what makes you uncomfortable. Whether you see it or not, you and Black have been dating."

Melissa wasn't as surprised by their revelation as she probably should be. She'd always felt like her sessions with Black were more like dates disguised as kink sessions.

"I think, deep down, you knew this already," Zoe said knowingly.

"If that's true, then you need to decide how far you're willing to take it. Fortunately, now that they've canceled your next session, you have some time to think about it while we spend a fabulous week in a villa they gifted you." Golden smirked.

"You two are enjoying this," Melissa said.

"No, we just think it's funny that you could be so worldly in all other areas of your life except dating," Zoe said.

"Oh, and being worldly in dating has helped you two?"

Golden and Zoe looked offended for a moment, then all three laughed uproariously.

"How did all three of us end up sucking so bad at romance?" Golden asked.

"Let's see." Melissa raised her hand and began ticking off why she thought that was. "I have self-esteem issues that lead me to believe I'm not worthy of being loved, Zoe is afraid of getting hurt so she ends things before that happens, and you're afraid of letting anyone close to avoid the pain of a tragic loss."

Zoe laughed. "Well, damn, Dr. Hart. Since you've analyzed us, are you going to offer some wisdom to help?"

Melissa smiled broadly. "Yes, in my nonprofessional opinion I suggest we direct our energy into deciding which concerts and parties we'll be attending at the music festival and forget, at least for a little while, about our present romantic entanglements."

Zoe raised her glass of Mimosa. "Cheers to that!"

Melissa and Golden clinked their glasses to Zoe's. Melissa wondered if she'd be able to take her own advice. Afterall, her romantic entanglement had gifted her the vacation home they would be staying at.

❖

After Melissa and Zoe left, Golden poured the last of the mimosa mixture into a glass and stepped out onto the upper patio that overlooked their small but neatly manicured yard. She thought about what Melissa suggested and didn't know how that would be possible since the Twins were headlining one of the shows at the music festival in St. Kitts. Jade's whispered words still rang in her ear, and the momentary hurt in her eyes at Golden's lack of response stabbed at her heart. Golden didn't know if Kendra had heard it as well, if so, she hadn't acknowledged it or repeated the declaration. They had all dried off, gotten dressed, and the Twins had walked Golden down to the lobby to await her ride. She had avoided making eye contact with Jade until she said good-bye. The hurt was gone, but the adoration was still there. Her hug and kiss lingered a little longer than Kendra's and Golden found herself wondering what the few people in the lobby wondered about the three of them.

Melissa's analysis had certainly rung true for Golden. She had purposely avoided serious relationships with anyone, originally using the excuse that work kept her too busy to devote time to a relationship, but even with the dance school, her troupe, and traveling for performances, she could no longer use that excuse. Golden didn't want to give her heart to someone who could be taken away from her at the drop of a hat. She had seen how devastating losing her father was for her mother and promised herself that she would never go through that if she could avoid it. She couldn't imagine what would have happened if her mother hadn't had her and Drew to worry about. Her parents were just as in love the day her father was taken from them as they were when they first declared their love for each other all those years ago. She had overheard her mother talking to someone on the phone and describing losing her father like feeling as if someone had ripped her heart from her chest and crushed it. She understood that feeling because it was pretty close to what she had felt as she watched the light leave her father's eyes. In the back of her mind, Golden knew she reasonably couldn't live her life that way. More afraid of losing someone than loving them but there was no room for reason when fear and grief were combined.

She had gone to youth grief counseling, but they didn't cover the fear of falling in love once you became an adult. When she became an adult, she had been too busy working to make sure her family didn't have to struggle financially to worry about getting further counseling. Now, at thirty-five years old, she was falling in love and allowing fear to keep her from accepting it. Golden finished off the rest of her beverage and went back into the house frustrated with herself for being so stupidly obstinate. Especially after seeing that her mother had found a way to love again. It might not be the all-consuming lifelong love that she had for her father, but it was still love. She decided to change her clothes and head down to her studio in the basement to work off her frustration. Her phone buzzed on the kitchen counter. It was a text from Jade.

Hi. Would you give me a call when you have some time to talk?

Golden stared at the text for some time before she called Jade via video out of habit when she meant to call via phone. She was already nervous about this conversation; it was worse doing so face-to-face.

"Hey, thanks for calling me," Jade said.

"Of course. Why wouldn't I?"

Jade gazed guiltily away from the screen. "I'm sure you heard what I said this morning. I was caught up in the moment and blurted it out without thinking."

For a moment, Golden considered acting as if she hadn't heard it but that would've just been cruel. "Yes, I heard it."

"I don't expect you to say it back. Kendra is of the mindset that we shouldn't say anything unless you say it first so that you don't feel pressure to make any decisions about the three of us pursuing a more permanent relationship. But I'm glad it's out there now. It's been difficult playing like this is some casual thing that we've been doing when it stopped being that before Paris."

"So, Kendra feels the same way you do?"

"Yes. Unlike me, she's just better at keeping her feelings to herself."

Golden had to sit down. Jade wore her heart on her sleeve so it wasn't a total surprise that she was the first to admit to feelings beyond their intimate friendship, but Kendra had given her no clue as to her true feelings. Especially since she was usually the one pulling Jade back from saying too much during their calls.

"Golden?"

Golden hadn't realized a moment had passed without her responding. "Uh, yeah, sorry. I'm just not sure how to respond."

"I understand. I kind of blind-sided you with what I said. I just want to be upfront with you because I honestly don't know how I'm going to be able to keep going on the way we are."

"Bro, tell me that's not Golden." Kendra said in the background.

Jade didn't verbally respond but her expression gave her away.

"I thought we talked about this."

"We did, but I thought it was important that we put everything out in the open."

Kendra stepped into view over Jade's shoulder with a look of exasperation. "Golden, I'm sorry. I told her not to call you."

"It's okay. We've been avoiding this discussion since Paris. It's probably about time that we have it." She sounded more confident than she felt.

"Only if you're ready," Kendra said.

She wasn't, but Golden knew she couldn't run from it anymore. "I'm ready."

Kendra gave her an understanding smile as Jade turned her phone to fit them both on screen.

"Well, as Jade already blabbered." Jade gave Kendra an angry glare. "We're both falling for you, but I didn't want to put any pressure on you by telling you right now. I'm honestly fine with the way things are until you figure out what you want."

Jade and Kendra seemed to wait patiently for the full minute Golden chewed on her bottom lip trying to figure out how to say what she knew would blow up their comfortable little threesome.

"Before I met you, if anyone would have told me that I would be involved with you two I would have laughed in their face. Full disclosure, I've never really done the dating thing with one person, let alone two at once. I didn't have time for all that. I appreciate that you respected my wishes to just be friends in the beginning and that you didn't pressure me for more after we became intimate. Jade, I've tried picturing what a life would be like with you and Kendra and realized that I'm not ready for a commitment like that." Jade started to speak, but Golden shook her head knowing that she was going to say that they had no problem waiting for her. "Or if I'll ever be."

Jade's expression became crestfallen.

Kendra nodded. "Golden, I know we can be a lot for one person, especially someone that's never been in the type of relationship Jade and I are asking for. So, if you need a break from this…from us…we'll give you all the time you need."

Golden smiled sadly. "I don't deserve such understanding."

Jade smiled for the first time during the call. "Golden, you deserve the world. Don't ever think any less."

Her phone screen became a watery blur for a moment, then she wiped away the tears. "I don't need a break. I think it would be best for all of us if I just ended this now. I don't want to continue dragging this on knowing it's not going to lead where you two would like it to."

"Fuck! I knew I should've just kept my mouth closed," Jade chastised herself.

"Jade, this isn't because of what you said. I've known for some time that although I care deeply for both of you, I can't give you and Kendra what you want. I don't think I'm capable of giving it to anyone." Golden couldn't stop the tears now. This was breaking her heart.

Although Jade looked devastated, Kendra still had her easy smile, but her eyes shone with unshed tears.

"We'll respect your decision. If you ever need anything that we can help with, please don't hesitate to call."

"And if you change your mind about us—" Jade began saying.

"Jade, let it go," Kendra said in frustration.

Jade looked duly reprimanded.

"Thank you for your friendship and support, personally and professionally. Take care." Golden disconnected the call before she could completely break down, which was what she did. Sobs racked her body and she felt as if her heart was shattering into a million pieces.

❖

Zoe returned home to find a note and keys on her kitchen counter.

Dear Zoe,
I didn't think it would be good for either of us if I stayed so I'm going
to stay at my sister's while I look for another place. I'm sorry and I truly
do love you.
Danice

Zoe thought that she knew what heartbreak felt like when Kiara's father walked out on her, but that was nothing compared to what she was feeling right now. It was like she'd just lost a part of herself. She began second-guessing even bringing up the conversation, then she thought about what it would have been like if she had let the situation continue the way it was and how she would feel if Danice decided that she wanted to see what else was out there for her or, God forbid, chose to go back to Malik. She had done the right thing. Feeling as if someone had ripped her heart from her chest would go away in time. Zoe fought back tears as she neatly folded the note and put it in her pocket. She gazed down at the heart-shaped key ring that had keys to the front door, the upstairs apartment, and to her place.

Zoe picked them up then headed upstairs to the apartment. She walked in and felt an immediate sense of loss. Danice had made sure not to leave anything behind. All the pictures and mementos that had made the place hers were gone. The only sign left that she had even been there was the faint alluring scent of her perfume, Nest New York Perfume Oil. Zoe loved to bury her nose in Danice's neck because she smelled like a warm spring day. She walked slowly around the apartment, running her fingers over the arm of the sofa where they would cuddle and watch movies. Over the kitchen island where Danice would create the wonderful dishes handed down from generations of women in her family. Then she stood over the bed, gazing down and picturing the nights spent in each other's arms, making love, talking for hours, or just holding each other when a long rough day didn't spare them much energy to do anything else.

"Zoe, are you up there?"

At the sound of her mother's voice, Zoe shook herself from her memories, wiped the tears they brought on, and took a calming breath.

"Yeah, Mommy. I'll be right down."

She had been so lost in thought that she hadn't even heard her come into the house.

Zoe gave her mother a hug and a peck on the cheek. "You're early. I thought we weren't seeing each other until dinner."

"Kiara called me and told me Danice had moved out."

Zoe sighed. "Why am I not surprised." She walked into the kitchen and took a bottle of water from the refrigerator.

"She was worried about you. She knew she wouldn't be home and wanted to make sure someone was here to check on you."

"You two do realize that I'm a grown woman who doesn't need to be looked after."

"You're also a grown woman who hasn't had her heart broken in a very long time. You know that you don't have to be so strong all the time. You're allowed to be soft and vulnerable. No one is going to think any worse of you."

"Mommy, I'm fine. Really. If you want to be helpful, you can go grocery shopping with me. I didn't have a chance to go yesterday and I really don't want another night of takeout."

Her mother looked as if she would argue then smiled. "Okay. I need to pick up some things for your grandmother anyway. You know I'm here to offer a shoulder to cry on or an ear to vent to if you need me."

"I know." Zoe pulled her into a hug, then quickly pulled away because she knew that if she stayed within her comforting embrace a second longer that she'd be blabbering like a baby.

CHAPTER TWENTY-SIX

G irl! If this is what you get for not having sex with Black, imagine what they would give you if you decided to become their boothang," Zoe said as the golf cart shuttle that picked them up at the front gate pulled up in front of the villa they would be staying in during their vacation.

"This definitely ranks up there with those over-the-water bungalows we stayed at in Jamaica," Golden said as their driver unloaded their luggage from the cart.

Melissa was still too shocked to speak. In place of the front door was a gate that looked to lead to a courtyard. The gate opened and a man who looked to be in his sixties dressed in a similar uniform as their driver stepped out with a broad friendly smile.

"Welcome, Ms. Hart. I hope you and your friends had a pleasant flight. My name is Aubrey and I'll be your butler. If you'll follow me, I will show you your home during your stay with us in St. Kitts." Just as with other resort staff they had encountered upon their arrival, Aubrey spoke with an easy lilting Caribbean accent.

Golden bumped Melissa with her shoulder, reminding her to speak. "Oh, uh, thank you, Aubrey. You can just call me Melissa, and this is Zoe and Golden."

"Enjoy your stay, ladies," their driver said as he climbed back into the cart.

"Oh, excuse me." Golden hurried over to him and offered him a folded twenty-dollar bill. "Thank you."

"It was my pleasure." He tipped an invisible hat at her then drove off.

Melissa, Golden, and Zoe each grabbed their luggage and walked through the gate Aubrey held open for them. They had decided long ago that if they couldn't fit anything into the one suitcase and one carry-on that they were each allotted for their trips, then it didn't need to go. They entered a beautiful courtyard with the same lush flowers and greenery as the front of the house, plus lounge chairs and a hammock big enough for two people hanging between two palm trees.

"If you don't find me in my room tomorrow morning, I'm probably sleeping out here," Golden said dreamily.

"Good thing I brought extra bug spray," Melissa said.

Zoe chuckled. "Mel, our overly cautious sister."

Melissa quirked a brow. "That overly cautiousness saved you from a horrible sunburn when I brought aloe on our last trip."

"You right. I can't even argue with that."

They all laughed, probably remembering Melissa slathering almost a full bottle's worth of aloe on Zoe's back after she'd fallen asleep beside the pool while Melissa and Golden had been out shopping. Just inside the door were two sets of stairs, one leading up to the second floor and one leading down to what must have been the entertainment room. Just past the stairs was a powder room. There was a collective gasp as they followed Aubrey into a large living area with a big screen television mounted on the wall, to the left of that an equally large dining area with a table big enough to seat ten people comfortably and a kitchen any home chef would drool over. But what caused the gasps was the entire wall of glass that opened and led out to an outdoor living area, dining area, kitchen, pool, and guest cottage.

Melissa's mind was blown by all of this. "This is crazy."

Aubrey walked over to the kitchen and returned with a tray of beverages. "Something to refresh you until lunch is served."

Melissa picked up the glass with a clear liquid and fresh limes and lemons floating and took a sip. The fruited water hit the spot after their journey. Next, Aubrey led them upstairs to the bedrooms.

"Ms. Melissa, the master suite has been reserved for your use." He indicated a room at the end of the hall with double doors. "Ms. Golden and Ms. Zoe, you have the choice of any three of our guest rooms. I'm sure you ladies would like some time to freshen up and get settled. A light lunch will be prepared for you shortly. I'll be nearby if you should need anything." Aubrey gave a slight bow then left them on their own.

"The master suite. I need to check this out." Golden left her suitcase in the hall and headed toward the double doors.

Melissa followed, pulling her suitcase along with Zoe in tow. Golden swung both doors open and Melissa's bottom jaw almost smacked the floor. The bedroom was bigger than her entire apartment. There was a king-size bed, a whole sitting area facing a large flatscreen television with surround sound speakers, a dresser and armoire, and a wall of glass like the one downstairs with a sliding door that led to a private patio. The bathroom had a private toilet room, a double sink vanity, and a walk-in shower with three shower heads. A rain shower head in the ceiling and an upper and lower massage head on the wall. Outside the shower was a touch panel with a selection of shower and spa settings. The décor throughout was cream, black marble, and natural wood accents.

"Mel, if you don't snag Black, I will," Zoe teased her.

"Stop it. This isn't a marriage proposal, it's a vacation rental." Melissa walked out of the bathroom and back out into the hall. "I'm sure the other rooms are just as nice."

To Melissa's chagrin, although the other rooms were nice with each having their own bathroom and access to a shared balcony, they weren't as nice as the one she was staying in. After suffering through more teasing, Melissa left her friends to shower and settle in before lunch. Despite feeling as if there had to be a catch for Black to give her such a luxurious gift, Melissa decided she was going to do her best to take full advantage of it and worry about the repercussions later. She unpacked her luggage, laid out her new bathing suit and matching coverup to wear since they had purposely arrived a couple of days before the music festival to enjoy the sun and sand before the nonstop partying began.

She tied her locs into a topknot, placed her extra-large shower cap over them, then turned on all three shower heads just for the hell of it. She almost drowned herself under the rain showerhead, but the massagers were pure bliss as the water pressure pounded out all the knots in her upper and lower back. She had also been provided with a plush sponge and tropical-scented soap to continue her luxuriating shower. By the time she finished, the bathroom looked like a steam room and the clock on the nightstand told her she had been in there for a little over a half hour. She'd never taken a shower longer than fifteen minutes. Knowing she was probably going to have to endure further teasing from Golden and Zoe because they were probably already downstairs, Melissa hurriedly moisturized and dressed, then practically ran downstairs. Just as she suspected, her friends, dressed in similar attire but with a lot more flesh showing than her modest swimsuit, were sitting at the outdoor dining table with half-filled glasses of probably some fruity drink, smirking.

"Go ahead, get it over with," Melissa said as she sat beside Golden.

Golden shook her head. "We're not going to say a word, but you do look extra refreshed."

"Must have been some shower. That lower one sure piqued my interest," Zoe said.

"It was a great shower, but not because of where your dirty minds are going."

"If you say so," Zoe said.

Melissa rolled her eyes in exasperation, then they all laughed.

A beautiful ebony skinned woman with a smooth bald head walked out of the house dressed in a chef's coat and khaki shorts carrying a tray of sliced fruit. She placed it in the center of the table and smiled at Melissa. She had been in such a hurry to get downstairs that she hadn't even noticed anyone in the kitchen.

"Ms. Hart, I presume. I'm Chef Warner. We were just awaiting your arrival." Unlike the other staff they had met so far, Chef Warner had a British accent. "Lunch today will be a light fare with ingredients all grown and bought locally. I hope you enjoy."

Melissa turned from her retreating figure to Golden. "We have our own chef?"

"Girl, there's a butler, a chef, two maids, and a gardener. Aubrey filled us in while we were waiting for you. We could also have our own personal driver for the entirety of our stay so we don't have to worry about getting back and forth from the festival venues," Golden informed her.

"Black must be Bezos rich to afford this level of vacationing," Zoe said.

Melissa was suddenly nervous about the idea of someone like that being interested in her. What could Black possibly see in her other than what she represented as Mistress Heart? The movie *Pretty Woman* came to mind, and Melissa felt her body flush at the thought of Black offering her millions to become their side chick which basically, as Mistress Heart, she already was.

Golden filled an empty glass that sat at Melissa's place setting with whatever was in a pitcher set in the middle of the table. "You look like you could use this."

"Thanks." Melissa took a hearty drink of the beverage and realized it was heavily laced with rum. Her second sip was smaller before she set the glass back down.

Zoe gave her a sympathetic smile. "Don't go freaking out over this. Just enjoy the moment and worry about the rest when we get back to the real world. That's what Golden and I are going to do."

Golden patted her hand. "Exactly. Here, there's no heartbreak or romantic complications. Just sunshine, alcohol, music, and parties to help us forget about all that for a little while."

Melissa nodded. "You're right. We're here to escape not talk about what's going on back home." She raised her glass. "Here's to another fabulous girls' trip."

Golden and Zoe clinked their glasses to hers then they all took a drink. They were filling their salad plates with fruit from the platter when Chef Warner and Aubrey brought out three more platters and set them next to the tray of fruit.

Chef Warner gave them another broad smile. She obviously loved what she did. "For your dining pleasure we have a mixed green salad, mango ginger barbecue chicken, and conch fritters. I'll be in the kitchen if you need anything else. Enjoy."

They all thanked her then she and Aubrey returned to the house. A moment later, the soft sound of Caribbean music drifted over them from the outdoor speakers.

"I feel so fancy." Golden picked up her glass of rum punch, holding her pinky out as she sipped delicately.

"That's because we are, dahhhling," Zoe said in her version of a high society tone as she did the same with her glass.

Melissa laughed loving her friends and how they always managed to make her life so much more fun. "You two are foolish."

❖

Golden regretted coming to tonight's concert, and it hadn't even begun. They were attending the second night of shows at the music festival which happened to be the one the Rhythm Twins were performing. Melissa suggested they skip this one and spend the evening hanging out on the Strip where they could grab dinner, listen to local bands and dance on the beach. It sounded like a great idea, but Golden couldn't bear the thought of not seeing Jade and Kendra, even if it was standing amongst an audience of hundreds.

"Are you okay?" Melissa asked.

Golden nodded, attempting a reassuring smile, but she knew it hadn't worked by the concern on Melissa's face.

"We can still leave, text our driver, and be on the beach dancing under the moon like some pagan goddesses within fifteen minutes."

Golden gave her a genuine smile at that. "No, I'm good. Really."

"Okay, but just say the word if you change your mind."

"I will."

The master of ceremonies stepped up to the microphone to introduce the Twins. If Golden hadn't ended their relationship, tonight would have turned out much different. The plan had been that she, Melissa, and Zoe were going to be given backstage access to hang with Jade and Kendra and watch the concert from there. Afterward, Mel and Zoe would head back to their villa and Golden would go back to the St. Kitts Marriott Resort where Jade and Kendra were staying. She had promised one night with them because she wasn't totally abandoning her girls on their vacation. Zoe had suggested the Twins just stay with them at the Villa, but Golden had squashed that idea before it even had a chance to take root. That would have sent a message that she hadn't been ready for. But none of that mattered now since they were no longer seeing each other.

Jade and Kendra jogged out onto the stage and immediately went into one of their biggest party hits "Bringin' Down Da House" which had a reggaeton vibe and got the crowd hyped. From their VIP seating, Golden could clearly see the joy on Kendra's face. It was one of her favorites because it represented her Jamaican heritage and gave her an excuse to be extra with her dirty wind and surprisingly good twerking skills while performing with their backup dancers. It also showed off Jade's linguistic skills as Kendra had taught her patois while they were growing up and had written an entire rap in patois for Jade to do during the dance performance. By the end of their first three songs, Golden was even sweating from dancing.

"Whew! I haven't danced like that in a long while." Melissa was dabbing her face with a face towel from the villa that she had tucked into her bag.

"You have another one of those tucked in there?" Zoe asked, fanning herself with the program.

Melissa grinned knowingly. "Because I knew you two wouldn't listen to me about bringing your own, I brought extras." She pulled two more neatly rolled towels out of her bag and handed one to each of them.

Golden laughed. "We know who we need to bunk with if the apocalypse ever happens. Are you ever not prepared for any situation?"

"Nope. I learned long ago that nobody's going to take care of me like me." Melissa's tone was matter-of-fact rather than bitter, which showed how far she'd come from the girl she'd met twenty years ago.

"Folks, we're going to slow it down and give you a chance to cool off before the next performers come out and get you jumping again," Kendra said.

"Have any of you heard a little number of ours that's been topping the charts for months now?" Jade asked.

The crowd cheered loudly while Golden's heart skipped.

Kendra walked to the edge of the stage. "Do you know what song Jade is referring to?" She held her microphone out to a young woman who gazed at her dreamily.

"'Golden Girl,'" the woman said in a sexy tone.

Golden actually felt a twinge of jealousy.

Kendra simply gave her a smile and nod then walked back toward Jade who was sitting on one of two stools and offered Kendra her guitar.

"We're going to give the band a break and do something a little different tonight."

Jade glanced at Kendra who began playing the opening notes of the song just as she had done on the video that they had sent her from the recording studio. The lights dimmed, then Jade began to sing but not in the jazzy vocals the song had been performed since its release. There was no band, just her voice and the acoustics from Kendra's guitar. It was a beautifully haunting ballad that made Golden's body ache with the need to run up on the stage, take Jade in her arms, and tell her that she was sorry and that she loved them both. As if they knew she needed to be held to her seat, Melissa and Zoe took her hands and became her anchors as her emotions bubbled over and tears that she thought that she had cried out on the day she broke the Twins' hearts flowed like a leaky faucet. Jade's voice trailed off with the final note, the stage went dark, and the audience was on their feet with loud applause. The lights came back up just as Jade was wiping something from her eye. She and Kendra thanked everyone for coming out, they wrapped their arms around each other's shoulders and walked off the stage.

Golden stood to leave. "I should've listened to you two and not come."

"Golden, wait, we'll come with you," Melissa said.

Golden shook her head. "No, I just need a minute. Stay, I'll be back before the next performers come out."

Melissa looked as if she would follow but nodded. "Okay. If you're not back in a half hour we're coming to look for you."

"I wouldn't expect anything less."

Golden left their section and made her way through the stadium and was about to head to the ladies' room but changed her mind. Instead, she texted their driver to ask him to meet her out front.

"Leaving so soon?" Godrick, their driver, asked.

"Yes. Would you please take me to the St. Kitts Marriott Resort."

"The St. Kitts Marriott Resort? You're not going back to your villa?" He gazed at her from the rear-view mirror with a look of confusion.

"No. The Marriott please then you can come back here for my friends who will need a ride back to the house." Golden used her former Financial Shark tone that brooked no argument.

Godrick quirked a brow then looked away from the mirror. "Yes ma'am." His tone said he was paid to drive, not argue.

She texted Melissa and Zoe and told them she'd gone back to the house.

We'll come back to the house.

No, stay and enjoy the show. I just need a bit of alone time.

How about this, we'll stay through two more performers to give you a couple of hours alone, then we'll head back. If you still want to be alone, then you can hide out in your room while Mel and I enjoy more of that rum punch by the pool until you're ready to have fun again.

Golden smiled. She didn't know what she would do without her girls, although she doubted that she'd be back by then, which meant she would have to tell them where she really was. She'd cross that bridge when she came to it. When they pulled up to the hotel, Golden took two twenties out of her wallet and offered them to Godrick with a smile.

"Thank you."

"No need, ma'am. Everything is taken care of as part of the resort fee."

"How about if I include, I'm sorry for being a rude American."

Godrick grinned. "In that case." He took the money. "Feel free to call if you need a ride back."

"I will. Thank you again."

Golden walked into the lobby, took out her phone, and opened the message Jade had sent her the day they had arrived in St. Kitts with their room number in case she wanted to see them while they were all there. She didn't know why she didn't delete it, but now she was glad she hadn't, although, they probably wouldn't be back for a for a few hours and she wasn't going to just sit outside their hotel room like some crazy stalker. Golden decided to have a drink at the bar to pass the time. She nursed it for a good hour before walking over to the desk and asking them to try Jade and Kendra's room. They still hadn't come back so she returned to the bar for another drink which turned into a third. She stood to go to the front desk again and felt light-headed. That's when she remembered she hadn't really eaten much all day because her stomach was in knots over seeing Jade and Kendra. She decided the best course of action was to just go up to the room. If she stayed down here, then she'd end up drinking herself into a stupor.

She got on the elevator, then took off the four-inch wedge sandals she was wearing because she felt too unsteady to keep walking in them. She found Jade and Kendra's room and knocked. She knew there was no one there to answer, but it didn't hurt to try. The numbers on the door swam before her eyes.

"I just need to sit down." She used the wall to guide herself to the floor then the hall began to spin. "Jeez, I shouldn't have had those drinks. I'll just close my eyes for a minute until everything stops spinning."

Somewhere in the distance, Golden heard her cell phone ringing but couldn't open her eyes or move to answer it. Then it stopped and she heard a familiar voice. She finally managed to blink her eyes open to see Jade kneeling in front of her.

"Hey, beautiful, are you all right?"

Golden lifted her hand to stroke Jade's cheek. "Are you real?" Why was her speech slurred? She only had three drinks at the bar. Oh, and one before they left for the concert and another at the concert. All with barely any food on her stomach.

"Very real and you're very drunk."

Kendra's face appeared beside Jade's. "C'mon, let's get you inside."

Kendra picked Golden up, cradling her in her arms as Jade opened the door to their room.

"Take her to the bedroom. I'll get her some water." Golden heard Jade say.

As Kendra carried her toward another door, Golden realized they were in a suite. Kendra laid her on the bed. As she did, Golden noticed the time on the bedside clock. It had been two hours since she'd texted her friends.

"Wait, I need to call Mel and Zoe. They don't know where I am."

Kendra sat on the bed beside her. "They were calling you when we found you outside our room. I answered and told them where you were."

Golden covered her face with a groan. "I'm so embarrassed."

Kendra gently removed her hands from her face. "Don't be. We're just glad to see you."

Jade entered, sitting on the other side of Golden, offering a bottle of water. "Here you go."

Golden took a few sips then gave it back to her. She could barely hold her eyes open. "If it's okay, I'll just lay here for a minute then call Godrick to come get me and take me back to the house. I shouldn't have come here." She settled back into the plush pillows and gave in to the heaviness making her eyes flutter closed. The last thing she saw were Jade's and Kendra's loving gazes.

CHAPTER TWENTY-SEVEN

As Melissa stretched, she thought to herself that she could get used to waking up in paradise every morning. The cool ocean breeze blowing in through the open patio doors, the sound of tropical birds squawking and chirping in the trees, and the ability to go out the back door, down a palm tree lined path to the private beach for resort residents only for her morning walk. She tied her locs up into a ponytail and put on a tank top and a pair of running shorts. She didn't need shoes as she liked to feel the sand squish between her toes as she walked. Finally, she grabbed her wireless ear buds and phone then headed out of her room. Zoe's door was still closed. She liked to sleep in when they were on vacation while Melissa and Golden were usually up early to work out or go for walks. Melissa shook her head as she passed Golden's room.

When she and Zoe returned to the house last night to find out from Aubrey that Golden hadn't been there since they left for the concert her first thought was that she'd gone for a walk and gotten kidnapped. She watched enough *Dateline* to know how often things like that happened. Zoe suggested that before she freaked out, they attempt to call Golden, which she did, twice with no answer. Aubrey called Godrick and found out that he had dropped her off at the St. Kitts Marriott Resort which had confused them until Zoe remembered that's where the Twins were staying. Since they didn't have their phone numbers, Zoe called the hotel and asked to be connected to their room. At the same time, Melissa tried Golden's number again, but Kendra answered. She explained that they had just come upon Golden asleep, and possibly drunk, outside their room. She and Zoe found it hard to believe that Golden would do something so out of character. Kendra promised that she and Jade would take good care of her and personally escort her back to the house in the morning. They trusted them enough not to promise bodily harm if they took advantage of her inebriated state, but Zoe felt the need to issue the threat anyway. Melissa just hoped that they'd work things out because she knew the Twins made Golden happy, and all she'd ever wanted for her was to be happy.

The smell of coffee drifted toward her as she walked downstairs. It was too early for Chef or Aubrey to be here preparing breakfast. She and Golden were usually returning from their walk at the same time Aubrey and Chef were arriving for the day. As she rounded the corner from the hallway into the living area, Melissa had a direct view of the kitchen and someone who wasn't Aubrey or Chef was standing there with their back to her pouring a cup of coffee. She knew she and Zoe had locked up everything for the night, yet the sliding glass wall from the backyard was partially open. Instinct told her to quietly back out of the room and run upstairs to wake Zoe up as she called resort security, but something familiar about the person made her hesitate long enough for them to turn around. Zoe's fear turned to confusion.

"Black?" Somehow, she recognized those eyes gazing over the top of the coffee mug raised to their lips.

They lowered the mug, giving her a sheepish grin. "Oh…uh…hey. I hadn't planned on popping in until later when you all woke up, but Aubrey hadn't resupplied the guest house since no one had used it in a while and I needed my coffee."

It took Melissa a moment to realize two things. She finally knew who Black was, and Zoe had been right. Without the mask, even after not having seen Alex in years, she recognized them. "This can't be happening."

Melissa turned around and practically ran back upstairs.

"Melissa! Wait, I can explain!"

Melissa ignored Alex, almost stumbling as she tried to take the stairs two at a time, forgetting her legs were too short for that.

Alex caught up to her as soon as she hit the top landing and grabbed her arm. "Melissa, please. Let me explain. It's not what you think."

Melissa rounded on them. "It isn't? So, you haven't been spending months deceiving me about who you are? About knowing who I was?"

"Well, yes, but it isn't as bad as it sounds."

"What is going on out here?" Zoe stepped out of her room yawning and dressed in an oversized T-shirt. "Oh, shit! Alex?"

"Hey, Zoe."

Melissa took advantage of the distraction to yank her arm from Alex's grasp, run to her bedroom, well, technically Alex's bedroom, then slam and lock the door.

"Melissa, please. I hadn't planned to come here, but I couldn't continue doing what we were doing. I came out here to explain." Alex pleaded from the other side of the door.

Melissa paced in front of it, torn between shock and relief that the truth had finally been revealed.

"Let me talk to her," she heard Zoe say followed by the sound of footsteps walking away. "They're gone."

Melissa opened the door just enough to peer out and make sure. Seeing that Zoe was alone, she opened it wider to let her in, then sat on the bed.

Zoe joined her. "Well, that was quite the wake-up call."

"Go ahead and say it. You were right. Alex and Black are the same person."

"I was just guessing. I never in a million years thought I'd be right about it or that they would show up here. Other than the obvious shock of it, how are you feeling?"

"Confused, strangely relieved, and pissed."

Zoe nodded. "I could see how all those would apply. The next question is, what do you want to do about it? If you want to hop on the next flight home you know Golden, assuming she's figuring out her own entanglement at the moment, and I are with you. It's been a great vacation, but it wouldn't be worth putting you in an awkward situation to continue."

Melissa considered it but knew running from the situation wouldn't make it go away. She was going to have to talk to Alex eventually if she was going to find out why they had done all of this. "No. I'll talk to Alex, but if anyone is going to leave it's them. They interrupted our vacation not the other way around."

Zoe grinned. "Go get them, girl. Do you want me to come down as backup?"

"No, I think I got it."

"Okay, but all you need to do is yell and I'll be there. After I put on something more suitable for an epic reality television confrontation." Zoe gave Melissa a wink as she bumped her with her shoulder before she left.

Melissa decided that it wouldn't hurt to change as well. She exchanged her walking attire for a red halter sundress covered in large white hibiscus flowers and a high-low hem. It was the closest thing she'd brought to the red and black she usually wore as Mistress Heart. She hoped the red would give her the confidence she needed to get through this situation with her Mistress Heart attitude. She even did the one last look in the mirror that she did just before meeting with a client, but Mistress Heart was nowhere to be found. With a sigh of resignation, she headed downstairs.

❖

Golden woke up with a pounding headache. She sat up in a bed she didn't recognize, dressed in just her underwear.

"What the hell?"

The door opened and Jade's head peeked through. "Hey, Sleeping Beauty." She opened the door fully and walked in carrying a tray. "I thought you might need something to put in your stomach before heading back to your villa."

Last night's activities came back to Golden in a rush of embarrassment. She flopped back onto the pillows, which didn't help with her headache, with the sheet over her head. "I can't believe I got drunk. This is so unlike me."

She felt the bed sink then the sheet was tugged out of her hand. "Hey, we all have that one drunken night we'd like to forget."

Golden bolted up. "We didn't…"

Jade frowned. "No, and I'm a little offended you'd think we would take advantage of you that way. It was bad enough that your friend felt the need to threaten us, but I thought you knew us better than that."

"I'm sorry. This is a first for me. I've never gotten drunk enough to not remember what I did the night before. Believe it or not, it's the only thing I haven't done that Melissa has." She smiled, hoping to put Jade at ease.

Jade gave her an understanding smile. "No worries. Here, drink this." She handed Golden what looked like a smoothie. "It's not a cure-all, but it will help ease your hangover better than greasy food or hair of the dog that bit you. There's also a bottle of water and a bagel on the tray over there." She pointed to the desk next to the bedroom door.

"Thank you. I hope I didn't put anyone out of their bed."

"Technically, you kicked us both out of our bed, but the sofa and chaise in the living room were comfortable enough for the night."

Despite Jade's teasing smile, Golden couldn't help but feel like a horrible person. First, she broke up with them, then she showed up sloppy drunk on their doorstep, then she took their bed.

"Golden, it's okay, really. Now, drink that. Eat if you can and when you're ready to go we'll get a taxi and take you back to your place."

"Thank you."

Despite Jade's reassurance, Golden still felt guilty. After Jade left, Golden sluggishly climbed out of bed to find her clothes. They were folded neatly on a nearby chair. Once she was dressed, she took a moment to sit and gather her thoughts before facing Jade and Kendra again. She sipped at the smoothie, feeling a little better having something in her stomach. She considered eating the bagel, but the thought made her nauseous so she finished half the smoothie then picked up the bottled water. Golden had expected to get a little emotional when she saw Jade and Kendra perform but nothing like the immense regret and loss that overwhelmed her. She had been able to hold back the nagging feelings bubbling up after they came on stage and performed some of their upbeat party anthems, but with Jade's raw performance of "Golden Girl," she lost the battle.

Golden finally had to face the truth that she loved Jade and Kendra with every fiber of her being. Despite all that she had going on, her life felt empty without their presence. She missed their early morning text messages even with the three-hour time difference between New York and California. She missed the weekly video calls whether they only had time for ten minutes or two hours. What she missed most of all was the possibility of sharing a committed life with both. Golden was tired of holding on to the past and running away from her future. Her father always told her that life was short and that you had to take as much good as you could get out of it. It was how he lived his life, and it's what he'd tell her to do today. She smiled when she thought of her father meeting Jade and Kendra. She knew he would love them. They say daddy's girls always ended up with someone who reminded them of their father. In many ways, Jade and Kendra did just that. Golden's father was affectionate, gentle, and loving like Jade, also confident, strong, and patient like Kendra. He had been with her in Paris when she performed with them, as if he had been giving his approval and to let her know it was time to live her life not in fear of losing love but in the joy of embracing it. Golden knew that if she walked out of that hotel room without telling Jade and Kendra how she truly felt she would never get the chance again.

❖

Melissa stood in the entryway of the living room watching Alex as they stood outside on the patio with their back to her, arms folded, gazing up at the sky as if all the answers to life's secrets could be found there.

"Ms. Melissa, your latte is ready."

Melissa turned away just as Alex turned around. She walked over to the kitchen island where Aubrey had set a mug on the counter for her. Through the rising steam, she smiled at the rose design in the foam, one of the many designs he made in her lattes that were waiting for her after her morning walks along with Golden's coffee made with brown sugar and vanilla-flavored creamer.

"Thank you, Aubrey."

It was too hot to drink right away, but she lifted the mug to her face and inhaled the mocha scent. She could feel Alex's eyes on her, but she refused to rush. Her morning routine had already been thrown into an upheaval with their appearance. Aubrey placed another mug on the counter. The scent of chai floated up from it.

"You're the man, Aubrey." Zoe picked up the mug and leaned against the counter. "How long do you plan on making Alex suffer? I don't know if I can take that sad puppy dog expression much longer."

"Just for another minute. They deserve longer for what they did."

Zoe chuckled. "The sooner you allow them to explain themselves the sooner we can get back to our vacation."

Melissa sighed in exasperation. "Fine."

As she walked out onto the patio, Alex looked like a student steeling themselves for a punishment from their teacher. The irony of it almost made her smile. She walked past Alex and sat at the dining table. Aubrey walked out, offering Alex a smoothie then left them alone, closing the patio door behind him. Melissa appreciated his discretion. Alex joined her at the table, sitting directly across from her.

"The floor is yours." Melissa sat back in her chair trying to appear nonchalant as she sipped her coffee while her body flushed in reaction to

Alex being so near and knowing that it was their fantasies that Melissa had been indulging in as Mistress Heart.

"Okay. First, my intention wasn't to deceive you."

"Could've fooled me."

"I honestly didn't know you were Mistress Heart at the fundraiser. A business associate had invited me to go, it was for a good cause, and Prince Property Management gets many of their art pieces from the co-sponsor Art is Life Gallery, so I figured, why not. Then I saw Mistress Heart walk out with so much sexy confidence. Controlling the room as if everyone were at her command, and I was intrigued. After my divorce I threw myself into work. My only outlet had been basketball, but after a while I wanted something different. Some companionship that didn't require a full-time commitment so I joined the Red Dahlia Social Club hoping to get that with Mistress Heart."

"You seriously didn't recognize me?"

"No. We hadn't seen each other in almost twenty years. As you can see, my appearance has drastically changed since we last saw each other so I assumed yours might have also. I tried looking you up on social media after we lost touch, but it seemed all your accounts except Facebook had been closed, then when I tried to reach out there, you blocked me."

Melissa looked guiltily down at her half empty mug.

"Besides, the Melissa I knew was a sweet, shy, conservative young woman. Not the sophisticated sexy woman sitting across from me now or the bold, sensual, and commanding Mistress Heart that I've gotten to know."

Melissa gazed up to find Alex looking at her in that seductive way they did as Black. It was distracting so she quickly got them back on track. "When did you find out that I was Mistress Heart?"

"Just after our consultation, I had received a thank you card from the gallery for the donation and one of the signatures was yours. I couldn't imagine Melissa Hart was a common name, so I went on the Gallery's website and there was your picture with *Melissa Hart, Gallery Manager & Art Curator* underneath it. I was pleasantly surprised by how much you had changed but also still stayed the same. I recognized that beautiful shy smile from the girl I once knew, but I still hadn't put two and two together. It wasn't until our first session when you walked out to greet me that it hit me with that smile." Alex smiled wistfully.

Melissa was no longer feeling the warmth of attraction. "So, you've known the entire time?" she said angrily.

Alex had the good sense to look guilty. "I'm not proud of myself for having led you on, but I saw a side of you I'd never seen before. You were sexy, vibrant, and uninhibited, it was too tempting not to explore."

Melissa frowned. To hear Alex basically telling her that they were more interested in spending time with her as Mistress Heart than revealing themselves to spend time with her as herself brought back old insecurities that she thought she'd gotten past.

"I know what you're thinking, and it's not true. I figured Mistress Heart was a part of you that you didn't feel comfortable enough to be outside of Red Dahlia. I wanted to get to know that part of you as well as I knew the Melissa I had cared so much about all those years ago when I let you get away because I was prideful and stupid. I owe you a huge apology for how I reacted to what happened that day at Coney Island. I'm sorry and I've regretted it for a long time." Alex seemed sincere but that didn't change the fact that they had deceived Melissa for months.

She shook her head. "That all sounds great, but it doesn't excuse what you did."

"What would you have done if I had revealed who I was and that I knew who you were? Or even come to you without the mask? Would you have still taken me on as a client?"

Melissa hesitated in responding. Because it was Alex, who she still harbored feelings for after all these years, would she have broken her own rule?

"I have a rule not to take on people I know as clients." She knew that didn't answer the question, but she hoped it would suffice.

Alex looked at her knowingly but didn't push it. "To be honest, I thought that if I had told you the truth that you would kick me to the curb. I didn't want that." Alex reached for Melissa's hand. She didn't pull away when they took it. "There were so many times over the past eighteen years that I wanted to ask Golden or Zoe how to get in touch with you. Then I remember how I was the one who pursued you, made you feel as if I understood about you not being ready to come out, then turned around and treated you like a criminal when all you were doing was protecting yourself. Golden told me what happened with your stepfather refusing to pay for you to go to Howard, and I wanted to call you then, but I thought that after what happened, I wouldn't want to talk to me if I were in your position."

Melissa gave Alex's hand a squeeze. "I probably wouldn't have talked to you. I was angry back then and had even shut Golden out for a while because she was going through enough at the time so I put all my focus on her."

"Melissa, what we've shared these past months has been like nothing I've experienced before. For the first time in a long time, I didn't need to be Alex Prince, the tough, ambitious, and driven real estate mogul. I didn't feel obligated by the woman I'm with to make a show of our appearance in public to be caught by the paparazzi. Or even be laughed at when all I want is to stay home to read a book or watch a movie together. Behind the mask of Black, I got to be just Alex spending a nice evening at home with an intelligent, witty, and beautiful woman."

Melissa slid her hand from Alex's. "But it wasn't real, Alex. You paid for an experience and that's what you were given. What happens behind closed doors at the Red Dahlia is pure fantasy. What happened between Black and Mistress Heart wasn't real."

It hurt Melissa to say that because there were moments when she just allowed herself to enjoy their time together not as Mistress Heart but as herself.

"You know that's not true. Are you going to sit there and tell me that it was ALL an act? That you felt nothing? Because I'm happy to remind you of several moments when the proof of your desire was very obvious."

Melissa wanted to smack the knowing smirk from their face. "Desire and affection are two different things. You don't need to care about someone to share a moment of passion with them."

"Is that so? Let's test that theory." Alex walked around to where she was sitting. "Would you mind standing?"

Melissa heard a hint of the tone Alex used as Black when giving her instruction. Without even thinking, she stood. Alex took her face in their hands. As they slowly lowered their head toward hers, the voice of reason in Melissa's head told her to stop them but the desire that she felt for them seemed to think that it was about time this was happening.

Alex stopped at the point where their lips were so close that they softly brushed along hers. "May I kiss you, Melissa Hart?"

It took Melissa a second to realize that Alex had used her real name, not her domme persona. "Is this your idea of testing my theory?" she said breathlessly.

"Maybe. Or Maybe I just want to kiss you."

"You have my permission."

The kiss was slow and sensual. It was the adult version of their first and last kiss on the Ferris wheel. Despite participating in the kiss, Melissa fisted her hands by her side, wanting to prove that what was between Mistress Heart and Black was nothing more than a physical attraction that she could walk away from now that the masks were off. Her heart was calling her a liar as the line blurred between her unrequited feelings for Alex and her growing feelings for Black. She almost whimpered when Alex's lips left hers.

"Do you know how long I've wanted to do that?"

"Why didn't you?"

Alex shifted their hand to gently rub their thumb across Melissa's lips. "Because I didn't want to break any rules that would get me kicked out of the club."

Melissa gave Alex a teasing grin. "What else have you wanted to do?"

Alex shook their head and released Melissa's face. "We're not in the club. After today, Black no longer exists."

Melissa could see by the look on their face that Alex was serious. "What are you saying?"

"I'm saying I came here to be open and honest. To tell you that I've fallen in love with you."

Shaking her head, Melissa wrapped her arms around herself feeling all those old insecurities. "You're in love with Mistress Heart, not me."

"Do you hear yourself? Mistress Heart is just as much a part of you as Black is me. Hiding behind a mask doesn't change who we are."

"It was a role, Alex. One that you paid to entertain you. Nothing more." Melissa turned to walk back into the house, her vision blurring with tears.

"The gifts I brought were for Melissa. The scenarios I created were for Melissa. The feelings I can no longer fight are for Melissa. Mistress Heart was just the means for me to show her that I've always regretted walking away from you that day in Coney Island. That I've compared every woman after that day to you. Do they smile as openly as Melissa does? Do they care for their friends as devotedly as Melissa? Are they as smart and quick-witted as her?"

Melissa still had her back to Alex as they came up behind her and wrapped their arms around her waist. "Do they make me want to dress up like some storybook knight in shining armor to rescue them from anything and anyone wanting to do them harm then whisk them away to a high tower where I can love and care for them the way they deserve like I do, when I think of Melissa?"

Tears ran down her cheeks as she stood tense and wary in Alex's arms. "I don't need anyone to rescue or take care of me anymore. I've been doing just fine on my own."

Alex placed their face beside Melissa's "I know. The last thing I want is to take away your strength and independence. I just want to be there when you need someone to help you hold the reins when you're tired of being in control. To show you that you're worthy of being loved when others have you believing otherwise. To be the soft place you land after a hard day."

Melissa didn't realize that she'd waited most of her life to hear someone say anything close to what Alex had said until now. She was tired of always being in control, believing vulnerability was a weakness and that love was out of reach for her. Being wrapped in their strong arms as they whispered sweet loving words in her ear was the balm needed to soothe her emotional wounds. Melissa relaxed, then turned in Alex's embrace, gazing up to see if the look in their eyes matched the words they spoke so lovingly. Alex looked at her the way Melissa would see Golden's father looking at her mother and hoping for the day someone would look at her with such love and tenderness.

Alex reached up to wipe her tears away. "Will you let me love you?"

"Why me?"

"Why not you?"

She snorted. "I can think of several reasons."

"None of them will deter me. It's always been you. It always will be."

That nagging little voice that had been with her since she was five years old when her father left them to start a whole new family with his side chick, treating Melissa like the unwanted stepchild when his other children came along, tried convincing her that she'd never be good enough for someone like Alex. After all, even her mother spent years choosing alcohol and drugs over taking care of her only to replace that with the reverend and the church when she found God. Then she really did become the unwanted stepchild. The love she saw reflected in Alex's eyes just as quickly quieted that voice and Melissa felt a peace that she'd never experienced before.

"You mentioned you were staying in the guest house?"

"Yes."

Melissa stood on her toes to place a soft kiss on Alex's lips. "Take me there."

"Is this Melissa or Mistress Heart making this command?"

Melissa smiled. "It's whoever you'd like it to be."

CHAPTER TWENTY-EIGHT

Zoe smiled as she watched Melissa and Alex walk to the guest house. "Chef, I guess it will be breakfast for one today."

Chef Warner grinned. "Yes, ma'am."

Zoe was happy for Melissa. Of the three of them, she believed Melissa deserved a happily ever after worthy of the sapphic romance novels she enjoyed reading so much. She believed Alex would give her that. The beep of the front door opening interrupted her thoughts. Zoe walked out to greet Golden, Jade, and Kendra. Golden was shushing them as they walked in.

"No need, we're all up." Zoe chuckled at Golden's look of surprise.

"I figured Melissa would be up, but this is early for you."

"Good morning, Zoe," the Twins said in unison.

"Good morning. We've had quite the morning already. I see you three have worked things out."

Golden looked from Jade to Kendra with a smile that lit her face with love. "We also had quite a morning."

"That's wonderful news." Zoe was genuinely happy for her friends. It was obvious that when it came to romance, she would have to live vicariously through them. "You're just in time. Chef is about to start breakfast. I thought I was going to have to eat alone."

Golden walked and looped her arm through Zoe's as they headed to the main area of the house. "Alone. Where's Mel?"

"We had an unexpected visitor this morning." Zoe quickly filled Golden in without revealing to Jade and Kendra about Melissa's side gig, but enough for Golden to figure out what had happened. "They disappeared into the guest house just before you arrived."

Golden gazed out the patio door toward the guest house. "Alright now, Mel."

"Chef, it looks like it will be four for breakfast."

"No worries."

Aubrey offered everyone a beverage then went about setting the indoor dining table as Zoe, Golden, and the Twins made themselves comfortable in the living area. As Golden explained what happened from last night until she finally admitted her feelings to Jade and Kendra. It seemed the Twins couldn't keep their hands from Golden and she was the same way. She sat between them with Kendra's arm around Golden's, her fingers lightly running over her shoulder, Golden's hand on Kendra's leg while Jade held her other hand, lifting it every so often to place a kiss on her knuckles.

As happy as she was for Golden and Melissa, Zoe found herself envying the obvious love between them and missing Danice terribly. She had been putting on a brave face during their trip, but at night she lay in bed on the verge of tears, aching to call Danice to tell her she was wrong for accusing her of putting Malik and her family before her own happiness. Then she would remember how Danice just left without putting up much of a fight or denying what Zoe had said. Unfortunately, none of that eased the pain of her heartache.

"Breakfast is served," Chef Warner announced.

"Wow, now this is a spread," Kendra said, rubbing her hands together in anticipation.

"You've outdone yourself today, Chef," Golden said.

Chef Warner shrugged. "Judging by all that's happened this morning, it seemed to be a special occasion so, with Aubrey's assistance, I prepared accordingly. Bon appetit."

There were scrambled eggs fluffier than the soft clouds in the sky, thick, golden slices of French toast with fresh berries, a bowl of fresh tropical fruits, a platter of various breakfast meats with ham, sausage, and bacon and three different fruit juices. It was a feast compared to the fresh fruit and omelets requested by the three of them every morning since they'd been there. They were obviously underutilizing Chef's skills. Not long after they sat down to eat, the doorbell rang. Aubrey left to answer it.

"Were you expecting anyone?" Zoe asked Golden.

"No. You?"

Zoe shook her head. They gazed curiously toward the entry way. Zoe heard a female voice but couldn't hear what was being said. The sound of footsteps followed, and Aubrey entered carrying a weekender bag followed by a surprise guest.

"Danice?" Zoe stood so quickly her chair scraped loudly across the floor.

Danice looked self-consciously at the group sitting at the table then back at Zoe. "I'm sorry to just drop in like this unannounced but I needed to talk to you."

"You could've just as easily called." Zoe didn't mean for that to sound as snarky as it did. She was just shocked at seeing Danice here, looking as beautiful as ever, after she had just been thinking about her.

Danice smiled softly. "This was a conversation that needed to happen in person."

"Zoe, can't you see that she's making a grand romantic gesture?" Golden said.

Aubrey cleared his throat drawing everyone's attention to him. "May I suggest utilizing the front courtyard for privacy while I will take Ms. Danice's bag up to the empty guest room."

That seemed to snap Zoe out of her shock. "Uh, yes, please. Thank you, Aubrey." She looked at the others around the table. "Excuse us." Then walked toward Danice. "Why don't we go outside and talk."

❖

"The floor is now yours," Alex said.

Melissa was suddenly at a loss as to what to do next. This wasn't like one of their sessions where they hid behind masks playing characters in a fantasy. This was real life. The girl of her teenage dreams had confessed their love to her and was waiting for her to take the next step. She closed the distance between them then reached for the buttons on Alex's shirt, but they covered her hands to stop her.

"If we're doing this, it's because you're ready for something more. I need to hear you say it."

"I'm ready."

Alex quirked a brow. "Ready for what?"

Melissa gave them a shy smile. She wasn't used to expressing herself in such a vulnerable way. As Black, Alex had managed to convince her to let her guard down and trust that they wouldn't do anything that would hurt her. They were asking the same thing of her, only as themselves, and it was her heart, not her body they were asking her to entrust them with.

"I'm ready to explore where this will take us. I'm ready to be just Melissa and Alex."

That was all she could give them for now because, despite her feelings for them, she wasn't ready to completely give herself over to the unknown. It must have been enough because Alex released their hold on her hands so that Melissa could continue unbuttoning the soft linen shirt. She laid the shirt over a nearby chair then tucked her thumbs into the elastic waist of the matching linen pants and slid them over their hips. The pants dropped to the ground, Alex stepped out of them, then Melissa picked them up to place them with the shirt. She stepped back as Alex removed the sports bra and briefs that they were wearing to admire their slim, well-toned athletic figure. The Alex she remembered wasn't much bigger than they were now, but they had softer, feminine features and curves. Now it was as if they had toned down any femininity for a more androgynous appearance. They were even more attractive than they were back then.

"It's a bit awkward to be the only naked person standing here."

"It's only fair that since I undressed you that you undress me."

Alex gave her a sexy smirk as they walked slowly toward her. They grasped the straps of her sundress and slid them off her shoulders, the backs of their long fingers brushing along her arms, making her stomach clench with desire, before releasing the dress to pool at her feet. She stood before them in a strapless bra and panties and despite them having seen her in nothing at all during most of their sessions, Melissa felt more vulnerable now than she did then because she had her mask to hide behind. She had to keep from attempting to cover herself with her arms. Alex walked around her, unhooked the clasp of her bra, tossed it on the chair, then ran their hands down her torso to the waistband of her panties.

Melissa gasped as she felt Alex's soft lips press against the nape of her neck. As they slowly lowered her panties, they continued placing gentle kisses along her spine until that article of clothing joined the dress at her feet. Melissa moaned with pleasure as their lips lingered at her lower back. Alex stood, walked back around her, then grasped her hand and led her to the bed. The guest house had a king-size bed, a desk, and a kitchenette where the small patio entrance was located across the pool with direct sightline of the main house. Alex had drawn the blinds when they entered so there was no chance of an audience.

"I'm actually nervous," Alex said.

That surprised Melissa. "Why?"

Alex stroked her cheek. "Because I've wanted this since our first session. It took everything I had not to walk out of that closet to join you on the bed."

Melissa grinned. "I probably would've had you immediately removed from the premises."

Alex chuckled. "Which you would've had every right to do. You didn't know me from Adam."

"You know what's funny. I felt something familiar about you the first time we met." She turned her head to kiss the palm of their hand. "Maybe subconsciously I recognized you."

"Maybe."

Alex lowered their head to kiss Melissa. Turning her body and brain to mush. She wrapped her arms around their waist and melted against them with a passionate moan. Alex steered them toward the bed then sat down with Melissa standing between their legs. They ended the kiss to forge a heated trail of kisses from her lips to her breasts, alternating taking a pebble hard nipple into their mouth. The volume of her moans increased as a wildfire of desire burned through Melissa. She arched her back then grasped Alex's head, tangling her fingers in the short curls. To her surprise, she felt an orgasm building already, but before it could reach its peak, the warmth of Alex's lips was no longer wrapped around her nipple. Melissa gazed frustratingly down at them.

Alex gave her a soft smile. "Not yet. I've waited too long for this moment to rush it."

They stood, pulled back the covers on the bed, climbed in then patted the empty side invitingly. "Join me."

Melissa joined them with nervous anticipation, desire, and happiness combining into a jumble of feelings fluttering in her belly. In the past, what little sex Melissa had had been with her following others leads. With Riley she had been in full control. With Alex, even though they hadn't had actual sex, their sessions that included mutual self-pleasuring had been with Alex guiding and her controlling the tempo. She wondered if that would be how their lovemaking would go as well.

Alex ran their fingers along Melissa's arms. "I'm going to ask you to do something for me."

"Okay."

"I know you're used to being in control and uncomfortable with being vulnerable, but I want you to trust me."

Melissa gazed at them warily. "What are you going to do?"

Alex grinned. "Relax, I'm not going to tie you up and suddenly break out a trunk full of spanking tools. I just want you to let go of all of that to allow me to make love to you."

"Okay," Melissa agreed hesitantly, but she could feel herself growing tense over the thought of just letting go.

Alex gave her a look of understanding. "Let's try something."

They got out of bed, walked over to a suitcase sitting atop a luggage rack, and began rummaging through it. Once they found what they were looking for they turned and Melissa noticed a bandana in their hand.

They must have noticed her look of concern because they gave her a reassuring smile before offering her the scarf. "Have I given you any reason not to trust me in our sessions?"

Melissa gazed suspiciously from the scarf to them. "No."

"Then, once again, I'm asking you to trust that I wouldn't do anything to make you uncomfortable or harm you."

Melissa took the bandana. "What's this for?"

"To blindfold you. I think it might help you to get out of your own head and focus on your senses."

Melissa knew what Alex was trying to do. Rose had once told her that one of the most erotic experiences of her life had been being blindfolded during sex. But it meant giving up total control of what was happening to her, which was difficult. She gazed back at Alex who patiently waited for her to decide what she wanted to do. She knew they would be fine if she chose not to be blindfolded. She also knew that she could trust them, especially after the spanking session. Melissa once again ignored that little nagging voice of insecurity as she folded the bandana, covered her eyes, and tied it around her head. Feeling a sense of panic, she lifted the scarf just enough to be able to see Alex and the concern in their eyes.

Alex reached for the scarf. "Okay, maybe this wasn't a good idea."

Melissa shifted away from them. "No. I can do this."

"I'm sure you can but now might not be the right time to try it."

Melissa ignored them, closed her eyes, took a couple of deep breaths then lowered the scarf. She slowly lay back on the bed, still feeling a little panicked, but she was determined to get through it because she knew Alex wouldn't hurt her. They had been right about her other senses being heightened. She felt the bed shift, then Alex's warm body lying beside hers.

"Tell me to stop at any time you're not feeling comfortable."

"Okay." She waited with bated breath then jerked in surprise when she felt Alex's fingers brush along her arm.

"Just relax and feel my touch," they whispered seductively in her ear.

Even with her eyes covered, Melissa kept them closed. It felt less restrictive if she felt like her eyes were just closed and not being kept from seeing things. She found that her senses weren't only heightened but so was her sensitivity to touch as Alex stroked and caressed her from her face down her torso. By the time they reached her hips, her inner walls were contracting in arousal. She felt the bed shift once again, then Alex was straddling her. Before panic could even raise its head, their lips coaxing hers into a slow sensual kiss knocked it right back down. Alex proceeded to take their time kissing, nipping, and stroking her until she was whimpering and squirming with desire. Being blindfolded seemed to give her permission to just enjoy being made love to, something she rarely did because she was always too much in her head about whether she was doing it right.

When Alex settled between her thighs, brought her to the edge of orgasm and back with her slow, intimately erotic kiss, Melissa wavered between never wanting the pleasure to end and wanting to beg for release. In the end her body made the choice for her when Alex suckled her clit into their mouth then eased two fingers between her now dripping lips. If Melissa didn't know any better, she'd swear that the entire neighborhood could hear her body explode with her orgasm as colorful lights bounced before her closed lids. Just when she thought it was over, Alex slid up the length of her body, their fingers still stroking in and out, pressed their lips to hers and shared the taste of her pleasure. Melissa felt another orgasm building, reached between them to ease her fingers between Alex's legs, finding them just as wet with arousal, and within minutes both were groaning and bucking against each other in orgasm.

They both were breathing heavily as Alex carefully rolled them onto their side. The bandana had shifted during her final orgasm and sat wrapped around her forehead. She blinked her eyes open to find Alex smiling.

"You're looking very smug right now."

"Not smug, just happy."

Melissa wanted to hold onto the happiness she was feeling as well but she hadn't been successful with maintaining romantic relationships in the past. The fact that this one developed because of Alex's aka Black deception and her work at the Red Dahlia didn't bode well in her mind, but she was determined to at least try.

"By the way, because I understand that being Mistress Heart gives you something that you obviously need in your life, I wouldn't ask you to give that up. If you decide to walk away from that part of your life that should be your decision."

Melissa gazed at Alex in surprise. "You'd date a woman that works in a fetish club?"

Alex shrugged. "You told me that sex is prohibited so it's not like you work in a sex club or brothel."

"True but it's still considered sex work."

"I understand that, but I also feel like I know you well enough to know that you aren't the kind of woman that would take money for sex."

"Although I don't look down on women that do, it's just not my thing."

"I respect that."

"Thank you." Melissa stood, but before she walked away, she leaned down to give Alex a soft kiss. "Despite the shock, I'm glad you decided to tell me the truth because I'd been agonizing over whether to end our arrangement or asking you out."

It was Alex's turn to be surprised. "Really? Why Mistress Heart, I think you like me."

Melissa gave them a sexy grin. "Maybe a little."

❖

Zoe led Danice out to the front courtyard. Once there she offered her a seat on one of the lounge chairs. She sat on the edge as if afraid to get comfortable. Zoe did the same on the one next to her so that they were facing each other.

"So, is it true what Golden said. You're trying to make some grand gesture by coming here?"

"Yes and no. I needed to talk to you, but it wasn't a conversation that I felt should be had over the phone. Especially after the way I just up and left."

"After our conversation I just assumed you left because there was nothing more to discuss."

Danice looked remorseful. "No, I left because you were right and I didn't want to admit it. I was falling back into old patterns of allowing my mother and Malik to guilt me into obligations that I willingly gave up when I signed the divorce papers. I was mad at myself for not recognizing what was happening and allowing it to come between us. I didn't want to continue hurting you so I thought it was best to just leave until I could figure out how to break away from all of that."

"Again, you couldn't have told me that over the phone?" Zoe didn't mean to sound so bitchy, but her heart was hurting just looking at Danice sitting across from her. She was doing her best not to pull her into her arms and tell her none of that mattered, but it did.

"Yes, but after a surprising talk with my father I decided that this was a first step in showing you that our relationship is a priority and that I'm willing to do whatever it takes to prove it to you."

Zoe looked at Danice in confusion. "Your father?"

"Yes. My father unexpectedly came to see me after he'd heard that I was back at my sister's place to tell me that he didn't agree with the way my mother and Malik were trying to manipulate me. He had hoped my relationship with you would finally bring me the happiness I deserved."

"He knew about us?"

"I guess so, which surprised me because I hadn't told my parents, but it turns out Malik was happy to do it for me."

"Why does that not surprise me."

"Well, he did it hoping my parents would try do what they did when I told them I was bisexual which was guilt me into getting married. It was mostly my mother doing the guilting. I thought my father hadn't spoken up about it all because he didn't think it was his place to get involved, but it turns out that my father had been struggling with his sexuality when his parents insisted that he marry my mother. He told me that he was at a loss as to how to help me when he couldn't help himself in the same situation."

"Wow. Did your mother know?"

"No one told her, but he suspects she figured it out after my sister was born and their sex life dried up."

"Wait, are you saying your parents have been together all this time without having sex? With each other or anyone else?"

"My father said he's been faithful and as far as he knows, so has my mother."

"That's crazy. My parents could barely keep their hands off each other up until the day my father died."

"Well, because of how things turned out for him, my father had hoped that I wouldn't take the same route and had been glad to hear that I'd found someone who made me happy. He told me that he thought I was making a mistake and could no longer sit by and watch me choosing obligation over my own happiness again. He told me that if you and I love each other, that's all that should matter and the only person I should be obligated to make happy is myself. Then he offered to pay for my ticket to fly here to win the woman I love back, so here I am," Danice slid off the chair, knelt before Zoe and took her hands, "making a grand romantic gesture to beg for your forgiveness and ask if you can find it in your heart to give me another chance to prove that you are my one and only."

Zoe could see the sincerity in Danice's eyes, but she needed to hear the words that would tell her that her heart would be safe with Danice. "What about Malik?"

"I told him before I left to come here that he's going to have to either figure out how to take care of himself, call his parents, or let my mother take care of him since she seems to love him so much. I think she sees in him what she had wanted in my father. Either way, they can have each other because I'm done with allowing them to dim my light and happiness. Zoe Grant, I love you with all my heart, which you have fully and completely."

Zoe smiled as tears of happiness blurred her vision. "I love you too and I expect a lot more groveling for forgiveness later when we have some privacy."

Danice gave her a sexy smile. "I'm guessing I'm going to be spending some time on my knees while I'm here."

Zoe took her face in her hands. "Your knees, your back, whatever position I feel provides the best groveling." She lowered her head and pressed her lips to Danice's for a kiss that made up for their time apart.

CHAPTER TWENTY-NINE

Golden removed the large filet of salmon she'd been cooking from the broiler then set it on the stovetop. She let it sit while she finished placing the rest of the food family style on the large dining table. This would be the first brunch with Melissa and Zoe in over three months. She couldn't believe she hadn't seen her girls in all that time. It had been crazy since all their lives changed in St. Kitts a year ago. Zoe and Danice had gotten married and instead of a honeymoon they had taken Kiara on a graduation trip to South Africa that turned into a two-month stay so that they could arrange for her to spend a gap year there before returning to go to school at New York's Fashion Institute of Technology in the fall.

Melissa had extended her stay in St. Kitts for a week after their girls' trip ended to spend some alone time with Alex to figure out if they could have a relationship without the masks. Now they were planning their own wedding. Well, at least the wedding coordinator they hired was planning it since they were busier than ever. Alex's parents had recently decided to retire so they were now running Prince Property Management with their sister and brother full-time. Vivienne had chosen to retire six months ago leaving Melissa with the responsibility of managing the gallery with the assistance of her own personal assistant while also still taking special request VIP clients one day a week as the mysterious Mistress Heart at the Red Dahlia.

Golden proudly gazed at the spread laid out before her. She and the Twins had worked hard on this feast to ensure that it represented their little family well. Golden had prepared soul food dishes, Kendra had prepared a few Jamaican dishes, and Jade had hand-rolled various sushi options. She couldn't imagine being happier than she was at that moment. The dance academy was so busy there was a wait list for students to get in. The burlesque school now did private home classes to accommodate the growing clients and the Satin and Lace Burlesque Revue had done their first European tour this past summer with a special show in Montmartre dedicated to the memory of her aunt Dinah that included a vintage fashion show dedicated to her love, Celine. That trip also included claiming her family's inheritance from her aunt Dinah.

After her first trip to Paris, she had been so busy because of the media attention from her performance with the Twins then shortly after found herself nursing a broken heart after ending her relationship with them. Anything that brought back memories of Paris had her weepy so she had never gotten around to opening the envelope that she had found tucked in the trunk of Dinah's costumes at the dress shop. It wasn't until she decided to see if the costumes could be repaired and altered for her and her troupe to wear that she remembered the letter was still in the bag she had used in Paris. The letter was addressed to Golden's great-grandmother who was no longer alive so she and her mother took it to her grandmother to open. As it turned out, the envelope didn't just include a letter but also notarized copies of two deeds and transfer of property to Bess Hampton and her descendants upon Dinah's and Celine's deaths. One deed was for the building that had once housed her dance school and Celine's boutique and the other for the cottage she and Celine had lived in during their life in Montmartre.

The letter had been written before Dinah and Celine had left Montmartre to escape the Nazi regime and tucked into the trunk for her to send to her niece. It had been a follow-up to one that Dinah had sent shortly before telling her family of their fear of being sent to a camp with some of their fellow Black expat entertainers as well as being caught for hiding their Jewish friends in the basement of the dance school to assist them in escaping Nazi-occupied Paris. Not knowing what would happen, they were making plans to send some of their belongings to New York for safekeeping before they left Montmartre for Cannes until they could safely return.

Golden's grandmother explained that Dinah and Celine had never been able to send their belongings because they had to hurriedly leave Paris, fleeing to Cannes until they could come home again. When the war ended and they returned, they learned that the building and cottage had been sold and any record of their ownership had gone missing. Golden couldn't imagine what her aunt must have been going through at such a difficult time. Fortunately, they were able to buy a house in Paris, Dinah found a studio to lease nearby to continue her classes, and Celine continued designing and making clothes for private clients but never reopened her boutique at another location. They spent several years trying to get their property back to no avail.

With Camille's assistance, Golden was able to find out that Dinah and Celine's cottage wasn't too far from hers and had been vacant for several years. Golden's grandmother agreed that they would only fight for the cottage as they had no desire to uproot the businesses that already occupied the former dance school and boutique so Camille also referred her to an attorney in Paris who could help them navigate the red tape and court system to get the property back. During Satin and Lace's Revue in Montmartre, Golden had flown her grandmother, mother, brother, and his family to Paris to visit the home their ancestor lived in and loved. Despite the previous tenant having taken pretty good care of it, the cottage still needed work after being vacant for so long. Golden immediately hired the same contractors who had done Camille's cottage to do the work. She had felt such pride standing with her family outside that little cottage that held such a vital history in their family. She wished her father had been there to see it but had a feeling he, Dinah, and Celine had been smiling down on them with just as much pride.

Golden and the Twins were planning a getaway there once the work was finished, but today, they were at the Long Island house celebrating the one-year anniversary of that day in St. Kitts when her and her sister-friends finally let love into their lives.

Golden felt arms wrapping around her waist. "Hey, babe, this looks great."

She turned to give Jade a kiss on the cheek. "Thanks. I haven't put your sushi out yet. I figured it was best to wait until everyone arrived."

"That's fine. I'll get the dipping sauces ready." Jade kissed her back then walked away.

The doorbell rang.

"I got it!" Kendra yelled from the living room where she had been programming her new toy, an automatic record changer Golden had given her for her vinyl record player.

Golden hurried over to the kitchen counter to where she'd left champagne chilling in a bucket and began filling seven glasses set on a tray.

"I got that. You go greet your girls," Jade said.

"Thanks." Golden hurried out of the kitchen and couldn't contain her excitement at seeing Melissa and Zoe.

There were squeals and a group hug followed by more squeals.

"You would think they hadn't seen each other in years," she heard Alex say.

"It might as well have been with those three," Danice said.

Golden ignored them for the moment. She spun Melissa around. "Girl, I know you said you were shortening your locs, but I didn't expect this much."

"Yeah, I'm just too busy. Zoe cut it yesterday. She said this length should be more manageable." Her formerly waist-length locs were now just past her shoulders.

"It looks good. So does the ombre blond highlights on you, Zoe. Is that the new wash-out hair color you're debuting at the Bronner Show?"

Zoe gathered a handful of her locs, studying the ends. "Yeah. I figured if anybody should be the guinea pig for testing it, it should be me. I've got a few more tweaks before I'll feel like it's ready, but we're ahead of schedule."

Golden turned to her other guests. "Hey, Alex and Danice, I see these two haven't driven you crazy yet."

Alex grinned. "We just hide it well."

Danice snorted. "Speak for yourself. I feel like I'm married to a mad scientist as much as Zoe's keeping me up with mumbling in her sleep about formulas and textures."

Zoe smiled sheepishly. "This hair color formula has been a tough one to figure out compared to any of the other Hair For You products."

"Yeah, but it will be worth it for your bottom line in the end," Golden said.

Melissa chuckled. "You can take the girl out of finance but you can't take finance out of the girl."

Golden looped her arms through both Melissa's and Zoe's to lead them toward the dining room. "True and look how well it has served all of our bank accounts."

Zoe nodded. "I'm not going to argue that point. If it weren't for you bringing Alex into my life I'd probably still be struggling trying to get just halfway to where I am today."

"Yeah, and I guess if you hadn't referred me for the personal assistant job with Vivienne, I'd still be a miserable overpaid babysitter for the Lees."

"All true, but you guys have helped me as well. Mel, I don't think I would have ever made it through the worst moment of my life without your love and support. Zoe, If we hadn't gone to Belinda Trent's birthday party, I would've never discovered burlesque."

"Or met the Twins," Melissa teased her.

Golden smiled. "Also true."

"So, basically, if the three of us had never become friends, we'd be miserable and lonely," Zoe said.

They gazed at each other as if the realization of what Zoe said hit home.

"Champagne anyone?" Jade announced as they entered the dining room. She met the group halfway carrying the tray of glasses as expertly as if she still waited tables like she did back in college.

As everyone took a glass, Golden gazed around at the people that had become her found family. She hadn't realized it until Melissa and Zoe pointed out that their connection had led them here to this moment. It only seemed right that one year ago today the three of them had let go of the pain and trauma of their past to make room for a love that, like their friendship, was as tough and malleable as leather, as intricate and complicated as lace, and as strong and binding as locs. Like all those, with the right amount of care and attention, would stand the test of time.

About the Author

Anne Shade is an incurable romantic with a passion for writing stories about women who love women. Whether it's contemporary, erotica, historical, intrigue, or fantasy, Anne's stories cross many genres with one common factor…BIPOC representation in all her main characters. When Anne isn't writing she's coordinating dream weddings and daydreaming about plans for her future bed and breakfast.

Books Available from Bold Strokes Books

A Case for Discretion by Ashley Moore. Will Gwen, a prominent Atlanta attorney, choose Etta, the law student she's clandestinely dating, or is her political future too important to sacrifice? (978-1-63679-617-8)

Aubrey McFadden Is Never Getting Married by Georgia Beers. Aubrey McFadden is never getting married, but she does have five weddings to attend, and she'll be avoiding Monica Wallace, the woman who ruined her happily ever after, at every single one. (978-1-63679-613-0)

Flowers for Dead Girls by Abigail Collins. Isla might be just the right kind of girl to bring Astra out of her shell—and maybe more. The only problem? She's dead. (978-1-63679-584-3)

Good Bones by Aurora Rey. Designer and contractor Logan Barrow can give Kathleen Kenney the house of her dreams, but can she convince the cynical romance writer to take a chance on love? (978-1-63679-589-8)

Leather, Lace, and Locs by Anne Shade. Three friends, each on their own path in life, with one obstacle…finding room in their busy lives for a love that will give them their happily ever afters. (978-1-63679-529-4)

Rainbow Overalls by Maggie Fortuna. Arriving in Vermont for her first year of college, an introverted bookworm forms a friendship with an outgoing artist and finds what comes after the classic coming out story: a being out story. (978-1-63679-606-2)

Revisiting Summer Nights by Ashley Bartlett. PJ Addison and Wylie Parsons have been called back to film the most recent Dangerous Summer Nights installment. Only this time they're not in love and it's going to stay that way. (978-1-63679-551-5)

The Broken Lines of Us by Shia Woods. Charlie Dawson returns to the city she left behind and she meets an unexpected stranger on her first night back, discovering that coming home might not be as hard as she thought. (978-1-63679-585-0)

Triad Magic by 'Nathan Burgoine. Face-to-face against forces set in motion hundreds of years ago, Luc, Anders, and Curtis—vampire, demon, and wizard—must draw on the power of blood, soul, and magic to stop a killer. (978-1-63679-505-8)

All This Time by Sage Donnell. Erin and Jodi share a complicated past, but a very different present. Will they ever be able to make a future together work? (978-1-63679-622-2)

Crossing Bridges by Chelsey Lynford. When a one-night stand between a snowboard instructor and a business executive becomes more, one has to overcome her past, while the other must let go of her planned future. (978-1-63679-646-8)

Dancing Toward Stardust by Julia Underwood. Age has nothing to do with becoming the person you were meant to be, taking a chance, and finding love. (978-1-63679-588-1)

Evacuation to Love by CA Popovich. As a hurricane rips through Florida, so too are Joanne and Shanna's lives upended. It'll take a force of nature to show them the love it takes to rebuild. (978-1-63679-493-8)

Lean in to Love by Catherine Lane. Will badly behaving celebrities, erotic sex tapes, and steamy scandals prevent Rory and Ellis from leaning in to love? (978-1-63679-582-9)

Searching for Someday by Renee Roman. For loner Rayne Thomas, her only goal for working out is to build her confidence, but Maggie Flanders has another idea, and neither are prepared for the outcome. (978-1-63679-568-3)

The Romance Lovers Book Club by MA Binfield and Toni Logan. After their book club reads a romance about an American tourist falling in love with an English princess, Harper and her best friend, Alice, book an impulsive trip to London hoping they'll each fall for the women of their dreams. (978-1-63679-501-0)

Truly Home by J.J. Hale. Ruth and Olivia discover home is more than a four-letter word. (978-1-63679-579-9)

View from the Top by Morgan Adams. When it comes to love, sometimes the higher you climb, the harder you fall. (978-1-63679-604-8)

Blood Rage by Ileandra Young. A stolen artifact, a family in the dark, an entire city on edge. Can SPEAR agent Danika Karson juggle all three over a weekend with the "in-laws," while an unknown, malevolent entity lies in wait upon her very skin? (978-1-63679-539-3)

Ghost Town by R.E. Ward. Blair Wyndon and Leif Henderson are set to prove ghosts exist when the mystery suddenly turns deadly. Someone or something else is in Masonville, and if they don't find a way to escape, they might never leave. (978-1-63679-523-2)

Good Christian Girls by Elizabeth Bradshaw. In this heartfelt coming of age lesbian romance, Lacey and Jo help each other untangle who they are from who everyone says they're supposed to be. (978-1-63679-555-3)

Guide Us Home by CF Frizzell and Jesse J. Thoma. When acquisition of an abandoned lighthouse pits ambitious competitors Nancy and Sam against each other, it takes a WWII tale of two brave women to make them see the light. (978-1-63679-533-1)

Lost Harbor by Kimberly Cooper Griffin. For Alice and Bridget's love to survive, they must find a way to reconcile the most important passions in their lives—devotion to the church and each other. (978-1-63679-463-1)

Never a Bridesmaid by Spencer Greene. As her sister's wedding gets closer, Jessica finds that her hatred for the maid of honor is a bit more complicated than she thought. Could it be something more than hatred? (978-1-63679-559-1)

The Rewind by Nicole Stiling. For police detective Cami Lyons and crime reporter Alicia Flynn, some choices break hearts. Others leave a body count. (978-1-63679-572-0)

Turning Point by Cathy Dunnell. When Asha and her former high school bully Jody struggle to deny their growing attraction, can they move forward without going back? (978-1-63679-549-2)

When Tomorrow Comes by D. Jackson Leigh. Teague Maxwell, convinced she will die before she turns 41, hires animal rescue owner Baye Cobb to rehome her extensive menagerie. (978-1-63679-557-7)

You Had Me at Merlot by Melissa Brayden. Leighton and Jamie have all the ingredients to turn their attraction into love, but it's a recipe for disaster. (978-1-63679-543-0)

All Things Beautiful by Alaina Erdell. Casey Norford only planned to learn to paint like her mentor, Leighton Vaughn, not sleep with her. (978-1-63679-479-2)

Appalachian Awakening by Nance Sparks. The more Amber's and Leslie's paths cross, the more this hike of a lifetime begins to look like a love of a lifetime. (978-1-63679-527-0)

Dreamer by Kris Bryant. When life seems to be too good to be true and love is within reach, Sawyer and Macey discover the truth about the town of Ladybug Junction, and the cold light of reality tests the hearts of these dreamers. (978-1-63679-378-8)

Eyes on Her by Eden Darry. When increasingly violent acts of sabotage threaten to derail the opening of her glamping business, Callie Pope is sure her ex, Jules, has something to do with it. But Jules is dead…isn't she? (978-1-63679-214-9)

Head Over Heelflip by Sander Santiago. To secure the biggest prizes at the Colorado Amateur Street Sports Tour, Thomas Jefferson will do almost anything, even marrying his best friend and crush—Arturo "Uno" Ortiz. (978-1-63679-489-1)

Letters from Sarah by Joy Argento. A simple mistake brought them together, but Sarah must release past love to create a future with Lindsey she never dreamed possible. (978-1-63679-509-6)

Lost in the Wild by Kadyan. When their plane crash-lands, Allison and Mike face hunger, cold, a terrifying encounter with a bear, and feelings for each other neither expects. (978-1-63679-545-4)

Not Just Friends by Jordan Meadows. A tragedy leaves Jen struggling to figure out who she is and what is important to her. (978-1-63679-517-1)

Of Auras and Shadows by Jennifer Karter. Eryn and Rina's unexpected love may be exactly what the Community needs to heal the rot that comes not from the fetid Dark Lands that surround the Community but from within. (978-1-63679-541-6)

The Secret Duchess by Jane Walsh. A determined widow defies a duke and falls in love with a fashionable spinster in a fight for her rightful home. (978-1-63679-519-5)

Winter's Spell by Ursula Klein. When former college roommates reunite at a wedding in Provincetown, sparks fly, but can they find true love when evil sirens and trickster mermaids get in the way? (978-1-63679-503-4)